THE ENEMY WITHIN

LARRY BOND

WARNER BOOKS

A Time Warner Company

Copyright © 1996 by Larry Bond and Patrick Larkin
All rights reserved.

Warner Books, Inc., 1271 Avenue of the Americas,
New York, NY 10020

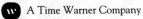 A Time Warner Company

Printed in the United States of America
First Printing: March 1996
10 9 8 7 6 5 4 3 2 1

Library of Congress Cataloging-in-Publication Data
Bond, Larry.
    The enemy within / Larry Bond.
       p.   cm.
    ISBN 0-446-51676-7
    I. Title.
PS3552.059725E54   1996
813'.54—dc20   95-15241
                                                               CIP

Book design by Giorgetta Bell McRee

To Jeanne and Mennette,
with all our love

Acknowledgments

We would like to thank Dwin Craig, Don Gilman, Dave Hood, Mennette Masser Larkin, Don and Marilyn Larkin, Colin and Denise Larkin, Ian, Duncan, and Chris Larkin, Erin Larkin-Foster, Kay Long Martin, Elaine Meisenheimer, John Moser, Bill and Bridget Paley, Barbara Patrick, Tim Peckinpaugh and Pam McKinney-Peckinpaugh, Thomas T. Thomas, Tom Thompson, and Brad Ware for their assistance, advice, and support.

Author's Note

After four books, you get to know a fellow pretty well. While there is still much to learn about Pat Larkin, I can honestly say that in ten years of working together he has always been a good friend and an excellent writer. He is good at his craft, and I've got to work like crazy to keep up with him.

Anyone who's read one of our other books knows that these are joint efforts. If this is the first one you've picked up, know that these truly are the work of two minds. This book is just as much Pat's as it is mine, and he deserves as much credit as I do for its success.

We both hope you enjoy it.

PROLOGUE

JANUARY 15

Benicia Industrial Park, California, Near San Francisco

The accident scene looked real—even to Shahin's skeptical eyes. A crumpled Toyota Corolla sat sideways across the narrow on-ramp to Highway 680, surrounded by fragments of smashed safety glass and puddled oil. Four emergency flares cast a flickering red light across a spiderweb of concrete pillars and rusting railroad bridge supports rising above the freeway entrance. As a final touch of authenticity, the sharp, sweet smell of leaking gasoline hung in the chilly night air.

The short, bearded man nodded to himself, satisfied that his deception would hold for the brief time required. He moved off the road and into the shadows beneath the overpass.

His cellular phone buzzed softly. He flipped it open. "Yes?"

The muffled voice of Haydar Zadi, his lookout, sounded in his ear. "Two minutes."

"Understood." Shahin slid the phone back inside his wind-breaker and checked the pistol in his shoulder holster. Their first target, their chosen weapon, was on the way.

Perched high in the cab of his big rig, Jack Briggs saw the flare-lit wreck up ahead in plenty of time. He swore once and braked smoothly, coming to a complete stop near the foot of the ramp.

Like most independent truckers, he preferred making his runs at night and in the early morning to avoid the Bay Area's god-awful traffic. It was a routine that worked well—usually. But not tonight.

Still growling to himself, he peered through the windshield. At least the Toyota's driver didn't seem hurt. The man had glanced around once when the rig's headlights hit him, but then he'd gone right back to staring down at his car's smashed front end. Might be drunk, Briggs decided. It was near closing time. Hell, only a drunk would wander off the main road into the lit-tle town of Benicia's deserted industrial park at this time of the night.

He shook his head angrily. Well, tanked up or not, the clown was going to have to help push that Japanese pile of junk off the ramp and out of the way.

Pausing just long enough to square up his battered, oil-stained baseball cap and shut off the engine, the trucker yanked his cab door open, jumped down, and started across the glass-strewn as-phalt in long strides. He was still several feet from the Toyota when the other man suddenly turned to face him, bringing the pistol he'd been concealing on target in one smooth, deadly, flowing motion.

Briggs stared at the weapon in shock. His mouth fell open. "What the—"

A single 9mm bullet caught him under the chin, tore upward through his brain, and exploded out the back of his skull.

Shahin knelt, retrieved the spent shell casing from the road with one gloved hand, and dropped it into his pocket. Neatness was a habit that had saved him so many times over the past several years that he indulged it without thought. There were many others in the HizbAllah who were less careful, but none who could match his record of operational success. He rose to his feet and turned away without giving the American he'd murdered more than a single disinterested glance.

Another pair of headlights swung across the scene and steadied as a small car, an old blue Nissan Sentra, pulled up beside the dead man's truck. Shahin stood motionless in the sudden dazzling brightness, waiting for the two other men who made up his special action cell to join him.

Haydar Zadi was the first out of the car. The lookout grinned in clear relief, showing a mouthful of yellowing, tobacco-stained teeth. "It went perfect, eh? Like clockwork!"

"Yes." Shahin nodded curtly, biting down an urge to snap at the older man. Didn't the fool know they had no time to waste? At most they had only minutes to clear away all signs of this ambush and move their prize under cover inside the warehouse they'd rented nearby. But Zadi was a "casual"—a fundamentalist radical recruited out of the local immigrant community for this one mission. Snarling at him would only make him more nervous, more prone to panic. Instead, the Iranian gestured toward the dead truck driver. "Toss that thing in your truck, my friend. We'll dispose of it later."

Zadi's smile vanished, wiped away by his first good look at the murdered man. In the glare of the headlights, the blood pooling around the American's shattered skull glistened black. He swallowed hard and hurried to obey.

Shahin shook his head in disgust. He disliked being forced to rely on a squeamish amateur, but he had no choice. The HizbAllah was one of the Middle East's largest and deadliest terrorist organizations, but outside of New York its network of covert operatives and sympathizers was still too poorly organized to support and conceal a larger force. He swung away and stalked over to the only other member of his small team.

Ibrahim Nadhir was the youngest of them all, barely twenty.

Taller than his superior, smooth-shaven, and slender, he stood staring up at the giant vehicle they had captured.

Shahin clapped him on the shoulder. "You can drive this monster, Ibrahim?"

"Oh, yes." Nadhir reached out a single hand and actually caressed the side of the big rig. His eyes were dilated. "It is a beautiful machine. A perfect machine."

Shahin suppressed a shiver. Tehran's revolutionary mullahs had refined the brainwashing techniques originally taught them by North Korean and Vietnamese instructors. He understood the value of what they had done to Nadhir. But surely no man could be at ease in the presence of one remade into the living hand of Allah.

He followed the younger man's fixed, adoring stare and smiled for the first time. The truck itself was nothing. Anyone with money could buy or lease such a truck. No, the real prize for this night's work was the big rig's cargo: a massive, cylindrical steel tank full of ten thousand gallons of high-grade gasoline.

Highway 101, north of San Francisco

The Marin County commuter tide was in full flood shortly before the sun rose. Tens of thousands of cars crept slowly south along Highway 101, inching through San Rafael, up the lone incline above Sausalito, through the Waldo Tunnel, and downhill toward San Francisco. Headlights glowed a ghostly yellow through the fog still shrouding the approaches to the Golden Gate Bridge.

Two vehicles ground forward with the rest. Four cars behind the lumbering gasoline tanker truck driven by Ibrahim Nadhir, Haydar Zadi gripped the steering wheel of his old, battered Nissan, darting occasional, frightened glances at the quiet, angry man seated beside him.

Shahin scowled at their slow, snail-like pace. As their local contact, Zadi had been responsible for scouting this section of their route. But nothing in the older man's reports had fully prepared him for this halting procession of luxury sedans, sports cars, and minivans. It was grotesque—an evil display of wasted wealth and power. Though a child on foot would arrive in San Francisco sooner, not one of these decadent, arrogant Americans could bear the thought of parting with his prized automobile.

Inside the Iranian, contempt warred briefly with envy. His scowl grew deeper. These people worshipped their creations of steel, chrome, fiberglass, and rubber above all other things— above even God Himself.

So be it, Shahin thought with grim finality. The HizbAllah would teach these idolaters a harsh lesson—a lesson scrawled in fire and blood. His dark eyes settled on the gasoline tanker truck up ahead. "How much further?"

"Two kilometers. Perhaps less," Zadi answered. He cleared his throat nervously. "The last exit before the bridge is very near."

Shahin nodded, ignoring the fear in his companion's voice. The old man would have to hold his cowardice at bay a while longer.

He leaned forward to get a better look at their surroundings. The steep hillsides of the Marin Headlands rose to the west— black masses still more felt than seen through the last remnants of night and fog. To the east, the ground fell away into the dark waters of San Francisco Bay. Distant lights twinkled along the eastern horizon, slowly fading as the sky paled before the rising sun. Ahead to the south, the Golden Gate Bridge's massive towers and suspension cables were already visible, rising out of the mist.

CHP Unit 52

Inside a sleek black-and-white cruiser parked just off Highway 101, California Highway Patrol Officer Steve Dwyer sat sipping the last cup of coffee from his thermos, studying the cars streaming past him through bleary eyes. He yawned, trying to get some oxygen into his bloodstream. After a long shift spent scouting for drunks, joyriders, and other lowlifes, the steady crackle of voices over his radio and the lukewarm coffee were just about the only things keeping him awake,

Dwyer stifled another jaw-cracking yawn and ran a hand over his scalp, frowning when his fingers slid along skin where only months before there had been hair. This goddamned job was getting to him, he thought. Hell, he was only thirty-two—way too young to be going bald. Maybe he could put in a stress claim and get the department health plan to cough up for some of that Rogaine stuff before he started hearing Kojak jokes and finding lollipops taped to his locker.

The sight of a gasoline tanker mixed in with the traffic streaming past him brought the CHP officer fully awake. For safety reasons, tankers and other carriers of hazardous materials were banned from the bridge and its approaches during rush hour. Everybody knew that, didn't they? For damned sure, every trucker who wanted to keep his license knew that. Everybody except this idiot, obviously.

Dwyer plucked his radio mike off the dashboard. "Dispatch, this is Five-Two. I have a HazMat rig trying to cross the Gate." He squinted into the slowly growing dawn. "Plate number is Delta, Tango, Two, Nine, Four, Five, Three. I'm making the stop now."

With its lights flashing, the CHP cruiser pulled onto the highway.

Highway 101

Shahin cursed as the American police car suddenly slid in right behind Nadhir's truck. The Iranian bent down to tear open the gym bag between his feet. He tugged a Czech-made Skorpion machine pistol out of the bag and checked its twenty-round clip. Satisfied, he flipped the weapon's folding wire stock into place and looked up. "Bring me close to that police car!"

When Zadi hesitated, the Iranian lifted the Skorpion's muzzle, aiming it casually at the older man's stomach. His eyes were cold. "Do it," he said softly.

Horrified, Haydar Zadi swerved left into the next lane and accelerated. Horns blared in outrage behind them.

Shahin ignored the noise, his eyes fixed on the patrol car still trying to pull Nadhir off the road. He could hear the policeman using his loudspeaker now. That was a wasted effort, he knew. The younger Iranian didn't speak or understand any English.

Weaving slightly under Zadi's unsteady hands, the Nissan drifted up alongside the black-and-white police cruiser. Still pinned by heavy traffic, neither vehicle was moving more than twenty kilometers an hour. Shahin held his breath, waiting for the right moment. Closer. Closer. Now.

The two cars were less than two meters apart.

He poked the machine pistol above the door frame, took careful aim, and squeezed the trigger.

The Skorpion stuttered wildly, bucking upward in Shahin's hands as he emptied a full magazine into the other vehicle at point-blank range. Sparks flew off torn metal, and glass shattered, smashed into a thousand fragments by the hail of gunfire. Blood fountained across the police car's dashboard. Still rolling forward, the black-and-white slowly veered off the highway, spun around until it bounced into the hillside, and came to rest with its lights still flashing.

Inside the Nissan, Zadi flinched, panicked by the sudden deafening noise. He yanked the steering wheel left again and then back hard right, narrowly missing another car. More horns sounded angrily behind and all around them.

"Fool!" Shahin snarled. He glimpsed a road sign ahead and off to the right. They were practically right on top of the last exit before the bridge itself. They had done their part. They had brought Ibrahim Nadhir safely to the brink of Paradise. Now it was time to pull away—to live and fight and kill on another day. He grabbed Zadi's shoulder and pointed. "There! The exit! Go! Go!"

Pale and shaking harder than ever, the older man obeyed. He jammed his foot down hard on the gas pedal. The Nissan sped off the freeway and flashed into an intersection without stopping. But they were moving too fast to make the turn that would have taken them back onto 101 heading north. Instead, Zadi skidded left, turning onto a small, two-lane road that snaked around and up the Marin Headlands, climbing ever higher along the sheer bluffs overlooking the Golden Gate and the Pacific Ocean.

Shahin whirled in his seat, straining to look through the Nissan's rear window. Behind them, the gasoline tanker continued straight on down the highway. It roared steadily past the exit, driving toward San Francisco.

On the Golden Gate Bridge

Sitting tall behind the wheel of the tanker truck, Ibrahim Nadhir paid little heed to the chaos and confusion breaking out on the road behind him. Zadi and Shahin were there. They would do whatever was necessary to safeguard his mission.

The young Iranian smiled gently. All the long months of his training and religious instruction were close to fruition. His full awareness, his very soul itself, was focused on one overriding objective: the huge structure looming out of the fog in front of him. Everything in his life had come down to this one moment. This one place. This one act of faith.

He crossed onto the Golden Gate Bridge. The sound of the road beneath the tanker's tires changed, becoming hollower and more metallic.

Taillights blazed a brighter red as the cars ahead slowed, preparing to wend their way through the tollbooth plaza blocking the bridge's southern end.

Still smiling, Nadhir brought the big rig to a stop right in the middle of the span. The situation was perfect. Cars crowded with Americans hemmed him in on all sides.

He lifted his gaze from the road before him and looked east. A bright glow through the mist marked the rising sun and a new day. His eyes alight with an inner fire, he murmured, "God is great."

Ibrahim Nadhir breathed in for the last time and reached for the detonator on the seat beside him.

The tanker truck exploded, spewing jagged pieces of steel shrapnel and ten thousand gallons of burning gasoline across the deck of the bridge. Vehicles inside the blast radius were shredded, smashed, and then set ablaze. Other cars and vans further out were hit broadside by the shock wave and blown completely off the span, plummeting into the icy waters below. Everywhere the gasoline landed, fires erupted, fed by new fuel from ruptured automobile gas tanks. Within seconds, the jammed center of the Golden Gate Bridge was a roaring sea of flame.

The Marin Headlands, above the Golden Gate

Half a mile away and five hundred feet above the bridge, Shahin tightened his grip on the car door handle, grimly holding on as Haydar Zadi took another hairpin turn too fast. The speeding Nissan skidded wildly, sliding across the centerline with its tires screeching.

The sky behind them caught fire, lit red and orange by an enormous explosion.

Zadi screamed, half blinded by the sudden glare off his rearview mirror. Still screaming, he spun the steering wheel around in a frantic effort to stay on the road. He turned the wrong way.

Moving at more than fifty miles an hour, the Nissan Sentra

flew over the edge of the cliff, tumbling end over end down a sheer slope in an avalanche of dirt, rock, torn brush, and shredded metal.

JANUARY 16

Building 405, Benicia Industrial Park

Building 405 had started its life as part of the Benicia Army Arsenal. Since the Army closed its base back in the early sixties, the warehouse had changed hands more than a dozen times, moving from owner to owner and landlord to landlord in a dizzying, confusing procession. All of them had valued its sheer size and easy access to the freeway, railroad, and waterfront. None of them had valued Building 405 enough to spend much time or money on maintenance. From the outside, the place looked more like a ruin than a going concern—a heap of flaking, cracked concrete walls covered by moss, rust stains from an old tin roof, and spray-painted graffiti.

FBI Special Agent Michael Flynn stopped at the entrance to the cavernous warehouse to watch his investigative team at work. More than a dozen agents were scattered throughout the building, poking and prying everywhere with gloved hands as they looked for evidence. Others were busy stringing yellow police tape around areas marked for closer inspection. Camera flashes went off in a rapid, uneven sequence as photographers recorded every aspect of their search.

Flynn followed every move intently, fighting hard to control the fury surging through him. The tall, grim-faced FBI agent had just come from the explosion site at the Golden Gate Bridge. Twenty-four hours after the bomb blast, firemen and forensics specialists were still prying charred bodies out of mangled cars strewn across the span. More than one hundred innocent men, women, and children were dead. Dozens more were

critically injured—all of them badly burned or maimed by flying chunks of steel. The bridge itself would be closed for days,
both by the investigation and by the need to make sure the
fires set by the tanker explosion hadn't affected its structural
integrity.

He shook his head. Over the years he'd seen a lot of dead
bodies and a lot of murder scenes. But he'd never seen anything
like that tangled, twisted slaughterhouse on the Golden Gate
Bridge.

Flynn wanted the bastards responsible for this massacre. He
wanted them more than he'd wanted any murdering thug he'd
hunted in his twenty-six years with the Bureau. His hands
clenched into fists.

He looked up as his top aide broke off a hushed conversation
with some of the other agents and hurried over. "What've you
got for me, Tommy?"

"Plenty." Special Agent Thomas Koenig nodded toward one
of the work benches surrounded by yellow tape. "We found
some cut strands of detonator wire over there. And the chemical sniffers are picking up definite traces of plastic explosive.
There and all over this dump."

Flynn grimaced. "So this was the bomb factory?"

"Yeah," Koenig said flatly. "The way I figure it is this: They
popped that truck driver out near the highway." He pointed to
the two massive ramps that led directly from the street into the
building's interior. "Then they drove the tanker right up one of
those ramps, parked it, and pulled down those steel doors. After
that, they had all the time in the world to wire it up for the big
show." He shrugged. "No muss. No fuss."

"Shit."

"Exactly." Koenig looked up at him closely. "Get anything besides a couple of John Doe stiffs out of that wrecked Sentra?"

Flynn nodded. Connecting the smashed-up Nissan they'd
found at the bottom of the Marin cliffs with the bomb blast and
dead CHP officer hadn't required brilliant detective work, just
common sense. "Weapons: a nine mil and a Czech machine pistol. They're on the way to ballistics. Plus, we found a coil of

wire and about a half-kilo block of plastic explosive in the trunk."

Koenig whistled softly. "Curiouser and curiouser." He frowned. "Think somebody else was out there yesterday morning cutting away a few loose ends?"

"Maybe."

"Sir!" One of the agents manning their bank of laptop computers and secure phones waved him over. "A fax just came in from D.C. They've got positive IDs on both those bodies."

Flynn arched a slate-gray eyebrow in surprise. That was damned quick work. Somebody was on the ball back at the Hoover Building after all.

He tore the paper straight out of the machine and scanned it rapidly. The Nissan's driver was pegged as a man named Haydar Zadi, a legal resident alien and Iranian national. His eyes narrowed. Zadi had been on the FBI's Watch List because of his reputed ties to Islamic radicals. No wonder they'd been able to identify him so quickly.

The biggest news was at the bottom of the fax. The other man they'd found wedged inside the crumpled Sentra was a bigger fish—a much bigger fish. Though they didn't have any fingerprints to match for a positive ID, the Bureau's counterterrorist specialists were virtually certain the dead man was one Rashim Mahdi, alias Mir Ahrari, alias Mohammed Shahin.

"Son of a bitch." Flynn ran his eyes down a long list of unsolved assassinations and bombings—some in Europe, some in the Middle East. This Shahin character had been marked by a host of Western intelligence agencies as one of the HizbAllah's key operational commanders. He looked up from the fax. "Put me through to the Director. Now."

JANUARY 20

The White House, Washington, D.C.

Outside the White House, the sun had long since set, bringing another cold, gray, and windy winter day to a dreary end. The streets around 1600 Pennsylvania Avenue were almost empty— abandoned by the capital's cadre of bureaucrats, politicians, and high-priced lawyers heading for plush suburban homes. Inside the executive mansion, however, staff aides, cabinet members, and uniformed military men still crowded the Oval Office.

Major General Sam Farrell knew it was considered an honor to be asked to offer advice to the President of the United States. Right now he was beginning to wish there had been some graceful way to decline that honor. He'd been invited to this high-level White House confab because he headed the Joint Special Operations Command, the headquarters controlling all U.S. military counterterrorist units, including the U.S. Army's Delta Force and the Navy's SEAL Team Six. That made him one of the Pentagon's top experts on terrorism. So far, though, Farrell, a sturdy six-footer with an open, friendly countenance, had been asked precisely two questions: Did he want coffee or a soda? And could he please move his chair over to make room for the Chief of Naval Operations?

To the general, the seating arrangements for this meeting reflected the current administration's fundamental priorities and power structure. The President's political gurus and media advisors filled the overstuffed chairs closest to his desk. Beyond them, the Director of the FBI, the head of the CIA, the Secretary of State, and the Attorney General sat in an awkward row, wedged together on a couch that was just a shade too small for all four of them. The Joint Chiefs of Staff, Farrell, and a few other subordinate officers were furthest back, relegated to seats lining the far wall.

At last, the President looked up from a thick, red-tagged briefing book he'd been devouring while the discussion raged around him. There were shadows under his eyes. Even in normal times the nation's chief executive often had trouble sleeping. Now his fatigue showed plainly. He fixed his gaze on the FBI Director. "You're sure the Iranian government was directly involved in this attack on us? That this wasn't just a couple of whacked-out crazies on a killing spree?"

Farrell shifted slightly in his chair, concealing his impatience. They'd already been over this same ground several times. The others around him didn't seem fazed. Apparently, marathon talkfests were the rule in this administration, not the exception.

"We're as sure as we can be under the circumstances, Mr. President," David Leiter answered carefully. At forty, the trim, telegenic FBI Director was young for his post, but he'd spent years as a prosecutor and he knew how to build a case.

Physical evidence from the site of the bridge massacre and the dead terrorists definitely linked the HizbAllah to the attack. And where the HizbAllah went, Iran was always close behind. Tehran's radical Islamic regime had helped create the shadowy terror group in the early 1980s. Tehran provided it with safe havens, training camps, and supplies. Tehran held the organization's purse strings and kept its ideological fervor burning at a fever pitch. For all practical purposes, Iran owned the Hizb-Allah. Given all of that, the consensus opinion among America's senior counterterror experts was clear: The HizbAllah's leaders would never launch an operation of such magnitude without direct authorization by Iran's Supreme Defense Council.

After all, Iran had plenty of its own reasons to strike hard at the United States. Since the fall of the Shah, the two countries had been more or less in a state of undeclared war. Iranian-sponsored hostage-takings had been met with American economic sanctions. During the 1980s Iranian attacks on neutral shipping during its war with Iraq had led to a series of fierce naval clashes in the Persian Gulf. In recent years Tehran's ambitious efforts to acquire missile and nuclear technologies had encountered stiff American resistance at all levels. With the collapse of the old Soviet Union, Iran's radical mullahs viewed the United States—the Great Satan—as the last remaining obstacle and threat to their revolution. And Tehran's state-controlled press had been quick to openly celebrate the "heroic martyrs who have plunged this dagger into America's heart."

Leiter paused, letting that sink in, and then pressed on. "Finally, Mr. President, we have hard evidence of official Iranian involvement." He nodded toward the CIA chief. "Several years ago, our intelligence services started making contacts in Eastern Europe's arms industries. We knew their desperate need for hard currency would make it difficult to completely block explosives sales to terrorist front groups. So we did the next best thing. We persuaded them to blend distinctive mixtures of inert chemicals into every batch of plastic explosive they manufacture. Essentially, every separate production run carries its own unique molecular signature."

The FBI Director paused again. "Our labs ran a trace on the explosives used in the Golden Gate Bridge attack. They came straight out of Iranian military stockpiles, Mr. President. Stockpiles the government of Iran purchased less than six months ago."

"I see." The President bit his lower lip, apparently still reluctant to make a final decision.

Farrell understood his hesitation. By their very nature, military operations involved killing. They were also inherently hazardous—both physically for the men tasked to carry them out and politically for the national leaders who approved them.

Still frowning, the President shut the briefing book in front of him and glanced toward the small man seated to his left. "Any thoughts, Jeff?"

Balding, scrawny, and often dressed in worn suits that were ten years out-of-date, Jefferson T. Corbell blended oddly with the rest of the button-down crowd inhabiting the White House. Despite that eccentric appearance, Farrell knew, the man wielded enormous power.

Corbell was the President's top political tactician, the keeper of his prospects for reelection.

"We have to hit the Iranians back, Mr. President. Hard." Corbell at least had no doubts. He leaned forward, stabbing the air with a finger to emphasize his points—speaking forcefully through a soft southern drawl. "When the American people find

out who was behind this attack, they'll want action on this—
not finger-wagging or U.N. resolutions."

The diminutive Georgian glared at the Secretary of State as if
daring him to disagree before he turned back to the President.
"Our focus groups all say the same thing: You can't afford to appear weak or indecisive. God knows, we can't afford to let this
thing linger on much longer. This foreign policy shit is dragging
all your poll numbers down."

Farrell hid his distaste for Corbell's reasoning. It shouldn't
take bad polling news to push and pull this White House into
retaliating for one of the worst acts of terrorism ever conducted
on U.S. soil, but he'd been around Washington long enough to
know that domestic politics played a role in every administration's foreign policy decisions. Civics textbooks aside, that was
the way the world worked, and you couldn't ignore it.

The President seemed to read his mind. He smiled wryly.
"Well, I guess I don't often get the chance to win votes by doing
the right thing. Admiral Dillon?"

"Yes, sir?" The white-haired Chairman of the Joint Chiefs
straightened in his chair, expectation plain on a face weathered
by years spent at sea in all seasons.

"Put your forces in motion."

FEBRUARY 5

In the Persian Gulf, east of Qatar

The still, calm waters of the Persian Gulf exploded, blasted
apart by a missile surging skyward from below the surface.
Boosted at first by a solid rocket, it climbed rapidly, deploying
tail fins, stub wings, and an intake for its jet engine. As soon as
the airfoils bit into the air, the Tomahawk cruise missile arced
over, diving for the concealment offered by low altitude.

The sea erupted again, eighty yards further north. Another

missile roared aloft. Tomahawk after Tomahawk followed, taking flight at precise, thirty-second intervals.

Several miles away, a four-engine, propeller-driven plane orbited slowly above the water.

Lieutenant (jg) Pat Royce sat in the right seat of the Navy P-3C Orion, watching the launch through binoculars, counting the missiles. They fanned out slightly over the deep blue water of the Gulf, speeding away to the north at just under the speed of sound. Not terribly fast for a jet, Royce thought, but compared to this bus, that's pretty zippy.

He keyed his mike, using the intercom to be heard above the thrumming roar of the Orion's engines. "I've got six good birds so far, all heading in the right direction, Dave."

The pilot and mission commander, Lieutenant Commander Dave McWhorter, nodded. He spoke into his own mike. "Sparks, pass the word, 'Launch made on time, proceeding smoothly.'"

Except for quick scans of his instruments, the P-3 pilot kept his own eyes on the skyline, ready to throw the Orion into evasive maneuvers at the first sign of trouble. So far the launch area was clear of air and surface traffic, and the Tomahawk missiles were working as advertised. But they were still attacking a hostile foreign power, close to its shores.

McWhorter could feel the sweat beading up on his forehead. There were Iranian jet interceptors based at Bandar-e Abbas, scarcely two hundred miles east. Loitering like this to observe and report on the missile launch wasn't terribly covert, and trouble could arrive a lot quicker than his old, lumbering turboprop could get out of it.

Six minutes began to seem an eternity.

As exposed as McWhorter and Royce felt two thousand feet above the surface, Commander Mark Marino felt even more so a hundred feet under it. USS *Helena*, a *Los Angeles*-class attack submarine, lived by stealth, and the explosions of water and spray above him sounded like a combination brass band and steam calliope. And in order to fire its salvo of Tomahawk cruise missiles, his boat had to steer a straight course at periscope depth at creep speed, ghosting north at no more than four or five knots. The noise also blinded many of his own sonar arrays. Not that they were much good anyway in the warm, shallow waters of the Persian Gulf.

If any of the ultra-quiet diesel subs the Iranians had bought from the Russians were lurking close by, Marino and his whole crew could be dead before they even knew they were under attack.

Ducking that unprofitable and unnerving thought, he scanned *Helena*'s control room.

Chief Walsh, the boat's senior fire control technician, hovered over his board, making sure that if the automated sequence went wrong, it didn't get any worse. Not far away, Master Chief Richards, chief of the boat, manned the diving panel, working hard to keep the boat level. Each Tomahawk weighed almost two tons. With that much weight leaving the submarine's bow every thirty seconds, Richards was kept busy trying to compensate for the rapid changes in *Helena*'s trim. The other officers and ratings packed into the control room were equally attentive to their duties.

Marino allowed himself to relax minutely. Except for a slightly greater air of concentration and a tendency to speak even more softly than usual, his crew might almost have been conducting a routine peacetime drill.

In a way, that wasn't surprising. Once started, the launch process was virtually automatic. The sub's navigation system gave the Tomahawks their starting point. Preloaded data packs fed in their destinations. Launch keys were turned and the fire control computers took over.

That all sounded deceptively simple, but Marino knew the reality was fiendishly complex. It had taken Navy planners days working around the clock to lay out and punch in each missile's flight path. Even with the space-based global positioning system—GPS—to help guide the weapons, landmarks had to be found, defenses plotted, and search plans determined, so that each Tomahawk had a near-perfect chance of reaching its target.

He glanced at the nearest clock. Precise timing had been as critical for this operation as it was for a space shuttle launch or an amphibious invasion. To make sure the missiles' GPS receivers could pull down enough data to get good navigational fixes, there had to be a certain minimum number of GPS satellites overhead. To guarantee the Pentagon and the White House near-instantaneous damage assessments, the missiles would strike right before a slated midmorning pass by U.S. recon satellites. That way the low morning sun would provide the contrast and shadows so useful for accurate imagery interpretation. Finally, the Tomahawk strike had to arrive between prayers. Devout Muslims prayed five times a day, and if missiles hit home during any of those periods, it would be seen as a blasphemous slap at all Islam—not just at Iran.

Helena shuddered one last time.

Marino had been counting silently to himself. He and Walsh straightened up at the same moment.

"Last bird's gone, sir," the chief reported formally.

Marino thought he heard a little relief creep into the older man's voice. He shook his head, half to himself. *Helena*, several of her sister boats, and the ships of a Navy surface task group had just fired what he hoped would be the first and last shots in a war. All in just minutes. Times had certainly changed.

He barked out a string of new orders. "Make your depth three hundred feet. Right standard rudder, steady on course zero four zero."

It was time to get out of here, back into deep water.

By the time Walsh reported and Marino issued his helm orders, their last Tomahawk was twenty nautical miles downrange.

The eighteen-foot-long cruise missile skimmed the sea surface, first steering west around the radar station on Lavan Island, then turning a little east to dodge another radar at Asaluyeh airfield. There were several paths through the Iranian radar net, and the missiles salvoed by the *Helena* and the other attacking ships were splitting up to use them all at staggered intervals.

Flying at nearly five hundred knots, Tomahawk number 12

made its landfall just ten minutes after launch, flashing low over a desolate, barren landscape. It climbed steadily, threading its way through the rugged Zagros Mountains littering the southern half of Iran. Tehran lay far to the north—almost at the outer limit of its range.

The weapon flew on, inhuman in the steadiness of its flight, the precision of its turns. Periodically, it would turn on its GPS receiver and fix its position. A conventional inertial guidance system could drift as much as half a mile over the flight time of a Tomahawk missile. The GPS unit would keep Tomahawk 12 accurate to within a few meters.

Six hundred seventy miles and seventy-five minutes after leaving the USS *Helena,* the missile crossed the Qom-Tehran Highway and came within sight of the Iranian capital.

Tehran's skyline was already marred by thick, billowing columns of smoke. Even in broad daylight, a burning oil refinery lit the inside of one black cloud with an ugly orange-red glow. The first wave of American cruise missiles had arrived only minutes before.

Although civil defense alarms were still sounding, the missile didn't hear the sirens. It was busy making another navigational fix. With four satellites above its horizon, the Tomahawk's GPS receiver established its position to within three meters—just half its own length. Still flying with impersonal, inhuman precision, it skimmed over the city, ignoring the few antiaircraft bursts beginning to pepper the air around it. The gunners were too late. *Helena's* Tomahawk 12 was the trailing edge of the American attack.

It passed over the Iranian Parliament building, already a shattered, burning ruin, and suddenly, matter-of-factly, dove down—aiming for the old Exxon building.

After being abandoned by its American owners following the Shah's fall, the ten-story concrete and steel structure had been taken over as headquarters for the Revolutionary Guards, the Pasdaran. Under their aegis, it also served as a center for planning terrorist raids. Members of the Pasdaran command staff routinely coordinated operations with the HizbAllah, provided its leaders with intelligence information, and supplied it with weapons and explosives.

Now the Pasdaran was paying for their actions.

Tomahawk 12 was the last of six cruise missiles targeted on the headquarters building. One missile's guidance unit failed in flight, sending it crashing into the side of a mountain near the southern Iranian city of Shiraz. But all four of the others screamed straight in on target, gutting the structure with thousand-pound warheads. Ripped apart by the repeated bomb blasts, the Exxon building's upper floors teetered and then collapsed into the street. Now this last missile dispensed tiny, HE-laden bomblets over the ruined Revolutionary Guards headquarters. Their rapid-fire detonations shredded steel and glass and flesh and anything else over a fifty-meter-square area.

White House Press Statement

"At 3:00 A.M. eastern standard time, elements of the United States Navy launched approximately one hundred Tomahawk missiles at Iran. Their targets were the military installations, economic facilities, and official ministries used by the Iranian government to plan or facilitate terrorist attacks against the United States, most recently the murderous and unprovoked bombing on the Golden Gate Bridge. Based on initial assessments, we believe this retaliatory strike inflicted heavy damage on all intended targets. Our own forces involved in the operation suffered no losses.

"Though we regret any loss of life, the government of the United States earnestly hopes the Islamic Republic of Iran will draw the appropriate conclusions from this action—and immediately and unconditionally abandon its support for international terrorism."

CHAPTER ONE
MANEUVERS

FEBRUARY 6

Near the Holy City of Qom, Iran

A cold, bitter wind whipped across Iran's barren central plain, whirling sand, dust, and charred bits of paper and clothing across a scene of utter devastation.

General Amir Taleh picked his way carefully through the rubble and uncertain footing, favoring his right leg. He stopped momentarily to get his bearings. Bearings on what? he asked himself angrily. Taleh fought the urge to pick up a piece of shattered concrete and throw it.

A slender, physically fit man, with a neatly trimmed black mustache and beard, Taleh wore a heavy winter coat over his light olive-green fatigue uniform. The only adornments on his clothing were the stars on his collar tabs indicating his rank in Iran's Regular Army. Nothing else showed his status as Chief of Staff of the armed forces. Even now, the self-appointed guardians of his nation's Islamic Revolution were not fond of rank and class distinctions.

He was standing amid the burned-out wreckage of what had been the most sophisticated electronics facility in Iran. Only a ragged outline of the exterior walls remained, showing its original size. Ten thousand square meters of factory space and sophisticated equipment lay jumbled inside—with no more value now than a slum's rubbish heap. Explosives experts picked their way carefully through the rubble, looking for unexploded bomblets, while in one corner two men with Green Crescent armbands wrestled with a body still partly buried in the debris. Police and Pasdaran guards kept civilians out, but just beyond the barrier a large knot of silent men and women waited for word of those still missing.

Almost nothing was left of the electronics plant—one of Iran's precious-few facilities able to fabricate and repair integrated circuits and other high-tech electronic components.

Taleh was tired, his leg hurt, and he was coldly furious with the fools who had poked and prodded a sleeping lion into swiping back. And for what? For nothing! A few newspaper headlines and a few more graves in the Martyrs' Cemetery. Certainly, nothing of lasting worth!

The Iranian general scowled. He had been at the Defense Ministry when the American retaliatory strike hit yesterday. He'd only escaped death because he had been visiting one of his subordinates when the missiles arrived. One Tomahawk had hit the corner of the building containing his offices—obliterating them.

As it was, his leg had been injured by falling debris, and many of his best staff officers were dead or in hospital. The Defense Ministry itself was a smoking ruin. Since then, Taleh had been busy, far too busy according to his leg, visiting the attack sites and assessing the damage and trying to decide what to do next.

He turned to his aide. "How many missiles impacted here, Farhad?"

Captain Farhad Kazemi's answer was immediate and precise. "Seven, sir, out of the one hundred and five we have accounted for." He added softly, "Seven technicians are known to be dead and twenty-two more were seriously injured. Another eight are still missing."

The tall, wiry officer was Taleh's constant companion. Almost three inches taller than the general, his youthful, unlined face stood in direct contrast to the older man's own war-hardened visage. Like Taleh, he was dressed in olive fatigues, the standard dress of the Iranian Army, but Kazemi was armed, carrying a holstered Russian Tokarev pistol at his side.

For more than seven years, Kazemi had been Taleh's secretary, bodyguard, and sounding board. As the long war with Iraq limped to its bloody, futile close, the general had saved him from a trumped-up charge before Iran's Revolutionary Courts, securing his absolute loyalty in the process. He was one of the few men Taleh could afford to relax with. As much as any general could relax with a captain, that is.

Taleh let some of his pent-up anger out. "Seven missiles out of one hundred and five. An afterthought! And look at this! Billions of rials lost, and more than a dozen irreplaceable men killed! Abilities so painfully built up, bit by bit, reduced to so much junk."

He strode to where a nervous civilian stood waiting, deferential almost to the point of cowering. Dust and dark, dried bloodstains covered the man's clothing, and his face showed the signs of strain and a night without sleep. Before the American attack, Hossein Arjomand had been the plant's assistant director. With his superior still missing and presumed dead, the engineer probably feared he would be the one held accountable by Taleh's notoriously unforgiving regime.

"I . . . I just learned of your arrival, sir." Arjomand swallowed convulsively. "How may I assist you?"

Taleh waved his hand at the man, as if to motion him away, then stopped. He should at least try to get an idea of the situation. "How long to rebuild?" he demanded.

The engineer turned pale. "At least a year, General, maybe more. International sanctions will not prevent us from obtaining the materials we need, of course, but it will cost more and take much longer." He paused, then continued with his head lowered. "But I have lost so many people. How can I replace them?"

Drawing a breath, he started to list his losses in detail, but Taleh stopped him impatiently. "Save that for your own ministry. Tell me this. This plant produced electronic components vital to our armed forces. Missile guidance units, radars. Can they be made elsewhere?"

"Not as many. Not a tenth as many, General."

Taleh nodded, then abruptly turned away with Kazemi in tow.

As they walked, the captain noted the near-instant response of two tough-looking men in his field of view. They turned, still keeping a lookout ahead and to the sides, and trotted toward the American-built Huey helicopter. If the general had ever seen any irony in trusting his life to a machine made by the Great Satan, it had long since passed.

Once clear of the rubble, Taleh strode purposefully toward the aircraft, its engines now turning over. Shouting to be heard over the whine, he asked, "How many more sites?"

"Two, General, a chemical plant and an aircraft repair facility."

"Skip them. The story will be the same as the three we've already seen today and the ones last night as well. We'll go back to Tehran. I have to prepare for the Defense Council meeting later this week. And I'll want to meet with my staff after prayers this afternoon."

Kazemi nodded and once again checked around them. This time he saw all six bodyguards, their German-made assault rifles at the ready, fanned out around the helicopter, all alert for any signs of trouble. These men, too, had been with Taleh a long time. His rank and position entitled him to have an escort, but he eschewed the customary Pasdaran detail. They might be ideologically correct, but the Revolutionary Guards were lousy soldiers, and one thing the general could not stand was a lousy soldier. Instead, he used his own detachment of Iranian Special Forces soldiers. All the men wearing the green berets were hardened veterans, and Taleh had seen combat with each and every one.

His care had paid off. The general had survived countless battles against the Iraqis and at least two attempts on his life—one by political rivals and one by leftist guerrillas.

The two officers climbed aboard, and the bodyguards, still moving by the numbers, ran to join them. Once the last pair of Special Forces soldiers scrambled inside the troop compartment, the pilot lifted off, using full torque to get the Huey moving as quickly as possible.

Buffeted by high winds, the helicopter raced north toward Tehran at two hundred kilometers an hour.

Taleh sat motionless, watching the ruined factory shrink and fall away behind him. His thoughts mirrored the bleak, bomb-shattered landscape below.

In the mid-1970s Amir Taleh had been a junior officer, freshly commissioned and serving under the Shah, Mohammad Reza Pahlavi. Those had been difficult times for any Iranian of conscience, especially for one in the Army.

Driven by the impulse to regain Iran's place as the Middle East's leading power, the Shah had embarked on a series of massive projects to modernize, to Westernize, his nation. There had been progress. Schools, hospitals, and factories sprouted across an ancient, once-impoverished landscape. But the price had been high. Precious traditions, customs, and religious beliefs had been ground underfoot in the central government's rush to ape the West.

Ironically, the rapid oil price hikes engineered by OPEC only made matters worse. The gushing flood of petrodollars had intensified corruption, always a way of life for many in the Pahlavi court. Billions had been squandered on extravagances and on ill-conceived public works. Through it all, rampaging inflation made life harder and harder for the vast majority of Iranians.

Stung by the first stirrings of mass dissent, the Shah's government had reacted badly, handing over more and more power to the dreaded secret police, the SAVAK.

Taleh remembered the ever-present SAVAK informers all too well. At the Tehran officers' academy, one of his classmates had disappeared one night. No one was sure of the young man's crime—certainly, Taleh had never seen him commit any treasonous offense. His friends had dared not ask his fate, and even his family had never been told what had happened to him. The SAVAK operated as a law unto itself.

After receiving his lieutenant's commission, Taleh had been fortunate. He'd been sent to the United States, one of the many talented junior officers selected for further military training by the Shah's patron country. The long, difficult months spent in Infantry Officers' Basic and Ranger School had taught him much. He'd come to know and respect many of his instructors and his fellow students. They were tough, dedicated men—soldiers to the core.

He had felt less admiration for America as a whole. Outside its military, American society seemed strangely lacking—somehow sadly incomplete. Its people were often spiritless, overly materialistic, and selfish. Taleh suspected it was because they had no unifying faith—no common bond to give them strength.

Despite that, Taleh had learned what he could, and he had learned it quickly and well. Then he had returned home to find a country in chaos.

SAVAK excesses had at last sparked the very unrest the Shah so feared. Confronted by mass demonstrations and riots, Iran's ruler turned to a reluctant Army, ordering it to impose martial law, to crush its own people at gunpoint.

Taleh grimaced. Those were ugly memories. He could still see the broken, bleeding bodies in his mind's eye. Hundreds had died in the street fighting: idealistic students, devout, gray-bearded clerics, and chador-clad women. Even children had been caught in the cross fire. But at least none of them had died at his hands.

He could still recall the look of mingled anger, pity, and understanding that had crossed his commander's face when Amir Taleh—one of the officer corps' rising stars—had refused to obey any order to fire on the crowds. There had been a blood price to pay for such defiance, of course.

Taleh shifted slightly, still conscious of the old scars across his back. He'd been arrested immediately and taken to a secret SAVAK prison. There he had endured countless beatings, countless acts of cruelty and torture. But he had survived. Scourged by men, he had grown ever more steadfast in his faith.

As God had willed.

When the Shah finally fell from power, he waited for his freedom. He waited in vain. The Islamic Revolution, which should have been his salvation, simply replaced one set of jailers with another. To the mullahs, Taleh's refusal to obey the Shah's martial-law orders meant nothing. In their eyes, his military training in America had "Westernized" him beyond redemption. They saw him and the other young officers like him as "a threat to the Islamic society" they planned to build.

And so the *faqih*, the Islamic judges who now ruled Iran, had ordered the armed forces "purified." Hundreds of field-grade and general officers were executed. Others escaped to the West and into a dreary, inglorious exile.

By some standards, Taleh was lucky. He was simply left in prison to rot—a captive languishing without trial and without a sentence. But just as a war against his own people had proved his downfall, so a war against an ancient enemy restored his fortunes.

When Saddam Hussein's Iraqi legions stormed across the frontier, Iran's purged, "pure" Army proved itself incapable and inept. In desperation, the Islamic Republic combed through its prison camps to find the veteran soldiers it needed to fight and win. It had found Amir Taleh.

Throughout the eight-year-war, he had fought two enemies: the Iraqis and many inside the Republic's own governing circles. In a way, the mullahs were right. He had been Westernized, at least in the sense that he had accepted the Western idea that tactics and military reality were not affected by revolutionary doctrine. Competence and sound planning mattered more on the modern battlefield than blind courage.

He'd proven that, in battle. Starting out in command of a company, promotion had come quickly to him, a combination of survival and skill. First an infantry battalion, then a Special Forces battalion. He'd spent more time in combat than almost any Iranian officer now alive—much of it behind Iraqi lines.

His decorations, grudgingly awarded, marked him as Iran's top soldier.

Those decorations had also saved him from falling into the hands of the Pasdaran, the fanatical Revolutionary Guards. Products of the Revolution, the Pasdaran's leaders viewed all Regular Army officers as potential traitors—or more dangerous still, as potential rivals for power within the Republic. For them Taleh was a walking nightmare: a decorated hero, a victorious leader, and a devout Muslim who ignored their authority. They'd never been able to touch him.

He frowned. Of course, he had never been able to touch them either. To his utter frustration, he had been forced to watch them send thousands of devout young volunteers to futile deaths in foolish frontal assaults, unable to speak out. The Revolutionary Guards had no grasp of tactics. They did not understand their enemy. Wrapped in a cloak of ideology, they never evaluated their actions against the brutal test of reality. Worse yet, the men at the top had never made the sacrifices they demanded so casually of others.

Since the end of the war, Taleh had devoted himself to rebuilding Iran's Regular Army. Despite continuing opposition from the Pasdaran and other radicals, he'd risen steadily in rank, climbing to the very top of his profession. He had never married. Surrounded by enemies as he was, a wife and children would have been little more than a point of weakness, a constant vulnerability. No, his soldiers were his only family.

Kazemi's voice broke into his thoughts. "Five minutes, General."

He could see Tehran now. A thin haze of smoke still hung over the skyline, almost twenty-four hours after the attack. Fires were still burning out of control in some parts of the city, spreading outward from the gutted shells of the Majles, the Parliament building, and the Defense Ministry. One bright spot in all this was the destruction of Pasdaran headquarters, but the capital had suffered more in one day than it had in the entire eight years of war with Iraq.

The American missiles had killed hundreds, and hundreds

more were in hospitals all over the north of Iran. Most of those
killed were government workers, technicians, military officers,
or officials. Every ruling body except the Council of Guardians
had suffered some loss.

The American message was clear. Payment for the dead in
California had been returned tenfold, and much of his nation's
military power had been savaged. And to what end? Was this
worth it? Taleh shook his head, still staring out across the city
flowing by below him.

Despite years of support from Tehran, HizbAllah and the
other groups had done nothing to improve the strategic position
of Iran or of Islam itself. Though occasionally stung by their
random bombings, hijackings, and hostage-taking, the United
States and its allies were still able to maintain their hold on the
Middle East—playing one Islamic country off against another.

The helicopter settled heavily onto a makeshift landing pad
set up near the office building he'd selected as the Defense Ministry's temporary quarters. Several staff officers were visible
through the swirling dust, anxiously awaiting his return.

As soon as the rotors slowed, Taleh was out, favoring his leg
but moving as quickly as he could. The Defense Council meeting was still four days off, but there were preparations to make.

Somewhere in the air over Tehran, he'd made his decision.
This waste and destruction must never be allowed to happen
again.

FEBRUARY 10

Tehran

General Mansur Rafizaden sat in the back of his speeding black
Mercedes sedan, angrily contemplating the upcoming meeting.
By rights the Supreme Defense Council should have been gath-
ering at his headquarters, not at those of the Army. He scowled.

That cunning fox Amir Taleh was growing bolder in his efforts to steal power away from the Islamic Republic's true and tested guardians.

For more than a decade, Rafizaden had led the Basij, the People's Militia. He and his officers had mobilized tens of thousands of teenagers into hastily trained battalions for service in the war with Iraq. Many had died in that service, but since their deaths assured them all a place in Paradise, he was sure they had gone gladly.

Now he found himself suddenly thrust into command of the whole Pasdaran, a promotion earned when American warheads decimated the upper ranks of the Revolutionary Guards. Though new to his post, he took his responsibilities most seriously and he had no intention of surrendering his organization's hard-won powers to Taleh or any other tainted soldier.

Rafizaden began considering plans to humble his rivals. A guardian of the Revolution had to be energetic. He couldn't wait for threats to appear. He had to find those who were dangerous and crush them long before they could become a threat. Well, Taleh and his fellows were clearly dangerous.

While he sat deep in thought, his black Mercedes sedan raced through northern Tehran, escorted by two jeeps—one leading, the other trailing. Each jeep was filled with teenage Basij soldiers carrying a collection of assault rifles and submachine guns. During the more violent days of the Revolution, and during the war with Iraq, such escorts had been a necessity. Now they were viewed as almost a formality, and positions in the jeeps were given out as honors to favored soldiers.

The ambush took them all by surprise.

Just as the Pasdaran convoy passed one intersection, an Army truck suddenly roared out onto the street behind them. Before the men in the rear jeep could react, the truck braked hard and turned sideways, blocking the street to any other traffic. At the same instant a panel van pulled out across the convoy's path. The van's driver scrambled out of his vehicle on the passenger side, diving out of sight.

Even as the surprised Basij troopers readied their weapons,

rifle and machine-gun fire rained down on the two jeeps from several second-story windows. Hundreds of rounds ricocheted off pavement and metal and tore the guards to pieces in seconds.

Both escort jeeps, their drivers killed by the fusillade, spun out of control and crashed into the buildings lining the street. The Mercedes, armored against small-arms fire, tried to steer around the abandoned panel van, bouncing up and over the curb in a desperate bid to escape the trap.

An antitank rocket slammed into the sedan's windshield and exploded, spewing white-hot glass and metal fragments across the driver and a bodyguard in the front seat. Rafizaden and an aide in the back ducked down and were spared the worst of the blast. The move bought them only moments of life.

A second rocket ripped the Mercedes' roof open, showering both the Pasdaran commander and the younger officer with lethal splinters. Then the first RPG gunner, hurriedly reloading, fired again. This third warhead streaked downward and exploded deep inside the vehicle, turning it into a shapeless pyre.

Defense Ministry, Tehran

General Amir Taleh supervised the last-minute arrangements for the Supreme Defense Council meeting personally.

It was a sign of the mullahs' confusion that they were unable to prevent him from hosting the gathering here on his own ground. Like the armed forces, their ranks had been thinned by the American missile strikes. Many of the ruling faction's top men were dead—buried beneath the rubble of the Parliament building and other official ministries. Power had been lost and gained, and political alignments were in flux.

Taleh stood near the door to the conference room, watching his nervous aides hurriedly arranging the maps and other briefing materials he'd ordered prepared. This was to be a critical meeting, one that would change the course of the Islamic Revolution, possibly even deciding its ultimate success or failure, and along with it the survival of Iran as a state. It was clear that changes were needed. Taleh understood that, even if the *faqih* did not.

Captain Kazemi appeared at the door to the meeting room, quietly waiting to be noticed. Taleh nodded to him, and the young officer strode over to the general, doing his best to look calm.

"Sir, we've just heard from the police. There's been an attack on General Rafizaden's car. He's dead."

Taleh's eyes narrowed. "Go on."

The staff clustered around Kazemi as he recounted the first reports flowing in: The convoy ferrying the new head of the Revolutionary Guards to the conference had been smashed in a swift, violent street ambush—wiped out by automatic-weapons fire and rocket-propelled grenades. The only clues to the crime were some pamphlets scattered over the scene. Written in Kirmanji, they demanded independence for Kurdistan.

Taleh sighed audibly, and inside, the knot of tension almost disappeared. "Very well, Captain. We'll move the meeting back an hour. The Pasdaran will need some time to appoint new representatives."

Kazemi asked, "Should we cancel the session altogether?"

Taleh shook his head. "No, Farhad, everyone else is already en route. Unless the Imam directs otherwise, we will meet."

He glared at the rest of his staff. "There's nothing we can do about Rafizaden. Everyone, back to your tasks."

The cluster of officers and civilians dissolved. Taleh turned back to his aide. "Do the police have any clues to the assassins' identity?"

Kazemi shook his head. "Nothing much. Nothing more than a description of well-armed men in civilian clothes. The entire attack was over in just a minute or two. They promised to send anything else they find to our intelligence office."

Taleh allowed himself a small smile. "Good. Carry on, Farhad. You know your orders."

The captain nodded crisply and hurried away.

The general also nodded, but inside, to himself. Over the next few weeks Kazemi would make sure that the Special Forces troops involved were transferred to other units in other provinces. As highly experienced soldiers they would be welcomed by their new commanders. At the same time, Taleh's net of die-hard loyalists in the Army would grow.

That was a sideshow, though. The most important thing was that Rafizaden was dead, and the Pasdaran would be confused and leaderless.

Taleh looked at his watch. In a little more than two hours, the President, Prime Minister, the remnants of the Defense Ministry bureaucracy, the armed forces, and the Pasdaran would meet to decide on a response to this latest American attack. He now anticipated little serious resistance to his proposals. Though they were both mullahs, the President and the Prime Minister were also canny politicians, adept at setting their sails to ride out every shift in the Republic's stormy factional politics. Neither man would choose to confront the man who led their nation's armed forces—not without assured backing from the Revolutionary Guards.

No, with the Pasdaran crippled, Amir Taleh would dictate Iran's future course.

MARCH 4

Defense Ministry

Perched on a small settee outside Taleh's private office, Hamid Pakpour waited in mounting dread. He mopped the sweat off his brow, cheeks, and neck with a large handkerchief, acutely aware that his nerves were stretched to the breaking point. Why had he been summoned here? What could the head of Iran's military possibly want with him?

Certainly, he was a prominent merchant—and one of the richest men in all Iran. But he had always been very careful to stay out of politics. Just as he had always taken pains to make public his intense devotion to Islam and to the Revolution. Many in the government had received tangible proofs of his devotion—discreet gifts of land or marketable securities.

Could that be the reason? Pakpour wondered uneasily. Did the general want his own "assurances" of the merchant's loyalty? He prayed fervently to God that was so. Anything else would be disastrous.

Only the blind and the deaf could not know that Taleh had emerged from the chaos of the past month as *the* power behind the President and the Parliament. Security duties once the exclusive province of the Revolutionary Guards were increasingly performed by Regular Army units. The Pasdaran was little more than a pale shadow of its former self. Its best men were being transferred to the Army. Many of the rest were simply being pensioned off. A few, the most radical, were said to be under lock and key—detained for certain unspecified offenses against the state.

"General Taleh will see you now. Come with me."

Pakpour looked up to find an Army officer standing beside him. Sweating again, he rose hurriedly and followed the taller man into the next room.

Even for temporary quarters, Taleh's office seemed spartan. Beyond a single desk and two chairs, there were no furnishings. Maps of Iran and its neighbors covered the walls. The general's desk held nothing more than a phone, a blotter, and a personal computer.

Taleh himself looked up from reading a dossier and nodded towards the chair in front of his desk. "Sit down, Mr. Pakpour."

The merchant obeyed, conscious of the taller Army officer still standing almost directly behind him.

"Your family? They are well?"

Pakpour moistened his lips, somewhat reassured by the other man's manner. No Iranian moved too quickly or too directly to the business at hand, preferring to open any discussion with small talk about small matters. Whatever Taleh wanted, he was evidently willing to observe the usual social niceties. "My wife and children are all in good health, General. They long for the spring, of course."

"Naturally. This winter has been bitter for us all."

Pakpour found himself relaxing minutely as the conversation drifted lazily through the prospects for warmer weather ahead.

When it came, the change in Taleh's manner was swift, sudden, and horribly direct. He leaned forward, all pretense gone from his voice and manner. "You have close ties to the West, Mr. Pakpour." He tapped the dossier in front of him. "Ties which many of our fellow countrymen would consider treasonous."

Pakpour paled. They knew. Despite all his precautions, despite all his clever bookkeeping, they knew. With inflation running at more than fifty percent a year, the sums offered him by America's CIA for snippets of political and economic information had been too tempting to refuse. Gold held its value at a time when the rials circulated by the Republic were scarcely worth the paper they were printed on. He tried to croak out a denial.

Taleh cut him off with a single icy glance. "In fact, I fear that many would consider your connections to a foreign spy agency worthy of a death sentence." He paused for a long moment before continuing. "I do not."

The merchant sat dry-mouthed, stunned.

Taleh smiled thinly. "I have messages I want you to carry to the West, Mr. Pakpour. Messages I cannot and will not entrust to regular channels." His smile disappeared, replaced by a frown. "The HizbAllah's foolish war of terror against America has gone too far and cost us too much. I wish to end it. We have been isolated from the world for far too long."

He closed the dossier on his desk with an air of finality and pushed it aside. "Will you act as my go-between in this matter?"

Pakpour, still trembling, was scarcely able to believe his ears or his good fortune. "Of course, General. I am your servant—your humble servant."

"Good." Taleh seemed satisfied. He nodded to the tall, silent Army officer standing behind Pakpour. "Captain Kazemi will show you out. We will speak more of this later."

When the door closed, Taleh rose from his desk. He stood for long minutes at the window, contemplating the city spread out before him. New-fallen snow carpeted the streets and rooftops and turned the rugged mountains lining the northern horizon white.

His eyes closed in concentration. He disliked having to rely on a fat, greedy fool like Hamid Pakpour, but he would not spurn the gifts laid before him by God. It was time to set his long-dreamed plans into motion. For years the radicals of the HizbAllah and other terrorist groups had been a constant drain on Iran and its armed forces, sucking up money, arms, and other resources for no worthwhile end. Well, he thought grimly, no longer.

CHAPTER TWO

THE VEIL

MAY 2

Over Iran

SwissAir Flight 640 rolled ponderously into its final approach to Tehran's Mehrabad International Airport. The huge DC-10 shuddered as it lost altitude, buffeted by columns of hot air rising off the sunbaked sand and silt below. Outside the jetliner, the clear blue sky faded abruptly into an ugly brown murk. Sited nearly a mile above sea level, Iran's sprawling capital city lay buried under a perpetual sea of smog.

Lieutenant Colonel Peter Thorn caught the first acrid, oily whiff of the polluted outside air slipping through the aircraft cabin's filters. He felt the hairs on the back of his neck rise. He frowned slightly, irritated at himself. The smell was unpleasant, but he knew his reaction was evidence of growing tension, not of a refined sensibility. The closer he got to Iran, the more the animal instincts buried below layers of intellect and training came to the fore, silently screaming out a warning to fight or flee.

Thorn shrugged inwardly, forcing himself to relax. In this case, his instincts could be right on target. Few Westerners would view a stay in the Islamic Republic calmly—no matter what combination of profit or curiosity drove them. The Revolutionary government was still too unpredictable and too arbitrary in its enforcement of the harsh Islamic code. The slightest slip in speech or action could land even an ordinary tourist in hot water. Three months after U.S. cruise missiles blew the hell out of Tehran and other Iranian targets, the stakes were far higher for an American soldier—especially for a high-ranking officer in the Army's counterterrorist Delta Force. Even for one carrying a safe-conduct pass personally signed by General Amir Taleh, the head of Iran's regular armed forces.

Taleh claimed he wanted to end Iran's undeclared war against the United States and its allies. The safe-conduct pass and the invitation to use it were intended as proof of his sincerity.

Discreet invitation or no invitation, there were plenty of high-ranking people in the Pentagon and the State Department who believed this mission's timing was an act of total insanity. Despite Taleh's cautious overtures through a CIA source, normal diplomatic relations between Iran and the United States were still nonexistent. Certainly, no U.S. analyst had an accurate read on the Islamic Republic's chaotic internal politics. Under those conditions, the nay-sayers argued, sending one of America's top commandos to Tehran was like handing Iranian extremists a gift-wrapped package for torture, interrogation, and ransom.

As the designated package, Thorn hoped like hell the nay-sayers were wrong. Neither he nor his boss, Major General Sam Farrell, the head of the Joint Special Operations Command, put much faith in secret messages and diplomatic feelers. Words didn't mean much when your life and freedom were on the line. Pictures and telecommunications intercepts were another story.

U.S. spy satellites were picking up solid evidence that Tehran was reducing its support for international Islamic terrorism. Transcripts of NSA-monitored signals between terrorist training camps in Iran and their headquarters in Lebanon, Syria, and

Libya were full of complaints about Iranian refusals to pay them or provide promised weapons. The latest satellite photos were also significant. Some of the camps run by smaller organizations now stood abandoned, apparently unable to operate without assured Iranian backing. But the larger, more self-sufficient groups—the HizbAllah, for one—were very much in business. Their facilities were still bustling, crowded with terrorists recruited from around the globe.

Those camps were the reason Amir Taleh said he wanted Western military observers on the ground inside Iran itself.

Hydraulics whined as the Swiss DC-10 slowly banked left and then leveled off, lining up with the unseen runway. Thorn felt a series of heavy thumps through the cabin floor beneath his feet. The landing gear was coming down.

He glanced out the window to his left. The smog pall cut so much sunlight that he could see a faint reflection of himself. Green eyes stared steadily back at him out of a lean, sun-darkened face. The face looked boyish, but he knew that was a measure of the reflection, not reality. He was thirty-eight and there were already a few strands of gray in the light brown hair he wore longer than Army regulations usually allowed. There were also tiny crow's-feet around his eyes—fine lines worn into the skin by wind, weather, and the pressures of command.

Thorn looked out past his own mirrored image, matching the countryside below to the memories of his youth. On the surface, nothing much seemed to have changed in the twenty-two years since he'd last seen Iran.

Clusters of drab, flat-roofed buildings were visible through the haze now, stretching along the straight line of the Tabriz-Tehran highway. Trucks, buses, and passenger cars crowded the wide, paved road, weaving in and out without apparent regard for traffic rules or safety. Mountains loomed in the distance, dark against the barren, treeless plain.

As a teenager, Thorn had come to Tehran to live with his father, a highly decorated U.S. Special Forces NCO assigned to help train the Shah's Army. Three years of his life had passed in a whirlwind of learning and adventure as he'd explored the maze of Tehran's narrow back streets and hiked through the rugged countryside outside the city. Along the way he'd acquired enough Farsi to mingle easily with every element of Iranian society—all the way from the ruling elites down to the poorest porters in the bazaars.

He had also made a number of friends. Some were American and British, the sons and daughters of businessmen and diplomats working in Iran. But chief among all his friends had been a young Iranian named Amir Taleh.

Taleh, four years older and already an officer cadet, had taken Thorn under his wing, showing him a side of Iran few Westerners ever saw and yanking him out of trouble whenever that proved necessary. Their personalities and interests were so similar that some of their fellows had begun referring to them teasingly as brothers. Neither of them had fought hard against the notion. Their friendship had seemed a great constant in a changing world. They had stayed in touch even after Thorn went home and while Taleh went through Ranger School in the United States.

Then Iran's Islamic Revolution shattered all normal ties between their two countries. Caught in the turmoil surrounding the rise of the radical mullahs, Taleh vanished—seemingly without a trace. Only in recent years had Thorn begun seeing references to his old friend in foreign military journals and intelligence reports. From then on, he had followed the Iranian's rapid rise through the ranks, greatly relieved to note that Taleh had avoided involvement in the terrorist schemes fomented by his nation's fundamentalist government.

He shook his head. After the Shah fell, the Iran he had loved so much as a boy had changed almost beyond recognition. Ironically, most of his professional life had been spent training to foil or avenge terror attacks sponsored by the Islamic Republic. Now it somehow seemed wrong to come back to this country unarmed and in daylight, flying in on a neutral airline.

Iran had been the site for Delta Force's first mission—and its greatest failure. When the aborted Iranian hostage-rescue mission came to its fiery end at Desert One, Peter Thorn had been just another second lieutenant, fresh out of West Point, green as grass, and fighting hard to survive Ranger School without being recycled. But even then he'd known he wanted more than any regular Army command could offer him—more challenge, more action, and more responsibility. Several years spent shepherding conventional troops through the dull grind of drill and paperwork only confirmed that. He'd jumped at the chance for a Delta Force slot like a drowning man grabbing for a rope. He'd never looked back.

Buoyed by the self-confidence and self-discipline instilled by his Green Beret father, he'd made it through a rigorous physical and psychological selection process designed to weed out all but the best. Those tests had been followed by six months of around-the-clock instruction in commando tactics and covert operations. Since then he'd climbed steadily from a captain commanding a twenty-man troop to a lieutenant colonel leading one of Delta's three assault squadrons.

Thorn rubbed his nose absentmindedly, feeling the thin, almost invisible scar that ran across its bridge and down under his right eye. The scar and a couple of metal pins in his right cheekbone were the only real reminders of a long-ago helicopter crash that could have been a lot worse.

He grinned suddenly. It was ironic. He'd been shot at in Panama, hunted through the Iraqi desert, and ambushed during a brief, nightmarish tour in Somalia—all without getting so much as a scratch. His only serious injury in sixteen years of active-duty service had come from an accident during a routine, peacetime training exercise. Not surprising, really. Delta Force operated under a single constant admonition: Train hard, fight easy.

"Seat backs and tray tables up, please. We will be landing soon." The flight attendant's pleasant, German-accented voice brought Thorn back to the present. The slender, good-looking brunette leaned across the empty seat next to him and deftly snagged the plastic cup of mineral water he'd been nursing for the last thousand air miles or so.

"*Danke schön.*" He brought his seat back upright. The flight

attendant smiled at him and moved off to check on the rest of
the main cabin, swaying in time with the increased turbulence.
She glanced back once to see if he was still watching and smiled
again.

Down, boy, Thorn told himself. Duty before pleasure. Uncle
Sam wasn't paying the airfare for this jaunt so he could make a
pass at a Swiss stewardess. Besides, she was probably more curious about him than seriously interested.

Even wearing a fashionable gray suit, button-down shirt, and
conservative tie, he didn't look much like his fellow passengers.
Most of them were older and heavier—solid-looking Swiss, German, and Iranian businessmen who were either still bent over
paperwork or sacked out under airline-issue blankets. There
were more than he'd expected. America's cruise missile strikes
and the political upheaval they'd sparked had been bad for business. But now, as the first rumors of changed Iranian government attitudes began filtering out, commercial travelers were
starting to return.

The DC-10 thundered low over the airport's inner beacon
line and dropped heavily onto the runway, braking hard after
one jarring bounce that rattled teeth and shook a few overhead
compartments open.

Thorn kept his eyes locked on the landscape sliding past the
decelerating jetliner. Mehrabad International was busy—
crowded with jets and turboprops in the colors of Iran's two national airlines and those of the major European carriers. Fuel
trucks and baggage carts rumbled across the tarmac, crisscrossing between taxiing planes.

At first glance, it could have passed for any major airport anywhere in the industrialized world. A closer look dispelled that
impression. Two camouflaged, twin-tailed interceptors were
parked just off the runway. Ultramodern MiG-29s on strip alert,
he realized—kept ready to take off at five minutes' warning.
Further out, near the perimeter fence, there were sandbagged
emplacements for antiaircraft guns and SAM launchers. Taleh
might be making overtures to the West, but the forces he commanded weren't letting their guard down.

Still bouncing slightly as it rolled across the rough, often-patched tarmac, the SwissAir jet turned off the runway and slowly taxied toward Mehrabad's single terminal building. The steady roar of the DC-10's engines faded to a high-pitched whine and then to silence. A bell chimed through the cabin loudspeakers. They had arrived.

Thorn sat motionless for a moment, breathing steadily to relax nerves and reflexes that were now on full alert. Then he unbuckled his seat belt, pulled a soft-sided bag out from under the seat in front of him, and stood up, leaning forward to keep from smashing his head into the baggage compartment above. Even though he stood an inch under six feet tall, his height exceeded the design specs for a window seat.

He ignored the standard announcements crackling through the intercom in German, French, Italian, English, and Farsi. If his old friend didn't really have enough power to protect him from Iran's radical Islamic fundamentalists, a knowledge of customs regulations and the local weather wasn't going to matter one damn bit.

Thorn suddenly missed the comforting weight of a pistol at his side. Cheer up, Daniel, he told himself, it's time to poke your head into the den and find out whether or not the lions really are friendly. He stepped out into the aisle and joined the other passengers already streaming toward the forward cabin door.

A lone Iranian Army officer in a neatly pressed dress uniform stood waiting at the end of the jetway. Thorn headed toward him, eyeing the tall young man's unfamiliar rank and unit insignia.

"You are Colonel Thorn?" The Iranian soldier's English was good, though heavily accented.

Thorn nodded. "That's right." He offered his passport and safe-conduct letter in proof. "Here are my credentials."

The Iranian shook his head. "That won't be necessary, sir." He smiled. "I am Captain Farhad Kazemi, General Taleh's military aide. Welcome to Iran, Colonel."

"Thank you, Captain." Thorn shook Kazemi's outstretched

hand, trying to conceal his surprise. Whatever he'd expected, it wasn't this casual, matter-of-fact reception.

"If you will follow me, sir." The Iranian captain nodded toward the main terminal area. "I have a staff car waiting to take you to your quarters."

Thorn moved off beside the younger man, striding easily through the men and chador-clad women waiting to board other flights. A few stared back at them, openly curious at the sight of an Iranian soldier escorting an obvious Westerner. He ignored them, more interested in getting an answer to the question uppermost in his mind. "And when do I meet with General Taleh?"

Kazemi turned his head. "Tomorrow morning, Colonel. After you have had a chance to rest from your journey."

MAY 3

The Manzarieh camp, northern Tehran

The Manzarieh Park camp sprawled across several acres in Tehran's fashionable northern quarter. Surrounded on all sides by pleasant, suburban homes belonging to wealthy businessmen and government officials, the camp contained barracks, classrooms, armories, and firing ranges. Shade trees lined the wide, well-paved streets and open grounds inside the walled compound. At its peak, Manzarieh Park had housed nearly a thousand terrorist trainees from around the world.

Now it was on fire.

Clad in a set of unmarked Iranian Army battle fatigues, a bulky flak jacket, and a steel helmet, Lieutenant Colonel Peter Thorn double-timed across a broad avenue, heading for a bullet-riddled, burning gatehouse that marked the main entrance to the camp. Tough-looking Special Forces troopers formed a protective ring around him, their assault rifles at the ready.

Black smoke swirled across the street, billowing from the wrecked gatehouse. The smell of cordite lingered in the air. Corpses littered the pavement—HizbAllah guards gunned down when Amir Taleh's assault force smashed its way through into the training complex.

The leader of his escort force, a short, swarthy sergeant, peered around one corner of the burning building and then motioned Thorn forward. "Safe! Safe! All ended." He pointed toward the sprawled bodies and drew one grimy thumb across his throat. "Understand?"

Thorn nodded. He loped through the gate with his escorts in tow.

The camp itself was a scene straight out of Dante's *Inferno.* At least half the barracks and other buildings were ablaze, gutted by rocket-propelled grenades, satchel charges, and cannon fire. Bodies dotted the streets and lawns. Most wore the shapeless fatigues or civilian clothes preferred by the HizbAllah. A few, very few, wore the olive-drab uniforms and green berets of Iran's Special Forces.

Soldiers combed through the burning compound, hunting for surviving terrorists with a care and precision that Thorn admired. Those moving were always covered by other teams prone and ready to fire. T-72 tanks and BMP-2 infantry fighting vehicles sat at key vantage points, turrets swiveling as the gunners scanned their surroundings for potential threats and new targets.

Still trotting forward behind the sergeant, Thorn whistled softly to himself. He'd read many reports on the Islamic Republic's armed forces. None gave them credit for the kind of professionalism he saw displayed here. Striking at first light, Taleh's handpicked troops had ripped through Manzarieh like a tornado through a Kansas trailer park.

"Come!" The Iranian sergeant pointed toward a small band of officers and NCOs clustered near one of the T-72s. Radio antennas and open map cases signaled the presence of a senior command group.

Thorn easily pinpointed Farhad Kazemi in the gathering. The

young captain stood several inches above his companions. His gaze shifted to the shorter, bearded man issuing a rapid-fire string of orders to the assembled officers. At one final word of command they scattered, moving off to rejoin their units. Only Kazemi and the man he'd been watching were left, heads bowed together as they conferred over a map.

His memories jumped more than twenty years into the past in the blink of an eye. Amir Taleh looked older, more care worn, and more serious, but there were still a few visible traces of the young cadet who had befriended an American teenager adrift in a foreign land.

The two Iranians turned at his approach.

Briefly unsure of how to proceed, Thorn fell back on formal military courtesy. He came to attention and snapped off a crisp salute.

Taleh returned his salute just as crisply. Then he broke the tension by smiling and holding out his hand. "Peter! Welcome! It has been too long—far too long, my friend! You look well. Soldiering must agree with you."

Thorn smiled back. Circumstances had changed. Amir Taleh had not. "You don't look so bad yourself." He nodded toward the general's stars on the other man's shoulders. "Soldiering seems to agree with you even more!"

The Iranian shrugged casually. "God has willed it." It was the expression his countrymen always used to turn away the bad luck believed to be inherent in a compliment. "Thank you for accepting my invitation, Peter. I know it took courage to make this journey."

Thorn fought down sudden embarrassment. His earlier concerns about this mission paled in comparison to the very real risks Taleh and his men had just run to smash the Manzarieh training camp. They'd just killed more terrorists in half an hour than Delta Force had taken out in its entire history. "Not much courage. I've often wanted to come back to your country." He glanced down at the Iranian battle dress he wore and smiled ruefully. "I just never thought I'd do it while wearing this uniform."

Taleh laughed softly. "Well said." He waved a hand at the shattered, burning compound around them. "Tell me, Peter, what do you think of my little demonstration?"

"I'm impressed," Thorn said flatly. He hesitated only a moment before going on. If Taleh had wanted to meet a smooth-talking diplomat, the Iranian wouldn't have asked for him. "But frankly, I'm also surprised. Cutting off supplies to the HizbAllah is one thing. Declaring open war on them is another."

He nodded toward the dead terrorists strewn in every direction. "What you've done here can't be undone. After today, the HizbAllah and the other radical groups will want your head on a pike. No matter what happens between our two countries, you've put yourself and your troops awfully far out on a very slender limb."

"True." Taleh seemed unworried. "And that is exactly why I wanted you to see this operation. I wanted you to see how deadly serious I am about ending Iran's connection with these extremists."

The Iranian shrugged. "Of course, I will not deny that I have my own reasons for destroying the HizbAllah and the others like them. Although I am a good Muslim, the terrorists and their supporters in the Pasdaran and the Parliament have often been my foes. Crushing them strengthens my own position."

Thorn nodded. That squared with what little U.S. analysts knew about the current state of Iranian politics. "Sounds like classic economy of force." He smiled. "I suspect old 'Gut 'Em' Duszinski would be pleased."

Taleh's dark eyes lit up in amused recollection. He had gone through the Ranger School a few years ahead of Thorn, and Sergeant Major Duszinski was a legend in the U.S.-trained special warfare fraternity. After surviving six tours in Vietnam, the hard-nosed veteran had come home to teach ambush tactics at the Ranger School. Generations of soldiers since then had grown to cordially hate the man's guts. But none of them had forgotten the commonsense lessons he'd pounded into their aching brains.

The Iranian leaned forward and tapped Thorn on the shoulder. "You understand me. This is why I asked your superiors to send you, a friend and a soldier—a fighting soldier—as their representative. I will be honest. I do not trust your country's politicians or your diplomats."

Taleh smiled briefly. "For that matter, I do not trust my own politicians or diplomats. None of them, American or Iranian, will tell the plain truth if they believe a lie will suffice."

Thorn nodded. Taleh's wry sense of humor was still intact.

He glanced again at the shattered terrorist training compound. In less than an hour, the soldiers commanded by his boyhood friend had crushed a powerful nest of terrorists who had haunted the United States for years. Both the magnitude of Taleh's operation and the size of the gamble the other man was taking overwhelmed and chilled him. In one fell, bloody swoop, Taleh had severed the Iranian military's ties to Islam's crazed extremists. It was astounding—almost unbelievable. But seeing was believing. Dead terrorists did not lie, and those Taleh's troops had gunned down were men who had tormented the West for decades.

Suddenly impatient at the prospect of further diplomatic sparring, Thorn turned back to the Iranian. By openly attacking the HizbAllah, his friend had performed a valuable service for America. Taleh had also put his own life and career on the line. That kind of commitment deserved plain talk. "I guess the question is: Where do we go from here? You know my country will be grateful for your actions today. But what do you want from us in return?"

"What do I want? I want many things, Peter." Taleh shrugged again. "But I do not expect too much too soon. Iran and the United States have a long history together—an unfortunate history in recent years. True?"

Thorn nodded silently, thinking of the long, sorry string of hostage crises, bombings, murders, and retaliatory strikes.

"It will take time and much hard work to dissolve the enmities built up over so many years," Taleh said quietly. "But in the short term, I would like to offer my cooperation in the fight against these terrorists. My forces will deny them further safe haven inside Iran. And I can offer documents, pictures, and other records that your intelligence services will find invaluable. In return I want assurances against renewed missile strikes or other hostile actions aimed at my forces."

"And later?"

"Later I hope that our two nations can work more closely on a number of fronts." The Iranian studied him closely. "We both know that Iran is a poor country. This mindless, uncoordinated campaign of terror has cost us dearly. We have been isolated politically and economically for far too long. I am hoping that your leaders will help me change that."

"I see." Thorn did see. He was enough of a strategist to know what Taleh's offer of closer ties with Iran might mean for the United States and the whole Middle East. Ever since the Shah's fall from power, the U.S. and its Western allies had been searching for a way to stabilize the vital region. Their first choice, Saddam Hussein's Iraq, had proved itself an untrustworthy ally and an incompetent foe. The current alternative, Saudi Arabia, was a weak reed—sparsely populated, corrupt, and cordially loathed by most of its neighbors. If there truly was a chance that Iran could be lured back into the community of civilized nations, he knew the White House and the State Department would jump at it.

Shots cracked nearby. Thorn's head lifted in surprise.

Squads of Iranian Special Forces troops were walking slowly through the compound, methodically firing into each of the bodies littering Manzarieh Park's streets and blood-soaked lawns.

Taleh saw the question on his face and nodded somberly. "Yes. My troops are killing any terrorists who may only have been wounded."

He held up a hand to forestall any protest Thorn might make. "I know what your codes of military justice say about such things, but you must understand our position here. As you pointed out, we are now at war with the HizbAllah. Since they will show me no mercy if I fail, I will show them none now. In any case, every fanatic we take alive is only another prisoner the others will try to free—a constant irritant, perhaps even a danger to us again someday. Dead, they may become martyrs, but martyrs cannot hold a rifle or turn a detonator key."

He was right, Thorn knew. The UCMJ contained specific procedures for dealing with prisoners—procedures laid out with lawyerly precision. But very few of the rules written for an antiseptic courtroom were easily applied under combat conditions. And by its very nature counterterrorism was a murky field—one full of moral ambiguity and cruel necessity. Very few people outside the tight-knit organizations dedicated to fighting the shadowy war against terrorism understood that. Look at the public furor that had erupted several years before when a British SAS team ambushed several IRA guerrillas in Gibraltar and shot them down without warning or mercy.

He looked up. Taleh was still waiting for his response. The hardships of the Revolution and the Iran-Iraq war had made his friend far more ruthless than he remembered. But this was the other man's fight and his home ground. Second-guessing his decisions now would serve no useful purpose. He nodded his reluctant understanding.

The Iranian seemed satisfied. "Good." He glanced at his watch and signaled Captain Kazemi over with a quick gesture. "Farhad will escort you back to your quarters for now, Peter. I will join you there after my prayers."

Taleh clapped him on the shoulder again. "Then we can eat together and discuss these matters at greater length. We can also talk of the old days—the better days of our youth." He swept his eyes over the smoldering ruins of the Manzarieh camp. "And in considerably more pleasant surroundings."

MAY 10

The U.S. State Department, Washington, D.C.

Twenty-four hours and seven thousand grueling air miles after leaving Iran, Lieutenant Colonel Peter Thorn finished debriefing the last set of self-proclaimed State Department experts on the results of his mission. He gritted his teeth as the door to the conference room swung shut behind him and turned to the senior officer at his side. "I swear to God, sir, I've never seen such a group of pompous, arrogant . . ."

"Calmly, Pete. Calmly." Major General Sam Farrell steered him away from the room and down a tiled corridor toward an elevator. He pressed the down button and stood back. "Our current lords and masters of the Foggy Bottom may be pompous. They are arrogant. But they most certainly are *not* deaf."

"Sorry, sir." Thorn took a deep breath and then released it slowly. Farrell was right. He would gain nothing by losing his temper right in the State Department's inner sanctum. He'd never thought debriefing this administration's coterie of foreign policy experts would be a walk in the park. So why should he kick when they turned out to be as obnoxious as he'd expected?

Oh, they had been polite enough—on the surface anyway. They'd listened fairly attentively to his outline of General Taleh's moves to rid Iran of the HizbAllah and to the recap of his conversations with the Iranian leader. But there had been a dead silence when he'd offered to take questions. More telling still, he and Farrell had been completely ignored during the prolonged discussion that followed his briefing.

In fact, it had become very clear that the band of corporate lawyers and former academics who made up the State Department's current policy elite were utterly uninterested in the views of those they saw as uniformed robots—as simple men suited only to obey orders from their civilian superiors. Instead, Austin Brookes, the elderly, courtly Secretary of State, and his inner circle were a lot more interested in claiming total credit for Iran's sudden change of heart. Thorn had heard enough abstract nonsense about back-channel diplomacy and geopolitical "levers" in the past two hours to last him a lifetime.

At least Taleh was proving a man of his word.

His troops had pounded two more HizbAllah camps while Thorn was still in Iran. And a preliminary analysis of the data he'd brought back from Taleh showed that many of the dead were terrorists who had been on the U.S. government's Most

Wanted lists for years. In the long run, Thorn thought, that mattered a hell of a lot more than which set of American bureaucrats counted coup for making the Iranians see sweet reason.

One thing more was sure. Taleh was thorough. He played to win at all times. He accepted no excuses—not from his subordinates and not from himself. That was something Thorn found familiar. It was the way he'd lived his own life from boyhood on.

"Coming, Pete?"

"Yes, sir." Thorn hurriedly collected his wandering thoughts and followed his commander into the elevator. Without talking they rode down to the car waiting to take them back to Andrews Air Force Base. He and Sam Farrell had been friends for more than ten years and the older man knew when to let him simmer.

But as soon as the staff car pulled out of the curving State Department drive and turned onto a busy, traffic-choked street, Farrell broke the silence. "Everything set for your change-of-command ceremony next month, Pete?"

"Yes, sir. And Bill Henderson's ready and raring to take charge." Thorn could hear the reluctance and regret in his own voice. He had commanded Delta's A Squadron for two years now—two of the happiest, most fulfilling years of his life. He'd relished every minute spent leading the officers and men widely regarded as the finest troops in the U.S. Army.

Nothing lasted forever, though—especially not in the Army. His command tour was up and it was time to hand the outfit over to his deputy. Time to take on a new assignment. Although that was long-hallowed Army routine, he knew that not even the colonel's silver eagles he'd be pinning on at his new post would ease his sense of loss.

Giving up command of the squadron was bad. Giving it up for a staff job was worse. And giving it up for a staff job at the Pentagon was awful beyond all measure.

On the strength of his successful covert mission to Iran, Farrell had wangled him a new post as the head of a special intelligence liaison unit, an outfit charged with tracking and evaluating terrorist groups that might become JSOC targets. It was just the kind of ticket he needed to punch to climb higher in the military hierarchy. Somehow that wasn't much comfort. Like many officers who saw themselves as "warriors" first and career professionals second, Thorn regarded an assignment to the Pentagon with sheer, unadulterated loathing. The massive building was a maze of interservice politics, petty backbiting, paperwork, paperwork, and more paperwork.

He frowned, aware that Farrell was watching him with just the faintest hint of mingled sympathy and amusement. Oh, he'd ride the desk he'd been assigned and he'd do his best, but that didn't mean he had to like it.

Thorn shook his head in frustration. Cut loose by Iran, the HizbAllah and the other radical Islamic factions were on the run. They were vulnerable. And now, no matter how he looked at it, he was left with the disquieting feeling that he had been shunted off to the sidelines right when all hell was breaking loose for the terrorist bastards he'd been preparing to fight all his life.

CHAPTER 3

SHARPENING THE STEEL

MAY 22

In Iran, west of Shiraz

(D-DAY MINUS 207)

The camouflaged UH-1H Huey helicopter clattered west, following the trace of a winding valley deeper into Iran's Zagros Mountains.

Seated right behind the pilot and copilot, General Amir Taleh found the view beautiful but daunting. Razor-edged mountains soared high above the helicopter, some three or four thousand meters high. The peaks were brown, tan, dun—every earth-colored shade imaginable. Naked to the harsh sun beating down out of a cloudless sky, every sheer rock wall and jumbled boulder field radiated heat.

He glanced down. The narrow valley they were flying over was also a stark unrelieved gray and brown, the color of rock and bare earth. Nothing green seemed to grow along the banks of a bone-dry stream bed that filled only during the region's short winter.

The Huey bucked up and down suddenly, rocked by strong gusts that clawed at the fragile craft. The deeper into the mountains they flew, the more turbulent the air became.

"Masegarh Base, this is Tango One-Four. Request permission to land. Over."

Taleh could hear the strain in his pilot's voice. Safe flying this far up in the Zagros required total concentration and pinpoint precision. Only the most skilled professionals in the Iranian Air Force were allowed to fly this mountainous route. Mistakes were too costly—in lives and, more important, in valuable machines.

He leaned forward slightly, craning his neck to see through the cockpit canopy. Several kilometers ahead, the valley widened, opening onto a broad natural amphitheater surrounded on all sides by jagged mountains. A dirt road snaked out of the valley and across the plain, visible from the air only where it cut through isolated clumps of weathered rock and withered brush. The road ended at a cluster of low buildings shimmering in the heat.

"Tango One-Four, this is Masegarh. You are cleared to land through Air Defense Corridor One. Winds are from the east at twenty-five kilometers an hour, with occasional gusts up to sixty kilometers."

"Roger."

Slowing now, the helicopter flew out of the valley and out across the barren plain, heading for a small cleared square of ground outside the Masegarh camp. A fuel truck and several jeeps were parked off to one side of the helipad. A Cobra gunship in Iranian Air Force markings sat nearby under camouflage netting. Needle-nosed shapes poking out from under more camouflage netting further away betrayed the presence of a SAM battery.

Engine whining, the Huey slid over the pad, flared out, and settled heavily onto the ground. Sand and small pebbles kicked up by the rotor downwash rattled off the helicopter's fuselage and skids.

Taleh could see a uniformed reception committee waiting beyond the arc of the Huey's slowing rotor. Ducking beneath the blades, one officer ran forward and slid the side door back.

Bracing himself against the heat, Taleh jumped down. Kazemi followed right behind him. They walked slowly over to the waiting officers.

One immediately stepped forward, came to attention, and saluted. "Welcome to the Masegarh Special Forces camp, sir."

"Colonel Basardan." Taleh returned the salute, eyeing the other man with approval. He'd handpicked Basardan for this assignment. During the war with Iraq, the colonel had proved himself a good soldier and a superb organizer, but he'd been letting himself go at a Defense Ministry desk job in Tehran. Now the incipient paunch and double chin were gone. Evidently, the mountains and the harsh training routine agreed with him.

"I believe you already know my senior officers?" Basardan asked.

Taleh nodded. He'd personally selected each and every man above the rank of lieutenant stationed at Masegarh.

The weapons, tactics, demolitions, and language instructors assigned to this training camp were among the best in the Iranian armed forces. They represented a sizable percentage of his country's relatively small pool of professional soldiers. In fact, the whole facility represented an enormous investment in precious time, scarce resources, and even scarcer military skills. Had they known anything about it, Taleh's surviving opponents inside the government would have been sure to decry the whole effort as an inexcusable waste. Others might argue that the officers based here would be better employed teaching their specialized skills to the broader mass of Iran's Regular Army.

He would have ignored them all. The elite commando teams being trained and hardened at Masegarh were vital to his future plans.

Taleh was suddenly impatient. Written reports meant nothing. He wanted to measure the progress being made here with his own eyes. He caught Basardan's eye and nodded toward the waiting Russian-made GAZ jeeps. "Let's proceed, Colonel. You can brief me on the way."

"Yes, sir." The commandant turned away, signaling his officers into their vehicles. "We have an exercise or two under way that I think you will find most interesting."

With Taleh, Basardan, and Kazemi in the lead jeep, the small convoy swung off the helipad, heading down the lone dirt road toward the base.

The sentries manning a checkpoint outside the main gate saluted and waved them through. Taleh noted with interest that none of them were Iranian.

Basardan saw his look and nodded, pitching his voice to carry over the sound of the jeep's motor. "They are trainees, General. We expect them to perform a wide range of routine duties— everything from manning our guard posts to working in the maintenance pool."

"Very good." Taleh was pleased. These men would have to function efficiently deep in enemy territory for several weeks and even months. Anything that enhanced their self-discipline and self-sufficiency was a welcome addition to the course.

The camp's "Main Street" was two rows of plain concrete barracks, an administration building, classrooms, an armory, and an elaborate obstacle course—all the trappings of a regulation Army training facility. There was only one unmilitary touch. The minaret of a small mosque built just beyond the compound stood as a constant reminder of God's dominion.

Masegarh had once been used as a Pasdaran camp for training foreign "freedom fighters." Taleh was having dozens of such places dismantled, but he had ordered this installation kept in operation and even upgraded slightly. But only slightly.

One had to be careful. The location of this place was certainly known to Western reconnaissance satellites. Still, he believed it would attract less attention to use an established base than to build a new one. Taleh's mind conjured up the English phrase that most closely captured his intention: to hide in plain sight.

He scanned the camp as they roared through it at high speed.

Everywhere, he saw groups of hard-working men jogging in formation, with an Iranian noncommissioned officer always close on their heels. Others scrambled under and over the obstacle course's maze of barbed wire, pits, walls, and ropes—all under a steady barrage of shouted criticism from unsmiling, eagle-eyed instructors.

More trainees were busy on firing ranges outside the base perimeter, honing their combat skills with a wide array of different weapons. The periodic crack of high-powered sniper rifles being zeroed in blended with the steady rattle of automatic-weapons fire. Other men clustered around Iranian Special Forces officers demonstrating rocket-propelled grenade launchers, mortars, plastic explosives, and shoulder-fired SAMs.

The convoy kept moving, accelerating down the road and out into the countryside. They drove for fifteen minutes before pulling up to a stone cairn by the roadside—the only landmark visible in the whole bleak landscape. Another GAZ jeep and two senior noncoms with clipboards waited near the cairn, occasionally consulting their watches.

Taleh turned to Basardan for an explanation.

"I sent a platoon of twenty men out on a twenty-kilometer hike this morning. They have three hours to complete the march." The camp commandant nodded toward the cairn. "That is the finish line."

Taleh waited. The glint in Basardan's eye told him there was more to this exercise than a simple road march.

"Each man carries a rucksack filled with thirty kilograms of rocks."

Taleh could hear Kazemi suppress a soft, astonished whistle. He understood his aide's amazement. The grueling march the colonel had outlined surpassed anything in the standard Iranian Army regimen.

Kazemi leaned forward from the back of the jeep. "And if they do not finish within the three-hour deadline, Colonel?"

"They fail the course," Basardan said flatly. "Permanently."

The young captain sat back, silent, while Taleh exchanged glances with the colonel. The trainees did not know it, but there were no return-trip tickets from Masegarh. His orders dictated the most extreme measures to maintain absolute secrecy.

Taleh saw the leading group of marchers first. He pointed down the road. "There they are, Colonel."

The four men were still several hundred meters away, tiny in the distance and barely visible through the shimmering heat waves. All wore the same olive-drab fatigues and reeled under the weight of the bulging rucksacks slung from their shoulders. As they came steadily closer, Taleh could hear their hoarse voices egging each other on.

He nodded. That was good. Very good. Even in pain and near the edge of utter exhaustion, these men were still a group—not a pack of lone wolves.

At last, half carrying one man who'd stumbled and nearly gone down, they trotted the final hundred meters to the cairn and collapsed panting on the ground. Taleh studied the four men with interest. One looked like an Arab, probably a Palestinian. Another might be a Turk or a native of one of the former Soviet republics. Two were Bosnian Muslims—one dark-haired, the other fair. All in all, a mix typical of the camp's population.

One of the noncoms who had been waiting checked their names off on his clipboard. The other stalked forward to the middle of the huddle of gasping trainees. "Congratulations, little children. You made it." He paused. "Trucks are waiting to take you back to the camp."

Still too breathless to speak, they looked up with smiles that were faint on worn faces. One by one they levered themselves off the ground and staggered painfully to their feet. Slowly the smiles faded. There were no trucks in sight.

The Iranian sergeant nodded pleasantly. "The trucks are eight kilometers that way." He pointed back down the road. Away from Masegarh.

All of them stared back at him, mouths hanging open in shock and despair. The dark-haired Bosnian shook his head wordlessly, moaned, and collapsed like a puppet with all its strings cut. The Turk simply sat down, numbly staring at the ground between his feet.

"Impossible. Impossible," the Palestinian gasped. He pointed a shaking finger at the stone cairn. "That is the end mark. The finish. You told us that."

"Yes, that is true," the Iranian Special Forces sergeant agreed patiently. His tone hardened. "But circumstances change. Plans change. You must expect the unexpected."

The fourth man, one of the Bosnians, silently nodded. His fair hair and pale blue eyes made him stand out from his darker companions. His actions were even more different. He turned to the others and began pulling them back to their feet, all the while urging them on. "Come on, Selim! To your feet, Ahmad! Up, Khalil! You want to rest? We'll rest at the trucks!" His voice, though hoarse, still carried a note of utter conviction and confidence.

Stooping, he slung his arm around the other Bosnian and moved off at a tired, weaving half-trot. The others followed him.

Taleh and Basardan looked at each other and nodded somberly. The attrition rate at the Masegarh camp was three out of four. It was easy to see which of these men would survive.

"What is his name?" Taleh asked as the trainees staggered off into the distance.

"Sefer Halovic."

Headquarters building, Masegarh Special Forces camp

By late afternoon, Taleh had seen enough to know that Colonel Basardan and his officers had grasped his vision for the special units he expected them to train. Using many of the same techniques employed by the American Rangers, the British SAS, and the Russian Spetznaz, they were molding a cadre of fierce, disciplined commandos—men schooled in the arts of intelligence-gathering, sabotage, and killing. Men who would act as his own "smart weapons" deep in the heart of an enemy homeland.

He had no illusions. Those who survived Masegarh would not be supermen. The time allotted was too short. But they were already infinitely superior to any forces the HizbAllah or the Pasdaran had ever managed to field.

"Trainee Sergeant Halovic is here, sir." Captain Farhad Kazemi stuck his head through the door of the office Taleh had commandeered for a series of interviews. He needed to know more about these men than he could glean from typed dossiers or from watching them maneuver through a series of set-piece exercises. Would they be able to do what he asked of them? Were they tough enough? Intelligent enough? Ruthless enough?

"Send him in, Farhad."

The Bosnian came into the office, obviously fatigued but still standing straight and reporting correctly. Taleh studied him quietly for a few moments.

Halovic had a lean, hungry look that the Iranian suspected had been there long before he began his training at Masegarh. His face was thin, almost gaunt. Even his hands were long and slender—a surgeon's hands. That was appropriate. According to his file, the Bosnian had once been a medical student at the university in Sarajevo. Clean-shaven and of average height, he appeared to be somewhere in his late twenties.

Halovic was also a quiet man, as might be expected under the circumstances. He met Taleh's probing gaze without blinking or looking away. Like any soldier, he'd apparently learned that meetings with superiors were usually a time to keep your mouth shut, your ears open, and to say what they wanted to hear.

Taleh finally broke the silence. Speaking in English, the lingua franca of the camp, he pointed to a chair. "Sit down, Sergeant."

"Thank you, sir." The Bosnian sat down easily, almost gracefully. Even off his feet he gave the impression of a hunter set to strike, of a predator poised to kill.

For a moment, Taleh felt as though he were staring into a

mirror. He shook himself mentally and went on. "You look like a man who has seen hard times, Sergeant."

Halovic thought for half a beat before replying. "Everything in Bosnia is hard, General."

Taleh nodded. He indicated the file folder open on the desk in front of him. "You have seen much fighting." It was not a question. Combat experience was one of the basic preconditions for admission to the Masegarh training course.

"Yes, sir," Halovic said quietly, firmly.

Before war tore his homeland apart, the Bosnian had been content to continue his studies in Sarajevo. The idea of being a soldier had been the furthest thing from his mind. Even when the killing and atrocities began, he'd only seen the need for another doctor. He had fully intended to serve his people as a healer.

But then Serb irregulars butchered his family, along with dozens of others in his home village. And something had died inside Sefer Halovic—died along with his elderly parents, his sisters, and his younger brother.

He had abandoned his medical training. It was pointless to heal the sick and wounded while the men with guns were free to act again—to slaughter at will. Coldly determined to kill as many Serbs as possible, Halovic had gone to war. The self-discipline, intelligence, and imagination that would have made him a brilliant doctor had instead made him an effective killer and a superb guerrilla leader.

At Taleh's prompting, the Bosnian outlined several different engagements, including ambushes, assassinations, and carefully planned assaults. His voice was calm, dispassionate—almost as though he were talking about someone else's actions. Only when he described his most spectacular exploit—a massive car bomb attack on the street outside the Yugoslav Defense Ministry itself—did any hint of satisfaction creep into his voice.

"The Serbs were still counting their mangled dead weeks later." He showed his teeth. "I believe that was when they truly began to know fear."

Halovic's face tightened. "Then the cease-fire came. The precious 'peace' imposed by the U.N. and by the Christian powers. The surrender that will strangle my people while the Serbs grow stronger on our stolen lands." His eyes were ice-cold now, full of remembered rage. "But I did not sign that surrender. I have not abandoned the struggle. And that is why I came here, General."

Taleh nodded, satisfied. It was a chilling tale, but one he knew was repeated many times all over the camp. Of the five hundred or so men at Masegarh, most were Bosnians, recruited out of the wreckage and despair in Sarajevo and the other butchered Muslim cities and villages. Others were ex-PLO fighters, African guerrillas, or Muslims from the former Soviet republics. There were thousands, tens of thousands, of such angry, dispossessed men all over the world. They were fertile ground for his recruiters.

He leaned forward. "I have one more question, Sergeant."

Halovic looked up at him, under full control again. "Yes, sir?"

"Those men today? Your comrades on the march? What would you do if they faltered the same way on a mission?"

Halovic's answer came swiftly, without even a moment's hesitation. "I would kill them, General."

After Kazemi ushered the Bosnian back to his squad, Taleh turned to Basardan. "How many are there like him, Colonel?" he asked softly.

The camp commandant shook his head. "Not many, sir. Oh, the rest are good," he reassured Taleh, "but Halovic is something special."

"Yes." Taleh's eyes narrowed in thought. "Keep me informed of his progress. I believe we will have work worthy of this young man."

CHAPTER FOUR

LEARNING CURVE

JUNE 10

The Pentagon

Colonel Peter Thorn rode the escalator up from the Pentagon Metro stop and stepped off into a crowded corridor junction. He paused to get his bearings. That was a mistake. Trying to stand still in all the chaos around him was like trying to stem an avalanche with a barbed-wire fence.

Uniformed soldiers, sailors, airmen, and marines of every rank pushed past on both sides, hurrying onward toward a staircase leading up to ground level. Civilians dressed in everything from business suits to electrician's coveralls joined them in equal or greater numbers. Strange faces streamed by in a dizzying, never-ending parade. More than twenty thousand military and civilian workers labored inside the labyrinthine five-sided building, and right now most of them seemed to be pouring up and out of the Washington, D.C., area's subway system in a lemminglike rush to start the workweek.

Thorn found himself moving forward with the noisy throng—propelled onward almost against his will, constantly jostled by elbows and by muttered, impersonal apologies as people bumped into him. He could feel himself tensing up.

He didn't like crowds. He never had—even as a child.

Thorn hated the feeling of anonymity, of being nothing more than a faceless member of the same herd. He'd worked hard all his life to excel, to stand out from those around him. You couldn't do that as part of a crowd.

Even worse, you lost total control over your own movements and actions. Like a naval convoy reduced to sailing at the speed of the slowest ship, any large group tended to act at the level of the lowest common denominator. No matter what the reason, if enough people in a mob started moving in a particular direction, you either moved with them or you got trampled.

Thorn narrowly avoided a collision with a coffee-carrying Navy captain apparently deep in his own morning fog. He shook his head. This was crazy. Every soldier in Delta Force knew the importance of teamwork—but their teamwork was based on a clear understanding of each man's distinctive strengths and skills. The only skill involved here seemed to be in putting one foot in front of the other with your eyes open. He had the sudden sinking feeling that he was going to miss the tight-knit professional community at Delta's Fort Bragg compound more than he'd ever imagined.

Beyond the staircase the stream of civilians and military personnel arriving for work began to assume some semblance of order, forming into long lines to funnel through the security station guarding the Pentagon's main entrance. Everyone entering the building had to flash a badge toward the bored-looking Department of Defense guards manning the station.

With a sense of relief, Thorn veered out of the line he'd been stuck in and headed for a desk near the guard post.

One of the DOD policemen behind the desk looked up from the sports section of the *Washington Post*. "Can I help you, Colonel?"

"Sure hope so." He held out his military identity card. "My

name's Thorn. I'm taking up a new post here, but I don't have a pass yet." He nodded toward the enormous entrance hall visible beyond the security station. "Plus I'm not real eager to wander around in there without a native guide."

The cop smiled in agreement. "It's a hell of a maze, all right, sir." He took Thorn's ID and flipped open a thick book in front of him. "Right. Let's see if we can find out where you're supposed to go."

Squinting back and forth between the card and the book, the policeman ran his finger down a long list of names, ranks, internal addresses, and phone numbers. "Thomas . . . Thompson . . ."

His finger stopped moving. "Yep. Here you are, Colonel. JSOC Intelligence Liaison Unit. Director: Thorn, Peter, NMI."

NMI. No middle initial. That was the bureaucratic abbreviation used to fill in forms for those without middle names. Thorn knew that wasn't really accurate in his case. He had been born and baptized with a middle name—Aloysius. But the name had been his mother's choice. He'd dumped it when he was eleven, right after she divorced his father and vanished to "find herself." That was just a year after his dad had come home from Vietnam, and just two years before they went to Iran.

He squared his shoulders, shrugging off the flash of pain that always came with remembering those events—even after all this time. He'd survived. His father had survived. And he knew lots of people who were worse off. A whole lot worse off.

The DOD policeman picked up a phone from his desk and punched in a five-digit internal number. "Intelligence Liaison? Yeah, this is the main entrance security station. Listen, your new CO is here." He listened to the voice on the other end and then turned to Thorn. "They're sending someone up to meet you, Colonel."

Thorn nodded his thanks and stepped back from the desk to wait. He was conscious of curious looks from some of those shuffling past him on their way to work. But not from many. Colonels were a dime a dozen in the Pentagon. Here you evidently had to have three or more stars on your shoulder boards before anyone paid any attention to you.

He'd been waiting for more than ten minutes with rapidly diminishing patience when his "guide" finally showed up. A young red-haired man wearing a white short-sleeved shirt, a loosely knotted blue tie, and a security badge clipped to his shirt pocket came zooming out through the entrance, dodged through the crowd funneling in, and hurried over to the desk.

"Colonel Thorn?" the young man asked anxiously, clearly out of breath.

"That's right."

"I'm Mike McFadden, sir. One of your junior analysts. The Maestro . . . uh, Mr. Rossini . . . sent me up to get you in." McFadden swallowed. "Sorry it took so long, but it's quite a hike."

Seen up close, the analyst's appearance inspired even less confidence. Pens and what looked like a pack of chewing gum bulged behind his security badge, and the bottom of his tie showed signs of having been dunked in coffee or a cola not long before. There were even tiny traces of powdered sugar caught in the scraggly mustache McFadden seemed to be trying to grow.

Thorn sighed inside. Like every other special warfare operative, he'd never been a spit-and-polish fanatic, but this was going to take some getting used to. Strike that, he thought, looking at McFadden again. This was going to take a *lot* of getting used to. He cleared his throat, searching for something diplomatic to say. "You *must* be very, very good at your job, Mike."

"Sir?"

"Never mind." Thorn motioned toward the security checkpoint. "Lead on, Macduff."

"That's McFadden, sir . . ." The young man stopped and grinned suddenly. "Oh. I get it. Shakespeare. Right."

The analyst moved off again, ushering him through the checkpoint and metal detectors. He paused on the other side. "Where to exactly, Colonel? Want to pick up your building pass first? Or go straight to the office?"

Thorn made a quick decision. He needed to find out just what and who he was dealing with in his job. "The office."

McFadden nodded rapidly and led him past a row of shops

selling everything from books to toiletries, walking fast at a pace that almost bordered on a trot. Thorn was glad to see that. It made him think that the red-haired young man might not have just been making excuses for his own tardiness earlier.

Within minutes he was sure of it.

By then they'd gone up and down so many ramps, staircases, and identical corridors that Thorn was starting to feel totally, hopelessly lost. A sign on one wall reading "C-Ring" gave him the only clue to their current whereabouts. They were in the third of the Pentagon's five concentric rings. Swell. That narrowed it down to somewhere within a few hundred thousand square feet. Real useful.

McFadden held open the door to another staircase. "We're almost there, Colonel. Like I said, it's quite a hike."

Thorn followed him down the stairs and out another door. He stopped dead in his tracks.

They were in a basement corridor. Fluorescent lights glowed overhead at wide intervals. Some were out. Others flickered wildly, throwing misshapen shadows against walls painted a faded institutional green and off the bare concrete floor. Electric trolleys piled high with tools, machinery, and boxes of files whirred by in both directions.

Thorn looked up. The low ceiling was a tangled maze of girders, pipes, and wiring. He lowered his gaze to McFadden. "Is this a shortcut?"

"A shortcut?" The analyst seemed confused. "No, sir." He pointed down the corridor. "Our office is just down there a little ways."

Christ. Thorn knew that some of the armed forces' more traditional-minded senior officers bitterly resented the special warfare community's growing clout and stable budgets. He guessed that someone in charge of Pentagon office space had decided to exact some petty vengeance by installing the JSOC's new intelligence outfit in the most godforsaken place possible.

He trailed after the younger man until they came to a brown steel door set into one of the corridor walls. It was equipped with an electronic card reader and a ten-key pad. The letters "JSOC-ILU" were stenciled at eye level in fresh white paint.

McFadden gestured toward the door. "Welcome to the Dungeon, Colonel." He reddened. "I mean, that's our nickname for it . . ." His voice trailed away.

Thorn took pity on him and smiled. "Seems appropriate, Mike. Okay, the Dungeon it is." He pointed his index finger at the door. "Now let's get inside and get to work."

"Right." McFadden moved in front of him to slide his ID card through the reader and to input the code needed to open the door. Thorn noticed that the other man was careful to block his view of the lock's keypad. That was a mark in his favor. Even though the analyst didn't pay much attention to his personal appearance, he obviously took the need for security very seriously indeed. So his priorities were straight.

The door buzzed suddenly and unlatched.

"We each have our own card, sir," McFadden explained, stepping back as the door swung inward. "You'll get yours and the number code when you sign in at the Security Office."

Nodding his understanding, Thorn walked briskly into what McFadden called the Dungeon. At first glance the accommodations looked better than the bare corridor outside—but not that much better. There was a lot more light, the walls were painted a pale blue, and at least someone had laid a worn brown carpet over the concrete floor.

Beyond the secure door a narrow hallway opened on to a common area. A large table surrounded by chairs filled the center of the room and a small table off to one side held a coffeemaker and a stack of paper cups. Other corridors led off from this central room into the rest of the complex.

Thorn didn't have time to notice more. Several men and a couple of women were gathered near the coffeemaker, clearly waiting to greet him. They ranged in age from their early twenties to their mid- to late forties. All of them were civilians.

One of the oldest, a tall, balding, heavyset man, stepped forward right away and held out a huge, bearlike hand. "Colonel

Thorn? My name's Joe Rossini. I'm your deputy director. Welcome aboard."

"Thanks." Thorn shook hands with the man who would be his number two for the next year. Steeling himself to make the white lie sound sincere, he said, "I'm glad to be here."

Rossini nodded toward the others. "The rest of these eager, shining faces are your section leaders." Dark brown eyes gleamed behind the thick lenses of his plain black-frame glasses. "They crack the whip on the other analysts, keep the computers humming, and generally do all the real work around here while I fill in the *New York Times* crossword puzzle and think deep thoughts."

Thorn grinned. Whatever else he was, at least Rossini wasn't the kind of pompous bureaucrat he'd feared being saddled with. He paid careful attention as the big man introduced the others one by one, matching faces to names for later reference. He hadn't wanted this posting, but he was here now and he planned to do the best job he could.

When Rossini finished the introductions, Thorn looked the group over one more time. "I won't make a speech right now. I'm sure you'll all hear my voice far too often and far too soon." There were a few mildly nervous chuckles at that. He waited for them to die away before continuing in the same easy, informal tone. "I do want to make one point, though. I care a lot about accuracy and about the truth. What I don't care much about is strict military formality. So you don't have to keep calling me 'Colonel' or 'sir.' My first name's Peter and I expect you to use it. Okay?"

They looked relieved.

"Great. That's it, then. I'll see you all later in the day." He turned and nodded toward Rossini. "Right now the Maestro here and I are going to get better acquainted."

His new deputy's thick black eyebrows shot up in surprise at Thorn's use of his office nickname. Half hidden behind the other analysts, Mike McFadden gulped audibly and faded away down one of the corridors.

Thorn smiled inwardly. He'd filed away his guide's first, accidental revelation of Rossini's handle for use at the first suitable opportunity. In his experience it never hurt to have a reputation for being ultra-observant.

The man they called the Maestro wasn't slow on the uptake himself.

Rossini saw McFadden vanish, glanced at Thorn, and pretty clearly mentally added two and two together. The big man shook his head in mock dismay. "So what do people call you behind *your* back, Pete?" he asked.

Thorn shrugged, smiling. "I suspect you'll find out a hell of a lot sooner than I will." He motioned in the general direction of the rest of the complex. "How about giving me the fifty-cent tour before we get down to business?"

"To hear is to obey." Rossini led the way down the right-hand corridor. "We'll start with the Regional Analysis sections . . ."

Beyond the meeting room, the Intelligence Liaison Unit's quarters branched out into a warren of small offices crowded with cubicles, desks, computers, and filing cabinets. Maps, blackboards, and bulletin boards hung from the walls almost everywhere Thorn looked. Every room held two or three people either hunched over computer keyboards or conferring together in earnest tones. Television sets flickered in several corners, tuned to the major news networks with the sound muted.

The whole organization gave off a feeling of energy and quiet excitement. One bulletin board held rows of small black-and-white snapshots showing the high-ranking terrorists confirmed killed in Amir Taleh's crackdown. Another tracked the ongoing disintegration of the HizbAllah's command structure.

Thorn liked what he saw so far. These people weren't just going through the motions. They were genuinely committed to their work.

He could also sense Rossini's pride in his creation. In a little over a month, the big man had molded a disparate collection of forty or so counterterrorism experts drawn from everywhere across the vast alphabet soup of U.S. intelligence agencies into a unified team. That was an impressive accomplishment. Thorn knew a lot about motivating soldiers to work hard when their lives and those of their comrades were on the line. He was savvy enough to realize that he knew a lot less about motivating people when the stakes were more abstract.

The JSOC Intelligence Liaison Unit might be Major General Sam Farrell's brainchild, but it was obvious that Joe Rossini's drive and dedication had brought it to life.

His office was about as far back inside the complex as it was possible to get—right next to Rossini's. They shared a secretary and a photocopier. Beyond that and the same basic floor plan, the two rooms didn't have anything in common.

The deputy director's office was a mess. A series of framed photographs on the walls gave the room a personal touch. They showed a smiling Rossini, his wife, and an assortment of four or five children in a variety of settings. Everything else was work-related. Almost every square inch of desk and floor space was piled high with computer printouts and floppy disks. And books. Books on terrorism and psychology. Books on weapons, explosives, and sabotage. Books on the climates, cultures, and histories of different parts of the world. Stacks of books that were piled so high and so precariously that you had the feeling the slightest tremor would start an avalanche.

Slightly stunned by the sight of so much crammed into so little space, Thorn pulled his head out of Rossini's room and ushered the big man into his own barren work area. None of his own personal effects had arrived from Fort Bragg yet—not that he would have very much to hang on the walls even when they did, he realized.

He shut the door behind them, tossed his uniform cap onto his empty chair, and perched himself on one corner of the desk. He gestured toward the room's only other seat. "Take a pew, Maestro."

"Thanks." Rossini sat down heavily.

Thorn watched the big man closely, noting the way he winced as he straightened his left leg out. He had been limping by the time they finished the brief tour. "Your knee giving you trouble?"

"A little. Too much football when I was younger and too

many extra pounds now. My wife and kids watch my calories for me, but the weight doesn't seem to come off." Rossini dismissed his personal problems with a disinterested shrug. "What would you like to know first, Pete?"

"Well, I'd like a rundown on exactly how the outfit's shaping up. Plus, where you see us fitting into the JSOC and Pentagon scheme of things."

Thorn had read a huge stack of reports before flying up from North Carolina, but he wanted to hear it straight, without the usual official gobbledygook. From what Sam Farrell had said, Rossini had a reputation throughout the intelligence community for not pulling any punches—even when keeping quiet might benefit his career. This seemed like a good time to find out how much of that reputation for candor was deserved.

Rossini didn't disappoint him.

"We've got some damned good people working here, Pete." The big man smiled gently. "Some of their social graces aren't exactly up to snuff, but they're some of the brightest puzzle-pushers I've ever seen. Too bright for the powers-that-be in their old agencies, I guess."

Thorn nodded. He'd been worried by some of the things he'd read during his first quick scan through the Intelligence Liaison Unit's personnel records until he'd begun to see the emerging pattern. Backed by Farrell's carte blanche, Rossini had recruited mavericks—men and women whose skills were undoubted but who were widely viewed as square pegs in round holes inside the existing intelligence bureaucracies. At a time of declining budgets, the CIA, the NSA, and the other agencies were under increasing pressure to cut costs and staff. In those circumstances, the first to go were usually those who didn't quite fit the button-down, yuppified tone emanating from each organization's upper floors.

Those were exactly the kind of people Farrell had said he wanted for the JSOC liaison unit: people who were independent-minded and "just plain ornery enough" to take the analyses generated by the rest of the intelligence community, shake them up, turn them inside out, and basically play holy hell with the conventional wisdom.

Well, Joe Rossini had taken the general at his word, Thorn realized. The offices outside this room were crawling with men and women who loved nothing better than poking holes in other government agencies' pet theories. Men and women who were now under his authority. Terrific. He had the sudden, unnerving feeling he'd just stepped out into a bureaucratic minefield.

He shook off the feeling and asked, "Any problems so far?"

"You mean besides our wonderful accommodations?"

Thorn matched Rossini's wry tone. "Yeah. Besides that."

"Frankly, not as many as I expected. The teams I've set up are shaking out pretty well. The data's starting to come in and most of the agencies are cooperating—or at least making a good first stab at it."

Then Rossini shook his head. "But we need more focus, Pete. More practical input on the kinds of intel Delta, the SEALs, and the rest of the Command really need for planning and conducting operations. Without that we're just another time-wasting loop in the information cycle."

Thorn nodded, starting to understand why Farrell thought he could do some good here.

Providing the Joint Special Operations Command with highly accurate, up-to-date intelligence on terrorist groups and their foreign backers was the whole rationale for this new unit's existence. The Special Operations Command already had a Directorate of Intelligence staffed by hundreds of dedicated professionals, but they were mostly sited far away from Washington, D.C. They were also often mired in the kinds of interagency rivalries and lockstep thinking that inevitably developed in large organizations.

For years Delta Force and the other American commando units had been complaining about the quality of the intelligence support they received. Delta even had its own detachment of covert operatives, nicknamed the Funny Platoon, to provide tactical intelligence just before any strike. The ILU was an effort to build on that—to expand JSOC's storehouse of reliable information to the strategic and operational levels. People outside JSOC saw Major General Farrell's new unit as simple empire-building. People inside saw it as a matter of survival. Bad intelligence got good soldiers killed.

Apparently, the general was counting on him to give Rossini and his civilian teams the military and operational insights they lacked. Now, that made sense, Thorn thought, feeling a surge of excitement and satisfaction at the prospect of real, meaningful work—work that could save lives. He wasn't an analyst, and he certainly wasn't a skilled "fixer" able to navigate the Pentagon's tangled administrative backwaters. But he did know the kind of data commandos needed to survive and succeed.

He leaned forward. "Okay. Let's concentrate on developing that focus first, then. We can't turn analysts into Delta commandos, but we can give 'em a clearer idea of just what's involved in putting a mission together and in pulling it off without getting killed. Here's what I think we need to do . . ."

Rossini listened intently while he outlined his ideas, interrupting only to clarify something or to offer alternate suggestions.

By the time they broke for a quick lunch, Thorn was feeling better about his new post. A lot of his success or failure in this assignment would depend on how well he and his deputy director worked together. Although it would take time to fully sort their relationship out, his first take was positive. Rossini might be carrying around a lot of extra weight, but none of that fat was between his ears.

JUNE 18

Fighting an urge to put a bullet through the computer screen in front of him, Peter Thorn forced himself to take another stab at understanding the procedures required to request photorecon satellite time. The acronyms and bureaucratic doublespeak glowing on his monitor were all starting to run together in one unintelligible mass.

Pursuant to AFR 200-11, NSDD-42, and DCID 1/13, requests to the NFIB's Committee on Imagery Requirements and Exploitation (COMIREX) must first be approved by the appropriate offices and suboffices listed in DOD Circular 18/307.5 . . .

"Got a minute?" Rossini's booming voice broke the spell.

Thorn looked up in relief and waved his deputy in. "Hell, Joe, take an hour." He nodded in disgust at the electronic text showing on his computer. "I'll be old and gray before this stuff makes any sense to me."

"If you ever do figure it out, you'll probably be the first person in DOD history," Rossini said sympathetically. "The rest of us just fill out as many random forms as we can find and hope to hit the right ones by luck."

"Swell." Thorn swiveled his chair away from the computer. "So what's up?"

"Mike McFadden came to me an hour ago with some interesting material." Rossini sat down and plopped a thin stack of papers down on the desk in front of him. "He's been digging through some of the data the CIA collects from the Brits, the French, and the rest of NATO. These pieces caught his eye."

Thorn paged through them. Most were intelligence reports from the international peacekeeping units and headquarters stationed in Bosnia. Somebody, either McFadden or Rossini, had highlighted the significant sections with a yellow marker.

His eyebrows went up. Buried deep among the routine descriptions of Serb, Muslim, and Croat troop movements and weapons deployments were some disquieting reports. There were rumors circulating through the Muslim armed militias and guerrilla forces—rumors of mysterious foreigners spreading money and plane tickets to men with good combat records and leadership skills.

He looked up at Rossini. "Somebody's recruiting terrorists again."

"Yep." Rossini spread his hands. "The question is, who?"

"The CIA have any ideas?"

Rossini shook his head. "Nope. Not that they're much interested. Langley doesn't see Bosnia as a priority. It's a European bailiwick. And there're no nukes involved to make it sexy for the Congress. Plus, they don't have anyone on the ground outside of Sarajevo."

"Shit." Thorn grimaced. "These recruiters could be working for almost anyone in the Islamic world. Iraq. Syria. Pakistan. Afghanistan. Even what's left of HizbAllah or Hammas. Hell, they've all got military training missions operating inside Bosnia."

"So do the Iranians," Rossini pointed out.

"True." Thorn nodded. He thought back over his conversations in Tehran. "Look, Joe, General Taleh promised to cooperate with us in the fight against terrorism. He's certainly kicked the hell out of them inside his own country. Maybe we should test his cooperation on a bigger playing field."

"You want to see if his own intelligence people have picked up these same rumors?"

"Right. Christ, one thing's sure. The Iranians are bound to have better sources in Bosnia than the Brits, the French, *or* the CIA." Thorn thought further for a moment. "Look, I'm flying down to Bragg next week for a conference with Farrell. Have McFadden put this together in an organized fashion and I'll take it with me. Then we'll see if the boss can shake loose a few more resources to follow this up on our own."

Rossini nodded. "Sounds good."

"In the meantime, we'll keep digging ourselves with what we've got now—including a call to Taleh." Thorn's jaw tightened. "Some son of a bitch is out there rebuilding a terrorist movement, and I want to find out who the hell it is."

CHAPTER FIVE

DRY RUN

JUNE 21

The Pentagon

Colonel Peter Thorn sipped his instant coffee and grimaced at the awful taste. Served him right for arriving before the coffeemaker's self-appointed caretakers turned the machine on, he thought. He bit down hard on a tired yawn.

He'd started coming in to the office before dawn—partly to get an early start on the day, but mostly to avoid the Pentagon rush-hour crush he disliked so much. Although the strategy worked, coming in early didn't mean he could leave any sooner. Mostly, he was still locked to his desk long into the evening. Since taking over the Intelligence Liaison Unit, he'd been putting in sixteen-hour days to bring himself up to speed on his analysts' work and on the way the DOD system ran.

Those extended days and nights were paying off in knowledge and understanding, but he knew he couldn't keep up the murderous pace for much longer. Falling asleep on a pile of reports during a meeting would probably not be the best way to build his new staff's confidence in him, he thought wryly.

His phone buzzed suddenly, bringing him wide awake. "Thorn here."

"Colonel, this is Sergeant Nyland in Communications. You have a secure call from Tehran. A Captain Farhad Kazemi?" The noncom stumbled slightly over the unfamiliar name.

"Put it through, Sergeant." Thorn glanced at his computer monitor. With a little software wizardry from Joe Rossini, he'd set it to continuously display the local time in both Washington and Tehran. With eight and a half hours between them, it was still morning in D.C. It was near evening in the Iranian capital.

He heard a series of clicks and then the low hum of a carrier wave as Kazemi came on the line. "Colonel Thorn?"

The captain's voice was slightly distorted by the satellite up-link and the scrambler but still recognizable. For the Iranians, the secure communications system they had been given was one of the first tangible technological fruits of Taleh's quiet cooperation with the U.S. It wasn't the newest equipment in the American electronics arsenal, but it was far more effective than anything else available to them.

"Go ahead, Captain, this is Thorn."

"It is good to speak to you, Colonel." Kazemi sounded genuinely glad to reach him, though he was clearly a bit surprised at the speed and ease involved in making a connection halfway around the globe. Nearly two decades of revolutionary turmoil and inadequate maintenance had left the domestic Iranian telephone system in complete chaos. "Please hold for a moment, sir. General Taleh will be here shortly."

Thorn arched an eyebrow in surprise. Although he hadn't known exactly what to expect when he and Rossini asked the Iranians for their take on the rumored terrorist recruiting in Bosnia, he certainly had not expected a direct response from Amir Taleh himself. Commanders of Taleh's high rank rarely worked the detail side of the intelligence game. With the radicals still in control of some parts of the Iranian government, he must be keeping the precise extent of his rapprochement with the U.S. a closely held secret.

The Iranian general's firm, confident voice came on the line. "Good morning, Peter."

Thorn sat up straighter. "Evening, sir."

"Shall we dispense with discussing the weather and the other usual pleasantries? I am afraid that my time is at a premium just now. Captain Kazemi guards my schedule like a jealous lion and he informs me that I have a staff meeting in short order."

Thorn smiled to himself. After days spent wading through Pentagon doublespeak, Taleh's plain, blunt manner was a welcome breath of fresh air. "Of course."

"Good," the Iranian said. "Then let us cut to the heart of the matter. I have questioned my intelligence officers about these rumors from Bosnia." He paused briefly before continuing. "They confirm some of the reports you passed on to Kazemi."

"So someone is recruiting Bosnian Muslims as terrorists?"

"So it appears," Taleh agreed somberly. "However, they do not believe this recruiting effort is as widespread as your own intelligence agencies fear."

"Oh?"

"It is the old story of the marketplace, Peter. One timid man sees a shadow and within the hour all have heard that an army of ghosts has gathered." Thorn could almost hear the other man's shrug. "I suspect such a process is at work in Bosnia. One man offered training abroad becomes ten men in the telling and retelling. And ten men recruited as terrorists becomes a thousand or ten thousand summoned to a new *jihad* as word is passed from wagging tongues to straining ears."

"I hope you're right." Thorn knew the Iranian had a good point. The rumors the various Western intelligence agencies were picking up could easily be stories blown out of proportion—"echoes" bouncing back and forth from a single, small kernel of truth. But even ten well-armed, well-trained terrorists could wreak almost as much havoc as a larger force.

He said as much to Taleh.

"That is true," the Iranian said. "I assure you, I do not take this news lightly, Peter. I have no wish to see our mutual enemies regaining any of their strength—no matter how weak they are now."

"Do your intelligence people have any kind of a fix on who's behind all this?" Thorn asked. If Taleh could just point him in the right direction, he and Rossini could put pressure on the CIA and the other agencies to focus the resources needed to find these bastards. To pinpoint them while they were still training. To keep them under close and constant watch. And then to smash them before they could act against the West.

The Iranian disappointed him. "I am afraid we have no solid evidence." He sighed. "It is a difficult matter. There are many different Muslim factions in Bosnia—almost as many as there are countries here in the Middle East. They have adopted as their own the quarrels and petty jealousies that tear us apart. They spend almost as much time killing each other as they do fighting the Serbs.

"In any case, the more radical groups have little use for Iran now," Taleh continued. "When I broke the hold of the Hizb-Allah over my nation, we lost what little influence we had over the fanatics. Their allegiances have shifted."

"To Baghdad?" Thorn asked, mentally fanning the deck of hostile Islamic powers and picking the most powerful among them.

"I think it is likely," Taleh agreed. "The Iraqis have ample reason to hate America and its allies."

Thorn nodded to himself. The Iranian general's theory fit neatly into the composite picture of the current Islamic terrorism threat that Rossini and his analysts were putting together. Communications intercepts and reports from human sources already showed that the surviving fragments of the HizbAllah, Hammas, and other radical groups were drifting into Baghdad's orbit. If Bosnian Muslims were being rounded up for a new terrorist campaign, the Iraq government was clearly the prime suspect.

"I wish that I could have been more helpful. I promise, you will be the first to know if I learn anything more."

"Thank you. I'll be grateful for any assistance you can provide," Thorn said. "In the meantime, we'll keep probing on our end."

"Of course. Go with God, Peter."

The connection to Tehran broke, leaving Thorn listening to a dial tone. He put the phone down, stood up, and poked his head outside his office.

His secretary, a prim, middle-aged woman, was just hanging her purse on the back of her chair.

"Peggy, will you ask Joe Rossini to see me as soon as he comes in? I just had a call we need to discuss."

Thorn pulled his head back inside before she could reply and sat down again at his keyboard. Hesitantly at first and then with increasing speed, he began typing in the commands needed to pull up the latest files on Iraq and its Ba'thist regime.

Defense Ministry, Tehran

(D MINUS 177)

General Amir Taleh turned away from his desk to find his military aide watching him intently.

"Do they know, General?" Kazemi asked quietly.

Taleh shook his head firmly. "No." He shrugged. "As we thought, Farhad, the Americans have heard whispers in the wind. Nothing more."

He thought for a moment longer, pondering what Thorn had told him. Abruptly, he made a decision. "Nonetheless, the risks of our Bosnian enterprise are no longer worth the reward. We already have the men we need. Instruct General Sa'idi to close down our operations there immediately."

"Yes, sir."

Taleh nodded to himself. The agents he had commissioned to find recruits had been cautious, using cutouts and false papers to shield their true identities. Even if Thorn kept "probing," there should be no direct trail for the American to follow back to Iran. He looked up. Kazemi was still watching him.

"Do you think the American colonel believed what you told him, General?"

"For now." Taleh smiled thinly at his subordinate. "Peter Thorn is a very determined, very intelligent man, Farhad. But he has one fatal weakness. He is an honest man who sees his own virtues in others. He does not understand that candor is a luxury for the strong. The weak cannot afford such nobility."

Kazemi nodded.

"My old friend also puts too much faith in the common bond between soldiers." Taleh frowned slightly. "There is such a bond, but there are ties which are stronger—those of blood and those to the one, true God. One may respect an enemy and yet remain committed to his destruction. After all, even the great Saladin and Richard the Lion-Hearted broke bread together and spoke as friends. But either would gladly have slashed the other out of the saddle on a battlefield."

He dismissed the whole question with an impatient wave. "We have more urgent matters to deal with than one American colonel, Farhad. Speak to Sa'idi and then bring me the latest personnel reports from the Masegarh training camp. I want to go over the composition of the strike teams again."

"Yes, sir." Kazemi hurried out to obey his orders.

Taleh moved closer to a large-scale map pinned to one of his office walls. He studied it for a few moments, weighing and rejecting alternate plans. Convinced again that his original strategic concepts were still valid, he turned his gaze toward the calendar posted beside the map. No, he thought in satisfaction, Thorn and his compatriots would not pierce the veil he had drawn across their eyes—not in the time left to them.

JUNE 24

Fort Bragg, North Carolina

Colonel Peter Thorn glanced at his team as they crouched to either side of a locked door. Like him, each man was clad from head to toe in dark-colored clothing and body armor. Black Kevlar helmets, shatterproof goggles, and flame-resistant Nomex balaclavas protected their heads. Their assault vests and leg pouches held an arsenal of grenades, spare pistol and SMG magazines, and other gear. Each of the four men held a German-made Heckler & Koch MP5 submachine gun in his gloved hands.

"Sniper One, ready. No target."

"Sniper Two, ready. No target."

Thorn tensed as the whispered reports from the two-man sniper teams he'd posted outside sounded in his earphones. They confirmed what he'd suspected from the moment his assault force infiltrated this compound. All the terrorists and hostages were inside the room in front of him. And the bad guys were being very, very careful. They were staying well away from the windows and any exposure to his long-range firepower.

Great. This was going to be a bitch.

He pointed to the door and held up two fingers, signaling the type of breaching charge he wanted.

Staff Sergeant Callaway, the team's demolitions expert, nodded sharply, eyes bright behind his thick goggles. The tall, broad-shouldered noncom laid his weapon aside, yanked open the Velcro tab on one of his assault vest's gadget pouches, and carefully extracted a thin sheet of explosive rolled into a cylinder. Moving slowly and surely, he straightened up, unrolling the demo charge at the same time.

Thorn spoke softly into the radio mike taped to his throat. "Team Lead. Five seconds." He tightened his grip on his MP5 and tugged a beer-can-shaped flash/bang grenade out of his left leg pouch. "Four. Three . . ."

Callaway slapped the paper-thin sheet of explosive onto the door, triggered the detonator, and whirled away.

"One."

WHUMMP! The door blew inward and slammed down onto the floor. Special timers had detonated the top of the demo charge a split second ahead of the bottom, directing the blast downward.

Without waiting, Thorn rolled out, lobbed his grenade through the smoke, and rolled back against the wall. "Grenade! Go! Go!"

His number two man glided through the doorway and moved left just as the flash/bang went off in a rippling, blinding, deafening series of flashes and staccato explosions that would confuse and disorient anyone inside the room.

Thorn followed him into the smoke, sliding to the right with his submachine gun at shoulder level, ready to fire. He kept moving along the wall, his eyes scanning back and forth through the arc he'd assigned himself. The adrenaline pouring into his system seemed to be stretching time itself. Every dazzling flash from the exploding grenade lit the room like a giant, slow-motion strobe light.

Motion tugged at the corner of his left eye. He spun in that direction, aiming, centering the target coming at him in his rear sights. A woman wearing a jacket and skirt loomed out of the smoke. His finger relaxed minutely on the trigger.

Her hands were full.

Thorn's trained instincts took over. He squeezed off a three-round burst that knocked the half-seen figure backward to the floor. He spun right, still moving forward, hunting new enemies in the gray haze. Submachine guns stuttered briefly off to his left as other members of the team engaged targets of their own.

He edged past an overturned desk. There! More movement off to his right. He whirled that way, seeing a man rising to his knees. His MP5 came up and centered on the man's chest.

Thorn fought off the urge to fire. The kneeling man was unarmed. He barked out a command. "You! Down! Now!" He emphasized the order with the muzzle of his submachine gun.

The man dropped facedown and lay still.

Thorn scanned through his arc again, searching for further signs of movement. Any movement. Nothing. He looked again, even harder this time. Still nothing. His pulse began slowing, falling toward normal. "Team Lead. Right side is clear."

His backup man echoed his assessment. "Number Three. Confirmed. Right side is clear."

More voices flooded through his earphones as the rest of the assault team checked in.

"This is Two. Left side is clear."

"Number Four. Confirmed."

Thorn waited for a final report from his snipers before allowing himself to relax. They had good news. None of the terrorists had escaped the room during the assault team's attack. He spoke into his throat mike. "Control, this is Team Lead. Exercise complete."

A laconic voice answered. "Roger, Lead. Exercise complete. Weapons safe."

Thorn and the others snapped their safety catches on and stood easy.

Recessed overhead lights came on suddenly, illuminating the shooting room. High-speed fans kicked in with a low, vibrating hum, clearing the smoke still hanging in the air.

Thorn glanced around at the assault team's handiwork. Mannequins and pop-up targets—the hostages and terrorists—were scattered through the make-believe office. Those shown carrying weapons were bullet-riddled. Those that were unarmed looked intact.

"Congratulations, gentlemen. You've survived another jaunt through the Delta Force House of Horrors. And better yet, you did it without killing any of the people you were trying to save. This time. By the grace of God."

The familiar sarcastic voice from the open doorway brought Thorn around with a smile on his face.

Sergeant Major Roberto "TOW" Diaz strode into the room and stopped with his hands on his hips, surveying the situation before him with a mildly disgusted look. The short, muscular, dark-haired man, the senior NCO in Delta Force's A Squadron, exuded raw energy and strength even at rest. Intensely competitive, he worked hard to stay in the kind of physical shape that routinely let him outmarch, outfight, and outlast men ten or fifteen years younger. No one who saw him in the field would have guessed that he was forty-five.

"Fourteen point two seconds to clear one friggin' room," Diaz announced, apparently to the world at large. He looked at each man in turn before shaking his head. "That's slow, gentlemen. Awful slow."

He paused significantly. "My arthritic grandmother could rip this place apart faster than that."

There was a low rumble from the back of the room. "Hell, Tow, your grandmother can fly to the goddamned moon on her own power. According to you, anyway."

Diaz grinned. "Maybe so, Nick." He glanced at Thorn and his grin got wider. "I guess I shouldn't have expected more from a team leader who spends most of his time these days sitting on his butt at the Pentagon."

Thorn hung his head in mock shame. "*Mea culpa*, Sergeant Major. I am but a lowly staff weenie now. Ignore my august rank and close, personal friendship with your new CO. Pour out your wrath on my trembling shoulders. But, please, oh please, spare my beloved men."

The room erupted in laughter.

Diaz was the first to sober up. "Okay, okay." He held up a hand for silence. "Let's run through the overall results before I walk you through one-on-one.

"First, you accomplished your mission. Four of four bad guys are down and dead. Four of four hostages are secure and safe." He shrugged. "Your time was bad, but your accuracy was good. The computer scores you at ninety-four point four percent. For those of you who barely scraped through first-grade math, that means that seventeen out of the eighteen rounds you fired hit their targets."

Thorn nodded to himself, pleased by that. Not many outfits in the world could go into such a confused close-quarters battle and shoot with such precision. At least some of his skills were still intact. He listened to the rest of the sergeant major's general critique with a somewhat lighter heart.

His satisfaction faded when the other man led him across to the dummy terrorist he'd gunned down.

Diaz prodded the shredded female mannequin with the toe of a combat boot. He looked up at Thorn. "You hesitated."

Thorn replayed the confrontation in his mind and nodded slowly. "Yeah."

"Don't do it again," the sergeant major said sternly. "A woman . . . a kid . . . it doesn't matter. The round they fire will kill you just as dead. Look at the hands first. Always. Got it?"

Thorn nodded again, acknowledging the fairness of the criticism. Delta Force troops needed lightning reflexes and absolute confidence in their own judgment. A soldier who was too slow or too unsure in action could get himself and a lot of other people killed.

Confident that his message had been heard and understood, Diaz turned away, focusing his mind and sharp tongue on the next man in line.

Thorn exhaled softly. It could have been worse—a lot worse.

Debrief over, Peter Thorn trotted down the central stairs of the House of Horrors—the Delta Force nickname for the three-story building it used to rehearse assaults and hostage rescues. Besides the areas used for room-clearing drills, there were stairwells and elevator shafts so teams could practice every aspect of urban warfare. One large room even held the mock-up of part of a wide-body airliner fuselage.

The House of Horrors was the centerpiece of the $75-million compound known rather unimaginatively as the Security Operations Training Facility. It was the home base for the Delta Force. Besides the shooting house, the complex contained vertical walls used to rehearse cliff climbing and rappelling. There were extensive firing ranges where commandos could hone their skills with a variety of weapons and explosives. Other areas allowed them to practice combat driving, escape, and evasion.

Racquetball and basketball courts, weight rooms, an Olympic-sized pool, and a sauna helped Delta Force soldiers stay in peak physical condition. And when they were off duty, they could relax in the compound's living quarters, cafeterias, and separate squadron bars. Essentially, the facility was a small, totally self-contained city hidden by berms, electric fences, and pine trees in a distant corner of Fort Bragg. Guards and sensors ringed its boundaries, making sure that nobody got in or out without a top-security clearance.

Thorn came outside into the sweltering heat of a North Carolina summer afternoon and immediately slowed to a walk. Breathing deeply to clear the last traces of smoke and cordite from his lungs, he yanked the helmet and black balaclava off his head and ran a trembling hand through his sweaty, tangled hair.

He frowned. Muscles that ordinarily wouldn't even have noticed the effort he'd just put them through were already aching. Jesus, he thought wearily, two weeks behind a desk and I'm already falling apart. Technically, he'd just come down to Bragg for a meeting with Major General Farrell and the rest of the JSOC staff. Tagging along on today's exercise had been his own bright idea. Well, maybe it hadn't been so bright. Disgusted, he headed toward the BOQ and the nearest cold shower.

TOW Diaz came up from behind and punched him lightly on the shoulder. "You're getting old, Pete. Or soft. Or both."

"No shit," Thorn growled. "Tell me something I don't know." He glanced at the barrel-chested noncom walking beside him. "How's everyone at home, Tow? Nadine and the kids all okay?"

"They're good. Real good." Diaz' leathery face wrinkled up in a smile that was pure paternal pride. "You heard that Jimmy got into the Point?"

Thorn nodded. "I heard." At eighteen, James Diaz was the oldest of the sergeant major's four children. Winning admission to the U.S. Military Academy had been the kid's lifelong dream—one aided and abetted by his soldier father. "That's great news, Sergeant Major."

"Sure is."

"So no big college tuition bills for you," Thorn teased.

"Nope." Diaz looked smug. "A few plane tickets, a few hotel bills for the Army-Navy game, and a little spending money. That's it."

"Uh-huh." Thorn paused significantly. "Of course, when Jimmy graduates, he'll outrank you. Could get kind of awkward saluting your own son all the time."

Diaz shrugged. "So maybe I'll just take my twenty-plus, retire, and go soak up the sun somewhere."

"Right." Thorn snorted. The sergeant major was as much an Army brat as he was. The only way the service would put TOW Diaz out to pasture would be at bayonet point.

He changed the subject by nodding over his shoulder at the building behind them. "Which outfit holds the House of Horrors' trophy these days? Still A Squadron? Or have you let your guys screw up and give it to B or C?"

Now it was Diaz' turn to look disgusted. "Would you believe a frigging HRT section eked out a win yesterday? Shaved a full quarter second off our best time."

Thorn whistled in amazement. The Hostage Rescue Team, or HRT, was the FBI's counterpart to the Army's Delta Force and the Navy's SEAL Team Six. The FBI had jurisdiction over terrorist attacks or hostage-takings inside the United States itself. All three organizations collaborated on counterterror tactics and training. All three were also highly competitive.

He shook his head. "The Hoover boys just got lucky, I guess."

"Sure they did," the sergeant major agreed. He motioned toward an eight-man section jogging past them in full assault gear. "That's why I have our guys out working night and day to develop *their* good luck."

Thorn winced inside. Diaz hated to lose—at anything. Maybe he had picked a good time to transfer to the Pentagon after all.

"You down here for much longer, Pete?" The NCO turned toward him. "Want to give the course another go-around tomorrow?"

Thorn laughed. "No thanks, Tow. I filled my monthly masochist quota today and I've got meetings all day tomorrow. Besides"—he smiled crookedly—"the general's wife wants us all at her big soiree on time and smelling like roses, not like the inside of an old gym bag. And you can guess the uniform of the day."

Diaz groaned softly. "Dress blues, Colonel?"

"Dress blues, Sergeant Major."

JUNE 25

JSOC headquarters, Pope Air Force Base, North Carolina

Officers, senior NCOs, their wives and sweethearts crowded the dimly lit, air-conditioned bar, chatting politely in small groups as white-coated waiters circulated deftly among them with trays holding drinks and hors d'oeuvres. A jukebox played in the far corner, lofting soft music, a mix of light rock and pop tunes, over the buzz of conversation.

Thorn stood close to the door with Sam Farrell and Lieutenant Colonel Bill Henderson, the tall, thin man who now commanded Delta's A Squadron. They were talking shop.

"You getting anywhere with the CIA on this Bosnia thing, Pete?" Farrell asked.

"Not very far." Thorn shrugged, wishing for the hundredth time that he hadn't tied his tie quite so tight. The dark blue jacket, starched white shirt, and black bow tie of the Army's regulation dress uniform won him a lot of admiring female glances at formal dinners and other official functions, but they never rested easily on his shoulders. He preferred more comfortable working clothes.

"What the hell is the CIA's problem?" Henderson frowned. "They fighting some kind of turf war with you?"

"Maybe a little." Thorn waved off another drink from a passing waiter and turned back to the subject at hand. He repeated Joe Rossini's reasoning. "But the main glitch is that Langley has different priorities. They're trying to keep Congress happy by looking for the next big issue. Nukes. Drugs. You name it."

He shook his head. "The way they see it, terrorism is pretty much a dead horse—for right now anyway. The Iranians knocked the crap out of the HizbAllah and the rest so badly that nobody believes they're in shape to do more than run for cover."

"You think Langley might be right?" Farrell eyed him closely over his drink.

"Could be," Thorn admitted reluctantly. "Like Taleh said, I could be chasing ghosts. We sure haven't been able to pin down anything solid in those first reports."

"But . . ." Farrell prompted him.

Thorn nodded. "That little prickling feeling at the back of my neck isn't going away. The HizbAllah may be on the ropes, but desperate men take desperate chances. I think there could be real trouble brewing out there somewhere—and I'd rather not find out about it the hard way."

"Okay," Farrell said firmly. "Keep after it. There may not be any pot of gold at the end of your rainbow, but looking can't hurt." His mouth tightened. "Starting tomorrow, I'll see if I can get you some satellite time and better access to Langley's HUMINT sources."

Thorn felt better. HUMINT, the intelligence jargon for information obtained from human agents, was crucial to effective counterterrorist work. Even the most sophisticated spy satellites couldn't find terrorist training camps unless you pointed them at the right general area. If the CIA could bribe, blackmail, or bug someone in Bosnia with direct knowledge of this rumored terrorist recruiting campaign, he and Joe Rossini could start zeroing in on the right target.

"That would be great, sir." He swallowed the last remnants of his gin and tonic and put the glass down on a nearby table. "I'll phone my office first thing and have them send down—"

A woman's languid southern drawl cut him off. "Why, Sam Farrell and Peter Thorn, I am appalled. Talking business on a social occasion? You ought to be ashamed. And you, too, Bill Henderson."

They turned in unison like guilty schoolboys to see Louisa Farrell, the general's wife, smiling at them. She wasn't beautiful in the classical sense, but her violet eyes, elegantly styled silver hair, and natural poise made her what TOW Diaz would call "a powerfully handsome woman."

She swept in among them and took Thorn by the arm. "Now, you just come with me, Peter. You can talk shop with these two boorish misfits anytime. But I don't see enough of you these days."

"Yes, ma'am." Thorn surrendered to the pleasantly inevitable. He half turned toward Farrell. "With your permission, sir?"

The general grinned. "I wouldn't dream of standing in my wife's way, Colonel. They don't pay me enough. I'll pick up the pieces later."

What exactly did he mean by that? Thorn wondered.

Louisa Farrell answered his unspoken question. "Come along, Peter. I have someone I'd like you to meet. A new friend of mine. I think you'll like her."

Oops. It must be his turn again in the pet bachelor circus center ring. Most Delta Force operators were married and none of their wives seemed able to resist playing matchmaker. The general's wife was one of the most determined.

"Look, Louisa," Thorn protested. "I'm not looking for a bride right now—"

"You hush up, now." She laughed. "You can squirm and toss and turn all you like, but it won't put me off my stride. You hear me, Peter Thorn?"

"Yes, ma'am." He shrugged inwardly. He'd just have to shut up and soldier through the rest of the evening. Idly, he wondered who the JSOC officers' wives' club had selected as the ideal Mrs. Thorn this time.

Louisa Farrell didn't keep him in suspense. She led him straight to a corner table near the jukebox. A tall, pretty woman rose gracefully at their approach.

"Peter, this is Helen Gray. Helen, I'd like you to meet Colonel Peter Thorn."

Thorn was busy reevaluating his first hasty impression. This woman wasn't just pretty—she was beautiful. Short, wavy black hair framed a heart-shaped face and the brightest blue eyes he'd ever seen. An elegant, form-fitting black dress showed off a slender body with curves in all the right places. He couldn't guess her age any closer than a vague feeling that she was definitely over twenty-five but probably under thirty.

He had to admit to himself that he was impressed. This evening might turn out to be a lot more enjoyable than he'd first imagined. He held out his hand. "How do you do, Miss Gray?"

She shook it firmly and smiled politely. "I do pretty well, Colonel Thorn." Her voice was quiet, but it held a note of utter self-confidence.

Thorn was even more impressed. Maybe the Fort Bragg ladies' circle was doing a better screening job these days. Helen Gray was certainly a far cry from the usual run-of-the-mill debutante or charm school graduate they tried to fix him up with. Whatever else she might be, this woman clearly wasn't a stereotypical, wilting southern belle. He wondered exactly what she was doing at the base.

When several minutes of friendly but noncommittal conversation failed to yield an answer, he decided on a direct approach. "So what do you do for a living, Miss Gray?"

He saw Louisa Farrell hiding a smile and wondered what was so funny.

Helen didn't bother hiding her own amusement. She smiled, impishly this time, over her wineglass. "It's Special Agent Gray, actually, Colonel Thorn. And I lead the HRT section exercising here right now."

It took an effort to close his mouth. "You're with the FBI?"

Helen nodded briefly. "You're not surprised that a woman can beat your men at their own game, are you?"

Thorn noticed that her blue eyes, once warm and maybe even inviting, were a little colder now. Clearly, this was dangerous ground. Screw it. He opted for honesty. "Not really, Miss Gray." He looked her up and down. "It's just that I'm having a lot of trouble visualizing you in a black ski mask and body armor."

He held his breath, waiting for either a verbal explosion or a glassful of Chardonnay in the face.

Instead, she laughed delightedly. "That's not exactly a politically correct thing to say, Colonel."

Thorn smiled broadly. "I'm not exactly a politically correct kind of guy."

Louisa Farrell patted his upper arm. "I can certainly vouch for that, my dear." She inclined her head toward Helen and loudly whispered. "But Peter's not all that bad—not for a Neanderthal door-kicker, that is."

Helen laughed again. "I believe it."

Somebody turned up the volume on the jukebox and put on one of the older, slower tunes—a fifties classic. Louisa took that as a clue to slip away. "If you'll both excuse me, I do believe I'll try to find my husband and force him to dance with me."

A few other couples were already out on the floor, swaying in time with the beat.

Thorn studied them for a few seconds, working up his nerve. Then he turned to Helen. "Much as I hate to spoil my knuckle-dragging image, I have to admit that looks like fun." He hesitated, suddenly surprised to discover how afraid he was that she'd refuse. "Would you care to dance, Miss Gray?"

"I'd love to, Colonel."

Thorn led her out onto the floor, still perplexed by his earlier hesitation. Up to now, he'd never let any woman, or anything else for that matter, throw him off his stride like this. So what was so different about this one woman?

He forgot to worry about it as she slid into his arms.

Thorn moved in time with the music and with Helen for several minutes, content at first in the comfortable feeling of her body pressed lightly against his. He was conscious, though, of a growing desire to learn more about her. When the song ended and someone else put on a louder, faster tune from the seventies, he seized his opportunity. "Mind if we sit this one out, Miss Gray?"

"Only if you stop calling me Miss Gray," she replied. "Deal?"

Thorn grinned. "All right . . . Helen." Her first name seemed to flow very easily over his lips. He followed her off the floor, again admiring her beauty and grace.

They found a table far enough away from the jukebox so they could hear each other speak. He smiled across at her. "I hope your shoes are still intact. I'm afraid that dancing isn't my strong suit. I took some classes at West Point, but not much stayed with me."

Helen laughed. "Lucky you! My father was so afraid that I was becoming too much of a tomboy that he made me take cotillion with my sisters—for three years!"

Cotillion. That explained some of her grace. Thorn flagged down a waiter and secured two fresh glasses of white wine. "Sisters? I guess the Gray family's a pretty big clan, then?"

She shrugged. "Not that big. I have two sisters, one older and one younger, and one older brother."

Thorn smiled crookedly. "As an only child, that sounds like a pretty big family to me." He took a drink, remembering the long evenings and quiet holidays. "I used to wonder what it would be like to have brothers and sisters. But I guess I wouldn't trade my relationship with my dad for anything. It seems like he and I did everything together when I was growing up. Hiking . . . kayaking . . . skiing . . . riding, you name it."

Helen shook her head. "Your dad sounds like quite a guy." She hesitated. "What about your mom?"

Thorn felt his jaw tighten. "I don't have a mother. Haven't had one since I was a kid."

"Oh, I'm sorry . . . Did she die?"

He paused, undecided about how much to tell her. They were treading in very private waters. On the other hand, he felt intuitively that he could trust this woman. "No, actually my mother left us when I was eleven—after my dad came home from Nam. She said she needed more 'space,' that she had 'grown up' while he was overseas. I'm not sure either my dad or I ever really understood what she meant by that. We pretty much lost contact with her and learned to manage on our own."

Thorn stopped almost abruptly, somewhat embarrassed at

having revealed so much. "Sorry, I didn't mean to sound bitter. It may have been a blessing in disguise. I probably got away with taking all sorts of crazy risks with just my dad looking after me. After she left, my dad wangled a transfer to Fort Carson, Colorado, for a couple of years."

He pushed the conversation and his memories on to more pleasant ground. "That wasn't a bad place to grow up, really. I rode horses all year round and skied in the winter. Heck, I even cross-country-skied to school. It was great. And then when I was thirteen we moved to Tehran so my dad could help train the Iranian Army . . ."

The stories of some of his teenage adventures and misadventures in Iran's crowded capital lightened the mood considerably. But Thorn suddenly realized he'd been monopolizing the conversation for far too long. He made a frantic bid to turn the spotlight back on her before she decided she had been trapped by an egomaniac. "What about you? Where did you grow up?"

"Nowhere quite so glamorous, I'm afraid." Helen's smile took the sting out of her words. "We lived in Indianapolis, where my dad was an executive with the phone company. Probably what you'd call a typical suburban existence. I had all the advantages of a close family, good schools with teachers who cared about me, and wonderful friends."

She grinned broadly. "I'm practically a poster child for solid midwestern values."

Thorn snorted. "Right. Lots of suburban girls go on to careers as an FBI commando."

Helen spread her hands. "Well, of course, since I was the third kid I was always jockeying for position in the family. And while my sisters fulfilled my mother's dream by becoming charming, pretty girls who married well, I was always chasing after my brother and building forts in the backyard. I think sending me to cotillion was a last-ditch effort by my parents to make me suitable company for men." She laughed. "Little did they know that I'd choose a profession where I'm almost exclusively surrounded by men!"

Suddenly, Helen's watch beeped. Thorn saw her stiffen and then relax.

"What was that?" he asked.

"Eleven o'clock. I'm afraid I have to leave soon."

"Does your ride turn into a pumpkin at 2400 hours or something?"

She chuckled. "No. But I do have an 0400 wake-up call, courtesy of your Sergeant Major Diaz. He's challenged my team to a rematch."

Thorn shook his head mournfully. "Remind me to see if I can get Diaz transferred to an Arctic weather station." He looked seriously at her. "I'd really like the chance to see you again."

"I'm based at Quantico," she said quietly.

"That's not very far from Washington, is it?" he asked.

"No." The smile reached her eyes again. "It's not." They stood up together. "I hope you'll call me."

Thorn nodded seriously. "You can count on it."

He watched her go, slipping through the crowd with a dancer's grace. She turned once, looked back at him, smiled one last time, and then vanished.

He shook his head, completely baffled. How had she got him to talk about his family and his childhood? Those were not things he usually discussed at the drop of a hat. Especially not to someone he'd just met. And just what the hell had he said? Whenever he tried to recall the conversation in detail, he remembered little more than a blur of voices and those warm blue eyes.

"A hell of a woman . . ." he murmured.

Helen Gray was still remembering the way he'd smiled back at her from across the room. Still holding her wineglass, she moved off to find Louisa Farrell and say her good-byes.

The general's wife found her first.

"Well," she said, nodding back toward the knot of officers standing near the doorway. "What did you think of Peter Thorn?"

"He's an interesting man." Helen took a last sip of wine, carefully considering her response. "A *very* interesting man."

CHAPTER SIX

INFILTRATION

JULY 8

Falls Church, northern Virginia

"Senior administration officials say that the most interesting development at this U.N. conference on security and international development is something that wasn't on the official agenda at all: a series of private meetings between U.S. Secretary of State Austin Brookes and his Iranian counterpart, Foreign Minister Ahmad Adeli. Sources close to both governments have characterized these meetings—the first between high-ranking American and Iranian officials in more than ten years—as surprisingly cordial and productive."

Colonel Peter Thorn turned his head toward the open bathroom door and paused with his hands halfway through the convoluted process of turning a thin strip of colored silk into a perfectly knotted necktie. He'd left the television on both out of habit and from a desire for some noise to break the silence enveloping his rented town house.

"During the talks, Minister Adeli is said to have confirmed his government's hopes for the eventual restoration of full diplomatic and commercial ties with the United States. Apparently, only the fear of angering Islamic radicals still entrenched in the Iranian Parliament remains a minor stumbling block.

"Appearing before reporters this afternoon, the usually reserved American Secretary of State seemed a different man—smiling broadly and even cracking a few jokes with members of the press. If these reports are accurate, it's not hard to understand his newly expansive mood. Long under fire for his dull personality and haphazard management style, Austin Brookes must be savoring the prospect of achieving the high-profile diplomatic victory denied his predecessors in three previous administrations.

"This is Terrence Nakamura, reporting live from Geneva, Switzerland, for CNN."

Thorn snorted and finished knotting his tie. Uninterested in world currency fluctuations, he tuned out the rest of the broadcast. He didn't know whether to be amused or simply disgusted. Like most lawyers and all politicians, the Secretary of State was only too happy to claim credit for the work done by others. If General Amir Taleh hadn't had the guts to smash the radical hold on his own government, Brookes and the rest of his State Department stuffed shirts would still be at receptions passing each other glasses of dry sherry and drier position papers.

He shrugged his momentary irritation away. You couldn't change the ways of politicians any more than you could repeal the laws of physics.

Thorn studied his reflection in the mirror, turning his face first one way and then the other to make sure he'd hit all the right spots with his razor. Satisfied, he tugged at the collar of his blue button-down shirt, loosening it just a touch to let some oxygen down his windpipe. He looked more critically at his reflected image, eyeing the shirt, patterned red tie, and lightweight gray suit with a slight frown. They made him look more like a typical D.C. bureaucrat than he cared to at the moment. As a Delta Force operator, Thorn was used to wearing civilian clothes, but his personal tastes off duty ran more to blue jeans and boots than wool slacks and dress shoes.

Buck up, boyo, he told himself sternly. This was a special occasion after all. It had taken nearly two weeks of fairly regular phone calls, but he and Helen Gray had finally managed to synchronize their busy schedules for an evening out. He intended to make the most of it. Besides, Washington's finer dining establishments usually had a particular place reserved for people who showed up in casual clothes. They called it the exit.

Thorn checked his watch, swore at himself, and grabbed his car keys off his nightstand on the way downstairs and out the door. He'd made a reservation at Stannard's—one of the capital's most elegant restaurants—for eight o'clock. It was already past seven.

Nearly an hour later, Thorn pushed his way into the Stannard Hotel's packed foyer. The blast of overworked air-conditioning came as a much-needed relief after his dash through the hot, muggy evening outside.

Despite his best efforts, he was late. First, some idiot had stalled out on the Fourteenth Street Bridge, tying northbound traffic into knots. That was bad, but even a few weeks in the D.C. area had taught him to allow for delays on the highways. What he hadn't anticipated was the near-total gridlock on the capital's downtown streets long after the normal working day had come to a close. For a lot of people in this town, parking apparently meant double-parking, turning their blinkers on, and then going off to run errands. As a result, the crowded streets off Pennsylvania Avenue were a zoo—down to one lane in places and full of pedestrians darting across without bothering to look for oncoming traffic.

Stannard's small, richly appointed lobby was a sea of suits and evening dresses—jammed with people waiting for tables who had spilled out of an adjoining bar with drinks in hand and their voices at full volume. Thorn slid through the throng, searching for Helen—half afraid she wasn't there and half hoping that she, too, was late.

"Peter! Over here!"

He turned toward the familiar voice with relief and saw Helen Gray smiling at him. Smart woman, he thought. She'd taken a station in a corner near the entrance to the dining room, shielding herself from the worst of the crush while securing a good vantage point. He made his way to her side with all possible speed.

"Sorry I'm late," he said hurriedly.

"You should be." Her eyes twinkled. "I've already been propositioned by an Arab sheik, a labor lawyer, and a dairy industry lobbyist."

Ouch. Thorn looked carefully at the floor and then back at her. He shook his head soberly. "I don't see any bodies. What happened? Your pistol jam?"

Helen laughed. "No. I left it at home. It didn't go with the dress."

She was right, Thorn decided, a 9mm Beretta would definitely look out of place on the elegantly dressed woman in front of him.

He'd thought the black number he'd first seen her in at Fort Bragg was nice, but the dress she had on now was stunning. It was cut low enough to show off her tanned shoulders and the upper curves of her firm, perfectly proportioned breasts. It was the kind of dress that invited open admiration from men and barely concealed envy from other women. It was a dress he thought would look even better on its way off. Down boy, down! he told his libido, wondering again what it was about this woman, out of all women, that made him think and act so much like an oversexed, underbrained teenager.

He cleared his throat and sought more neutral mental ground. "Maybe we'd better see about getting our table."

"Absolutely," Helen agreed. From the satisfied look on her face she'd probably been reading his mind.

She nodded toward the tall, imposing figure of a maître d', stiff and formal in a tuxedo and firmly ensconced behind a lectern at the entrance to Stannard's oak-paneled dining room. "I tried to check in earlier, but Prince Charming there seems to think that only someone named Thorn can confirm a reservation made by someone named Thorn."

Her voice left no doubt about her feelings toward the kind of person who would uphold such an idiotic policy. Thorn had a sudden vision involving punji sticks, barbed wire, honey, and an anthill. He shook his head, very glad he wasn't in the other man's pointy black shoes, and led her up to the lectern.

Thirty seconds later he was beginning to plan his own prolonged and painful revenge on the maître d'.

He gritted his teeth and tried again. "Look, my name is Peter Thorn. I made a reservation for eight o'clock tonight two days ago. Check your book."

"Yes, sir." The restaurant's maître d' seemed completely unimpressed. "I *have* checked. Your reservation is perfectly in order." He offered them a bland, disinterested smile. "But I am afraid we are running slightly behind schedule this evening. I will be happy to seat you as soon as the first available table opens up."

"And just when will that be?"

"Not very long." The other man pursed his lips, making a pretense of giving the matter some thought. "Not longer than half an hour, I would guess. Certainly not more than forty-five minutes."

"Forty-five minutes?" Thorn held a tight rein on his temper. He'd only picked Stannard's because some of the other officers in the Pentagon mess had described the place as a Washington landmark. He was beginning to realize that wasn't any kind of guarantee of good service. More and more, John F. Kennedy's description of the capital city as a place that combined southern efficiency with northern courtesy seemed right on target.

The maître d's bored eyes slid past him and brightened. "Ah, Senator! It is delightful to see you."

"Thank you, Henry. My committee meeting ran a little over tonight. Can you squeeze me in?"

Thorn glanced around far enough to catch a profile made famous by years of network television news coverage and tabloid scandal.

"Of course, Senator." The maître d' snatched up a leather-bound menu from his stand and gestured toward the dining room. "Please follow me, I have just the right table for you."

Thorn watched him go through narrowed eyes. Why, that pompous, lying, no-good son of a bitch. Overhearing snatches of some of the snide, cynical conversations going on around him only fed his growing anger.

"So the chairman said to him, 'You either play ball on this amendment, Phil, or you can kiss that new overpass good-bye . . .' "

". . . the old bastard's screwing his administrative assistant worse than he is the taxpayers . . ."

"We slipped some language into the rider to smooth the hicks over, but Morgan may be a problem . . ."

Thorn shook his head in disgust. D.C. landmark or not, this was not his kind of place. Worse, he was probably batting a big fat .000 in Helen's eyes. He heard a muffled chuckle from her direction and turned toward her.

The look of amused sympathy on her face restored some of his good humor. If she wasn't holding this fast-developing fiasco against him, it still wasn't too late to salvage something from this evening. He shrugged ruefully. "Are you thinking what I'm thinking?"

She grinned back. "Yep. I certainly am. I say we blow this Popsicle stand. I prefer eating without all the pomp, circum-stance, and hot air."

Thorn started to relax. Maybe he'd been trying too hard to impress her. "How about Thai food?"

Helen nodded vigorously. "Now, that sounds wonderful. And the hotter the better."

"Yes, ma'am," he said, smiling. "There's a little mom-and-pop Thai place not far from my house that's pretty good. If you don't mind following me out there, that is."

She arched an eyebrow. "I think I can manage it. You are looking at an Academy grad with straight As in surveillance and close pursuit, you know." She paused. "Do they offer take-out at this restaurant of yours?"

He nodded.

"Great. Then we can eat at your place."

"My place?"

Helen laughed. "Don't tell me you're one of those messy bachelors, Peter. The kind that lets dirty clothes and dirty dishes pile up."

He felt a slow, wide grin forming on his face. "Nope. I come from a long line of God-fearing men with clean bodies and dirty minds."

She reached out and took his arm. "Oh, good. Those are the best kind."

When Thorn first moved to the Washington, D.C., area, he'd seriously considered renting a studio apartment in one of the cookie-cutter Crystal City high-rises overlooking the Pentagon. Living there would be convenient and reasonably inexpensive, he'd thought. Three days spent in one of the neighboring hotels had wiped that plan right out of his mind. Holding down a staff billet in the Pentagon's bureaucratic swamp was draining enough. Combining that with being cooped up in a noisy cage a couple of hundred feet above street level seemed a surefire recipe for going buggy in record time.

Determined to keep as much of his sanity as possible, he'd gone house-hunting with a vengeance, scouring the northern Virginia neighborhoods he'd ringed on a map until he found quarters he could tolerate for a year. He'd finally decided to rent the upper half of a red-brick town house right on the border between Falls Church, Arlington, and Alexandria. It was just off the Columbia Pike and an easy twenty-minute commute to the Pentagon. Better still, the town house complex backed onto a tiny, wooded state park. It was quiet and private enough so that he could at least pretend he wasn't living elbow-to-elbow with several million other people.

Thorn pushed the front door open with his foot and stepped aside to let Helen in first. His arms were full of warm take-out containers. Delicious smells wafted up from them—a mouthwatering blend of garlic, peanut sauce, onion, chicken, and shrimp.

Helen was already down the hall and inspecting his kitchen

by the time he finished closing the door. He followed her in and deposited their dinners on a tile counter near the empty sink.

She straightened up from his open refrigerator. "Well, I see you have plenty of the two basic bachelor food groups—beer and microwave dinners."

"Hey!" He pretended to be hurt. "I'm not totally uncivilized. There are plates in one of those cupboards over there. Heck, I've even got silverware somewhere around here."

Her eyes sparkled again. "My, oh, my. I am impressed."

Helen drifted out into the combination living and dining room while he pulled out plates, forks, and spoons. Except for a sofa, a coffee table, and a wall unit for his CD player and television, the room was empty. Boxes stacked neatly beside the sofa held an assortment of hardbacks, paperbacks, and professional military journals. There were no pictures on the walls. A sliding glass door opened onto a narrow balcony overlooking the woods.

"It certainly looks like you're settling right in, Peter," she teased, poking her head back into the kitchen.

"Now, there's a direct hit," he admitted. "I left most of my stuff in storage. The people renting my house outside Fort Bragg said they were looking for a furnished place anyway."

She nodded. "Plus, I guess that moving everything up here and unpacking it would give this new assignment of yours an awfully permanent feel?"

"Exactly." Thorn smiled at her. "Mind you, there are compensations for being so close to Quantico."

"Really?"

"No doubt about it."

Helen lowered her eyes, looking even more pleased. She nodded toward the living room again. "I thought you'd at least have some pictures of you and your father together. You told me so much about him when we first met that I've been dying to see what he looks like."

Dying. Thorn felt the smile on his face freeze solid.

"Peter?" She was staring at him now. "What's wrong?"

He swallowed hard and forced another faint smile. "Sorry. It's just that my dad passed away last year. It still takes some getting used to, I guess."

"Oh, Peter." Helen touched his arm. "I'm so sorry."

"It's okay. I'm fine," he murmured. "I'm fine."

That wasn't true, he realized. Whenever he thought the sorrow of his father's death was finally behind him, some word or phrase or picture would conjure up that whole bleak period all over again. His mind was still wrestling with images of the proud, strong man who'd raised him. And with the images of that last terrible year.

His father had fought hard against the cancer that had invaded his body—just as hard as he had fought against the NVA in the Vietnamese jungles. In the end, though, even big, tough John Thorn hadn't been able to beat impossible odds.

Thorn knew that he should have visited the hospital more often during that long, lonely battle. He should have been there when his father died. But he hadn't been able to stand it. Watching the powerful man who had been his first and only boyhood hero growing weaker with every passing day—slipping away by inches—had been too painful to bear. And his father had understood, even forgiven, his absence. Somehow that only made his betrayal seem worse.

He forced himself back to the present. His guilt over his father's death was a burden for him to shoulder alone, not to inflict on Helen.

"Are you sure that you're okay?" she asked softly, shared sorrow clear in her warm blue eyes.

He nodded decisively, determined to keep his memories and his grief to himself. "Oh, yeah. No problem." He motioned toward the living room, seeking refuge in rough good humor. "Now clear out and let me work, woman. Unless you want cold food, that is."

"Oh, no. Anything but that."

Grateful that Helen understood his reluctance to dwell on the past, Thorn followed her out of the kitchen. He finished laying out their place settings on the coffee table and started opening containers with a flourish. In an attempt to chase away the blues, he announced, "Dinner is about to be served, madam. Would you care for a single main course, or would you prefer a gourmet sampling of the best of Thai haute cuisine?"

"A little bit of everything, of course." Helen sat down on the sofa and watched him closely. "Does this mean that I don't get a guided tour of the upstairs?"

"You actually want to see the vast, inner expanses of my mansion? All two bedrooms and two baths?" Thorn asked casually, instantly aware that he awaited her answer with anything but casual interest. He leaned over the steaming assortment of different dishes, carefully doling out portions onto each plate.

"I'd love to." She watched his head come up in a hurry and laughed gently. "But after dinner, Peter."

To Thorn's considerable relief, the Thai restaurant hadn't let him down. Each dish tasted as good as it had smelled—a rare achievement for any prepared meal, let alone takeout.

At last Helen pushed her empty plate away with a small sigh. "Now, *that* was worth waiting for."

"Better than Stannard's?"

"Much better than Stannard's," she agreed. She leaned back against the sofa and closed her eyes for a moment. "This is really nice, Peter. It's peaceful and quiet, and best of all, it's away from work. Miles and worlds away."

"Have a bad week?" he asked quietly.

Helen opened her eyes and made a face. "Just a typical week." She shrugged. "Sometimes I think half the senior men in the Bureau believe I've gotten to where I am on the Hostage Rescue Team solely because I'm a woman . . . a real affirmative action aberration. The rest only want to trot me out as a showpiece for Congress or the media. You know, with a little sign around my neck that reads, 'See, we do get it. We're hip. We're with it on equal rights.' "

Thorn snorted. "Not many showpieces kick Sergeant Major Diaz' butt in a shooting-house competition."

Helen smiled in fond memory. "That's for sure." Then she shook her head in frustration. "It just doesn't seem to matter to the older guys in gray suits, though. I still have to prove myself to them all over again every single day."

"But not to your section," Thorn suggested.

"No. Not to them." She smiled. "They're a pretty good bunch of guys. For Neanderthal door-kickers, that is."

"Yeah. I've heard that some of us are even almost human." Thorn started clearing dishes. "So what made you decide to go for the HRT anyway?"

"You mean as opposed to choosing the normal career path for a young, ambitious FBI agent?" Helen shrugged again. "I wanted more action and excitement than I thought I'd get behind a desk in Omaha or Duluth or Topeka. Besides, it was a chance to break some new ground. To be one of the *first* to do something."

She looked up at him. "Does that make any sense?"

Thorn nodded. It made a lot of sense—especially to him. They were a lot alike despite their very different upbringings, he realized. Both of them were driven to win, to succeed, to be perfect. If anything, Helen had it a little harder than he did. As one of the first women assigned to the FBI's traditionally male counterterrorist unit, she would always have to fight the unspoken presumption that she was only there as a token female. He knew her well enough now to realize just how galling that must be.

He was also positive that Helen Gray would never take anything she hadn't earned in a fair and open competition—not a job, not a promotion, and not a trophy. The day after they'd first met, he'd gone back to Fort Bragg to review the videotapes of her section's winning run through the House of Horrors. Any thoughts that her victory was a fluke had gone right out the window after seeing those tapes. She was good. Very good. Her assault tactics were brilliant, she improvised rapidly when things went wrong, and she was a crack shot. She made up in agility, accuracy, and intelligence whatever she might lack in raw physical strength.

Helen touched his shoulder lightly. "What are you thinking, Peter?"

Honesty overrode his native caution and fear of sounding

corny. "Just that you're the most beautiful and intelligent woman I've ever met."

She laughed deep in her throat. "One hundred points for flattery, Colonel Thorn." She shook her head in wonderment. "Louisa Farrell said you were dangerous. And she was right."

Still sitting, Helen stretched lazily, arching her back and shoulders in a way that sparked a definite rise in Thorn's pulse. He moved closer.

Helen turned her face toward his, her lips slightly parted. He kissed her, gently at first, then harder. After he'd spent what seemed an eternity exploring a soft, warm sweetness, she leaned back and looked intently into his eyes. "And what are you thinking now, Peter Thorn?"

He smiled slowly. "I was wondering just when you had to report back to Quantico."

She pulled him down to her again. "Not until tomorrow night."

JULY 11

Sofia, Bulgaria

(D MINUS 157)

Colonel Shalah Haleri paced across his small, shabby room, reached the faded, yellowing far wall, and turned back toward the window. There was nothing much to see. Bulgaria's capital city sprawled at the foot of 2,300-meter-high Mount Vitosa, but he had chosen this run-down hotel for its anonymity, not its tourist value. The thick smog hanging over this industrial working-class neighborhood hid any clear view of the mountain's forested slopes and ski runs.

Abruptly, he stopped pacing and returned to the battered chair and scarred writing table that were the room's only other pieces of furniture besides an iron-frame bed and a washstand. Fifteen years as a covert operative in Iran's intelligence service had taught him many things—patience among them. When you were deep in an enemy land, haste was almost always the path to failure and to death.

Mentally, he reviewed his cover story yet again. He could not afford any mistakes. This meeting he had scheduled was too important to his mission.

The fractured states of the former Warsaw Pact were rich with pickings—if you had the money to spend. And Bulgaria had special items that were available nowhere else. General Taleh intended to add those resources to his arsenal. Haleri was the man charged with making the general's intentions a reality.

Haleri's lips twitched upward in a one-sided smile as he examined his passport. It had been issued under the name of Tarik Ibrahim, and even an intensive search would only lead any hunters back along a false trail laid all the way to Baghdad. It amused him to travel as a member of Iraq's spy service. There was a delightful irony there, he thought.

A soft knock on the door brought him to his feet. Instinctively, his hand slid under his jacket and then stopped. He was unarmed. Even in postcommunist Bulgaria, carrying a firearm was more trouble than it was worth. If things went wrong, he would simply have to trust in God, and in the suicide capsule his masters in Tehran had thoughtfully provided.

"Come in."

The colonel relaxed as his visitor stepped inside and pulled the door shut behind him. It was the man he had been expecting—the go-between. He called himself Petko Dimitrov—at least this week. The Iranian suspected his real name was long forgotten.

Dimitrov was as nondescript as himself—a middle-aged man with gray hair, a plain face, and expressionless eyes. We are two of a kind, Haleri thought with a touch of perverse pride. We are men who can walk through life without leaving any lasting trace of our coming or going.

"Good afternoon, Mr. Ibrahim."

"And to you." Haleri indicated the single chair. "Please, be comfortable."

Dimitrov set his briefcase carefully on the writing table and sat down.

The Iranian sat across from him, perched on the edge of the bed. He cleared his throat. "You have news for me?"

The Bulgarian nodded. A faint smile flashed across his lips and then vanished. It never reached his eyes. "I have spoken to my principal," he said slowly. "The work you have requested can be done. And it can be completed in the time you have allotted."

"Good." Haleri paused briefly. "And the price?"

Dimitrov shrugged. "The price will be high." He lowered his voice. "The encryption software you need is easy. The other . . ." He shook his head. "The other item is difficult. It will take a great deal of thought and effort."

Haleri nodded. He understood that. A complex task required a complex and extraordinary weapon. He pursed his lips. "How much?"

"Eight million." Dimitrov's eyes hardened. "There will be no bargaining, you understand? That is our price—no more and no less."

"Very well," Haleri agreed readily. The price was higher than he had hoped, but no one in Iran could produce the weapon he sought. "Eight million dollars?"

"Dollars?" Dimitrov smiled wryly. "I hardly think so. You will pay us in German marks. Half in a week's time. The rest on delivery."

Again, the Iranian agreed. Within minutes their business was concluded.

As he escorted the Bulgarian to the door, Haleri asked, "Does it have a name, this weapon of yours?"

Dimitrov shrugged again. "Once you have paid, you may call it whatever you wish." He smiled coldly. "We call it OUROBOROS."

AUGUST 3

Clearview Motor Lodge, Arlington, Virginia

(D MINUS 134)

Sefer Halovic let the door close behind him. The sound of it slamming shut was his signal to relax—however minutely. The first phase of his mission was over. He'd made it. He was safely in America.

Out of habit, the lean, cold-eyed Bosnian scanned the motel room. It would have looked commonplace, even drab, to any American, but it seemed luxurious to him. Two single beds half filled the room, which also held a chair, table, and television on a battered stand. The covers on the beds were a faded lime green. They almost matched the stained, gold-colored carpet. He could see several spots where the wallpaper, a speckled, ugly yellow-brown, was peeling away from the walls. He peered through an open door and saw a small bathroom, with a shower and a dripping sink.

Halovic nodded, satisfied by what he saw. Compared to the Masegarh barracks, this was palatial. More important, it was anonymous. He'd paid in cash and he'd been careful to avoid eye contact with the bored clerk. They'd barely exchanged a dozen words during the transaction—hardly a serious test for his English skills.

Throwing his bag on one of the beds, he collapsed onto the other. He'd been traveling for more than three days, following a long, circuitous route specifically designed to confuse anyone trying to retrace his path later.

First he'd flown from Tehran to Rome using false papers that identified him as Hans Grünwald, a German salesman. From there he'd taken the train to Paris and then a flight to Montreal.

Crossing from Canada had been the mission planners' masterstroke, Halovic realized. The U.S.-Canadian border was notoriously porous. Passport and customs checks there were infrequent at worst, nonexistent at best. He'd been lucky. The bus he'd hopped in Montreal had taken him all the way to New York without incident. From New York, he'd taken a train south to the vast, renovated bulk of Washington, D.C.'s Union Station. A taxi had brought him to this motel, one he'd picked at random out of a telephone book.

Halovic closed his eyes, trying hard to get some sleep. It was two in the afternoon, and the short nap he'd caught on the train had been no more than dozing, the uneasy rest of a soldier in enemy territory. He'd spent most of his time watching the scenery slide by while keeping a wary eye out for suspicious officials or police.

Images from the journey rolled through his restless mind. America was huge, bigger than he had imagined. A three-hour train ride would have taken him halfway across the former Yugoslavia. Here, it covered only a small fraction of one coastline.

He was also unaccustomed to a country at peace. He'd bought a newspaper and several magazines at Penn Station. To his amusement and disgust, Americans seemed wrapped up in trivialities. While the world exploded around them, they argued about scandals and fashions and the latest movies. His lip curled in contempt. If this country was a giant among nations, it was a distracted, childish giant.

These people did not know what real war was. To them, it was nothing more than a video game or a sporting event. Their brief news reports of the continued fighting in Bosnia seemed utterly abstract and dispassionate. His jaw tightened. Because the Serb murderers posed no threat to America and because their victims were Muslim, the American people were content to do nothing. They would let his homeland boil in its own blood because it was too distant for them to care.

Well, Halovic thought grimly as he slid into an uneasy, nightmare-filled sleep, I will show them what war is like. I will make them bleed.

The frantic chirping of his watch alarm roused him. He opened his eyes, rolled over onto his side, and turned it off in one smooth, graceful motion. It was six o'clock in the evening. It was time to move. Time to make his most recent incarnation disappear.

Halovic levered himself off the bed. He was still weary, but he could run on willpower and adrenaline for a while longer. He showered and changed into casual clothes—jeans and an open-necked shirt. He also shaved off the light blond beard and mustache that had hidden most of his face as Grünwald. Smooth-cheeked now, he shredded his old passport, plane, bus, and train tickets and flushed them down the toilet.

Back in the room, he opened his hard-sided travel bag and cut away the inner lining with a pocketknife to retrieve another set of identity papers, including a Virginia driver's license with his picture and the name of Frank Daniels. Bulging envelopes taped next to the forged documents held cash, a lot of it. More than thirty thousand American dollars—all in twenties, fifties, and hundreds.

Halovic regarded the money with cool calculation. Although he'd entered the United States unarmed, the cash in his possession was as much a weapon as any rifle. He planned to make sure that it was used wisely and not wasted—just like ammunition.

The hot, humid summer air hit him as he stepped outside carrying his travel bag. He left nothing behind in his room except the key, which the cleaning staff would find in the morning.

Halovic spotted a pay phone next to a fast-food restaurant across the street. After crossing at the light, he discarded the pair of wire-frame eyeglasses he'd worn as Grünwald in a nearby trash bin. He noted the street names in passing.

At the pay phone, he dialed a number he'd memorized in Tehran. It rang once before being answered.

"This is Arlington Transport."

"You have a pickup at Arlington Boulevard and Courthouse Road," Halovic replied. "Near the hamburger restaurant."

"Do you have the fare ready?" the voice asked.

"I'm from out of town. Can you take a check?"

"Yes." There was a pause. "It will be about ten minutes. Expect a green sedan."

"I will be waiting." Halovic hung up. He moved further down the road and pretended to be waiting for a bus. Vehicles flowed past in a steady stream as the evening rush hour built to a climax. Though nobody paid the slightest attention to him, the ten minutes seemed to pass very slowly.

A large green car—a Buick—drove by the phone booth, circled back, and turned into the fast-food restaurant's parking lot. Fighting his instinctive caution, he stood up with his bag in hand and strode up to the waiting vehicle.

The driver's window slid down noiselessly as he approached. A face turned in his direction, but the man's hands were hidden. Halovic knew that the Buick's driver had a weapon ready. He approved of that. He had no use for overconfident fools.

"I'm looking for Arlington," he said flatly. "I'm meeting a friend there."

"This is Arlington," the driver replied. Halovic noted that the man's English was heavily accented, but understandable. His face was half hidden in the shadows, and his hands were still not visible. "Your friend must be elsewhere. Perhaps he is in Alexandria?"

Halovic sighed. Sign. He spoke distinctly, careful to keep his hands in plain view. "Then I need a lift. I can pay you well." Countersign.

"Get in."

Halovic quickly walked around the front of the car and slid into the passenger side. He glanced once at the man beside him. "Drive."

Obeying the single terse order, the driver immediately put the Buick in gear and backed out. As he signaled to turn onto the street, he said, "Fasten your seat belt, please. The local traffic regulations require it."

Halovic complied, fumbling with the unfamiliar fittings. Then he turned toward his associate. Khalil Yassine was a short, dark-complected man in his late twenties. Until General Amir Taleh had plucked him out of a terrorist camp he'd slated for destruction and brought him to Masegarh for further training, Yassine had been a guerrilla fighter in a radical offshoot of the PLO.

The Palestinian spoke in a respectful tone. "There is a residential area ahead on the left. We can lose any possible trailers in there."

"Excellent. My name now is Daniels. So then, who exactly are you?" Halovic asked him, just as he might prompt a child to recite its catechism.

"I am George Baroody, a naturalized American citizen. I was born in Lebanon and emigrated ten years ago to escape the civil war there. I am a car mechanic, but I've been laid off and am looking for another job."

Halovic arched a skeptical eyebrow. "Lebanese? Don't the authorities keep a close eye on people from your country?"

Yassine shook his head. "They cannot. There are thousands and tens of thousands of immigrants in this region—some are legal, many are not. From all parts of the world. So I stay away from politics. I don't cause trouble. I stick to my own affairs." He shrugged. "In effect, I am invisible."

Halovic nodded, satisfied by the other man's confidence in his cover story. As an area leader, he'd been allowed to choose his own people, and he knew Yassine intimately. They were both the products of bitter wars fought against hopeless odds. They were both survivors of Masegarh.

As a teenager and a young man, Yassine had caused a lot of trouble for Israel and for Israeli forces in Lebanon. He knew Beirut and the Christian strongholds in southern Lebanon like the back of his hand. So his cover was a good one. He also had extensive experience with automobiles. More useful to Halovic, the Palestinian had demonstrated a remarkable talent for operating "behind the lines" in disguise.

Yassine was his driver and scout. The first cell member to arrive in the United States, he'd spent the last week securing lodgings and transportation—and learning the ins and outs of the area's roads and highways.

Halovic, as the team leader, was the second man to arrive.

More were on the way, leaving Iran by differing routes. A dozen or so were assigned to infiltrate America's eastern seaboard. Other groups were earmarked for other regions. The initial orders for all the cells were explicit: Arrive safely and undetected by the Americans. Submerge yourselves in their midst. Gather information and make plans as directed by Tehran. And then wait. Wait for the code words that will unleash you.

Yassine turned left off the wider boulevard into an area of narrower, tree-lined streets, single-family homes, and sidewalks. Driving smoothly and staying well within the speed limit, he took a series of twists and turns down the quiet suburban roads to clear their tail. Anyone trying to follow them would have stood out like a sore thumb.

Halovic took his eyes off the passenger-side mirror and nodded to the Palestinian. "We're clear."

Yassine took them out the other side of the residential development and onto a wider, arterial street. Ten minutes' drive took them to a small brick house with white-trimmed windows. It lay in the middle of a row of identical houses, all built beside a busy four-lane avenue. Bushes bordered a small, well-kept lawn.

Halovic nodded approvingly. The busy street would make their own comings and goings less conspicuous.

"What about the neighbors?" he asked as they pulled off the street and onto a concrete driveway beside the house. They parked behind an old Ford minivan. "Will they pose any problems?"

"I haven't seen anyone, and I've been here a week," Yassine reported. He nodded toward the houses on either side. "They all work. Both the husbands and the wives. We will have no trouble with them."

"Good." Halovic got out of the car and pulled his bag out after him. The sooner they were inside, the better he would feel.

Yassine handed him a set of duplicate keys before he unlocked the front door. It opened into the living room, illuminated by a single floor lamp. It was furnished with a secondhand couch, a few chairs, and a television set. The walls were painted an unremarkable beige, and a worn brown rug covered the floor. He could see into the kitchen beyond, also furnished. A short hall led off to his right.

Halovic followed the Palestinian down the hall.

"There are three bedrooms. This is one." Yassine gestured to a small front bedroom, sparsely furnished. He opened another door. "I have been using this one."

It was a corner room, larger and with nicer furnishings. The driver's tone made it clear that he would move out in a second if the team leader said the word.

"Keep it," Halovic commanded. "I'll only be here a few nights anyway." Once the rest of his force began arriving, he would find other quarters. Even the busiest locals were bound to grow curious if they noticed the house was occupied by several young men.

He opened the door into what had been the third bedroom. Brightly lit by an overhead fluorescent fixture, it was now a work area. Near one wall a cheap folding table supported a brand-new laptop computer and stacks of papers, while another table next to it was covered with gunsmith's tools and a partially disassembled pump-action shotgun. A third held power and electronics tool kits, all still sealed in their original packages.

Halovic wandered over to the first table. It was stacked high with maps, realty brochures, and classified ads. Most of the maps looked new, but he could see that Yassine had studied and marked several of them, concentrating on those showing the Washington metropolitan region.

He turned toward the silent Palestinian and nodded. "You've done well."

Yassine swelled with pride. The months they'd spent together at Masegarh had taught him that the Bosnian never offered praise lightly.

Halovic tapped the computer keyboard idly. He looked up. "Do you understand this machine yet?"

Yassine lowered his eyes, clearly embarrassed. "No. It is difficult." He shrugged. "The operating manuals are very hard to decipher."

"Difficult or not, you will learn to use this machine," Halovic said coldly. "Is that understood?"

"Yes." The Palestinian stood motionless for a moment with his head slightly bowed. "It will be done."

"Good." Halovic strode to the second table and picked up the disassembled shotgun. He recognized it as a Remington Model 870 and nodded to himself. A good weapon—at least in close quarters. Such weapons and the ammunition for them were also readily available in the United States.

A wooden rack against the wall held another Model 870, but this one had been radically modified, its barrel shortened and its stock sawed off and shaped into a pistol grip. Hunting rifles and pistols completed the small armory. All were common makes, firing widely available ammunition.

More powerful and more sophisticated arms and armaments would come from overseas—usually smuggled across America's wide-open border with Mexico. One of the twelve-man cells dispatched by General Taleh was solely responsible for shepherding those weapons shipments to secure drops scattered across the continental United States. Once the shipments were delivered, each regional cell would break them up, moving some of the gear to safe houses and hiding the rest in separate small caches.

Halovic put the shotgun back on the table and wiped the oil off his hands. "How far away is the first drop site?"

"I estimate a three-hour drive to the southeast. Somewhere near a town called Virginia Beach."

Halovic shrugged. The name meant nothing to him. He stabbed a finger toward the pile of maps. "Show me."

He peered intently at the map Yassine pulled out and unfolded, orienting himself—memorizing the astonishingly complex network of highways and major roads that fed in and out of America's capital city and surrounding suburbs. It was time to begin preparing in earnest for the war he would ignite.

CHAPTER SEVEN

FALSE COLORS

AUGUST 18

Walker's Landing, Virginia

(D MINUS 119)

Walker's Landing was a tiny Virginia hamlet nestled against the southern bank of the James River roughly two and a half hours south of Washington, D.C., and west of Richmond. Surrounded by tangled woods, gloomy swamps, and small, run-down farms, it was little more than a cluster of houses and stores centered around Route 250, a two-lane blacktop highway that crossed the river.

Sefer Halovic peered through the dirty windshield of his Buick LeSabre and nodded in satisfaction. He'd been guided to this part of Virginia by pamphlets carefully collected by Yassine and other Iranian agents. Walker's Landing seemed perfect for his purposes. Isolated, confined, and impoverished, the place appeared a likely breeding ground for the narrow minds and festering hatreds he sought. Country villages had produced some of the most savage killers in the Bosnian war. He saw no reason why it should be any different here.

He pulled off the main road and into a gravel motel parking lot at the southern end of town. A row of ten dilapidated cinder-block bungalows surrounded the parking lot. Each had been divided into two motel rooms. A car and an old pickup were parked out in front of two of the bungalows. The rest appeared unoccupied. The building closest to the highway had a sign in one of its unwashed windows identifying it as an office.

Halovic stepped out of his car and into the sticky warmth of a late summer afternoon. His nose wrinkled in disgust. From the smell and the flies buzzing around his head, he guessed that the owners of the StarBrite Motel rarely bothered to have their trash removed. Or perhaps they simply could not afford it, he thought coldly, eyeing the deserted parking lot again.

The contrast between this place and the tidy suburban communities he'd grown used to seeing around Washington was striking. It was a reminder to him that America's elites built their fortunes on the backs of the poor, both abroad and here in their own land.

The StarBrite Motel's office was no cleaner or fancier inside than its exterior suggested. Dust covered a rack of sun-faded tourist brochures and local maps near the rusting front screen door. Flies circled lazily around the room. The smell of fried food and stale beer hung in the air.

Halovic let the screen door spring closed behind him and walked up to the deserted front desk. The sound of a television filtered out through an open door behind the desk. From the muted crowd noises he heard, he assumed the set was tuned to one of the mass sporting events which seemed to preoccupy so many Americans. A baseball game, perhaps?

He stood waiting for a moment, listening, and then cleared his throat. "Excuse me, please? Is anybody there?"

Halovic was proud of his assumed German accent. Together with his own native speech patterns, simply substituting "t" for "th" and "v" for "w" made his words decidedly Teutonic. The accent lent credence to his new alias as Karl Grüning, a German postgraduate student on an extended vacation to America.

"Be right there, mister," a slow, southern drawl answered him from the back room. The owner of the voice, a wizened old man, emerged a few seconds later, blinking rapidly against the sunlight streaming in through the windows. He finished buttoning a plain white shirt that had clearly seen cleaner days and smiled nervously, showing an uneven row of yellowing, tobacco-stained teeth. "Now, then, what can I do for y'all?"

"I would like a room, please. You have a vacancy?"

"A room?" The old man seemed surprised by the notion that anyone would want to stay at his establishment. Then he roused himself. "That ain't no problem, mister. I've got plenty of rooms."

He looked Halovic up and down, clearly weighing what the traffic would bear. "Now, I charge twenty-five bucks a night—cash. In advance." He looked almost defiant as he continued: "I don't take no credit cards. And no checks, neither. Too much danged trouble."

Halovic nodded. Better and better. He had hoped that the motel owner's record-keeping would be on a par with his cleanliness. Carrying out this phase of the mission already entailed more risk and personal exposure than he would have preferred. At least staying in this rattrap would not require leaving a paper trail for the police to follow. He reached into his pocket, pulled out a full wallet, and carefully counted out fifty dollars in crisp ten-dollar bills. "That is not a problem. I would like to stay at least two nights, please."

"Two nights?" The old man seemed even more astonished, but not so astonished, Halovic noted, that he neglected to grab the money in front of him. "You can have number five. Tidied it up myself yesterday."

He reached under the counter for the right key and dropped it onto the desk in front of Halovic. "Scuse me for asking, mister, but you're a foreigner, ain't that right?"

The Bosnian smiled politely. "*Ja*, that is right. I am German."

"Thought so," the old man said with satisfaction. "I thought so." His eyes narrowed in speculation. "Now, I don't mean to pry or nothing, but I was wondering what you're doing here in town. Can't say as we get many foreign tourists here in Walker's Landing."

Halovic allowed himself to look embarrassed and eager at the same time. "I have come for the shooting. To shoot the guns, you understand?"

"The shooting?" Understanding dawned on the motel owner's lined face—mixed in with some surprise. "You mean you come all the way from Germany to fire off a few rounds at our local gun club?"

"Oh, no. That is, not only to shoot." Halovic paused, pretending to search for the right English words. "I am in America on a holiday. A sabbatical. I was in Richmond when I was told of your gun club." The Bosnian shrugged. "It seemed a good opportunity, you understand? Firearms are restricted in my country. There are few places to shoot. It is not like here."

The old man nodded slowly. "I've heard about them goddamn gun control laws like they got over there in Europe." Although obviously still puzzled that anyone would come all the way to Walker's Landing when there were more and better firing ranges closer to Richmond, he had clearly decided not to look a gift horse in the mouth. "Well, mister, I sure do hope you enjoy your stay."

He nodded toward the door. "There's a working phone in number five. You need anything, you just give me a holler, you hear?"

"*Danke.*"

"If you get hungry or want a drink, there's a couple of bars and a diner in town, just up Route 250. Okay?"

Halovic politely nodded his understanding and turned to leave. He could feel the old man's interested gaze as he walked back to his car. That was not surprising, really. In fact, he fully expected the story of the gun-crazy foreigner to be all over Walker's Landing by nightfall.

That was exactly what Sefer Halovic wanted.

It was still daylight when he wandered up the road into town, trudging slowly along the grassy verge in the stifling heat. Although an occasional car or pickup truck passed him, the traffic was extremely light. Walker's Landing was not really on the road to anywhere in particular. Certainly, the hamlet had very little to attract anyone to itself, he decided. Two churches, wood-framed houses, and a combination general store, post office, and pharmacy lined Route 250. Poorly paved streets on the right and left led off to more houses and a tiny school.

He stopped first at one of the local bars, the Riverfront. He didn't stay long.

A loud rock sound track pounded at him as he walked in the door. Four or five customers were scattered around the bar, all of them in their early to mid-twenties. Halovic frowned at the bare wood dance floor and drum set that dominated one end of the interior. This place was not what he was looking for. This was a dance club, not a drinking saloon. Besides, the bartender and two of his patrons were black.

Halovic made sure that everyone noticed the hard, angry scowl he directed at them before he spun on his heel and stalked out. He had an image to create and maintain.

The Riverfront's sole competitor looked more promising.

The Bon Air Bar sat at the north end of town, flanked on one side by a rutted, boggy field the bar's customers used as a parking lot, and on the other by a small stand of trees. The brick building's brown-painted wood-shingle roof might seem rustic or even homey at night, but the harsh late afternoon sunlight would not tolerate such friendly illusions. Right now the Bon Air Bar looked bleak and shabby. A neon sign on the roof advertised Budweiser beer, but Halovic wasn't sure it would actually light once the sun went down.

This time he heard country-western music coming out of a corner jukebox. There was no sign of a dance floor. The room smelled of tobacco smoke and beer, and its dark wood paneling seemed to absorb the dim light. The only bright color in the bar was a five-foot American flag tacked up across one wall. Two middle-aged men sat together, talking, while a younger man, thin with long hair, tended bar. A TV blared in one corner, tuned to yet another baseball game.

Halovic stood in the doorway for a few moments, taking in the scene in front of him. He actually liked country-western music, which had a fair-sized following in Eastern Europe. And this appeared a quiet place, one not used to strangers, but certainly more restful than the Riverfront. It should suit his needs.

He walked over and sat down on a red plastic barstool. When the bored-looking young bartender glanced in his direction, he asked for a beer, carefully picking an American brand.

He sipped the pale, cold brew cautiously, comparing it unfavorably to the darker, warmer European beers he'd first tried as a student in Sarajevo and then again as part of the intensive preparation for this mission at Masegarh. Alcohol was forbidden to followers of the Prophet under normal circumstances, but God would understand the need to camouflage himself in this land of unbelievers. He was supposed to be a German and Germans drank beer.

Still drinking slowly, he let his eyes focus on the unfamiliar game being played out on the television set. And then he waited.

"I don't guess they have much baseball where you come from, mister."

Halovic looked away from the TV to find the bartender looking at him. He shrugged and smiled politely, clearly puzzled by what he had been watching. "That is true. In Germany we play football—what you call soccer. It is a fast game and very simple. But this"—he nodded toward the set—"this baseball of yours is so difficult. So complicated."

"It's not all that tough, actually." The bartender grinned and held out his hand. "My name's Ricky Smith, by the way."

Halovic shook hands with the younger man and introduced himself. "Karl Grüning. From Leipzig."

"Pleased to meet you." Smith nodded toward the television again. "You want me to explain the finer points of the game?"

"I would be very grateful," Halovic lied smoothly. He sat back on his stool and sipped at his beer, content to let the bartender's gibberish about double plays, foul balls, and the rest wash over him.

The afternoon and early evening passed quietly. Halovic studied the men coming into the bar, noting faces and even names when he could hear them. Most wore work clothes, faded blue jeans or coveralls. Some had obviously come straight from their jobs or farms. While there were men in their twenties and thirties, the bulk of them were older.

By six-thirty there were ten or twelve men inside the Bon Air—all familiar to each other. Most came up and greeted the bartender, who in turn introduced the German tourist, "Karl."

Halovic answered their questions easily, describing Germany and the journey he planned across America. But he was always quick to turn the conversation back to baseball or to firearms and sport shooting.

One of the men talking to him paused to light a cigarette and then spoke around it. "I heard it's real tough to buy guns overseas. That true?"

Halovic nodded. "Ja. That is so. The authorities, they do not like citizens to own weapons. Even for hunting or sport. It is strictly forbidden in many places."

The man and several of his companions shook their heads in disgust. One muttered something about "goddamn guv'mints."

Their heads turned toward the TV as a sudden roar burst from the televised crowd. The man with the cigarette whistled and nudged the others. "Well, I'll be damned! Will you look at that! A grand slam! That boy hit a goddamn grand slam!"

Halovic carefully concealed his contempt. These people were like children—easily distracted and amused by trivialities. No wonder they were held in thrall by the rich and powerful in this country's cities and suburbs. Perhaps it was time to begin shaping the conversation to suit his purpose in coming to this backwater town.

He waited until the cameras cut away from the stadium and back to the network studio for a recap of the other games played that day. The commentator was a black man.

After listening to the sports anchor rattle off meaningless statistics for a few moments, Halovic suddenly remarked sharply, "Ah, get him out of here. I don't want to see him."

One of the older men seated nearby shook his head slowly. "He ain't that bad, Karl. You should hear—"

"No, no, I don't care if he is good or bad," Halovic countered. He grimaced. "I am just tired of all the blacks I see on television all the time. It's worse here even than in Germany."

Without pausing, he launched into a bitter fusillade against "the Turks, Arabs, and Africans who infest Germany's streets and steal jobs from true Germans."

As he spoke, Halovic carefully noted the reaction from the group. The four men he'd been talking with all frowned slightly or showed neutral reactions. When he finished, there was a small embarrassed silence. To his chagrin, nobody took the bait he'd laid out, and someone quickly changed the subject to the latest movies and TV shows.

Dinnertime came and Halovic ordered a barbecue sandwich. The crowd thinned only slightly during the dinner hour, then grew again until the Bon Air was comfortably filled.

The group sitting near him changed as men drifted in and out, and he took advantage of that to occasionally throw out a biting reference to the problems caused by blacks in America, comparing them to similar situations in Europe. He also complained about the interracial marriages and about black people's "low intelligence and tendency toward crime."

Most ignored his remarks, or changed the subject, or simply left quickly. A few argued the points with him, or even agreed to some extent. Despite that, none of them reacted in the way that he had hoped.

By ten o'clock Halovic was beginning to feel the effects of the beer he'd been drinking, even at his limited rate. His eyes smarted from the tobacco smoke and the stuffy air, so he made his excuses, paid his bill, and left.

The walk back through town to his dingy motel room helped ease some of his frustration—but not all of it. Although he had known that this part of General Taleh's master plan would take time and some risk to implement, he was all too aware of the days slipping past.

AUGUST 19

(D MINUS 118)

Halovic rose early the next morning. He exercised in his room, showered, and changed into jeans and a short-sleeved shirt. It was just after dawn when he stepped out into the muggy air.

Already aware of the sweat beginning to soak the back of his shirt, he crossed the highway and walked back to the diner he'd spotted the night before. There were three waitresses working that morning, one of whom was black. He was careful not to sit at one of her tables and he took pains to make his disdain for her known.

After a light breakfast he returned to his room, grabbed the Remington .30-06 rifle Yassine had procured for him earlier at a northern Virginia gun shop, and pocketed a large handful of cartridges. Before heading to his car, he also loaded a small 9mm pistol and tucked it away into a holster concealed in the small of his back. In Halovic's experience, it never hurt to have a hidden edge.

The Walker's Landing Rod and Gun Club lay right next to the James River, three miles west of town and down a winding country lane. A faded sign by the side of the road directed him to the clubhouse, an old concrete-block building topped by a rusting aluminum roof. Several other vehicles were already parked out front, and he could hear the steady *pop-pop-pop* of small-arms fire from off behind a row of trees.

With his rifle tucked under his arm, Halovic walked into the clubhouse to pay the five-dollar fee it would take to make him a member for the day. He paused just beyond the door to let his eyes adjust to the interior light.

Display cases containing rifles, pistols, shotguns, fishing rods, and other sports gear filled half the tiny shop. The rest seemed full of a hodgepodge of U.S. Army surplus clothing and military collectibles: World War II Wehrmacht helmets, fur-lined Soviet tanker's hats, knives, bayonets, and boxes full of decorations, service ribbons, and unit patches from a dozen different countries.

How ridiculous, Halovic thought icily, these Americans play so hard at being warriors. And yet, how little they understand about real war.

He stepped up to the counter with his five dollars already out and ready.

The proprietor, a large, bearded fellow wearing a white T-shirt with a fish on the front, took his money with a smile and passed him a photocopied sheet. "Those are our range safety instructions," he explained. "They're pretty basic. No booze, no automatic weapons, and no explosive targets are allowed here at the club.

"Now, when somebody yells 'clear,' it means they want to retrieve their targets. When you hear that, you immediately cease fire and put your weapon down. And then you yell 'clear' back so they know you heard 'em. Once everybody's stopped shooting, you're free to go out and check your own targets. Okay?"

Halovic nodded his understanding.

The other man eyed his rifle appreciatively. "That's a nice piece. Brand-new?"

"It is." Halovic patted the stock fondly. "I bought it just last week. A real beauty, eh?"

"Uh-huh. You need any ammo today? I've got a good special running on boxes of .30-06."

Halovic nodded again. He didn't really need more ammunition, but it made little sense to risk antagonizing this man. "One box, please. And a map of the area, if you have such a thing."

While the big, bearded man rang up his purchases, he used the opportunity to study his surroundings a little more closely.

The owner and most of his customers were white, but one black couple was also there, perusing the racks of handguns and hunting rifles. Halovic took pains to shoot several hard looks at them, some of which, he noted, were spotted by others in the shop.

With the racial views of Karl Grüning once more made plain, the Bosnian cradled his rifle and headed outside toward the sound of gunfire.

By four o'clock Halovic was back in the Bon Air Bar, this time perched well away from the television set.

He scowled to himself. The shooting range had been another waste of time. The people he'd met had been friendly enough, and they were certainly well versed in the workings of their various weapons, but none of them had been the least bit interested in his racial or political views. Worse from his viewpoint, the Walker's Landing Rod and Gun Club had seemed merely a well-armed version of the Elks, or Lions, or some other kind of American civic organization. It was not the sort of place that would attract the kinds of men he had come looking for.

So again he quietly sipped beer and conversed with the regulars. They seemed to accept him more today—at least in the sense that they were willing to challenge some of his wilder statements. One fellow named Jeff Dickerson, short, pudgy, and in his thirties, seemed to have come in with that as his express purpose. Halovic remembered him from last night. Dickerson had walked out right after he had uttered something about blacks and Jews causing most of the problems in the world. Now the man was back.

That played right into Halovic's hands. This man Dickerson was intent on a reasoned debate, so he gave him one. He was careful to keep the conversation unemotional, since an argument might cause them to be ejected from the bar. At a minimum an argument would drive other listeners away. And Halovic wanted listeners.

Speaking softly and calmly, he articulated a carefully thought-out worldview in which "lesser races" were the cause of many of the world's current problems. Knowing he would need such information, he had spent many hours studying the neo-Nazi pamphlets and other literature Taleh's agents had obtained in the United States and Europe. Now he repeated some of those same phrases, and quoted from German and American fringe writers who'd published books like *The Jewish Crime* and *Genetics and Race*. He also mentioned the Christian Bible frequently, selectively citing passages that supported his views.

Halovic didn't believe any of it himself. In fact, he found their arguments and "facts" pathetic—almost comical. Islam, true Islam, recognized no racial divisions among the Faithful. Nevertheless, the man he was supposed to be would have believed in his hatreds with his whole heart and soul, and he had no compunctions about spouting such nonsense as long as it furthered his mission.

It was not a fair fight. The American was motivated by honest conviction and limited by logic. Halovic, whose only goal was to widely air a racist philosophy, used or abandoned logic as he chose. Always friendly, always convincing, he manufactured facts and statistics, the more outrageous the better. And in the end, after almost an hour of intense discussion, the other man stormed out, thoroughly disgusted.

Inside, Halovic smiled. He'd watched the others in the bar while he'd argued with Dickerson. Most had at least been aware of the conversation. Some had tuned in surreptitiously, listening to the verbal cut and thrust with interest.

Nobody else seemed immediately eager to take up the racial gauntlet he'd thrown down, so he sat alone quietly, watching television while he waited again for his efforts to bear fruit.

A little after seven, two men entered the bar. Halovic, who reflexively kept one eye on the door, only noticed their arrival among the after-dinner crowd because one of the pair gestured in his direction and said something to his companion.

Both came over to him right away. The first offered his hand and said, "I'm Tony McGowan. We talked yesterday."

Halovic took it, remembering the tall, black-haired man. He hadn't said much, but he'd always been nearby, in easy earshot.

The other man was older, in his fifties, with rougher features and brown hair cropped almost as short as Halovic's. He was built like a wrestler gone to seed, bulging muscles gone slack or turned to fat. He also extended his hand. "Name's Jim Burke. I hear you're looking to do a little shooting."

Halovic nodded. "Ja. I shot some today—at your gun club here." He allowed his disappointment to show on his face and in his voice.

Burke smiled thinly. "Pretty tame, isn't it? Nothing much exciting to shoot at out there. A few regulation targets and some old cans and bottles."

McGowan chimed in. "Real little-old-lady stuff."

Halovic nodded cautiously.

Burke took the barstool next to him and signaled the bartender for three more beers. He leaned closer. "A few of us have a range we've set up on some private property. We can cut loose a little more out there than they do at the gun club. Anyway, we were wondering if you'd like to join us out there tomorrow. Say, around noon."

Halovic thought fast.

Were these men what they claimed to be, friendly locals simply looking for a chance to show off their weapons and skills to a foreign visitor? Unlikely, he decided. Tomorrow was a weekday, a workday for most of these people.

Or were they provocateurs, law officers of some type on the prowl for potential troublemakers? That was doubtful too, he realized. Walker's Landing seemed too small and isolated to warrant much attention from the authorities.

Halovic felt a sudden thrill—the same kind of thrill he always experienced when his crosshairs first settled on his chosen target. It was far more likely that Burke and McGowan were two of the very men he had come hunting. He smiled slowly at the man sitting beside him. "Thank you, yes. I would like to shoot with you very much. It would be an honor."

AUGUST 20

(D MINUS 117)

The red Blazer that picked up Sefer Halovic in the morning held three men: Burke, McGowan, and another man, much younger and in excellent physical condition, behind the wheel. He introduced himself as Dave Keller.

Halovic climbed into the backseat beside McGowan. He was already starting to sense the hierarchy involved here. Burke was clearly the leader and the man he must convince. The others would look to him.

Their shooting range was a fifteen-minute drive south of Walker's Landing, well off Route 250 down a narrow, wooded private road. Frequent signs warned trespassers to stay out. Those closest to the highway threatened legal action against anyone caught violating private property. The notices further down the road carried more ominous warnings.

Halovic shifted slightly in his seat. He had been right. Whatever else they were up to, these men were not just being friendly to a foreign tourist. The shape of the pistol he carried concealed in the small of his back was suddenly reassuring.

Keller wheeled the Blazer off the road and into a long, narrow clearing separating dense woods on either side. More trees at the far end closed off the clearing entirely. The four of them piled out and began pulling their gear out of the back.

The Bosnian finished loading his rifle and straightened up. He looked down the clearing with interest. Burke and his companions had accumulated a wide variety of potential targets for their private shooting gallery. There were old oil drums, rusting refrigerators, and even a couple of abandoned cars scattered at varying distances all the way back to the distant woods. Most of them were shot full of ragged holes.

Keller nodded toward the optical scope Halovic had fixed to his rifle. "You got that zeroed in yet?"

He shook his head. "No, I would like to do that now."

Keller pointed toward an oil drum someone had painted red. "That's two hundred yards. Give or take a foot or two." He grinned mirthlessly.

"*Danke*." Halovic dropped into a relaxed kneeling posture and chambered a round. This would be an easy shot. There was no appreciable wind, and he knew the precise range to his target. He took a breath, let it out, took another, sighted, and then gently squeezed the trigger.

A puff of dirt appeared six inches in front of the barrel and a few inches to one side. After making a minute adjustment to the sight, he fired again.

This time the barrel rocked slightly—punched clean through the center.

"Damned good shooting," Burke remarked casually from beside his ear.

"*Ja*. Well, I was in the Army," Halovic lied.

"What did you do?"

"I was a sniper." That much at least was true.

Burke smiled. "A sniper, eh? That's interesting." He glanced at the others briefly and then turned back to Halovic. "See the crooked tree just past that old Dodge? The black willow? Now take a good look just to the left."

Halovic swung the rifle left slowly, hunting through the scope for the spot the older man had indicated. He stopped as a figure dressed in camouflage fatigues and hunched beside the tree trunk leaped into focus.

He took his eye away from the scope in surprise and glanced at Burke. "There is a man out there!"

The older man grinned. "Not really." He nodded downrange. "That's just a dummy we dressed up. Adds a little kick to the target practice."

Halovic nodded slowly. "I understand." Then he allowed a smile to form on his face. "That is much better than shooting at old metal!"

McGowan slapped him on the shoulder. "You got it, Karl!" He tapped the Remington rifle in Halovic's hands. "That .30-06 is nice, but how about handling something with a little more kick? You know, some real rock-and-roll?"

"Rock-and-roll?" Halovic didn't have to pretend any confusion this time.

"Yeah. Something that can go off on full auto. Something like this baby." McGowan held out an assault rifle—a weapon the Bosnian recognized as a Chinese-made variant of the old Russian AK-47.

Halovic laid down his .30-06 and took the assault rifle Mc-Gowan offered. Although thousands had been sold in the U.S. as semiautomatic weapons, someone had reconfigured this one to allow full-automatic fire. He looked up. "This rifle . . . isn't it against your American gun control laws?"

Burke shrugged. "Maybe. But this is private property, Karl. And we're a long way down the road. So what we do here is our own damned business. Nobody interferes with us. Understand?"

Halovic nodded firmly. "I understand."

"So let her rip."

"As you wish." With the ease born of long practice, the Bosnian flipped the safety off and began shredding a series of targets, walking his fire from right to left as he pumped short bursts into each. In seconds, he'd emptied the thirty-round magazine. He turned to the other men with a broad grin on his face, slapped the AK's stock with one hand, and exclaimed: "*Ausgezeichnet!* Very good! A beautiful weapon!"

Burke, McGowan, and Keller were staring openmouthed down the range.

Finally the older man spoke for them all. "Goddamn, Karl! That was some beautiful shooting." He looked at the row of mangled barrels and torn-up refrigerators again and shook his head in admiration. "Now, that calls for a drink! And for something to eat, by God."

Galvanized by their leader's decision, McGowan and Keller hurried to the Blazer and brought back a cooler containing a couple of six-packs, a loaf of bread, condiments, and an assortment of lunch meats. The four of them found shade under a nearby tree and sat back at ease, swapping sandwich fixings and cans of ice-cold beer.

Burke broke the companionable silence first. The burly man brushed the crumbs off his lap, drained his beer can, crumpled it, and tossed it casually aside. "Tony tells me you've got some pretty strong views on race problems, Karl. Is that a fact?"

Ah. Now it begins, Halovic thought. He nodded firmly. "That is a fact, Jim." Then he shrugged. "I know these views are not popular in America, but truth is the truth. The white races all over the world are being buried by a sea of inferiors—of blacks, of Jews, of Arabs . . ."

He was heartened by the other men's reactions as he continued his often-rehearsed tirade. Burke and McGowan both smiled and nodded as he made his points, clearly pleased by what they were hearing. Even Keller seemed to relax slightly.

Burke nodded sharply again when the Bosnian wound up his peroration with the assertion that "time is short. We must act soon and in force before we are drowned—and our race with us."

The older man pursed his lips. "You've sure got that right, Karl." He scowled. "God only knows the niggers and the rest are getting uppity as hell in this country."

That brought rumbles of assent from both Keller and McGowan.

Burke took another beer out of the cooler, drank deeply, and began outlining his own extremist views. Not surprisingly, they paralleled those Halovic had just laid out in every significant detail. He seemed delighted to find a kindred spirit from overseas—especially from Germany. His two followers chimed in occasionally, but they always deferred to the older man.

They are sheep, Halovic thought with contempt, all the while smiling and nodding himself. They go wherever they are led.

"Are there many others like you over there in Germany, Karl? Men who're willing to stand up for the white race?" Burke asked at last.

"Yes. Many." Halovic paused significantly to make sure he

had their full attention. "And not just in Germany. There are others like us all over Europe."

He stabbed at the grass with his finger as he continued. "We are organizing. Mobilizing. Arming! We are strong and growing stronger. The moment of truth is drawing near. Soon we shall strike. First in my homeland. And then in the other nations of Europe."

"Outstanding!" Burke's enthusiasm, unlike Halovic's, was wholly unfeigned. He turned to McGowan and Keller. "What'd I tell you boys? We're not alone in this fight. See, all we've got to do is provide some goddamned leadership and the pure whites will rise up to join us!"

Halovic took a deep breath. "So you have organizations such as mine here in America?" he asked carefully.

"Hell, yes, Karl!" Burke grinned proudly. "You're looking at the leader of one of the biggest!"

The Bosnian listened with hidden disdain and open admiration as the older man outlined his plans to "retake" America from its racial and genetic enemies. His wild-eyed schemes—a linked series of attacks and assassinations—were intended to spark a nationwide rising of the white race. To fire a revolt that Burke believed would be spearheaded by his own fanatical group—the "Aryan Sword."

Madness, Halovic thought coldly. But perhaps he could make it a madness tinged with a tiny grain of truth.

"We don't have the numbers I'd like. Not yet," the older American admitted. "But we're recruiting pretty fast. People around here are waking up to what's going on."

"That's true!" McGowan asserted loyally, backing up his leader. "With the Ramseys, we've got fifty-two members—counting the kids who're old enough to carry a gun."

Halovic tried hard to look impressed. In truth, those numbers were somewhat larger than he'd expected. Under all his drunken bluster, this man Burke must have the charisma needed to draw ignorant and gullible people together under a banner of hate.

He leaned closer to the older man. It was time to make his

move. "That is wonderful news. Great news. I had hoped to find a movement of courage here in America. You see, I am here to build an alliance across the seas. The war begins soon and we must fight together—side by side against the Jews and the blacks and the rest."

The Bosnian pulled a crumpled pamphlet out of his shirt pocket and handed it to Burke. Titled "The Jewish Plan," it had been picked up months ago at a white supremacist rally in Maryland by an Iranian agent posing as a journalist. "This was my guide."

"Jesus! That's Harry's pamphlet. I helped him run it off," Mc-Gowan exclaimed in surprise.

The atmosphere changed abruptly. Burke's face was suddenly a mask, unreadable. Halovic noted that Keller's hand now rested on the barrel of his rifle. He fought the temptation to reach for his own concealed pistol. He had known that this would be a moment of crisis. By their nature, hate groups like the Aryan Sword were run by secretive, paranoid men. They would not like the notion of a stranger actively searching for them.

He pointed toward the pamphlet still clutched in the older man's hand. "This was passed to us in Leipzig," he lied. "We knew that there were centers of resistance here in America, so I was sent to find them. But I am not alone. Others are looking too—in other parts of your country."

Burke shook his head in evident disbelief, but Halovic could see the excitement bubbling up beneath the older man's inbred suspicion.

He allowed himself to relax—however minutely. Everything was as the mission planners in Tehran had foreseen. People like Burke often talked in grandiose terms of forging an army, of leading a revolution, of blood and fire and sword. But they never seemed completely prepared to see their ideas taken seriously. The idea that someone might actually begin the race war they had predicted had them off balance.

The silence stretched.

McGowan reacted first. "This is bullshit!" he exploded. He

stood up, pacing stiffly over to Burke. "What's this guy talking about? Even assuming he's telling the truth, what do we care about Europe?"

Halovic checked Keller, who had not moved. The younger man's hand still rested on his rifle.

"Tony had a good point, Karl," Burke said carefully. "Why should we stick our necks out for you? What do we have to gain?"

"Arms. Sophisticated weapons."

McGowan snorted, but Burke held up a hand to silence him and only said mildly, "We're pretty well fixed for guns, Karl. As you should know."

"Small arms, yes. But I can get you automatic grenade launchers, antitank rockets, mortars, land mines, even antiaircraft missiles. Ammunition, explosives, and detonators too. Do you have these things?"

"No." The older man looked more interested. "At what price?"

Halovic shrugged. "Well below the price on the black market. Just enough to cover our own costs and shipping."

"Sure," McGowan sneered. "Now it comes out. This bastard's a con artist. I say we let him walk back from here." He nodded angrily toward the dark woods around them. "Or maybe we just make sure he doesn't go back at all."

A grim-faced Keller nodded slowly in agreement.

Halovic tensed.

"Sit down, Tony," Burke snapped. He turned back to the Bosnian. "You're talking pretty big, Karl. You'd better be able to back up what you say. Now, how the hell did you lay your hands on mortars and the rest? And what makes you think you can get that kind of hardware over here without the feds going apeshit?"

He had them, Halovic realized. He shrugged. "When the two Germanys merged, there was much confusion. The old communist Army built hidden arms bunkers all over East Germany. Their record-keeping was very poor." He smiled coldly. "My comrades and I found it easy to make some of those bunkers disappear from the files.

"As for transport . . ." He shrugged again. "That is simplicity itself. We have friends like you in position in ports like Hamburg and Rotterdam. And more friends in Canada who will handle transshipment for us."

Halovic fixed his gaze on Burke. "I say we can get you the arms you want. The arms you will need. I tell you again most solemnly, the war of blood and race you have foretold is upon us all."

The older man licked his lips, clearly tempted but still uncertain. He glanced swiftly at McGowan and Keller as though seeking their silent counsel. At last, he shook his head and stood up. "I've got to think more on this, Karl."

Halovic and the others stood up with him.

Burke looked at Keller. "You take him back to his motel for now, Dave." Then he turned back to Halovic. "And you be waiting outside your motel room at nine tomorrow morning. We'll talk more then. Clear?"

The Bosnian nodded silently, satisfied. He would let their greed and ambition war with their cowardice and caution through the night. He was over the first hurdle.

AUGUST 21

(D MINUS 116)

Wearing a light jacket over an open-necked shirt, Sefer Halovic stood waiting outside his motel room early the next morning. He didn't have to wait long. A rusty blue sedan—an old Chevrolet—turned off the road and roared straight across the gravel lot toward him at high speed. He forced himself to stand still as the car squealed to a stop right beside him.

Burke and McGowan were in front. Keller sat in the back.

"Get in," the older man ordered.

Halovic obeyed, careful to keep his hands in plain view at all times. He didn't like the tone of Burke's voice or the strain he could see on his face and those of Keller and McGowan. These men were operating on a hair trigger and that was dangerous—both for him and for them.

With McGowan at the wheel, the Chevrolet skidded out of the motel parking lot and turned north onto Route 250. They crossed the James River in silence and headed east on Route 6.

After several minutes, Halovic risked a question. "Where are we going?"

"Richmond," Burke replied tersely.

Richmond? Why there?

Keller handed him a manila envelope. "Read this."

Suppressing any questions, Halovic leafed though a sheaf of newspaper clippings and typewritten pages. They all concerned one man—a prosperous local black businessman named John Malcolm. The first clipping, a few years old, described a new youth training program launched by Malcolm. Other articles described the success of the program and his further ventures. He was active in several social circles, and he was a popular speaker at local schools and community meetings. One of the last clippings speculated on Malcolm's chances as a candidate in an upcoming congressional race.

The typewritten pages were a detailed dossier on Malcolm. They listed his home and business address, his children's schools, his wife's work, his church, his closest associates, and every aspect of his daily routine.

Halovic was impressed. Someone had done a great deal of research on this man and his movements. Its purpose was obvious. Malcolm was targeted for some sort of action by Burke's group. He was precisely the sort of black man they would hate and fear most—prominent, successful, and socially accepted. Judging by the dates, it was something they had been planning for quite some time.

He finished reading and looked up at the older man. "For what reason do you show me this?"

"We want you to kill him."

Halovic nodded slowly. Two possibilities confronted him. If

these men really were neo-Nazi radicals, this was a test of his sincerity, and by their standards, of his bravery. That was understandable. On the other hand, if Burke, McGowan, and Keller were police informers or agents, this was a trap—a ploy to have him condemn himself out of his own mouth.

To buy time to think, he stared for a moment at the quiet wooded countryside streaming past before glancing back at Burke. "And if I do?"

"We'll deal. Weapons for cash."

Halovic considered his chances coldly. If they were serious, his course of action was clear. Killing Malcolm meant nothing to him. All that mattered was the risk of discovery. Of capture. Of failure. Of course, refusing would also mean failure. Burke and his followers would never risk continued contact with a man they did not trust. That much was certain.

He studied the dossier again. The material it contained was well organized and complete. There were no airy assumptions, no unnecessary rhetoric. It was all very professional. And his companions, while reactionary, did not appear excessively sloppy or wholly stupid.

Questions swirled in his mind. Why hadn't they assassinated this man themselves? He wasn't naive enough to think he'd just happened to show up at the right time.

Halovic sensed the others waiting with mounting impatience. He had taken a reasonable amount of time to ponder his answer, but if he waited any longer, he would be stalling, both them and himself. There was no other data to be had. And delay could be fatal in more than one way. Decide, he told himself sharply.

Stung into action, he nodded. "Very well. I will kill this black man for you." Almost by reflex a workable plan popped into his brain. "You have a weapon for me?"

Burke glanced at Keller. "Show it to him, Dave."

The younger man reached into a brown paper bag between his feet and pulled out a brand-new pair of gardening gloves, a 9mm automatic, a separate eight-round clip, and a bulky, cylindrical silencer.

Halovic recognized the weapon as a Smith & Wesson Mark

22—a silenced model first used during the Vietnam War by U.S. Navy commandos. They had called it the Hush Puppy.

"There's a rifle in the trunk if you want it instead," Burke said.

Halovic shook his head. He would complete this operation at close range. "The pistol will suffice."

"It's cold," Keller said reassuringly. In answer to Halovic's questioning look, he explained, "It's not traceable. A dealer at a gun show traded it to us years ago. He doesn't keep records."

"That is very good." Halovic slid the clip into place, worked the action, and screwed the silencer into the pistol's muzzle. He nodded, satisfied by what he saw. The weapon was in excellent condition.

He looked out the window again. There were more houses and stores lining the highway. A sign informed him they were nearing the outskirts of Richmond.

Burke watched him closely. "You got any idea of how you want to do this thing, Karl?"

"*Ja.*" Halovic thumbed through the dossier until he came to a map showing Malcolm's movements. Then he leaned forward and jabbed a finger at the spot he wanted. "Drive here, to Elkheart Road. We will go directly to his office."

Burke nodded slowly after studying the map himself. "Okay. Do what the man says, Tony."

McGowan complied.

Ten minutes later, they were in a quiet, suburban section of Richmond. The small professional building that housed Malcolm's office lay a few tree-lined blocks from a large shopping mall. A parking lot surrounded the two-story brick and glass structure on three sides.

"Pull in here," Halovic ordered. He pointed to an empty space near the exit to the street. "There. Back in."

Sweating now, McGowan cranked the wheel over hard and carefully backed the Chevrolet into place between two other cars.

Moving slowly and methodically, Halovic donned the gloves Keller had given him and began to carefully wipe the metal surface of the pistol with a handkerchief. He was aware that all three men were staring at him. Burke seemed pleased. Mc-Gowan was wide-eyed and looked increasingly nervous. Keller was poker-faced.

The three Americans exchanged quick glances and then nodded to each other.

"We've seen enough," said Burke. "We believe you."

"Excuse me?" Halovic said. He tucked the pistol under his jacket.

"I said, we've seen enough," repeated Burke. "That's it. You were ready to go through with it. That's all we wanted to know."

Halovic frowned inside. His first contemptuous suspicions had been right. All of Burke's talk about waiting for the right moment, his elaborate plans, their stockpiled weapons, it was all just a fantasy.

He stared hard at the older man and shook his head. "No. It is not enough."

"Huh?" Burke was clearly bewildered. "What do you mean, Karl?"

"This was a test, true? To see if I would kill?"

The older man nodded rapidly. "Yeah, that's right."

Halovic smiled coldly. "Very well. I accept that." He pointed toward the office building. "Now I will test you. This black man will die and you will be a part of his death."

He glanced at Keller, the man he judged the toughest and most reliable of the three. "You. You will come along as my lookout."

The younger man stared at him for a moment, plainly taken aback.

"Hold on just a minute, Karl," Burke interrupted. "There's no need to go off half-cocked. I told you that we're satisfied you're one of us. We don't need to take any unnecessary risks here today."

A pale, terrified McGowan mumbled his agreement with his leader.

"Risks? You fear risks?" Halovic said scornfully. "And yet you call yourselves soldiers?" He shrugged. "My people will not deal with cowards or shirkers. Either this black man dies, here, today, or you will see no advanced weapons from me. Is that clear?"

He waved a hand toward the office building. "I tell you that your plan is good. This man can be killed with ease. But you must act—not sit and dream." He turned back to Keller. "Decide. Will you come with me?"

The younger man stared first at Halovic and then at Burke. "Jesus, Jim . . . what do you think?"

Clearly torn, the older man chewed his lower lip. He wanted those grenade launchers and explosives. He just hadn't expected to be asked to help kill anybody to prove his *own* good faith. Finally, he shrugged. "It's up to you, Dave. We need those guns."

"You are afraid," Halovic said flatly, forcing the issue. "Stay behind, then."

"Hell, no!" Keller flushed, unwilling to admit his fear. "If you really want to kill this nigger, I'll help you do it."

Halovic popped open the car door and got out quickly, before the stunned Burke could say anything else. The Bosnian worked hard to keep his expression neutral. These American fools were about to learn the difference between fantasy and deadly reality—a reality he already knew all too well.

Keller followed him without evident hesitation.

That was good, Halovic decided. He had no intention of trusting his life to this man, but at least he showed some backbone.

The office building's glass double door led into a small lobby. He checked the building directory, reconfirming the information contained in the dossier. Malcolm's offices were still on the second floor—suite 215.

Nobody else was in sight.

With Keller at his heels, Halovic walked down a short hall to a door marked "Stairs." He ignored the elevator.

Two flights of bare concrete steps led up to an unlocked steel fire door. Halovic paused long enough to make sure that it could be opened easily from either side. If anything went wrong in the next few minutes, a rapid exit might prove to be the difference between life and death.

The door opened up on a long hall that ran the length of the building, widening in the middle for the elevators. John Malcolm's office was down at the far end of the hallway.

With Keller still following him, Halovic walked briskly past a series of other offices. The sounds of typing and soft music filtered out from behind closed doors. The hallway was empty.

He stopped just outside suite 215. Painted lettering on a frosted glass door identified it as the offices of Malcolm Accounting. After checking the hallway again, he slipped the bulky Smith & Wesson out of his jacket. Then he turned toward Keller, measuring him one last time.

The American licked his lips, clearly nervous, but still in control of himself. Halovic knew the look well. He'd seen it on dozens of men just before their first real action.

Readying his automatic, he commanded softly, "Do not let anyone in behind me."

Keller nodded quickly.

With the pistol held out of sight, Halovic opened the door and walked through it into a reception area. Dark wood furniture, soft carpeting, and original oil landscapes on the walls conveyed a reassuring air of stability and success. A middle-aged black woman with snow-white hair sat behind a desk.

She looked up with a polite smile. "Good morning. Can I help you gentlemen?"

Halovic smiled back. "I certainly hope so. Is Mr. Malcolm in?"

"Yes, but he's with a client . . ."

Good enough. Halovic brought the Smith & Wesson up in one smooth motion and shot the woman in the chest. Blood spattered across the painting hung behind her. Even silenced, the pistol's report seemed shockingly loud, like someone dropping a heavy telephone book on a tile floor. He worked the slide rapidly, chambering another round, and fired again.

The woman slumped forward across her desk, scattering papers and a bound appointment book onto the carpeting.

"Oh shit."

Halovic glanced behind him. Keller's eyes were wide, almost

white with shock. He stood frozen in the doorway, staring at the carnage. He had clearly completely forgotten his duties. The Bosnian had expected that. The American's only real function was to act as a witness.

"Shut the door and be silent." Halovic swung away toward the entrance to Malcolm's inner office.

He knocked twice and went in without waiting for a reply. There were two men inside, one seated behind a large mahogany desk. The other occupied a Queen Anne chair in front of the desk. The furniture looked expensive, the men prosperous.

Malcolm, his primary target, was the one behind the desk. He matched his newspaper photos perfectly. A large, balding black man in his mid-fifties, he wore a subdued gray suit and conservative red tie. The other man, also black and similarly dressed, was younger. Halovic didn't recognize him, and didn't care. His presence here marked him for death.

Both looked toward the door, clearly surprised at being interrupted.

"You are Mr. John Malcolm?"

The man behind the desk nodded slowly. "That's right."

Halovic took three steps into the room, moving left to clear his field of fire. Perfect.

"Look, who are you?" Malcolm asked, still perplexed.

The Bosnian brought his pistol up, fired at Malcolm, swiveled slightly, and fired at the younger black man—all within a single murderous second. Both shots struck home.

Without hurry, Halovic strode to the desk. Malcolm sprawled back in his chair, a bright red stain spilling across his stomach. One hand clutched at his belly wound, but the other just twitched feebly, pawing toward a phone just out of reach. The businessman's eyes were open but unseeing, glazed with pain.

He had fired too low, Halovic thought coolly, displeased by the evident imperfection of his marksmanship. Stomach wounds were rarely immediately fatal.

This time he aimed carefully at Malcolm's head and fired twice more. The black man's face dissolved into red ruin and his body twitched violently as each 9mm round tore a path through his brain.

Without moving, the Bosnian turned to check the other man. Malcolm's visitor was still alive. He'd fallen forward out of the chair onto the carpeted floor. Now, moaning loudly, he was crawling through his own blood—inching in agony toward the open door.

"No, no, my friend," Halovic said softly. "You do not escape." He walked toward the crawling man, stood behind him, and fired two more shots into the back of his skull. Brains, blood, and skull fragments sprayed across the carpet. The young man shuddered once and lay still.

Halovic quickly stepped back and behind the desk, double-checking Malcolm's throat for pulse. Nothing.

About thirty seconds had passed. He walked out of the inner office. Again acting on trained reflex, he checked the white-haired receptionist, making sure she was dead. She lay as he had left her, facedown on a desk almost completely covered in her own blood. He dropped the automatic. Nothing about it would lead the police back to him, so there wasn't any need to risk being caught with it later.

Keller stared at him both in horror and in admiration. "Oh, man. You did it. You killed everyone. Didn't you?"

"You saw me," Halovic said coldly. He motioned the American out into the hallway, turned the snap lock on the door, and closed it behind him. They were done here.

He half expected to find Burke, McGowan, and the car gone, but the Chevrolet was still parked where they had left it. He and Keller piled in and he ordered, "Drive. But take your time. No traffic accidents, please."

"Sure. Sure. No problem." McGowan put the car in gear and drove slowly away. His knuckles were white on the steering wheel.

Burke furtively studied the two men in the backseat. From time to time he opened his mouth as though to ask exactly what had happened inside Malcolm's office, but each time, he closed it without speaking. Halovic ignored him, calmly studying the city streets, checking to make sure they weren't under surveillance.

Still pale and in a state of shock, Keller slumped back against the rear seat, staring straight ahead, shivering occasionally. But when they turned onto the highway leading out of Richmond without any sign of police pursuit or even interest, he seemed to settle down. His shivers died away and his color began coming back.

Halovic watched the younger man with some interest. Keller was apparently learning how to come to terms with the bloodbath he had witnessed. That was good. Given time, he might even learn to control his fears and to act with the discipline and ruthlessness a successful secret war required.

They were ten miles outside the Richmond city limits when Keller leaned forward, closer to Burke, and nodded toward Halovic. "Jesus, Jim, you should've seen it. Karl blew that damn nigger away like you'd put down a stray dog! He offed two more of 'em, too. Just like that!" He snapped his fingers.

Burke stared at Halovic. "You shot three people?"

"It was necessary." The Bosnian shrugged. "One man or three—it makes no difference." He smiled crookedly. "You cannot keep count in a war, Mr. Burke."

His own calm was not an act. He had killed many times in Bosnia, so many that he had lost track somewhere along the way. The faces of the dead sometimes came to haunt him in nightmares, but they faded in the waking day. Besides, eliminating Malcolm had proved to be child's play—an act without significant risk. These Americans were all so open, so unprepared—so unsuspecting. Killing them required less real effort than posting a letter.

"Then all this stuff about your group, about the alliance, about the guns and bombs you can get for us . . . that's all true? No bullshit?" Burke asked rapidly.

Halovic could hear the excitement building in the other man's voice. This was the reaction he had hoped for. Confronted for the first time by a man who would do what he had only dreamed about, Burke was beginning to see the prospect of his hate-filled rhetoric bearing real fruit.

He nodded somberly. "What I have told you is true. My comrades and I in Europe have the weapons . . . and the will to use them." His eyes narrowed. "The question I put to you, Mr. Burke, is this: Do you and your men of the Aryan Sword have the courage to join with us in this war? Can you really kill to save the white race in America?"

"Hell, yes!" Burke exclaimed. He sounded almost surprised by the certainty in his own tone. Then he thumped his fist on the seat back for emphasis. "You get us that heavy-duty hardware, Karl, and we'll set this whole goddamned state on fire before we're done! The blacks and Jews won't know what's hit them!"

Keller nodded sharply, seconding his leader's sudden resolution. "That's right!" He slapped McGowan on the back. "Ain't that right, Tony?"

The driver flinched and mumbled a tentative assent.

Halovic ignored him. McGowan was nothing—a drone. Burke and Keller were the key men in their twisted group, the brains and the muscle of their so-called Aryan Sword.

He hid a satisfied smile as Burke started bargaining in earnest, making the complicated arrangements needed to covertly acquire a wide range of weapons and explosives. Clearly, the older man now believed they would help make him a leader in the new crusade to "purify" America.

Well, Halovic thought grimly, let him dream. If Burke and the other extremist leaders truly believed in the coming Armageddon, they might even work up the courage to act on their own when the time came. And if not, the armaments they were about to receive would still make them useful stalking-horses for General Taleh's special action teams.

Either way these foolish Americans would be made to serve a greater purpose.

CHAPTER 8

LOCK-ON

SEPTEMBER 11

32nd Armored Brigade exercise area, near Ahvaz, Iran

(D MINUS 95)

Three Russian-made GAZ jeeps were parked on the crest of a low, boulder-strewn rise north and east of the industrial city of Ahvaz. Iranian Special Forces troops in full combat gear stood guard at key points on the hill, forming a protective perimeter around the high-ranking Army officers clustered near the three vehicles.

Standing at the center of the small group, General Amir Taleh swept his binoculars slowly back and forth, carefully scrutinizing the area selected as a training range for the newly reequipped 32nd Armored Brigade. He nodded to himself in satisfaction. It was good ground.

Regular patches of green dotted the distant northern and

western horizons—some of the date and sugar plantations that made Ahvaz Plain an important agricultural region. Oil wells were visible to the south, marking the edge of one of the vast gas and petroleum fields that had made the province both one of Iran's richest regions and a prime objective for neighboring Iraq during their bloody, endless war. Brown, rugged slopes rose to the east—the foothills of the Zagros Mountains.

No plantations or oil wells marred the emptiness of the stony, uneven landscape immediately to Taleh's front. There were only the rusting hulks of obsolete tanks and armored personnel carriers. Thousands of track marks were visible crisscrossing the barren plain, silhouetted by the slanting rays of the late afternoon sun. Heat waves shimmered among the abandoned fighting vehicles, distorting distances and shapes.

The long, low, deadly silhouettes of modern T-80 tanks and BMPs crammed with Iranian infantry maneuvered in and around the hulks. Dust kicked up by their speeding treads merged into a single, ragged brown cloud. The tanks and infantry fighting vehicles were firing on the move, all the while smoothly deploying into platoon-sized wedge formations.

As each T-80 fired, 125mm shells screamed through the air. Even at more than two thousand meters almost all of them burst somewhere around the target hulks. Taleh smiled, pleased by the accuracy the 32nd Brigade's tank gunners were demonstrating.

One round triggered a bright, orange-red ball of flame.

Taleh turned in surprise toward the bearded, hawk-nosed brigadier who commanded the 32nd. There shouldn't have been any reaction from those burned-out vehicles.

"We place tanks of diesel fuel and a few rounds of outdated ammunition inside the hulks before each exercise. My crews are trained to shoot until they see a fireball or explosion," the other man explained. "I have found that it increases the realism of the battle drill."

"An excellent idea, Sayyed." Taleh nodded approvingly. Like the other armies in the region, too many of Iran's battalions and brigades were hollow units—accumulations of first-rate hard-

ware and second-rate, poorly trained men. Leaders who understood the danger of that and who could forge their commands
into capable units were rare and valuable soldiers. Clearly, he
had chosen the right man to command this formation.

He glanced at Kazemi and indicated the burning wreck now
visible through a gap in the smoke. "Make a note of this,
Farhad. We will recommend the technique to all units."

Taleh swung back to watch the rest of the armored assault as
it swept across the barren, explosion-torn landscape before him.

An hour later, with the exercise complete, the small convoy
of three jeeps rolled through the gates of the Ahvaz Garrison,
heading for a long, low building that contained the brigade
headquarters. Barracks, maintenance sheds, and storehouses
lined the paved road on either side. Most were dark in the fading light.

Taleh glimpsed bright arc lights shining inside one of the
sheds. Technicians were hard at work inside, scrambling over
and under an armored behemoth like ants ministering to their
queen. He leaned forward and tapped the bearded brigadier on
the shoulder. "Stop here, Sayyed. I want to see this."

He never kept to a rigid itinerary, especially on inspection
tours. Part of that was for security reasons. He still had enemies,
now perhaps more than ever before. Randomly changing his
schedule kept them guessing, especially those with lethal plans.
But mostly, it was because he wanted to make sure his officers
learned to expect the unexpected—in peace as much as in war.
Above all, he thought, they must come to understand that uncertainty is the central feature of any battlefield.

At the brigadier's direction, the jeeps pulled up and parked
beside the floodlit maintenance shed.

Without waiting for his subordinates, Taleh jumped out and
strode into the building. His bodyguards hurried to take up their
positions around him, shooing away startled technicians and
mechanics like so many frightened geese. He paid only cursory
attention to the sweaty, oil-smeared men as they formed ranks

under the brigadier's glare. His gaze was focused on the mammoth T-80 they had been working on.

Taleh hauled himself onto the tank's chassis and clambered onto the turret. He slid through the open hatch with the ease of long experience and settled himself inside the T-80's cramped interior. He ran his eyes and fingers lightly over the dizzying array of dials, switches, scopes, cabling, and machinery—all still labeled in Russia's Cyrillic script.

On the whole, he was pleased by what he saw. His agents had purchased several hundred T-80s—Russia's most advanced battle tank—at ridiculously low prices from the cash-hungry bureaucrats in Moscow, who found it cheaper to sell a tank than to scrap it. Melting down a forty-ton chunk of armored steel was not a simple operation.

But this vehicle was far more than a simple chunk of metal.

He laid a hand on the massive breech of the T-80's 125mm main gun and nodded to himself. Powerful gas turbine engines, sophisticated fire control and gun stabilization systems, and reactive armor designed to foil enemy armor-piercing rounds and missiles gave this tank and the others like it speed, deadly force, and survivability that matched some versions of the American M1 Abrams. And once they were installed, the German-manufactured thermal sights his purchasing agents had acquired would make Iran's T-80s even more advanced than their Russian counterparts.

Truly, they should prove formidable weapons in the hands of trained crews.

Taleh frowned. There was the rub. Training. Training and maintenance.

Inspired by the will of God, Iran's Regular Army had no shortage of fighting spirit. What it had lacked was a sizable cadre of trained professionals who could integrate new weapons into competently prepared plans and keep the combat units properly supplied and all this newly acquired hardware up and running.

Shoddy staff and maintenance work had always plagued the Iranian armed forces—problems exacerbated by the militant creed imposed by the Ayatollah Khomeini and his radical successors. When anyone who deviated from the revolutionary ideology they preached ran the risk of arrest and even execution, it had proved almost impossible to form a professional officer corps.

Taleh was determined to change that. Iran could not afford to have an army of inexperienced zealots. His Western training had shown him the importance of proper planning and logistical support. The time to worry about details was before the battle started. Once the shells began to fly, it was too late—far too late. As his American Ranger instructors had said again and again, combat was the ultimate stress test. War found every weakness in men and in their machines.

He scowled, mentally chiding himself for the sudden burst of defeatism. He had made progress. Iran's military was no longer a clumsy giant. The religious monitors were gone, and the cowards and incompetents were going. The aggressive young officers who shared his vision were forging the rest into a true army—an efficient, professional force wholly subordinated to his will.

Another skilled observer loitered near the maintenance sheds—a thin-bearded, hook-nosed man dressed in ragged, dust-colored clothes and battered sandals. Hamir Pahesh watched the activity with an air of boredom, but with more interest and knowledge than might be expected of the average truck driver.

Pahesh's face had been weathered by the harsh Afghan climate and scarred by guerrilla war. Although only in his forties, he looked ten years older. Time had not been kind to him.

For most of his life he had been a farmer and part-time mechanic, scratching out a bare living in an arid, impoverished land. But then the Russians had come, razing his village simply because it might supply the mujahideen. Most of his family had been killed in the attack—the rest had died in the terrible winter that followed.

He'd fought the Russians, first as a member of a small band, then as part of a larger mujahideen group that had hit the invaders again and again. They'd had help, from the Pakistanis and the Chinese and the Americans. That was where Pahesh had first worked with the CIA.

He'd heard the stories about the American spy agency, of course. Propaganda from the Russians and their Afghan government puppets had labeled the CIA a sinister cabal dedicated to murder and chaos. That was nonsense, of course. The men he met in Pakistan gave him food, medicine, and weapons to kill Russians.

In the end he and his comrades had won. They had driven the Russians back across the border. But the civil war had continued, with Afghan killing Afghan now that they lacked a common enemy. His tortured, fragmented homeland had drifted from battle to battle as old tribal hatreds flared anew.

Pahesh felt adrift as well, his hate spent, but nothing to replace it.

He'd gone to Iran, seeking work and some new purpose. Instead he had been crammed into a refugee camp with thousands of his countrymen. Most Afghans were members of the Sunni branch of Islam. Most Iranians were Shiite. And evidently, the Iranians were willing to take Muslim brotherhood only so far. Pahesh had skills, though, as a mechanic and driver, and he'd been able to get a job driving a battered old truck.

Even out of the camp, he still felt unwelcome. Able to live only in ramshackle housing, paid a pittance for backbreaking labor, the ex-mujahideen felt the Iranian snubs every hour of the day.

Only with others from home could he find any peace. He'd run into one of his old guerrilla comrades, who had passed him on to an old American friend, now working in Iran. It didn't take a deep thinker to realize what he was doing there, or what he wanted Pahesh to do.

And Pahesh had been willing, more than willing, after seeing Persian hospitality. Since that day, many years ago, Pahesh had driven the length and breadth of Iran. He tried to get work near or on military bases wherever possible. There was much to see and more to overhear. He could speak Farsi as well as his own Pushtu, but he made sure the Iranians didn't know that.

Over the years, the Afghan had seen many things that interested the CIA. In return for the information, the Americans gave him money, as well as the high-tech equipment needed to do his work for them. The money kept Pahesh's truck in good condition and many of his refugee countrymen fed and warm.

Now his experienced eye roamed over the compound. He could see five tanks in the maintenance bays and at least a score more parked in back, waiting for their turn. He'd identified the T-80s the instant he'd spotted them. He also heard a lot of Russian being spoken. The Iranian military buildup was accelerating.

An Iranian sergeant walked around the corner. "There you are," he remarked. "Get moving, you're blocking the loading dock," the soldier ordered harshly.

Pahesh pretended ignorance and incomprehension, and with a disgusted look, the noncom spat out a few words slowly. "Go. Drive truck. Understand?"

Nodding, keeping his eyes down, the Afghan walked the short distance back to his truck, got in, and pulled out. The engine growled comfortably as he drove out of the base and away from its guns and fences.

He'd pick a safe place to work tonight. Although slow and somewhat cumbersome, the covert communications system he normally used was secure and fairly reliable. After coding and microfilming, his latest report would go through the regular mails to a friend in Pakistan, piggybacked on a personal letter. His friend would in turn pass it to a CIA controller working out of the embassy in Karachi. Depending on the vagaries of the Iranian postal service, his information should reach America in a few days.

SEPTEMBER 12

Lonestar Business Park, Dallas, Texas

(D MINUS 94)

Salah Madani stared out the dark, tinted windows of his rented office. He had a perfect view of the busy airport just across the road. Jets in different corporate and airline colors lumbered by, some heading for runways, others for the terminals and air freight buildings. Voices crackled through a bank of radio receivers tuned to the frequencies used by air traffic controllers, ground crews, and the airport's security personnel.

More than 50 million passengers and hundreds of thousands of tons of cargo flew in and out of the Dallas/Fort Worth airport each year. Dozens of hotels, warehouses, and office complexes bordered its outer perimeter—all built to profit from their proximity to the world's second busiest airport.

But Madani and the men in his action cell were not interested in profit. The office suite they had leased the week before offered a secure location from which to monitor airport operations and security. Operating in shifts, they maintained an around-the-clock surveillance, accumulating data on approach and departure flight paths, police activity, and ground traffic.

The risk of discovery was minimal. As the region's economy rose and fell and businesses prospered or went bankrupt, tenants moved in and out with astonishing frequency. So the local landlords were used to a high turnover. More important, they valued clients who paid well and in advance.

The Egyptian watched an airport police patrol car cruise slowly down the wire fence that marked the airport's perimeter. He noted the time and typed another entry into the laptop computer on the desk beside him.

He pursed his lips, considering what he and his comrades had learned so far. For anyone used to operating in security-conscious Europe or the Middle East, the Americans seemed almost unbelievably lax. They relied almost entirely on a few television cameras and an occasional sweep by the airport police. That was all. Amazing. How could they be so overconfident? So stupid?

Madani shook his head. Their reasons were unimportant. What mattered was that the Americans were vulnerable. Tehran would be pleased.

SEPTEMBER 14

New York City

(D MINUS 92)

Alija Karovic took the steps up out of the subway station two at a time, joining a steady stream of passengers eager to escape from the crowded, noisy platforms to Manhattan's crowded, noisy streets. Short, with dark brown hair and dark brown eyes, the Bosnian Muslim attracted no attention from the throngs hurrying to work. He wasn't surprised. Even when he spoke, the faint Eastern European accent coloring his English excited little curiosity. Decades after Ellis Island had closed its doors, New York was still a polyglot mix of races and nationalities, of immigrants from every corner of the globe.

At the top of the stairs, Karovic checked his watch. He was a few minutes early. He turned right and started walking, dodging preoccupied pedestrians coming the other way and panhandlers trying to cadge enough spare change to buy liquor or illicit drugs. Since infiltrating the United States, he'd spent nearly two months in this city and its surrounding suburbs, but New York's jammed streets and sidewalks still seemed strange to him. They stood in stark contrast to the desolate, war-ravaged boulevards of his homeland. In Sarajevo the sight of so many potential victims outside and unprotected would have sent Serb snipers and gunners into a killing frenzy.

A familiar car drew up beside him and pulled over to the curb. The driver reached over and popped open the passenger door.

Karovic slid inside and shut the door without speaking.

"Well?" the driver asked flatly, keeping one eye on the rearview mirror as he inched out into the stop-and-go traffic of the morning rush hour.

Karovic shrugged. "It will be simple. The system is practically undefended."

"Explain."

"There are no metal detectors. There are no bomb sniffers."

"What about the police?" the driver asked. "They have guards on the trains and platforms, do they not?"

Karovic nodded. "Yes. But they are no problem." He spread his hands. "The transit police are far too busy watching for petty criminals or crazy people. They will pose no significant threat to us."

The driver smiled. "This is excellent news, Alija."

"Yes." The Bosnian nodded somberly, staring out the car window at the Americans scurrying across the streets in every direction, seemingly heedless of the oncoming traffic or each other. They were like locusts, he thought angrily. Soulless and almost mindless—concerned only with self-gratification and endless acquisition. The time had come to sweep these creatures of the devil into the everlasting fire. He glanced at the driver. "I will transmit a full report later tonight."

SEPTEMBER 16

Near Manassas, Virginia

(D MINUS 90)

Sefer Halovic lay motionless in the tall grass beside an old fallen tree. From his vantage point on the forward slope of a thickly wooded hillside, he had a clear view of the isolated side road he had selected as a drop point. He could hear the low hum of traffic on Route 28 drifting through the forest, but nothing closer in. This small part of the rural northern Virginia countryside was still relatively untouched by all the new housing developments and shopping malls spreading southward from Washington, D.C.

The Bosnian stiffened as a red Blazer came into view, driving slowly up the rutted dirt road. Through his binoculars he could make out the faces of the three men inside the vehicle. They were the men he had expected to see: Burke, McGowan, and Keller.

The Blazer stopped beside an almost-overgrown road sign twenty yards below his hiding place. Burke and Keller got out and stood looking warily in all directions. Both carried hunting rifles. Halovic considered their caution a mark of some intelligence. Prearranged drop points were the usual setting for double crosses or ambushes.

While the older neo-Nazi stood guard, Keller moved off into the woods behind the sign, his rifle held at the ready. Although the American was out of sight in moments, his excited shout soon echoed up the hillside. "The stuff's here! Four crates! Just like Karl promised."

Halovic sneered. Amateurs. In a less secure location, the noise Keller was making could have been disastrous.

"Check it out!" Burke yelled back. "Make sure we got what we paid for!"

The Bosnian knew what they would, find. He'd helped Yassine pack the shipment himself. The crates contained Czech-made Skorpion machine pistols, AK-47 assault rifles, a PKM light machine gun, ammunition, several kilos of high-grade plastic explosive, and an assortment of sophisticated detonators. He'd told Burke that the weapons came from secret stockpiles of the East German Army. That much was true. Acting through several layers of middlemen, the Iranians had purchased them from ex-members of the Stasi—the East German secret police— who now controlled the criminal gangs in their former country.

Halovic watched closely as the three excited Americans began loading their new military hardware into the back of the Blazer. He was still faintly astounded by their greed and ignorance. Apparently, they really believed that someone would sell them equipment so far below the black-market price without expecting anything in return.

He stayed motionless until long after Burke and his companions were gone, making sure nobody else had observed this covert transaction. Then, as quietly as he had come, he slipped back down the hill to the spot where he'd concealed his own vehicle.

Like fat, lazy fish, Burke and the others had swallowed his lure. And when at last they were reeled in, the lines attached to them would lead the American authorities only in directions General Taleh wanted them to go.

SEPTEMBER 18

Special operations headquarters, Tehran

(D MINUS 88)

The squat, drab concrete building just off Khorasan Square had an evil reputation among the poverty-stricken residents of central and southern Tehran. Built decades ago as a local headquarters for the SAVAK—the Shah's feared secret police—the deep basements within its massive walls were rumored to contain torture chambers and mass graves. When the Shah fell, the Pasdaran, the Revolutionary Guards, moved into the building. Their fanaticism and heavy-handed repression soon blackened its name further. Now new masters ruled the roost.

Soldiers in the camouflaged battle dress and green berets of Iran's Special Forces manned checkpoints closing off the nearby streets. More troops garrisoned sandbagged emplacements on the roof, wielding an array of machine guns, light antiaircraft guns, and shoulder-launched SAMs. Nobody went in or out without an escort provided by soldiers personally loyal to General Amir Taleh.

Although the Khorasan Square building showed up in official documents only as an "auxiliary command post," Taleh had turned it into his principal special operations headquarters. More than a hundred handpicked staff officers were stationed there—each part of a giant analysis and planning cell charged with shepherding his complex master plan to completion. To maintain airtight operational security, they worked, ate, and slept inside the facility.

The general himself had an office buried deep in the building's basement. Detailed maps and operations orders covered each of the room's four walls. Those showing the United States displayed a spiderweb of safe houses, arms caches, and targets spreading across the country at an ever-increasing pace.

As the schedule tightened, Taleh found himself spending more and more time poring over the daily status reports transmitted by each team. To ensure that he could wield the different cells as a coordinated weapon when they took action, all command and control functions were channeled through his headquarters. Under no circumstances were the teams allowed to communicate with each other. If American counterintelligence penetrated one, they would learn nothing that could lead them to the others.

He flipped through the latest sheaf of computer printouts brought in by Farhad Kazemi, noting potential problems and successes with a dispassionate eye.

SITREP: LION 46

LION Prime Via MAGI Link to MAGI Prime:

1. LION confirms special weapons drop made to Aryan Sword contact BURKE. Payment received. Further direct contact evaluated as unnecessary, possibly hazardous. Aryan Sword behavior is undisciplined and erratic. They will not respond to positive control, but may well undertake actions on their own initiative.

2. LION sections have now completed strike reconnaissance on all first-wave assigned targets. All targets are viable.

3. LION Prime recommends Target BRAVO TWO for the initial action. Information contained in today's Washington Post suggests the following options . . .

Taleh read Sefer Halovic's latest situation report with growing satisfaction. He'd made the right choice there, he decided. The young Bosnian was proving a superb team leader in a critical sector—intelligent, ruthless, and obedient to orders. Just look at his success in achieving useful contact with the American extremists. Only four of the other action cells scattered across the United States had made similar contacts—and none to the same degree.

Halovic had exactly the right mix of cool calculation and daring required to conduct the covert war Taleh envisioned. Training and preparation could only carry one so far, the general thought. They had to be built on God-given talents . . .

Taleh brought himself up short. He sounded more like a proud father than a military commander. Halovic and his men were weapons—to be saved if possible, to be expended if necessary. They existed only to serve God and Islam. To serve as he himself served—and to lay down their lives for the greater good of all the Faithful.

He rubbed briskly at weary eyes. Too many days spent away from the sun and fresh air were exacting a toll on his endurance. Perhaps he should pay heed to Kazemi's nagging suggestions that he take more rest.

With an impatient snort at the weak longings of his own mind, Taleh thrust the thought away. He flipped through another report and then another, searching as always for signs of trouble that he had not anticipated. There were none. At least none of any consequence. No matter how hard he looked, he could see no indication that his plans had been discovered. The Americans seemed utterly unaware of the invaders hidden in their midst.

When he had finished, the Iranian general sat in silence at his desk, feeling again the sheer exultation of the great power he had harnessed. The arrow he had fitted to his bow was drawn tight, straining to be free, to fly toward the heart of his foes.

The Americans were rich. Then Taleh would strike at their wealth. The Americans had pushed their God aside in favor of a life of ease and materialism. So be it. He would strip them of ease and turn their goods into the instruments of their own destruction.

He closed his eyes, savoring the prospect. It would be as God willed.

CHAPTER 9

MISFIRE

SEPTEMBER 27

HRT headquarters, Quantico, Virginia

Helen Gray lay alone under her covers in that warm, comfortable zone halfway between drowsy wakefulness and true sleep. After the focused intensity of every day on duty, the chance to let her thoughts and feelings run free at night was a luxury she prized. In the peaceful darkness she had nothing to prove and no one to impress.

The clean, crisp smell of pine drifted in through the window she had left cracked open, caught and carried by a cool breeze blowing off the nearby Potomac. She burrowed deeper under the blankets. Autumn was on the way, and though the days were still warm, the nights were growing steadily colder. Helicopters clattered somewhere off to the north, muffled by the distance and the forests crowding both sides of the river. The familiar sounds meant the marines based at Quantico were practicing night flying again.

The FBI's Hostage Rescue Team had its headquarters on the edge of the Bureau's wooded Quantico academy campus. Firing ranges, an old airliner, and a smaller version of the Delta Force killing house gave team members a chance to hone their specialized skills. Beyond the ranges, a central building provided administrative offices, conference rooms, and temporary living quarters for HRT sections rotating through for refresher training or on routine alert.

As a section leader and one of the HRT's only women agents, Helen had a room all to herself. It wasn't fancy. Just a place to wash up and bunk in some privacy during the days and nights when she and her men took their turn as the team's ready-response force. A duffel bag beside the single bed held her gear, sidearm, and a change of clothes. Nothing else.

Not that she would mind having Peter Thorn here beside her right now, she realized. They'd known each other for only a few months, but Helen was already growing used to having him with her at night. She smiled drowsily at the thought of sneaking him into her room past her fellow agents. That would certainly shatter her Bureau reputation as an "ice maiden" once and for all!

Thoughts of Peter spun away in a dozen different directions.

She loved the way his face lit up when he smiled at her—a sunburst of joy on a face normally so serious and reserved. Or the catch in his voice when he shared memories of his childhood and his father with her, revealing a vulnerability he kept hidden from others. Their time together had been a revelation for both of them as each learned to lower carefully constructed defenses, discovering the intense pleasure two people could find in shared laughter and comfortable silence, and the touch of hand on hand, body on body.

But it was also confusing. She was having to face questions she'd been avoiding ever since leaving the Academy for her first assignment. What did she really want? A husband? Or something less? She had sacrificed much for her career. Could she risk all she had won for the love of a man? Even this man?

And what did Peter want from her? So far they'd both been

careful to stay very much in the present moment—to avoid any real discussion of a future together. That couldn't last for much longer. She realized that, although she wasn't sure he did. And what then? What would happen when the time came to think beyond the next evening out? He hardly ever spoke of it, but she knew that his mother's desertion of his father had left scars that ran deep. Would he shy away from her when their affair turned serious?

The phone by her bedside rang sharply, ripping through her sleepy, wandering thoughts. Helen rolled over, suddenly wide awake, and answered it. "Gray here."

"This is Lang. Sorry to wake you."

She sat up in bed, still cradling the phone. Special Agent John Lang commanded the Hostage Rescue Team. She could hear the tension in his voice. Something big must be in the wind. "Go ahead."

"We've got a situation developing up near D.C. I need you and your section in the briefing room in five minutes."

"On my way." Helen hung up, slid out of bed, and began pulling gear out of her duffel bag—a whirlwind of brisk, economical movement. She was aware of the excitement suddenly coursing through her veins. A situation, Lang had said. That single, flat word meant someone was in trouble—big trouble. But it also meant a chance to prove herself in action after all the years and months of training and simulations.

Still moving fast, she fastened Kevlar body armor over her black coveralls and then zipped an assault vest over the Kevlar. Sturdy rubber pads to protect her elbows and knees came next. Then she checked her service automatic and snapped it into the holster rigged low on her thigh. Done.

Helen went out the door and headed down the corridor to the briefing room at a trot. She could hear agents stirring behind her as the phone alert rippled through the building.

The briefing room contained all the tools needed to plan and prep HRT missions. Chairs faced a wall given over to a screen for an overhead projector, blackboards, and a large video monitor. A computer terminal linked them to databases at the

Hoover Building and at other federal agencies. A locked armory downstairs held still more gear: submachine guns, assault rifles, sniper rifles, shotguns, climbing gear, portable electronic surveillance systems, even the demolition charges used to breach locked doors, walls, and roofs.

John Lang, tall, gray-haired, and in his late forties, was there ahead of her. He looked up from the secure phone he was on and waved her to a chair up front, all the while talking in a clipped, tense tone. "Yes, sir. I understand. We're moving now."

Helen waited for him to finish, working hard to control her growing impatience. One by one, the other agents in her ten-man section hurried in through the door and dropped into seats beside her. Their eager expressions mirrored her own.

Lang finished his conversation and spun around to face them all. "Okay. I'll make this short and sweet. We have a hostage situation just outside D.C. This is the real thing. This is not an exercise."

Helen leaned forward, intent on his every word.

"There are terrorists holding a rabbi, some women, and some kids inside a synagogue in Arlington, Virginia. A place called Temple Emet. We don't know who the bad guys are. We don't know how many of them there are. But we do know they're serious. We've already got one confirmed fatality—a father who drove there to pick up his kid and apparently just stumbled into these bastards."

Helen's initial excitement faded, replaced by a growing sense of anger and outrage. Hostage-taking was vile enough. But murdering an unarmed innocent simply because he was in the wrong place at the wrong time marked the thugs inside the synagogue as either truly vicious or truly cowardly. The thought of children held captive in such cruel, capricious hands was chilling.

"The Director wants this section en route to the scene pronto," Lang continued. He looked straight at her. "Questions?"

"No, sir." Helen shook her head, She had questions, but none important enough to slow them up now. She stood up and faced her team members. "All right, people, you heard the man. You know the drill. Prep for a possible building assault. Let's move!"

Time seemed to fly by as she and the others scrambled to gather the weapons, ammunition, and other gear they might need. Minutes were precious and she begrudged every moment it took to collect their gear, but they were outside and jogging toward the helipad next to the headquarters building in less than ten minutes.

Two FBI-owned UH-60 Blackhawks were there waiting for them, already spooling up. Her section split up, one five-man team heading for each helicopter. That was a safety precaution in case one of the birds went down. Would-be terrorists had too much access to shoulder-launched SAMs these days for any mission planner's peace of mind.

Ducking low under the spinning rotors, Helen clambered into the lead Blackhawk and took the flight helmet offered her by the crew chief. She would need the intercom system to hear and talk over the helicopter's engine noise.

Lang pulled himself inside right behind her. Although she would plan and lead any assault on the synagogue, her chain of command ran through him. Once they were on scene he would set up an HRT command post and generally run interference with the locals and the FBI agent in charge. Ideally, that should free her to concentrate entirely on the mission at hand. The system worked well in training exercises. She only hoped it would work as well under the stresses and strains of a real operation.

The Blackhawk lifted off in a shrieking, teeth-rattling roar as its engines came up to full power. It then spun right as it climbed and then slid forward, heading northwest at nearly two hundred miles an hour. Helen glanced through the open side doors, her eyes drawn to the eerily beautiful spectacle of the moonlit, wooded countryside rippling past below them.

"ETA is ten minutes." The pilot's voice crackled through the headphones built into her helmet. "They're clearing a corridor for us now through National ATC."

"Understood."

Lang leaned closer. "You ready for me to fill you in on the details?"

Helen pulled her gaze away from the moonlight-dappled landscape and nodded. "What have you got?"

The older man shrugged. "Not much. And none of it good." He sat back against his thin metal and canvas seat and started ticking off what he knew. "This whole thing first blew up about three hours ago."

She checked her watch. "Around nine?"

Lang nodded. "That's when the local police got the initial reports of shots fired. The first squad car on the scene found a dead man lying in the temple courtyard. When the cops started to investigate further, they were warned off by somebody inside the synagogue claiming to hold hostages."

Helen frowned. "And we know that's true?"

"Unfortunately, yes." Lang matched her expression with a frown of his own. "Tomorrow's the first day of a major Jewish holiday—something called Sukkot."

"That's right. The Feast of Tabernacles." She saw his questioning look and explained. "I had a Jewish roommate at the Academy. It's some kind of harvest festival, isn't it?"

"Correct." Lang hunched his shoulders. "Part of the celebration involves building a wood hut, a tabernacle, outside and decorating it with autumn crops—pumpkins, Indian corn, that kind of stuff. This year the folks at Temple Emet decided to make the tabernacle a preteens-youth project."

Helen's jaw tightened. "How many kids are we talking about?"

"We're still trying to get an exact count from the parents, but it looks like at least ten to twelve boys and girls, two or three mothers who were chaperoning them, and the assistant rabbi in charge of the temple's youth group."

"God."

Lang nodded somberly. He had two small children of his own. "This could be a real bad one, Helen." His mouth turned down. "I don't know why, but my gut's telling me the negotiators aren't going to be able to talk these bastards outside. I think it's going to be up to us to get those kids out alive."

"Yeah. You could be right." To hide a sudden fear that they might fail, Helen turned away from him, staring blindly out the helicopter's side door. She'd already been seeing horrifying mental images of what might happen to those children and their mothers if things went wrong.

She looked at the ground. There were man-made lights down there now—the regular glow of streetlamps that told her they were already flying over the capital's southernmost suburbs.

The Blackhawk rolled right suddenly, altering course to the north.

"ETA now three minutes," the pilot warned.

Helen squared her shoulders, pushing her doubts away for the moment, and turned back to Lang. "Who's already on scene?"

"Last I heard, the Arlington cops had most of their patrol force and their SWAT team deployed around the perimeter. Plus, the Virginia state police have their people on the way. It's going to get crowded."

Helen nodded, unsurprised. Major hostage situations were like criminological black holes—sucking in every local and state police agency within driving distance. Waco, the standoff with Mormon extremists in Utah, and all the others in recent history had wound up involving hundreds of police officers, state troopers, and federal agents. By definition, domestic counterterrorism operations came under the FBI's control, but it often took hours to confirm those lines of authority. Nobody local willingly surrendered power to the feds before making absolutely sure they were dealing with a real terrorist incident and not just with a burglary or robbery gone sour.

She asked about that. "So exactly how did we get jurisdiction here so early, John?"

He shrugged. "We don't have jurisdiction. At least not yet. But we will."

"What?!"

For the first time, Lang looked slightly abashed. "One of the hostages is the nine-year-old daughter of Michael Shorr."

"Shorr?" Helen mentally paged through a list of VIPs. "The President's economics advisor?"

Lang nodded. "That's the guy. I guess the President's already been on the phone to the Director. I know the Director has a call in to both the mayor of Arlington and the governor of Virginia." He shrugged. "And you're aware that the Director is a very persuasive fellow."

Helen shook her head, even more troubled now. Starting off with a set of crossed administrative wires and with nervous politicians hovering over her shoulder sounded like a ready-made recipe for disaster. She rechecked the magazine on her submachine gun as the Blackhawk dipped lower, clattering toward a floodlit football field.

Outside Temple Emet, Arlington, Virginia

The Arlington police and the Virginia state troopers had set up their command post in a two-story brick high school down the road from Temple Emet. Patrol cruisers and unmarked cars crowded the parking lot. Policemen wearing bulky bulletproof vests and carrying rifles and shotguns stood in small clumps outside the front entrance, all talking at once and gesturing excitedly toward the distant bulk of the synagogue complex caught in the glow of the full harvest moon.

Other uniformed officers were busy directing a steady stream of men, women, and children down the street and away from possible danger. Most of the civilians were still in their pajamas with jackets and coats hurriedly thrown on against the brisk night air. Some were clearly confused, still sleep-fogged. Others were obviously angry at being rousted out of their beds without notice. Most were just plain curious, turning back now and again to stare at the synagogue before being ushered on by the police.

Helen followed Lang up the steps leading into the school, letting him clear the way through the curious cops with his FBI identity card. She'd left the rest of her section back at the makeshift helicopter landing pad to avoid getting them mixed up in the media circus she saw developing there. Print reporters and TV news crews were already starting to swarm on the street outside the police command post. And, like other special tactical units, the HRT worked best outside the glare of publicity and camera lights.

When they were through the high school's big front doors, Lang stopped a police technician wheeling in a cartload of radio gear. "Where's the CP, son?"

After a cursory glance at his ID card, the radio tech nodded down the hall. "Principal's office, sir. End of the corridor. Captain Tanner said it had the best line of sight to the synagogue."

Lang headed that way after signaling Helen to close up with him. "Tanner's the local area commander for the state troopers. I guess we're not in charge here yet."

She glanced at him. "You know him?"

He nodded. "I've met him at a few conferences. He's a good guy. Tough. Smart. Pretty levelheaded." His tone left a few other things unsaid.

"But he's not the kind of guy who's going to enjoy seeing the feds bulling their way onto his patch?" Helen prompted.

Lang's thin lips creased into a slight sardonic smile. "Not hardly, Agent Gray."

Wonderful.

The principal's office was a sea of uniforms: blue for the local police, brown and khaki for county sheriffs, black for SWAT personnel, and blue-gray for the state police. Helen found her eyes drawn to the one man out of uniform. Everything about him shouted FBI to her—everything from his well-tailored gray suit, power tie, starched white shirt, and shiny black shoes to his close-cropped blond hair and chiseled chin. He was busy talking earnestly into a cellular phone, cupping one hand over his unused ear to shut out some of the pandemonium around him.

She frowned. She knew Special Agent Lawrence McDowell all too well. They'd had one date a couple of years back. That

was before she'd instituted her self-imposed ban on office ro-
mances. In fact, he was the reason she'd laid down the ban.

McDowell was a climber, an ambitious prima donna with his
eye firmly fixed on sitting inside the Director's corner office
someday. Right now his star inside the Bureau was rising fast—
boosted both by some solid investigative work and by constant
self-promotion.

He was also a first-class jerk. He toadied to his superiors and
politicians of all stripes, yelled at his subordinates, and generally
rubbed most law officers outside the FBI the wrong way. He'd
also taken Helen's refusal to sleep with him very hard. She suspected he was the one behind a series of nasty little rumors per-
colating through the Hoover Building that she was either frigid
or a lesbian.

She nudged Lang. "Is Mr. Wonderful here for a reason? Or
just to have his picture taken?"

The older man hid a sudden smile. He didn't like McDowell
much either. Then his mouth turned down. "He's got a reason."

"Oh, crap," Helen muttered. "Don't tell me we're going to be
saddled with him as the AIC for this op."

Lang nodded flatly. The AIC, or agent in charge, was the top-
ranking FBI officer on the scene.

"Perfect." She eyed him sharply. "Any other pieces of good
news you've been waiting to dump in my lap?"

"Not at the moment."

A brawny, balding man with captain's bars on his state police
uniform suddenly pushed through the milling crowd and strode
toward them. He held out one large paw to Lang. "John, how
the hell are you? Did you bring any of your Bureau cutthroats
with you? Or just your ugly self?"

"I brought ten of them, Harlan." The HRT commander shook
hands with him and turned to Helen. "This is their section
leader, Special Agent Helen Gray. Helen, this is Captain Tanner of the Virginia state police."

"Pleased to meet you, Agent Gray." Tanner's right hand came
out again and engulfed hers in a firm, dry grasp. If he was surprised to see a woman wearing the HRT's black coveralls and

body armor, he hid it well. He pulled the pair of them aside to a slightly quieter corner of the office.

"So what's the drill, Harlan?" Lang asked softly when they were out of earshot of the assorted policemen setting up phone lines and radio gear and laying out maps of the surrounding neighborhoods.

"It's a mess. A great big goddamned mess," Tanner replied bluntly. He nodded angrily toward McDowell. "But we were getting a handle on things when Jesus Christ over there showed up and announced himself. I expect he'll put that cell phone down anytime and come tell me that God Almighty and the governor have jointly decided to put him in charge."

Helen winced. McDowell was working his own personal black magic again, pissing off every sheriff and state trooper he came in contact with.

Lang hastily started to offer his own embarrassed apology. "Jesus, I'm sorry about that, Harlan. I wish . . ."

Tanner shrugged. "Hell, it's not your fault, John. I knew you feds would butt in sooner or later. Anyway now that you and Agent Gray here have arrived, we'll just put our heads together and work around J. Edgar Junior over there if need be. Okay?"

Helen nodded firmly and was relieved to see Lang doing the same thing. Tacitly agreeing to side with local law enforcement against their own anointed Bureau superior might not be strictly kosher, but the truth was that they needed the manpower Tanner controlled a lot more than they needed to stroke McDowell's overinflated ego. For the two HRT agents, getting the hostages held inside Temple Emet out safely took precedence over every other consideration, even their careers.

Tanner seemed satisfied. He began briefing them on the latest developments. "My boys and the Arlington SWAT have had a pretty tight perimeter set up for the last couple of hours. Nobody's gotten in or out of the synagogue complex during that time."

That was one piece of good news, Helen decided. Containing the terrorists and their hostages within known geographical bounds was a key first step. It froze the tactical situation in place and lowered the odds of an accidental contact that could panic the hostage-takers into killing their captives.

"Any further word from the people inside?" Helen asked.

Tanner shook his head grimly. "Not a peep. We've tried calling every number listed for the temple, but they're not answering."

Helen frowned. That was not a good sign. Close communication was always a crucial part of ending any hostage crisis peacefully. At best, the FBI's skilled negotiators could often persuade the bad guys to surrender or to release some of their prisoners as a show of good faith. Even at worst, voice contact between the two sides played an important role in keeping the surrounded terrorists on a relatively even keel. And conversations with them always provided significant information on their numbers, behavioral patterns, motivations, and intelligence.

She shook her head suddenly. Unless they could find a way to make contact with the terrorists holding those kids, she and her teams would have to go in after them blind. And that was the way people got killed.

Lang's grim face showed his own comprehension of the mounting risks. He lowered his voice even further. "Any better idea of the numbers we're up against?"

Tanner spread his hands. "Zip. But the way I figure it, we're talking at least two bad guys . . . probably more." He gestured toward the windows. "I've got troopers out canvassing the neighborhood right now, looking for cars or trucks that don't belong around here at this time of night."

Helen nodded to herself. Lang's assessment of Tanner's competence had been squarely on target. Pinpointing the terrorists' vehicles would give them a much better idea of their likely strength. She looked up at the big state police captain. "What about hard data on their weapons?"

The corners of his mouth turned down. "They're heavily armed. There's at least one full-auto assault rifle in there. That poor dumb bastard who walked in on them got cut almost in half. No semiauto could do that."

Helen nodded her understanding.

Lang pointed out the nearest window toward the synagogue. "You know much about the temple layout yet, Harlan?"

"Not as much as I'd like to, which is why I'm having somebody dig the blueprints out of the county records office," Tanner admitted. He pursed his lips. "I do know it's a hell of a big place, John. See that large building on the eastern end? That's the centerpiece. Got a worship hall in there that can seat six hundred and an adjacent auditorium that'll hold as many more. Plus a slew of offices, dressing rooms, kitchens, classrooms . . . and that's just the main building. The whole complex takes up a full city block. And there's wide-open ground on all three sides facing away from the street."

Helen fought down the urge to swear out loud. This situation was sounding worse and worse. They were up against an unknown number of enemies, holding an as yet undetermined number of hostages in an unknown location somewhere inside a labyrinth. Just terrific. She focused her attention on the main building, trying hard to concentrate on possible solutions instead of intractable problems. "That roof's flat all the way around?"

Tanner nodded slowly. His eyes gleamed. "You thinking about working this one from the top to the bottom, Agent Gray?"

"Maybe. I'd like to—"

"Mind if I join your little planning session, Captain Tanner?" Lawrence McDowell's perfectly modulated voice broke in on the conversation. He looked triumphant. "Especially since your governor has now agreed that I'm in command here?"

"Fine by me." The Virginia state police officer nodded dourly. He stepped back slightly to make room for the other man.

"Good to see you, Larry," Lang lied smoothly, apparently determined to avoid a scrap with the agent in charge until it proved necessary.

McDowell smiled thinly. "You too, John." He glanced at Helen briefly, frowned coldly, and immediately turned his attention back to the two men. "I don't usually work this informally, but since you've already begun, let's just carry on from here, shall we? Now, as I see it, our first order of business is to conduct a covert reconnaissance of the synagogue grounds. Once we know where these terrorists have barricaded themselves, we can work on establishing communications with them. Our negotiating team is en route by helicopter. I expect them no later than 0100 hours . . ."

Helen listened to him regurgitating the Bureau field manual with mounting irritation. The son of a bitch apparently intended to ignore her whenever possible. Very well. That suited her just fine. Let him pass his orders through Lang, then. He could play his inside-track power games, and she would get on with the business of rescuing those kids.

Suddenly, she noticed him eyeing her again, nervously this time. She made him nervous? Why, for God's sake? As the agent in charge, he held all the cards here. What kind of threat did she pose to him?

Then she understood his reasoning and hurriedly tamped down a crooked grin. McDowell was deathly afraid that her presence would jinx his chance to be a media superstar. If the press found out that the Hostage Rescue Team's tactical commander was a woman, they'd trip all over themselves making her the story—and not him. He evidently judged everyone else by his own low standards. Didn't he realize that the very *last* thing a counterterrorist assault section leader wanted during a hostage standoff was publicity?

She was still shaking her head in disbelief when McDowell finished issuing his orders with a terse "Very well. You know what I want done. Now let's go do it."

While a rigid, poker-faced Tanner stormed off to marshal his own forces, Helen followed Lang out into the hall. They walked a few steps away from the crowded doorway and then paused, looking closely at each other.

"Can you put up with McDowell's shit? Or should I try to have him yanked off this operation?" the HRT commander asked abruptly. His tone was dead serious, and he clearly expected a carefully considered response from her. During any hostage crisis, tension between different agencies and different branches of the same agency was normal and expected. But bitter dissension between the overall commander and his ranking subordinates was another matter entirely. When you were dealing with terrorists holding prisoners, success or failure often hinged on a snap judgment made in a split second. Under those circumstances, uncontrolled personal disputes and rancor carried far too high a price in lost innocent lives.

Helen faced her superior full on. She wasn't going to be sidetracked by personal animosities—not now and not ever. Besides, laying her squabble with McDowell in front of the Bureau's higher-ups was more likely to hurt her than him. He had more pull with the FBI brass than she did.

With that in mind, she spoke firmly and with absolute determination. "I won't lie to you, John. I don't like him, and I don't like his attitude. But I do know who the real bad guys are here. And you know my troops and I are the best there are. You keep McDowell off my back and let us do our job, and I promise you we'll bring those hostages out alive and in one piece."

Lang nodded sharply, making up his mind with the swift assurance that characterized all of his decisions. "Okay, Helen. That's good enough for me." He clapped her on the shoulder. "Carry on, Special Agent Gray. Let's go pinpoint those terrorist sons of bitches."

She flashed a quick, lopsided smile at him and then whirled toward the exit, her mind already busy grappling with the tactics necessary to implement her first set of orders.

Above Temple Emet

Moving slowly, Helen Gray wriggled closer to the western edge of Temple Emet's flat roof. Her right hand swept back and forth across the rooftop in front of her, feeling for unseen obstacles or soft spots that might creak under her weight. This close to the terrorists barricaded somewhere inside the synagogue, the slightest noise might result in disaster.

A faint rustle of clothing from behind told her that Special Agent Paul Frazer, her number two, was right on her heels. For a tall man he slithered on his belly with surprising grace, silence, and speed.

It was nearly pitch-black. Dawn was still three hours away, the harvest moon had finally gone below the horizon, and the star-filled sky provided very little ambient light. She had decided against using night vision gear for this part of the jaunt. The goggles amplified all available light, turning even the darkest night into something resembling blue-green daylight, but you paid a price for that in reduced depth perception and peripheral vision. For now she planned to rely on her own, unfiltered senses.

She poked her head carefully out over the edge and peered down into a dimly lit courtyard. Temple Emet was built in a horseshoe shape around a parking lot and a landscaped quarter acre used for dancing and as a playground for children using the school. The tabernacle, a half-built wooden hut, stood abandoned in the center of the open area. Ears of corn and smashed pumpkins lay scattered across the grass and pavement. Her eyes rested briefly on the dark, broken shape sprawled awkwardly near the tabernacle. They hadn't yet been able to retrieve the body of the man the terrorists had gunned down at the very start of this mess.

She shook her head sadly and looked away, continuing her scan. The dead would have to wait. She was more concerned with finding the living.

Helen craned her head further out over the edge of the roof, studying the main entrance to the synagogue. Shallow steps led up to a pair of massive doors right in the middle of the main building. This was by far the largest and the oldest structure in the complex. The others were clearly add-ons built as the temple's congregation grew and prospered. And an Arlington SWAT contingent attached to her command had already carefully combed through those outbuildings and confirmed that they were empty.

She had two of her four snipers posted inside one of those

outbuildings, ready to provide covering fire for her six-man recon party if the terrorists spotted them first. The section's other pair of sharpshooters was deployed inside the treeline about a hundred yards away from the synagogue's eastern face. Most of the doors and windows in the complex opened onto the inner courtyard, but there were two enormous stained glass windows on the eastern wall. The windows themselves were famous works of art—each separate pane contained a representation of one of the Twelve Tribes of Israel.

A soft voice crackled through the earphones built into her helmet. "One, this is Romeo Three. In position. Ready to deploy."

Helen stared into the darkness, searching the rooftop thirty or so yards from her own position for Romeo Three and Four, Special Agents Brett and DeGarza, the second of her two-man recon teams. Nothing. She gave up, flipped the night vision goggles down over her eyes, and switched on the battery that powered them.

Two equipment-laden figures leaped into focus. One perched on the roof edge with his back to the courtyard, ready to rappel down the side of the building. The second HRT trooper sat facing him, braced to pay out a length of climbing rope for his partner.

She keyed her mike. "Three, this is One. I see you. Go ahead." She loosened the strap on her submachine gun and brought it around in front of her. Frazer crawled into place beside her and unlimbered his own weapon.

Romeo Three, Tim Brett, stepped back into the open air, dropped a couple of feet, and then swung back lightly against the temple wall. Then he repeated the process, slowly and gently making his way down the side of the building toward a window facing into the courtyard. He was using one hand to control his descent while the other held a sidearm ready.

Helen held her breath until Brett stopped moving, dangling only a foot or so from the window, just out of the line of sight of anybody looking outside. She watched closely as he holstered his automatic and reached inside one of the equipment pouches on his assault vest. Then he leaned over, slapped the piece of electronic listening gear now in his hand onto the top part of the window and rolled away.

His whisper ghosted through her headset. "Probe active. Live on channel three."

Helen switched the setting on her radio, shifting to the broadcast from the bug Brett had just put in place. Nothing. Just the soft hiss of static and dead air. There was no one inside the room behind the window. She swallowed her disappointment. On paper, the senior rabbi's office had seemed a logical spot for the terrorists to hole up in. According to the blueprints Tanner's men had liberated from the county records, the room had just that one narrow window and only one easily guarded door leading out to a secretary's office. Well, she thought coldly, they would just have to try again, somewhere else.

At her quiet command, Brett began climbing, hauling himself up hand over hand easily, despite the weight of equipment and weapons he carried.

"Romeo One, this is Romeo Five. I think I've got something." Special Agent Frank Jackson's normal stoic calm was gone.

Helen glanced behind her in surprise. She'd deployed Jackson and his partner, Gary Ricks, along the synagogue's eastern wall, more to cover all the bases than from a real belief they might hear anything in that area. She could just make out Ricks hunched over near the edge of the roof. So Jackson must be suspended somewhere beside one of the two huge stained-glass windows that opened up into the temple's worship hall. "Go ahead, Romeo Five."

"I have audio on channel six."

"Switching now." Helen changed the setting on her radio again.

She tensed as a number of different voices suddenly boomed hollowly through her headphones. Some were higher-pitched—children's voices, several of them crying softly while others tried to console them. Others were deeper, but still identifiably belonged to women—mothers trying desperately to hush their weeping sons and daughters. There were other voices too—

louder, harsher, and angrier. They belonged to men riding on the knife edge of sudden violence and bloody murder. The terrorists.

One guttural drawl in particular caught her horrified attention. "Tell those brats to shut up, or I swear to God, I'll blow them and this whole damned Jew rat's nest to kingdom come!"

Another masculine voice sounded in her headset, but this one was younger, calmer, and more educated. "I will do my best. But I tell you again this exercise is futile. Surely you must know that the police are all around this temple by now? What do you hope to gain by holding these children and their mothers prisoner? Let them go and I will stay behind. Surely I am hostage enough for you?"

Helen nodded to herself. That must be Temple Emet's assistant rabbi. A brave man. She only hoped his courage didn't get him killed before she and her troops could rescue him.

The guttural voice spoke again, even angrier now. "One more word out of you, Jew-boy, and I'll splash your goddamned brains across that organ there, you hear?"

Helen breathed out. She had heard enough. The terrorists and their hostages were in the synagogue's choir loft. It was time to leave before they realized just how close the HRT had gotten to them. She switched back to her section command frequency. "All Romeo units, this is Romeo One. We've pinged 'em. Pull back to RP Alpha. Verify."

One after another the men in her recon team checked in and confirmed that they were moving back to the rally point to await further orders.

SEPTEMBER 28

FBI command post, near the Temple

Helen stood at one of the large windows in the principal's office they had commandeered as a command post, staring out across

the open ground that separated the high school from Temple
Emet. The sun was going down, spilling gold and red light
across the synagogue complex. Pushed by the setting sun, the
shadows were lengthening. It would be dark in less than an
hour. But the full moon would rise a short time later, again making it too dangerous for them to move in until the very early
hours of the next morning.

"Special Agent Gray?"

Helen turned away from the window. One of Larry McDowell's assistants stood there—a young man, fresh-faced, and probably almost straight out of the Academy.

"Agent McDowell would like you to join them across the hall
for a planning conference."

"I'll be right there." Helen watched the young man scurry off
and then followed him. She was almost amused. So the all-
knowing agent in charge had finally decided to acknowledge
her existence. That must mean he was starting to feel the pressure from above and was looking for possible scapegoats.

Lang, Tanner, and McDowell were all gathered in the teachers' lounge he had turned into his own private command center.
One other man was there beside them, and she recognized him
as the head of the FBI negotiating team.

McDowell preferred deliberating outside the organized chaos
of the primary operations center, and she couldn't blame him for
that. The lounge was a small, quieter place. The four senior men
stood grouped around a coffee-stained worktable, intently studying blueprints of the temple complex. Along the wall behind
them, a small cadre of junior FBI agents in their trademark gray
suits manned a bank of tactical radios and secure phones.

Lang looked up at her approach. "You feeling okay, Helen?"
he asked.

"Fine." She'd made sure her troops slept through the morning
and early afternoon and she'd managed to grab a quick catnap
herself. Sleep discipline was emphasized by HRT training. Of
course, if this siege dragged on much longer, Lang would have to
bring in another section to spell them. She shied away from that

thought. Hearing those bastards inside the synagogue only made her more eager to be in at the finish. "What's up, John?"

"Nothing good."

"Still no word from inside?"

Lang shook his head grimly. So far, despite every effort, they'd failed to establish two-way communication with the hostage-takers. There were no phones in the temple choir loft and the terrorists were apparently too afraid of police sharpshooters to risk venturing out of their improvised fortress to find one down-stairs. Even an offer the FBI negotiators had made by loud-speaker to hand-carry a portable phone inside had so far gone unanswered and unheeded.

And an early hope that the unknown terrorists might be driven out of the choir loft by thirst had been quickly dashed by the discovery that it had a small adjoining washroom. Right now the FBI's only source of information on the bad guys was strictly one-way—eavesdropping via the listening device her team had planted early this morning and now supplemented by laser microphones aimed at the synagogue's large stained-glass windows.

"Now that we're all here, let's recap this thing and see if we can come to a consensus. Okay?" McDowell said brusquely.

Typical, Helen thought wearily. He locks me out of the room and then he acts as though I've been goofing off when he finally condescends enough to invite me in on the planning. But she kept her irritation off her face. Showing anger would serve no purpose and might only encourage him to needle her further.

"First, Captain Tanner's men have finally located the vehicle we believe the terrorists used as their transport. Correct, Cap-tain?"

Harlan Tanner nodded slowly, his own face impassive despite McDowell's barely concealed dig. "That's right." He didn't bother referring to his notes. "We've identified a 1985 Chevy Suburban parked down the street from Temple Emet as having been stolen from outside a Richmond home earlier yesterday. Every other car, truck, and van in the neighborhood belongs to someone with a legitimate reason for being in the area."

"Did your people find anything in the Suburban that might give us a handle on what we're facing in there?" Helen asked, butting in before McDowell could push on.

"Yeah." Tanner looked straight at her. "Forensics is still going over it with a fine-tooth comb, but they've already found traces of a lot of bad shit."

"How bad?"

"Carrying cases and cleaning kits for assault rifles—probably AKs." He paused significantly. "They also found the chemical signature for some high-grade plastic explosive—maybe four or five kilos' worth."

"Christ." Helen was appalled. That much explosive power, properly emplaced, could easily turn Temple Emet into a smoking pile of rubble. She turned to the head of the negotiating team—an agent named Avery, she suddenly remembered. "You've been listening in on these goons. How many are we dealing with exactly?"

"Three, Agent Gray. We've identified three separate voices belonging to the terrorists," McDowell cut in sharply, clearly irked that she'd been taking control of his meeting.

Avery nodded. "That's right. The accents are a little blurred because of the distance between our mikes and the choir loft, but my linguists believe two at least are originally from the Tidewater section of Virginia. The third man is definitely an American English speaker, but his precise origins are indeterminate. Their politics are pretty clear, though. We've picked up a lot of radical, neo-Nazi jargons and sloganeering. They also keep referring to someone they call 'a brother-in-arms.' A German national apparently named Karl."

"And their mental state?" Lang asked.

Avery hesitated briefly, apparently reluctant to theorize without more hard evidence, but then he plunged on. "Very bad. And deteriorating. This was not a planned confrontation. Instead, it's clear that these terrorists only intended to blow up the synagogue itself right before a major Jewish holiday. They stumbled on to the children's decorating party by accident. Right now they're pretty well locked into a classic paranoid state—

compounded by isolation, sleep deprivation, growing hunger, and alcohol abuse."

He saw their appalled glances and amplified that last comment. "We've heard fairly clear signs that at least one of them is already very drunk and may still be drinking."

"Damn it." Tanner spoke for them all. Alcohol would slow the hostage-takers' reflexes and reaction time, but it would also impair their judgment, perhaps making them more likely to start killing their captives.

McDowell took center stage again. "Right. You've heard the bad news. As I see it, the situation we face is inherently unstable. These creeps won't communicate with us. And now they're starting to lose it. So we're getting nowhere fast out here and the media vultures are out in full force, circling thicker and thicker." He paused. "I've been in constant touch with the Director. He's personally stressed that the Bureau cannot afford another Waco. We can't let this thing drag on indefinitely, and we can't have this siege end in another pile of dead women and kids."

Great, Helen thought to herself, talk about mixed messages. Risk an attack to end the standoff, but don't take any risks with the lives of the hostages. And that was impossible.

"I'm soliciting opinions here, folks," McDowell said. "Do we wait longer? Or do we strike now?" He turned to Lang. "John?"

"I say we go," the HRT commander said flatly. "Time is clearly not on our side."

"Avery?"

The negotiator took a deep breath and then sighed. "I concur. We should go."

McDowell stood silently for a few minutes, pondering his options and not liking any of them. Finally, he looked up. "Okay, I'll phone the Director and pass on our recommendation." He turned to Helen. "If he approves direct action, when can you and your section be ready to move?"

She didn't hesitate. "Early tomorrow morning. When it's dark." She glanced at Lang for confirmation. "We can move sooner if they start to unravel faster, but it would be a lot more dangerous."

He nodded his agreement.

McDowell frowned. "All right, Agent Gray. Assemble your section, make your plans, and then brief us."

"Of course."

But then he stopped her on her way out the door. "Don't screw this up, Helen. We've all got a lot riding on this one."

She smiled sweetly at him and pulled his hand away from her arm. "Not as much as those poor kids inside Temple Emet, Larry. Maybe you forgot about them."

She didn't wait to see what effect her parting shot had on him. She had work to do.

SEPTEMBER 29

The moon was down.

Helen Gray checked the fastenings on her Kevlar armor and assault vest one last time and then slung her submachine gun from her shoulder. She glanced at Rabbi David Kornbluth, Temple Emet's spiritual leader. "You understand about the stained glass, Rabbi? If there were any other way . . ." She left the rest carefully unsaid.

The rabbi, an elderly man, turned his shrewd gaze on her and shrugged. "I would prefer that these barbarians had never invaded my synagogue, Miss Gray. But they have. And now you must root them out." He gently took her hand. "May God go with you."

Helen ducked her head, already knowing how much depended on her. "Thank you. I will." She strode away quickly, desperately hoping she could fulfill the promise she had just made.

Oh, her plan was sound. Very sound. But she knew only too well how swiftly the most carefully crafted plans could disintegrate in practice.

She trotted down the steps of the high school and out toward the pair of parked school buses that sheltered her assault force from both media scrutiny and detection by those inside the temple. Her four snipers were already in position on the eastern edge of the synagogue roof.

Paul Frazer was there waiting for her. He stepped out of the shadows. "What's the word, boss?"

"We go in." Helen felt again the thrill that rippled through her at those three simple words. Her emotions were racing in full gear—crashing back and forth between anxiety and exultation. "The Director confirmed the assault orders to McDowell five minutes ago."

"Outstanding." Frazer clapped his hands together, put two fingers to his lips, and whistled softly. The rest of her section materialized seemingly out of nowhere and crowded around her.

Helen glanced around the tight circle, making one last check. Their weapons and gear were in perfect order. They were ready. She nodded toward the synagogue, invisible behind the school buses and in the growing darkness. "We've trained hard for this chance. You all know what to do. When we go in, we go in fast. No stopping. No hesitating. If you see a terrorist, you put him down. Three rounds and down. Clear?"

They nodded fiercely. Teeth gleamed in the darkness.

"Okay, let's go! Alpha team takes the lead. Bravo takes overwatch. I'm with Alpha."

Helen led the six men to the edge of the open ground surrounding the temple complex and crouched low. She keyed her radio mike. "Sierra One, this is Alpha One. We're at the starting gate. Are we clear?"

Lang's confident voice came through her earphones. "Roger, Alpha One. Your birds are all in the nest. You're cleared to move."

"Moving." Helen suited her actions to her words. She loped out across the open ground, sprinting for the southern edge of the temple. Three men followed her. Frazer and the rest settled in to cover them during the long run up to the wall.

Heart pounding hard, she ran right up to the synagogue and

dropped prone with her submachine gun aimed at the ground-floor windows in front of her. The rest of her assault team followed suit—peeling off to either side until they were ranged in a ragged line facing the building.

She spoke into her throat mike again. "Come ahead, Bravo One."

"On our way," Frazer said.

Her tall deputy and his two-man team reached her position in less than thirty seconds. They dropped prone beside her.

Helen crawled right up to the wall and then raised her head slowly until she could peer in through one of the windows. Her night vision gear showed her an empty classroom. The classroom door was shut. Perfect.

She turned and waved her team forward. Then she smashed one of the lower windowpanes with the butt of her submachine gun and froze. The tinkling of glass shards falling onto a tile floor suddenly seemed very loud. "Sierra, this is Alpha. Any reaction to that?"

Lang's voice was reassuring. "Negative, Alpha."

"Entering now."

Helen reached in through the broken window with one gloved hand and fumbled with the latch. It came free and she pulled the window frame outward. Moving rapidly, one after the other, the men of her two teams scrambled inside and fanned out through the classroom. She hopped lightly over the windowsill after them and glided quietly to the door.

It opened on to a small empty corridor. All the overhead lights were off. She signaled an advance.

Leapfrogging in pairs while the rest knelt to provide covering fire, the HRT agents slipped out through the door, turned left, and moved down the small hallway until it intersected another, much larger corridor running the entire length of the temple. Helen poked her head around the bend, risking a quick peek.

The central corridor was wide enough for several people to walk abreast. Dark wood paneling and a marble floor gave it an elegant appearance. Points of brightness gleamed amid the blue-green sheen her night vision gear gave the world. She flipped the goggles up for a quick scan with the unaided eye. Small lights twinkled at eye level along the walls, blazing out of the darkness. The walls were coated with banks of bronze plaques. Each was inscribed with a man or woman's name, date of birth and date of death, a tiny, stylized tree, and a pair of lights, one on each side. The rabbi had briefed her on those plaques. Each commemorated a founding member or important contributor to Temple Emet.

Helen pulled her eyes away from the tiny lights and lowered her goggles again. The corridor ended in a pair of double doors leading into the synagogue's worship hall itself. The doors were closed.

Keeping her back to the wall, she slid around the corner and crouched. Frazer and the rest followed her. They deployed on both sides of the corridor—Alpha team on the right, Bravo on the left.

Helen looked across at Frazer. He nodded once.

Using bounding overwatch, the two FBI teams advanced cautiously to the large double doors—silent as ghosts on the slick marble floor. When they were within a few yards, she held up a hand, signaling a halt. They froze in place.

Helen went down on one knee, half turned, and motioned Tim Brett forward. The stocky agent was her surveillance specialist.

Brett crawled forward to the doors with Helen right in his wake. By the time she reached him, his hands were already busy fitting a length of flexible fiber-optic cable into a palm-sized TV monitor. Then he plugged the whole assembly into a battery pack hooked to his assault vest.

Helen crawled closer until she could watch the monitor picture while he gingerly fed the cable through a slight crack under the right-hand door. The tiny TV showed a worm's-eye view of the worship hall's thin carpet. She saw nothing out of the ordinary and motioned to the left. Brett obeyed, sliding it back and forth to scan the carpet near the other door. Still nothing. At another signal from her, he withdrew the cable, bent it almost into a right angle, and then slid it back under the door. By rotating the angled portion of fiber-optic cable, he gave the monitor a clear view of the areas near the door hinges and latches. Again, she saw nothing. There weren't any trip wires connected to explosives and not even anything as simple as tin cans rigged to sound a warning if someone burst through the doors.

Helen shook her head in mingled relief and disgust. These so-called terrorists were rank amateurs. Of course, that actually made them more unpredictable and potentially more dangerous. Professionals often followed set patterns that could be exploited.

Hand signals brought the rest of her assault force right up to the doors while Brett repacked his camera gear. She risked another whispered radio transmission. "Charlie One and Three, this is Alpha One. We're outside the hall."

"Acknowledged, Alpha," the gravelly voice of her senior sniper said. "We're ready."

From her crouch, Helen reached up and gripped the handle on the right-hand door. Slowly, carefully, she turned the handle and pushed gently. The door swung inward silently.

For the first time they could hear sounds from the choir loft overhead—muttered growls and curses from the terrorists and the soft sobs and moans of frightened children. Grim-faced now, the FBI agents wriggled through the narrow opening and split up. Helen and her Alpha team went right. Frazer and the rest of Bravo went left.

They came out into a vast open space. Temple Emet's worship hall centered on an altar positioned dead-center between the two enormous stained-glass windows. Behind the altar stood the Ark—a sliding curtain fifteen feet high and six feet wide that concealed the synagogue's Torahs, the scrolls of the Old Testament and Jewish law. Two lecterns stood beside the altar—one for the rabbi and one for the cantor. Rows of chairs for the congregation faced east, toward the altar and the Ark. Just inside the big double doors, carpeted staircases on the north and south walls led up into the choir loft.

Helen knelt by the southern stairs and peered upward with the submachine gun cradled in her hands. The terrorists and their hostages were still out of sight—above her and around a bend in the staircase. She glanced over her shoulder. Frazer and his men were set.

She took a deep breath, trying to settle her racing pulse, and then let it out. She keyed her mike. "Charlie Team, this is Alpha One. Go! Go! Go!"

Before she finished speaking, four sections of the huge stained-glass windows shattered inward. Four muzzles poked through the jagged holes. Two of the weapons were Remington-made sniper rifles. The other two were M16s equipped with the M203 grenade launcher.

WHUMMP. WHUMMP. The launchers coughed once each, hurling two flash/bang grenades into the loft.

Helen was on her feet and charging up the stairs even before the grenades went off. Bursts of blinding light and deafening noise smashed at her senses. She rounded the corner and threw herself up the last few steps into a wild, shrieking tumult. Women and children and grown men staggered everywhere in utter confusion.

With her submachine gun held at shoulder level, Helen yelled, "FBI! FBI! Everybody down!"

Deeper voices echoed her shouts from behind her and from the other side of the loft. Most of the disoriented people in her field of view began diving for the floor. All but a few.

Out of the left corner of her goggles, Helen saw a young, hard-faced man whirling toward her with an assault rifle in his hands. She spun left and squeezed the trigger on her submachine gun. Three rounds fired at a point-blank range slammed into the terrorist. His chest and neck exploded and he toppled backward out of sight over a row of chairs.

A sniper rifle cracked off to the right. She glanced that way in time to see a tall, black-haired man shriek in horror and agony, stagger backward, and tumble over the railing into the synagogue below.

Two down.

Still probing for targets, Helen advanced through the tangle of seats and writhing bodies. Purposeful movement near the organ caught her eye. She turned that way and saw a third man in camouflage fatigues, older and gone to fat, painfully crawling toward a metal box. Different-colored wires led out from the box to all four corners of the loft.

She fired another three-round burst. So did several of her men. The older man's body literally disintegrated under a hail of steel-jacketed bullets. Blood, shattered bone, and torn flesh sprayed across the organ keyboard.

Helen looked away, choking down a sudden urge to vomit. Three terrorists down. She moved away, hunting through the muddle for more bad guys. Frazer, Brett, and the rest fanned out with her, their weapons still ready. But there were no more men to kill.

The ringing in her ears faded away, making room for the terrified whimpers of the women and children she'd come to rescue. Helen turned slowly through a full circle, checking them over. Beyond a few bruises and scrapes, nobody seemed seriously hurt. At least physically. They would all have nightmares for years, she knew.

She spoke into her radio again. "Sierra One, this is Alpha. The loft is secure. Repeat, the loft is secure."

But she barely heard Lang's jubilant response. It was as though her words had broken through a massive dam inside, opening the way for the great wave of weariness and sorrow that came crashing over her.

Helen found herself staring through a numbed haze at the mangled remains of the older man she'd shot. Then her knees buckled and she sat down hard with her head spinning. She heard retching noises from close by as other men under her command threw up. Most of them had never killed anyone before. Even the veterans who had seen death before stood silent and hollow-eyed. She closed her own eyes tightly, shutting out the carnage.

When she opened them, she saw Lang kneeling beside her, watching her closely.

Helen smiled faintly. "Well, John, I guess we won."

He nodded somberly. "You won."

CHAPTER 10

BACKGROUND NOISE

OCTOBER 9

Public Broadcasting Service *Newshour*

The producers of the PBS *Newshour* were delighted with their Washington-based anchor's interview of the U.S. Attorney General. Normally dour and reserved, Sarah Carpenter was in full swing and high dudgeon—the very picture of official outrage at the terrorist attack on Temple Emet. She was making her anger and disgust plain with every icy word.

"According to reports this morning, the FBI has now positively identified the three dead terrorists—James Burke, Anthony McGowan, and David Keller—as ringleaders of a neo-Nazi fringe group located just outside of Richmond, Virginia. Are those reports accurate?" the interviewer asked.

The Attorney General nodded briskly. "They are. Our investigation has revealed that these men were the leaders of a white supremacist organization called the Aryan Sword. We believe this organization may also have been involved in the earlier murder of a local civil rights leader, John Malcolm." She pursed her lips. "Past administrations have turned a blind eye toward the activities of fanatical, right-wing hate groups. This administration will not."

"In what way, Ms. Carpenter?"

She leaned forward. "With the President's approval, I have instructed the FBI and all other appropriate federal law enforcement agencies to immediately redouble their efforts against these potential terrorists."

"And can you give us the broad outlines of these expanded efforts?"

"Certainly. We intend to mount a coordinated campaign on a number of fronts. First, we will increase our surveillance of known and suspected neo-Nazi terror groups. Second, I will direct the Bureau of Alcohol, Tobacco, and Firearms to take other steps to boost its seizures of illegal weapons and explosives. We will also take legal measures against illicit underground publications that advocate violence or promote bigotry and race hatred." The Attorney General tapped the table in front of her for emphasis as she spoke. "Perhaps most important of all, I intend to seek immediate congressional action to toughen and expand our federal gun control laws. We must make it impossible for these criminals and right-wing hatemongers to acquire weapons of death and destruction."

The PBS anchorman arched a skeptical eyebrow. "Surely only a very small proportion of the American people espouse such extremist views?"

"On the surface, the numbers are small," she agreed. "But I believe it would be a grave error to underestimate the threat the radical right poses to this nation. We live in an increasingly complex and fragile society. In such a situation, even a tiny number of fanatics are capable of causing enormous damage."

"You sound as though you anticipate more terror attacks like the one at Temple Emet, Ms. Carpenter."

The Attorney General nodded grimly. "In my considered judgment, we now face a much graver threat from within our borders than from without. I'm afraid that the new terrorist threat we must combat is largely homegrown—the terrible product of American racism and bigotry."

OCTOBER 11

Special operations headquarters, Tehran

(D MINUS 65)

General Amir Taleh watched the images flickering across his television screen with satisfaction. This American official, Sarah Carpenter, was unknowingly sowing the seeds for his own campaign.

Monitoring U.S. news broadcasts for items of special interest was one of the primary duties of the Iranian Interest section in Washington, D.C. At Taleh's express order, tapes that met certain preselected criteria were flown to Tehran via diplomatic pouch for further study and analysis by his special intelligence staff. And so the full tape of this *Newshour* interview with the American Attorney General had made its way to his office within forty-eight hours.

Captain Farhad Kazemi waited until the picture faded to black before punching the eject button on the general's videotape player. He straightened up with the tape in hand. "This was good news, sir?"

"Very good news," Taleh confirmed. "As always, the Americans see only what they want to see. We *shall* have the element of surprise." At that thought he felt again the surge of fierce joy that burned away much of his fatigue. But not all of it. After so many months spent in this office and in the field, he was all too aware of the enormous mental and physical strain he incurred by managing almost every aspect of this complex operation.

In theory he should have delegated more of that work to his subordinates.

Taleh snorted to himself. Theories were rarely worth the space wasted on them in textbooks. In the real world of the Iranian Army, there were few junior or senior officers with the grasp of strategy, logistics, and politics needed to fully comprehend his master design. And there were fewer still he could fully trust.

His mind turned to the staff conference scheduled for that evening. He had intended to use the meeting to finalize a decision to proceed with his plans. But why? He already knew what his decision would be. Seeing the news reports of the foolhardy Aryan Sword terror attack and watching the Americans rushing to confuse themselves only strengthened his resolve. After all, had not God Himself joined the fray—drawing a concealing cloak over the marshaling armies of the Faithful?

Taleh nodded abruptly. Why waste more time? He looked at his military aide. "Cancel the staff conference, Farhad."

"Sir?"

"Instead, contact London and all first-wave field commands. Instruct them to activate SCIMITAR as planned."

OCTOBER 12

Tehran

Hamir Pahesh closed and locked the door of the small, rundown apartment. When he was in Tehran, he shared the apartment with another man, his wife, and their four children. There really wasn't room for Pahesh, but both men came from the same village, and ties like that, especially in a foreign, hostile land, were almost as good as family. Besides, the truck driver was gone a lot and always returned with gifts: usually food, sometimes medicine. Mohammed Nadhir, his host, worked as a day laborer for even worse wages than he did, and the man had a family to support.

Pahesh would have helped a fellow countryman out in any case, and now because of his "extra income," he was the Afghan equivalent of the rich uncle. Thus, whenever he asked after the health of their nearby friends, the whole family packed up and left, usually bearing one of his gift packages. They thought he was a smuggler, which explained not only his need for privacy but his extra income.

After double-checking the drapes to be sure they were closed, Pahesh pulled out his duffel. The green canvas bag held his whole life: the few clothes he owned, a comb and brush, a few photos, and some mechanic's tools. It also held another small satchel.

He unzipped that, pulled out a cloth-wrapped bundle, and unwrapped a small gray plastic case, no bigger than a telephone book and half the thickness. Half the top surface was taken up by a keyboard and a yellow-green window high enough to display two lines of type. The display ran the width of the keyboard.

Working from memory, Pahesh typed quickly if not smoothly. He knew enough English to use a standard keyboard, but he had no real expertise with the thing. Allah help him if it ever broke.

It took him no more than half an hour to report his findings for the week. Not only did he have his own observations, but he also found rich pickings in the gossip exchanged by other truck drivers plying Iran's highways and military bases.

Something was going on. Stockpiles were being built up to an unheard-of level. New equipment was flowing into the combat units, and what was most interesting, they were in a terrible hurry to get it running. The Iranians were moving toward some sort of deadline.

Pahesh said as much in his report and provided the facts and figures that had brought him to that conclusion. Satisfied, he pressed a button. The machine hummed and then spat out a dot of plastic with his message microfilmed on it.

He picked it off the tray and using a bit of glue, attached it to a letter he'd already written, then sealed and addressed it. Packing up took only a few moments. Pahesh felt pleased, even proud of himself. It was a good report. He hoped the nameless men who read his work appreciated its worth.

OCTOBER 14

The Pentagon

Colonel Peter Thorn slid the bulky set of reports and attachments back across the desk to Joseph Rossini. He sighed and shook his head. "It's not enough, Joe. We've invested a few thousand hours of staff and computer time in a hunt for these Bosnian Muslim terrorists, and we're coming up with a big fat negative. No Bosnians. No training camps. No nothing."

He nodded toward the ceiling. "And I'm afraid we're about out of leeway for what seems more and more like a wild-goose chase. Farrell's under pressure from the JCS, and the Chiefs are under heavy pressure from the White House. The attack on that synagogue has everybody all shook up about right-wing terrorism. The brass can see the way the budgetary winds are blowing inside the administration, and they want us to 'refocus' our resources on what are called 'more pressing problem areas.' "

"Like Germany?" Rossini asked skeptically.

"Yeah. Apparently, the FBI believes some of the weapons and explosives the bad guys used came from a Nazi group in eastern Germany. So everybody's in a hurry to find and rip up the links between our crazies and theirs."

"Jesus Christ, that's even a bigger waste of resources!" Rossini exploded. "The Krauts are already working hard on their neo-Nazi problem, Pete. We'd just be plowing the same ground with every other intelligence agency from here to Tokyo."

"I know that," Thorn said. "And Sam Farrell knows that. But we just can't keep coming up dry and expect the money and satellite time to flow our way. A lot of people higher up the ladder want to close us down entirely. They're arguing that the

CIA and the State Department can do a perfectly good job of monitoring Middle East terrorism."

He shrugged. "I don't know, Maestro. Maybe General Taleh was right. Maybe those reports from Bosnia really were just meaningless rumors. Sergeant Major Diaz has a saying, 'If the complex answer doesn't fit, try something simpler, stupid.' "

"Another gem from the Little Green Army Manual of Chairman Tow?" Rossini murmured.

Thorn grinned and nodded.

"There is another possibility," Rossini argued. "Maybe we're just looking in the wrong place."

"Oh?"

Rossini tapped the sheaf of papers in front of him. "Look, so far we've been concentrating our search on Bosnia and Iraq, right?"

"Right," Thorn agreed, curious to see where his subordinate was going with this.

"Well, maybe we're taking too much for granted. Maybe Taleh doesn't have as much control inside Iran as he thinks. Maybe there are still people in power in Tehran who would like nothing better than to stick a knife between our ribs."

"That's a lot of maybes, Joe," Thorn said.

"True." Rossini spread his hands in frustration. "I can't point to any hard evidence. Hell, I can't *get* any goddamned hard evidence. You remember the NRO turned down my last request for another pass over southern Iraq?"

Thorn nodded. He'd had a testy run-in with his opposite numbers at the National Reconnaissance Office and the Defense Intelligence Agency's Directorate for Imagery Exploitation over that—to no avail. Control over America's sophisticated spy satellites was one of the most valuable commodities in the intelligence business, and you had to have a lot of clout to win extra time on a KH bird these days. Unfortunately, he and the JSOC Intelligence Liaison Unit had long since exhausted what little clout they had.

"Well, part of that pass would have taken the KH over the central Zagros Mountains. I've been seeing reports passed to us

from the Mossad network inside Iran. The Israelis keep men-
tioning persistent rumors of some large-scale commando training facility out in the middle of nowhere in those mountains."

"And you think that might be our missing terrorist camp?"

Rossini shrugged. "Possibly."

Thorn shook his head. "I think you could be on the wrong
track there, Joe. From what I saw and from what I've heard
since, Taleh is firmly in control of the Iranian military. And
remember, he has an Iranian Special Forces background. It
wouldn't surprise me one bit if he's building up Iran's commando
units along with the rest of his Army."

In fact, Thorn thought that was the most likely explanation.
The DIA's Weekly Intelligence Summaries were full of stories
on Taleh's efforts to modernize the Iranian armed forces. Iranian
purchasing agents were procuring supplies of modern armored
vehicles, artillery, ships, and aircraft in immense quantities—
mostly from Russia and the other former Soviet republics. Those
purchases were matched by increasingly realistic training and by
a series of purges that seemed aimed at ridding Iran's military of
incompetent officers. The conventional wisdom was that the
general and his supporters were preparing to fight and win a
possible rematch with their old adversary, Iraq.

In this case, Thorn thought the conventional wisdom was
right. He knew personally how much Taleh loathed the Iraqis.
The chance to smash them and restore Iran's position as a regional superpower would probably seem a godsend to the Iranian general. He said as much to Rossini.

The larger man's shoulders slumped slightly. "So you think we
should drop this investigation, Pete?"

Thorn hesitated. Though he believed Rossini's latest hypoth-
esis unlikely, he wasn't ready to dismiss all of the analyst's work
so readily. Given the necessarily limited nature of the data they
had to work with, intelligence professionals like the Maestro
were often guilty of seeing "tigers in every patch of tall grass."
On the other hand, he also knew how easy it was to fall under
the spell of the "rosy scenario"—to see events and data through
a mental filter that blocked out inconvenient facts. And he'd

worked long enough with the older analyst to respect both his intelligence and his intuition. If something about the situation in Iran was niggling at Rossini, now was the time to pin it down.

At last he shook his head. "No. I don't think we should drop it. Look, Joe, I'm scheduled to see Farrell the day after tomorrow. Do what you can to refine that"—he pointed toward the bulky report on their Bosnian probe—"and I'll try to wangle a little more time and some more resources from the Boss."

OCTOBER 16

JSOC headquarters, Pope Air Force Base, North Carolina

The long-drawn-out rumble of jet engines penetrated even the thick walls of Major General Sam Farrell's personal office. The C-141 Starlifter pilots assigned to fly the 82nd Airborne Division into any battle were practicing touch-and-goes on Pope's mile-long runways.

"Let me get this straight, Pete," Farrell said wryly. "You want me to tell the Joint Chiefs *and* the White House to take a hike because Joe Rossini still has a mental itch he can't scratch."

"Well, maybe not in so many words, sir." Thorn smiled. "I thought you might phrase it a little more diplomatically."

Farrell chuckled. "Since I like my job, I probably would." His expression turned serious. "But I don't know how much slack I can cut for you and your team, Pete. We've got some serious budget battles on the horizon, and I can't piss off too many people now who I'm going to need down the road later."

Thorn nodded his understanding. He'd been hearing the rumors on the JSOC grapevine for weeks. Faced with threadbare defense budgets and a reduced worldwide terrorist threat, some in Congress and in the SecDef's office wanted to disband at least one of Delta's three squadrons—with commensurate reductions in force for the 160th Aviation Regiment and other support units. There were senior officers in the Army's hierarchy who supported those proposals. Some were motivated by continuing doubts about the real military utility of "special operations." Others believed the Army would be better served by reintegrating Delta's highly trained noncoms into regular combat units. With his command under such close congressional and JCS scrutiny, it was no wonder that Farrell was reluctant to rock the boat very much right now.

He pulled his cap off the general's desk, preparing to rise.

"Not so fast, Pete." Farrell waved him back down. "Don't give up so easily. I didn't say I couldn't do anything at all."

"No, sir."

"But you will have to compromise," the general said. "Assign most of your people to research this European neo-Nazi connection the FBI is all hot and bothered about. In turn, I'll pull some strings with the powers-that-be. I should be able to make sure you can keep Rossini and a small team at work on this Bosnia problem. I know that'll slow you down some, but it's the best I can do. Fair enough?"

"Fair enough, sir." In truth, that was more than Thorn had expected.

"Good." Farrell rocked back in his chair. "Before you go, my wife wanted me to ask you how Helen's doing. That was one hell of a piece of work she did inside that synagogue. But I understand she had a rough time of it afterward."

Thorn nodded, remembering the exhaustion and regret he'd heard in Helen's voice during their first phone conversation after she came off duty. "It was the first time she'd ever shot anyone," he explained.

Farrell nodded sympathetically. "Killing's never easy on the conscience."

"No, sir." The image of a young Panamanian Defense Force soldier rose in Thorn's mind. The kid couldn't have been much more than seventeen years old. He shook off the memory. "But

Helen's tough. She's recovering pretty well. In fact, I'm supposed to see her this weekend."

"That's good." The general smiled broadly. "I know Louisa
would give me holy hell if anything went wrong between you
two now. I think she's already planning your rehearsal dinner."

Thorn suddenly felt like a deer standing frozen in the headlights of an oncoming truck. And curiously, he wasn't sure that
he really wanted to spring out of the way.

CHAPTER 11
DETONATION

NOVEMBER 5

Washington, D.C.

(D MINUS 40)

The National Press Club was located in a nondescript, almost seedy, concrete office building on Fourteenth Street, right in the heart of Washington, D.C. Typical drab 1940s architecture, the National Press Office building reflected the age of the organization, but only hinted at its power.

Although technically only a professional organization for journalists, the press club was much more. Its members included the cream of the national and even international media. Their reporting could help make or break political careers, and no self-respecting political figure could pass up the opportunity to bring his or her message before such an influential body.

Since its founding in 1908, presidents had sometimes used the organization's forum to announce major new policies and programs. Foreign heads of state had argued their sides in international disputes. Interest group leaders of all stripes and persuasions had earnestly proclaimed their manifestos from its dais. In fact, over the years, the list of National Press Club guests had become so august that simply being invited to speak there was now a newsworthy event in and of itself.

The Reverend Walter Steele had addressed the National Press Club twice before. His first appearance, eleven years before, had come shortly after his election as the leader of one of the nation's leading black civil rights organizations. His speech, labeled "visionary" by those in attendance and endlessly replayed on the nation's television screens and over the radio airwaves, had firmly established him as a major player on the American political scene. His second oration, six years later, had been sharply critical of the then administration's civil rights record—further cementing his reputation as spellbinding firebrand, one with political ambitions of his own.

Since then, he had appeared on news programs, talk shows, and campaign platforms across the country, eloquently pushing a range of programs and proposals for everything from urban renewal to radical shifts in American foreign policy. He was a man of influence. A man who inspired blind devotion in some and blind hatred in others.

And now Walter Steele had asked to be "invited" to speak at a National Press Club luncheon. The rumors sweeping the capital's cocktail circuit said he planned to announce a bid for his party's presidential nomination—and failing that, he would announce backup plans to run as a third-party candidate. Political observers ranked him as a viable contender—one capable of siphoning away several million votes from an administration that had only narrowly squeaked into office.

Preparations for the Reverend Steele's visit began that morning.

At ten o'clock Sefer Halovic crossed Fourteenth Street with the light and ambled into the National Press Office building. He was dressed casually in jeans and a long-sleeved flannel shirt, with only a bright green, reversible windbreaker as protection against the cold, blustery autumn day. He listed slightly under the weight of his equipment—a full load of cabling and electronics gear. Black lettering spelled out "ECNS" across the back of the jacket. The same logo was repeated in smaller letters across the windbreaker's upper right front, with the name "Krieger" printed underneath. The name matched the one on the press pass clipped to his shirt pocket.

Obtaining the pass had been child's play. With the explosion in cable channels both in the United States and overseas, hundreds of reporters and television and radio technicians flooded the Washington, D.C., area—especially right before any scheduled event that might generate headlines and airtime. And, politically correct or not, journalism was still a hard-drinking profession. Halovic smiled inside. Last night, it had taken Yassine only seconds to separate a beer-laden cameraman from his pass inside the noisy, jam-packed confines of a hotel bar. The young Palestinian scout's fingers were deft—the by-product of a boyhood spent living hand-to-mouth in southern Lebanon refugee camps.

There should also be little risk in using the stolen pass. The cameraman might have reported his credential missing, but that would scarcely raise a serious official stir. Too many IDs were already adrift in this city of badges and cards for the police to zero in on one more among the missing. In any event, the pass now bore little resemblance to its original appearance—thanks to a skilled forger on his special action team. It had been carefully doctored to show his new alias. A Polaroid photo displayed his new appearance. Barring close scrutiny by unusually suspicious security personnel, the alteration should not be noticed.

To change his looks, Halovic had dyed his blond hair a light brown and let his mustache grow out for a few days. He also wore a pair of tinted, black-frame glasses that hid his eyes.

Still, the Bosnian didn't believe in taking unnecessary chances. That was why he had waited so long to enter the press club building and ride its small elevator up to the third floor. With less than two hours to go before the day's luncheon, the corridors should be comfortably crowded. He followed several other technicians out of the elevator. Like him, they were draped in coils of cable and weighed down by tripods and other equipment.

As he had hoped, the building's third floor looked even busier than usual. This was Halovic's second visit to the press club. The first had come more than three weeks before, shortly after he and his team received General Taleh's go code and began making the final scouting trips laid out in his operational plan.

The Bosnian joined the bustling crowds moving slowly through the lobby across a floor of heavily veined, polished tan marble. To his left was the Members Bar, dark-paneled and comfortable, with windows that overlooked the street. Even at this hour it was smoke-filled and noisy, already packed with reporters swapping drinks and stories.

He drifted right, heading for the entrance to the dining room.

A table blocked most of the entrance and a man in a suit sat behind it, checking badges. Suppressing a moment's nervousness, Halovic joined the short line waiting to pass through the barrier. Intellectually, he knew that the odds were in his favor. Since the Reverend Steele was not yet an announced presidential candidate of any sort, the hard-faced men of the U.S. Secret Service were not here in great numbers. Certainly, the man behind the table seemed more a functionary than a watchdog.

He shuffled forward and, without unclipping it from his shirt, turned his press pass to face the checker. He was careful not to make eye contact. The man glanced up, focused on the picture for barely a second, then waved him through with a bored nod.

Hiding his sudden surge of relief, Halovic shouldered his gear and trudged down a short hallway into the main dining room. He had crossed the wire without tripping any alarms.

The dining hall itself was not as large as he had expected. While it was not shabby, it had a low ceiling and wasn't nearly as ornate as the cavernous meeting rooms maintained by the area's better hotels. Speakers appearing before the National Press Club were interested in exposure, not in decor. And the members themselves preferred to invest their limited resources in items closer to their hearts than fine furnishings, china, and silverware. Apparently, they reserved most of their funds for keeping the club bar well stocked.

Halovic briefly paused in the doorway to get his bearings. Toward the rear of the room, technicians swarmed over a tangle of cameras, video monitors, and boxes full of electronics gear. Waiters moved briskly among the round tables arrayed before a long head table, laying out white linen tablecloths and place settings. Everyone in view seemed busy. By 11:30 the room had to be ready for two hundred of Washington's movers and shakers: working reporters, congressmen, administration officials, and influential lawyers and lobbyists.

He checked his own watch: 10:17 A.M. More than enough time. Sidling through the crowd in the rear, he studied the room layout with greater care. As expected, television cameras lined the back wall, stationed on an elevated platform so they had a clear shot of the head table and speaker's podium. The floor underneath the platform was littered with dark-colored cables and brightly colored boxes that were labeled "CBS," "CNN," and a host of other networks, both large and small. Behind the camera platform was a ten-foot-wide area where technicians crouched over video recorders and miniature TV monitors. Wearing headphones and mikes, they spoke constantly to their opposite numbers in other cities, fiddling with the connections and praying their satellite uplinks wouldn't fritz just before they went live.

Halovic wended his way through the muttering crowds to a relatively clear spot and brought out his own gear. The VCR came first, and he found a power strip with an open socket. He was rewarded with a bright green power light. Next came several gray metal junction boxes and black cabling. Hooking one end of a cable to the VCR, he carefully screwed the jack in, then payed the cable out, walking toward the aisle in the center of the room.

Out of consideration for the luncheon guests and their feet, all of the electrical cables to the podium were being kept to one side of the center aisle, and Halovic fitted his own into the midst of the thick bundle. Almost immediately, he came to the end of the first twenty-foot segment. Most video cable came in longer lengths, but the Bosnian was ready with a junction box. The size and shape of a small shoe box, it was labeled "European Cable News Service" in neat white letters. There were jacks on all four sides. He connected the first piece of cable to one of the narrow ends and then unwound a second length before hooking it into the other side. He was careful to look for another green power light before continuing.

The next twenty feet of cable brought him halfway up the room. He stopped and attached a second junction box, identical to the first. He could feel his nerves twitching, sending out warning signals. Although he knew the room was swarming with technicians, he felt certain every eye was on him. He surreptitiously scanned the room, determined to bury his irrational fears. No one was watching. There was even another network engineer coming up behind him laying more wire.

When he reached the open-backed speaker's podium with its nest of microphones, Halovic strung his cable around the edge and inside it. After a short pause to consider his options, he placed a third junction box inside the podium itself. Two more segments led out from there to two more junction boxes—one under each of the head table sections closest to the podium. More green power lights glowed.

In all of the confusion as technicians from more than a dozen competing news organizations worked frantically to set up their own equipment, nobody thought to ask Halovic why ECNS needed to wire up so much of the room.

Moving methodically now and with greater confidence, the Bosnian returned to the media area at the rear of the dining room, inspecting all the connections on the way. The boxes were in series, but he felt compelled to check and double-check his work. He would not get a second chance at this if something went wrong.

He scrambled onto the far end of the platform and began setting up a video camera on a collapsible tripod. It was a smaller camera and not as sophisticated as those of the other networks, but ECNS was supposed to be a new service—one based in Eastern Europe. They'd only recently established themselves in the United States and funds were still short. Nobody asked for an explanation, but Halovic wanted his cover story ready if anyone did.

Another length of cable connected the camera to the VCR. He checked the power light again. He didn't bother checking the picture.

By the time Halovic finished, it was close to eleven o'clock. He stepped out into the lobby and stood in an out-of-the-way corner, watching people come and go through narrowed eyes while he pretended to flip through a newspaper he'd bought at the nearest Metro station. He felt alone and increasingly secure. The point of maximum danger was behind him. His greatest fear during the setup had not been discovery by the minimal security forces present, but a simple encounter with another technician. He had studied the television equipment and media jargon as much as possible, but a professional would have spotted him as a phony in a heartbeat.

At about 11:20 A.M. Halovic looked up from the classified ads. Men and women in business attire were flowing past him, some talking, some laughing. The man at the table took their names and checked them off on a list. According to the schedule the Bosnian had memorized, the luncheon would begin at 11:30, with Steele's speech and a question-and-answer session slated to begin at noon. The Bosnian buried his head in the paper again, waiting.

At 11:40 the man at the table counted up the names, nodded to himself, and turned the table so that it was tight up against the side of the entrance to the dining room. He left, and a few minutes later, a young woman walked up and placed several stacks of paper on the table. Copies of Steele's oration, Halovic realized. The reverend evidently wanted to make sure his words were remembered and widely aired. Well, the Bosnian thought coldly, he could be sure of that.

He pushed off the wall and strolled back inside the dining room. Every chair around every table was filled, and the buzz of conversation and the clatter and clink of glasses and silverware were startlingly loud. He knelt, checked his VCR, and saw that all the junction boxes and the camera responded to a test signal. Good.

With a polite nod to the other cameramen closest to him, Halovic stepped up onto the media platform and manned his own minicam. He peered into the small viewfinder and swept the lens over the section of head table to the right of the speaker's podium. Four men and two women sat there, but none of them were Steele. He panned left. Ah, there.

The Reverend Walter Steele was a tall black man in his late forties. His hair, though still untouched by gray, had receded slightly from his temples. He was dressed in a well-tailored, dark gray suit, and a dazzling black, red, and green tie. As if the colorful tie were not bold enough, he had a piece of orange-striped kente cloth draped over his shoulders.

Halovic waited patiently, intent on the scene in front of him. Steele chatted with those closest to him—all older, distinguished-looking men. The Bosnian recognized one as a senior member of the Congressional Black Caucus. Another headed the Washington bureau of one of America's leading television networks.

He glanced down. His watch showed 12:04 P.M. One of the men at the head table pushed away his wineglass, stood up, and made his way to the microphones. The room quieted.

"Ladies and gentlemen, we're honored this afternoon to have as our speaker the Reverend Walter Steele. He is a man whose many accomplishments are so well known that . . ."

Taking care not to disturb the camera, Halovic stepped back off the platform and walked quietly over to his VCR. The technicians and cameramen around him spoke in hushed tones now, respectful of the speaker but intent on their own business. He pressed a button on the VCR and saw a new row of green lights appear. The junction boxes were armed.

Satisfied, Halovic returned to the camera just as Steele stood up and took his place behind the podium. He peered through the viewfinder again. The image was a little off center, but the Bosnian ignored the picture.

Instead, he pressed the record and the focus buttons simultaneously. A flashing red dot appeared on the viewfinder image. A thin, ugly smile crossed his face and then vanished without a trace.

Without pausing, Halovic turned, stepped off the platform, and walked briskly out into the lobby. Ignoring the elevator, he took the stairwell down. As he trotted down the stairs, he stripped off the green windbreaker and reversed it so that it was a more sedate and less memorable blue. The black-frame glasses went into a spare pocket. He would dispose of both later and in a safer place.

He was outside and crossing Thirteenth Street on his way to the Metro Center station when the National Press Club vaporized in a searing sea of fire and shrapnel.

Each of the junction boxes Halovic had so carefully placed contained two pounds of plastic explosive and hundreds of small nails. The VCR, larger still, held five pounds of explosive. All were linked to a five-minute digital timer accurate to the millisecond. When the timer counted down to zero, the six separate bombs went off in one simultaneous, shattering blast.

Those few who survived said it was as if the air itself had exploded.

Driven by each explosion, fragments sleeted through the crowded dining room at thousands of feet per second, splintering tables, smashing glass and china, and ripping flesh apart. Dozens of men and women were killed instantly. Dozens more were maimed almost beyond recognition.

Caught by the bomb planted less than a foot from his stomach, the Reverend Walter Steele—one of the most powerful and prominent black leaders in the United States—was literally torn apart. His mangled remains were later identified only by dental records.

The members and guests seated closest to the speaker's podium and the central aisle were wiped off the earth in the blink of an eye. Only a few, those furthest away, near the walls or corners of the dining room, survived.

They would later recount seeing the center of the room erupt in flame, feeling their lungs fill with choking smoke, and hearing the anguished screams of those who were dying. With shaking voices, they would describe it as a frozen moment of utter terror, of unimaginable horror.

Falls Church, Virginia

Helen Gray shifted sleepily under the bedspread, curling up closer to Peter Thorn. Her right hand toyed with the curly hairs on his chest.

She felt his lips brush against her forehead and smiled in lazy contentment.

"You keep doing that with your fingers, lady, and you'll have to take the dire consequences," she heard him say in a mock-serious tone.

Helen's smile widened and she opened her eyes. "Oh, good." She rolled over on top of him.

She was on leave and Peter had taken the day off work at the Pentagon to spend some time with her. But their plans to tour a museum or two and eat lunch in the city had fallen prey to deeper, more passionate needs. And every hour she spent in his company helped her push away the dark memories of the carnage at Temple Emet.

Her cell phone rang.

"Damn it," she growled. "Not now!"

Peter chuckled. "Go ahead and answer it, Agent Gray. I'll stay right here. I promise."

She poked a finger into his chest. "You'd better, Colonel Thorn. Don't forget, I'm an officer of the law." Then she slid out from under the covers and pulled her phone out from the tangle of clothing on his bedroom floor. "Gray."

"Helen, this is Lang." The HRT commander sounded strangely shaken. "I hate to disturb you, but I'm afraid your leave's been canceled. I need you to meet me at Hoover ASAP."

"What's up?" she demanded.

"Turn on CNN."

Helen turned toward the television at the foot of Peter's bed. Reacting to the sudden tension in her voice, he was already up and getting dressed. He saw her urgent gesture and switched the set on.

She gasped as the first pictures filled the screen. Fire trucks and ambulances crowded a city street near the center of Washington, D.C., surrounding a blast-shattered building. A dark haze hung over the site—smoke from the still-burning structure.

"To recap what we know so far, at ten minutes after twelve this afternoon, a huge explosion ripped through the National Press Club during a speech by the Reverend Walter Steele, one of the country's foremost civil rights leaders and a rumored candidate for the presidency. Unconfirmed reports from the scene indicate that Steele and as many as two hundred others were killed in the blast. Among those known to be attending the luncheon were several congressmen and high-ranking administration officials." The CNN announcer's voice wavered. "As well as some of the world's top reporters, including several who work for this network."

A poor-quality still photo of an American flag emblazoned with a swastika replaced the chaotic street scene. "Police sources have reported that, shortly after the blast, calls were received by the two major D.C. area newspapers claiming responsibility for the attack in the name of the New Aryan Order, a little-known, extreme right-wing group. The callers have been quoted as demanding that 'the white race in America begin a war of purification.' "

The CNN anchorwoman appeared on camera, still clearly shaken. "We will bring you the latest information on this tragedy as it arrives . . ."

Thorn snapped the television off and Helen turned back to the phone. Lang was still waiting on the line for her. "Jesus Christ, John."

"Yeah. It's pretty bad." The HRT commander fell silent for a few seconds. When he spoke again, his voice was calmer. "How long will it take you to get to D.C., Helen?"

"Forty-five minutes," she replied, already sorting out her clothes from the pile on the floor.

"Good. The Director is putting together a special task force to investigate this bombing, and I'm putting you and your section on it."

Helen nodded. The evidence was that this was a terrorist attack. If they could pinpoint the people responsible, whoever headed the task force would need an HRT force under his immediate command to round them up. "Who's in charge? Not McDowell, I hope."

The ghost of a smile sounded in Lang's reply. "No, not McDowell. They're flying Mike Flynn in from San Francisco."

Flynn. The name tugged at Helen's memory. "The guy who investigated the Golden Gate Bridge bomb attack?"

"That's him," Lang said. "He'll be here by seven. I want you here to meet him and the rest of the task force. I'll brief you on the other details in person."

"Understood." Helen hit the disconnect button and started throwing on clothes with reckless haste. She could sort out her appearance in one of the women's washrooms at the Hoover Building later. The most important thing was to get on the road before the highways clogged up for the afternoon rush hour.

Her last sight of Peter Thorn as she hurried out of his town house was his frustrated face. He'd spent his career preparing to hit terrorists overseas and now all the action had shifted to the U.S.—out of his jurisdiction and out of his control.

CHAPTER 12

PRESSURE COOKER

NOVEMBER 6

Outside the National Press Club, Washington, D.C.

Under a dismal, overcast November sky, throngs of onlookers, reporters, and camera crews pressed against the police barricades deployed to maintain a security zone around the bomb-gutted National Press Office building. The FBI-led task force charged with investigating the bombing had sealed an area a full city block wide around the crime scene.

Helen Gray stopped short of the police line, taking a good hard look at the organized pandemonium gripping the area just two blocks from the White House. Parked squad cars, ambulances, fire engines, and official vehicles belonging to nearly a dozen different federal and District of Columbia governmental agencies jammed almost every square foot of Fourteenth Street. Hard-faced D.C. police officers, wearing rain gear against the impending storm, manned the barricades, checking identity cards before allowing anyone in or out of the secure zone. Cars and trucks were backed up nose-to-tail for blocks in every direction.

The entire downtown was in gridlock, generated by the bomb-related street closures and by the tidal surge of the morbidly curious who were flocking to the site. To avoid the worst of it, Helen had walked from her temporary office at the Hoover Building instead of trying to drive the relatively short distance. This was her first visit to evaluate the evidence accumulated in the first few hours of the investigation. She'd stayed away until now to allow the technical experts some room to work. But from the number of vehicles parked outside the press club, she was one of only a handful of people in official Washington who had been able to resist the temptation to play backseat driver.

"You still think this is a good idea?" Peter Thorn said quietly into her right ear, eyeing the crowded street in front of them. "I've an idea that your bosses might not welcome another busybody poking his nose into their business just now."

Helen turned toward him. Like her, he was in civilian clothes instead of uniform. With the media already deep in a feeding frenzy over the press club bombing, neither saw any point in attracting attention to themselves. She shook her head decisively. "You're a recognized expert on terrorist tactics and weapons, Peter. I'd hardly call somebody with your experience a busybody."

"Maybe you wouldn't. But I'd say you're biased." He smiled tightly. "Truth is, this is way off my patch and you know it."

Helen shrugged. "So? Last time I looked, the Bureau didn't have a monopoly on brainpower. You might see something our people have missed. And if you don't, there's still no harm done."

Privately, she was less certain about the wisdom of her actions. She'd invited Peter to come along on her own initiative—without permission from Special Agent Flynn. Some of her reasoning was soundly professional. But she couldn't deny that many of her reasons were more personal. And by involving an outsider in an FBI investigation, she risked a reprimand if Flynn officially objected to his presence—despite the kudos she'd earned by smashing the Temple Emet attack. She looked inward for a moment, again considering whether or not she was willing to accept a black mark on her near-perfect record for his sake.

The answer was yes.

She still remembered that look of anguished frustration on Peter's face when they first heard the news about the bombing. Standing idle on the sidelines in the aftermath of the deadliest terrorist attack in U.S. history would have been more than he could bear. Besides, Helen admitted to herself, she treasured every moment spent in his company. Being completely separated from him for the long days and nights her work on the task force would probably require might have been more than *she* could bear. If involving him meant breaking every single one of her precepts about keeping her work and personal lives separate, so be it.

Certainly, the prospect of even an unofficial role in the search for the press club bombers had worked wonders on Peter. Despite his worries that his presence might get her in hot water, he couldn't hide his eagerness to join in the hunt—an eagerness that mirrored her own. The death toll from the attack was still climbing as crews found more bodies inside the wreckage, but it had already soared to nearly two hundred. She wanted to find the terrorists who were responsible for the bloodbath—to find them and destroy them before they could strike again.

Helen felt something patter down on her hair and looked skyward. The first full drops of cold rain spattered across her upturned face. She grimaced. There probably weren't any significant clues outside the building for the storm to wash away, but the worsening weather would make their job even harder and more depressing than it already was. At least it might thin some of the crowds surrounding the explosion site.

She tugged at Peter's elbow. "Come on, Colonel Thorn. Let's get inside."

He nodded gravely. "After you, Agent Gray."

They made their way through the milling crowds to the police line. A young cop stepped forward to meet them. His rain poncho whipped in a sudden gust of cold wind. "Sorry, folks. You'll have to move back. No one's allowed any further."

Helen pushed her Bureau ID under his nose. "I'm on the task force." She nodded toward Peter, who held his own identity card in plain view. "Colonel Thorn is a liaison officer from the Pentagon."

The policeman scanned both cards quickly but thoroughly, carefully comparing the pictures with their faces. He looked up. "Okay, you can come through." He pointed toward a temporary trailer parked just outside the entrance to the National Press Office building. "Just sign in at the command post, please. You'll be briefed on site protocol there."

The rain was falling even harder by the time Peter Thorn and Helen Gray strode across the narrow gap between the command trailer and the press building. Both of them carried sealed bags containing sterile, white plastic suits and plastic booties that would go on over their shoes. Special Agent Flynn's instructions to his special task force were clear. He wanted to make sure the investigators themselves didn't track in clothing fibers, dust, or mud that might confuse the forensics experts combing through the explosion site. They'd also been issued hard hats that were color-coded to indicate status and function at a glance. As a member of the FBI task force command section, Helen's was black. After minor haggling with the agent manning the security desk, Thorn had been issued a blue hard hat. The color proclaimed his status for now as an on-site observer.

Thorn looked up for a moment before entering the building, ignoring the rain sleeting into his face. From the outside, there was little visible bomb damage. The windows on all the top floors were blown out, and there were scorch marks visible on the concrete facade—either from the blast itself or from the resulting fires—but beyond that, the structure itself seemed largely untouched.

But when he and Helen stepped out of the central stairwell a few minutes later, he realized how horribly deceiving those external appearances were. It was hard to believe that this charred

slaughterhouse had once been the third floor of the National
Press Office. Rust-brown smears of dried blood were splashed
everywhere on the scorched floor and walls. Massive hydraulic
jacks braced the ceiling and some of the walls, indicating the
immense force of the explosion.

Teams of coroners' assistants in white protective suits were
hard at work in every corner of the room, still tagging bodies
and parts of bodies for eventual removal. Similarly clothed photographers moved among them, taking hundreds of pictures to
build a coherent record of the scene for later use in the investigation. Even the distribution of the dead could provide important clues to the number, distribution, and types of bombs that
had gone off inside the room.

Other teams of FBI agents and forensics specialists worked
around and among the coroners, making precise measurements,
sifting through the rubble, and collecting even the tiniest fragments of metal, plastic, paper, and cloth for more detailed lab
work and analysis. In what was almost an obscene parody of an
archaeological dig, even the smallest pieces of possible evidence
were carefully tagged with the time of discovery and their precise location. Bright red hard hats identified experts in explosives. White, yellow, and green helmets signified fingerprint,
fiber, and electronics specialists. Everyone wore the same plastic
suits and thick rubber gloves.

Thorn breathed in and fought down a sudden impulse to gag.
A foul stench hung in the air—a stomach-turning blend of
smoke, blood, the sickly sweet odor left by explosives, and the
acrid reek of powerful disinfectants. He heard Helen coughing,
but though pale, she was in full control when he looked at her.

She swallowed hard and motioned toward the near corner of
the dining room where several other members of the task force
command section stood conferring over a set of blueprints. "I've
got to check in. Coming?"

Thorn nodded and trailed her through the tangled heaps of
smashed, burned tables and chairs, careful to stay inside the
cleared paths marked by yellow police tape pinned to the floor.
He was already treading on ice just by being here without ex-

press authorization, so there wasn't much sense in trampling ungathered evidence.

The shortest of the men grouped around the blueprints glanced up at their approach. "Helen, glad to see you made it through the mob out there." He looked curiously at Thorn, clearly not able to place him.

"Tom, this is Colonel Peter Thorn. He's with the JSOC and one of the Army's top counterterrorism experts," Helen said, accurately if somewhat disingenuously. She turned to Thorn. "Colonel, this is Special Agent Thomas Koenig. He's the number two man on the task force."

The two men shook hands and stood sizing each other up while the other agents introduced themselves in a blur of names Thorn forgot almost as soon as he heard them. Aside from Special Agent Flynn himself, Koenig was the man who could make or break this informal consulting role Helen envisioned.

"You here on a mission, Pete?" Koenig asked finally.

Thorn shook his head slightly. "Just a watching brief, Tom. This is the FBI's solo show as far as I'm concerned."

He noticed Koenig relax minutely and hid a wry smile. Despite the clear edicts placing domestic terrorism incidents under the Bureau's jurisdiction, turf battles with other interested agencies and departments like the DOD were not uncommon, especially in such a high-profile case.

"Where's Flynn?" Helen asked, scanning the room.

"On the phone with the White House again, I think," Koenig answered. He sounded disgusted. "Between the National Security Advisor, the press secretary, the head of the Secret Service, and half a dozen other lesser lights, I suspect Mike's talked to half the goddamned executive branch already."

Thorn shook his head. As much as he wanted in on this investigation, he didn't envy the FBI the task of trying to cope with the nation's rattled political leaders. By targeting so many congressmen, opinion leaders, and important journalists, whoever had masterminded the press club bombing had struck squarely at the heart of the current political elite. From everything he'd seen on TV and read in the papers last night and this morning, both Congress and the administration were undeniably and understandably in a panicked uproar. They wanted concrete results, and they wanted them now.

He suspected that was part of the reason the FBI had summoned Flynn to Washington from the West Coast instead of handing the task force command to one of the Director's immediate subordinates. Ever since he and his investigative team had cracked the Golden Gate Bridge massacre in less than forty-eight hours, Special Agent Michael Flynn had a media reputation as a miracle worker.

From what Helen had told him, Flynn's reputation inside the Bureau was equally impressive—but very different. He didn't try walking on water to obtain results, he drained the whole pond. He was a detail man—a man who paid attention to every piece of evidence, no matter how insignificant it seemed at first. As a rookie, Flynn was said to have solved his first big case—a kidnap-murder—by following up on what at first seemed only a typo on a bank deposit slip.

That was just as well, Thorn thought, carefully studying the bomb-shattered dining room. He doubted there would be any miracles this time. Everything he'd seen so far seemed professional to his practiced eye. The timing, the way the charges had been placed to maximize the damage and casualties. Everything. He said as much aloud.

Koenig shrugged noncommittally. "Maybe." He nodded toward the red-helmeted explosives experts scouring the wreckage. "Our boys have already identified at least six separate devices. There may have been more."

"All triggered simultaneously?"

"Or so damned close together it makes no real difference, Colonel," Koenig said.

They were definitely up against a pro, then, Thorn decided. Bomb-making was a far more sophisticated and dangerous art than most people realized—knowledge that several vaporized sixties radicals had acquired the hard way. Rigging a series of six charges to go off at the same time required either enormous luck or practiced skill. Right now he would put his money on skill.

"And the explosive used was plastique?" he asked.

Koenig nodded again. "We're picking up residues all over the place. The lab work will take some time, but we're pretty sure it was standard commercial-grade C4."

At least that was good news. Explosives intended for peaceful civilian use included chemical tracers that would help law enforcement zero in on the manufacturer and even on the specific batch. Given enough time and a lot of legwork by its agents, the FBI should be able to track the plastique used here back to its source.

"What about those phone calls claiming responsibility? You think they were genuine?" he asked.

Koenig frowned. "They were genuine, all right. Both came in before the news of this massacre hit the wires. We've got partial audiotapes from the two newspapers, but I don't know that they'll lead us anywhere."

"Oh?"

"Whoever made those calls used a lot of electronic filtering on his voice," Koenig explained. "Plus, he was reading from a prepared script. We've got our sound techs trying to pick up what they can, but they tell me it's like listening to a robot, not a man. Hell, the call could even have been computer-generated."

That was another indication that they were up against at least one professional, Thorn realized. He shook his head. No matter what the politicians wanted to hear, he suspected that finding those responsible for this butchery was not going to be fast or easy. "Does the Bureau have any data on this New Aryan Order? Anything that would make you believe they could mount a strike like this?"

"Not much," Koenig admitted. "We've got a handful of groups calling themselves that in our database—one in Maryland, one in Idaho, two in the South, and a couple more in the upper Midwest." He scowled. "We spent most of last night poring over the bios of the top wackos and their chief lieutenants, but I'll be damned if we could see anyone with the guts or the brains needed for this stunt."

The FBI man spread his hands. "Of course, this could be a whole new set of slimeballs calling themselves the New Aryan Order—one we hadn't picked up before. Hate groups don't pay much attention to copyright laws."

"Or they might be getting help from someone you don't have on file yet," Thorn suggested quietly. "Somebody with a good working knowledge of demolitions and security procedures."

"You have a candidate in mind, Colonel?" Koenig asked, narrowing his eyes. "Does DOD have some psycho ex-Ranger or Green Beret on the loose that we should know about? Is that why you're here?"

Thorn shook his head and then stopped. He hadn't seriously considered that possibility before. Much as he disliked the prospect, he had to admit that the FBI agent's suggestion might have merit. The Army's special forces put a great deal of effort into screening out the bad apples, but no psych profile ever developed could guarantee one hundred percent perfection.

"We might also be looking at an overseas link between extreme rightist groups," Helen broke in. "Don't forget those references to a German neo-Nazi we picked up from Burke and the rest during the synagogue siege. We know the Aryan Sword was getting sophisticated military supplies from old East German arsenals. Maybe this mysterious 'Karl' and his friends have started supplying military expertise as well."

"Could be," Koenig agreed slowly. Ties between the National Press Club bomber and a foreign terrorist group would complicate the whole investigation. Because the attack took place on U.S. soil, the FBI would still have primary jurisdiction, but the State Department, CIA, and Pentagon would have a much louder voice if there were a connection to radicals overseas.

Another agent joined the small circle, a taller, older man with slate-gray eyebrows and a harassed expression. The badge clipped to his protective suit read "Flynn." "What's up, Tommy?"

Koenig swiveled toward his boss. "Just batting around a few theories, Mike. About whether or not the bastards who blew the hell out of this place were ex-military or might have had help from foreign terrorists." He nodded toward Thorn. "This is Colonel Peter Thorn. He's with the JSOC."

"I see." Flynn turned his gaze on Thorn, clearly taking in his lean, well-muscled form. "You're with Delta Force, Colonel?"

Thorn nodded. "Until recently. I run a special intelligence outfit out of the Pentagon now."

"I see." Flynn's gaze sharpened. "You're not on my official observers' list, Colonel."

Thorn noticed Koenig and the other FBI agents stiffen. Hell. He nodded again, speaking before Helen could intervene on his behalf. If Flynn was going to be a hard-ass about this, there wasn't any point in dragging her name and record through the procedural mud. "That's right. I came down on my own hook."

"I've already got more than four hundred agents and other personnel working this case, Colonel. Is there something we're not doing to your satisfaction?" Flynn's voice was dangerously quiet.

"No, sir." Thorn stood his ground. With all the pressure the FBI agent was under from above, he couldn't blame the older man for bristling at yet another outsider tramping through the crime scene. If their roles were reversed, he would probably feel much the same way. "But I've spent close to ten years studying terrorist tactics. I thought you might find that useful—on an unofficial basis."

"I see." Flynn gritted his teeth. "Look, Colonel Thorn, besides the experts going over this building with a fine-tooth comb, I have agents out interviewing every survivor—some under hypnosis. There are others checking the records of every parking garage and taxi company in the metropolitan area. I even have teams reviewing every inch of footage shot by the Metro security cameras for every station within walking distance—just on the off chance we might spot something. So I'm going to ask you again. Is there some solid angle you think we're missing?"

Reluctantly, Thorn shook his head. "No, sir. Not at the moment."

"Fine. Then please go back to the Pentagon and let us get on with the job. There are already investigators from every damned agency and police force known to mankind crawling through this mess, and I sure as hell do not need the U.S. Army's Delta Force adding its own two cents." Flynn raised his voice, addressing his next comments to the poker-faced agents in earshot. "This is real life, not a movie, and this task force is not going to go running off at half cock to hunt for some supervillain. That's not the way I work, and that's not the way to produce results. Instead, we're going to work systematically through the facts as they exist. I want hard evidence, not fancy theories. Is that clear?"

The senior FBI agent waited briefly to make sure the others had heard him before turning his attention back to Thorn. He lowered his voice again. "Wait until we've found these bastards, Colonel. Then you or Agent Gray here are perfectly welcome to shoot them."

Great, Thorn thought, I didn't fool him at all. He knows exactly who brought me inside.

Flynn looked at Koenig. "Have somebody escort the colonel through the security barrier, Tommy. I'm sure he has work of his own to do."

Thorn nodded stiffly and did an about-face, following the shorter FBI agent back toward the staircase. He studiously avoided looking at Helen. Seeing the concern for him on her face would only make things worse. The FBI was within its rights, and he was out of line. But knowing that didn't make it any easier just to walk away.

The Pentagon

Thorn was alone in his office, staring at nothing in particular, when Joe Rossini stuck his head in through the door. "You have a minute, Pete?"

"Hell, I've got days." Thorn heard the unfamiliar bitterness in his voice and clamped down on it. Self-pity was for five-year-olds. He nodded toward the empty chair in front of his desk. "What can I do for you, Maestro?"

Rossini gingerly lowered his bulk into the seat and leaned forward. "Heard you had a rough time of it with the FBI today."

"Word travels fast."

The analyst nodded. "Better than light-speed."

Thorn snorted. He shrugged his shoulders. "I tried sticking my nose in where it didn't belong and got slapped down. End of story. The FBI has the domestic counterterrorism ball, and we're out of the game."

"You really think that?" Rossini asked.

"No," Thorn said flatly, surprising himself. He shook his head. "Flynn and his team are good. Hell, they're better than good. But I can't help feeling that we're all behind the curve on this one. Somebody out there blew the shit out of the National Press Club, and he and his friends are still on the loose. Hunting these bastards down strictly by the book might take too damned long."

"You think they'll hit again," Rossini said, more as a statement than a question.

"Why not? Whoever they are, they just killed two hundred people within walking distance of the White House. Why should they stop now?" Thorn sat up straighter. Flynn had every right to keep him off the official investigation, but the FBI couldn't stop him from using the resources at his own disposal. But what more could he do? As part of a larger U.S. intelligence effort, his analysts were already pressing ahead to learn more about the suspected links between American neo-Nazis and those in Europe.

Then he remembered something Flynn's deputy had said. "I think we should start pulling some personnel files from Army and Navy records. I want the name and service record of every Green Beret, Ranger, and SEAL who's been booted for bad conduct, race prejudice, or mental problems. Say over the past fifteen years."

Rossini whistled softly. "You really think we're dealing with one of our own guys who's gone off the reservation?"

"Maybe. Maybe not." Thorn shook his head angrily. "I don't know, Maestro. This could be just a worthless shot in the dark, but I'm damned if I'll sit idly by while somebody starts burning this country down around our ears."

NOVEMBER 8

Sea-Tac truck stop, near Seattle, Washington

(D MINUS 37)

Hamid Algar scouted the parking lot carefully and covertly. A chill, light rain was falling, and he zipped up his leather jacket, trying to get the collar tighter around his neck. The dampness seemed to soak into his bones. He hated the rain the way a soldier hates mud or dust or flies. The Syrian had seen nothing but rain since coming to Seattle. The climate was as foreign as the food and the language and the people. He sustained himself with the knowledge that this campaign would not last forever, and that however uncomfortable he was, he would be making a lot of the Americans he despised even more uncomfortable.

The lot was full despite, or perhaps because of, the rain. At this predawn hour the lot was crowded with semis, their drivers taking time for a quick breakfast before pulling back on Interstate 5 and heading north. Located between Tacoma to the south and Seattle to the north, the truck stop provided food and showers, even beds, besides diesel fuel.

The Syrian moved deeper into the parking lot, paying careful attention to each vehicle. Glowing overhead lights highlighted the moisture that coated every surface. He was looking for a specific kind of truck driven by a certain kind of company. Nothing local. He needed someone heading on through the city, which was why he was here at this misbegotten truck stop at this accursed hour in this unholy rain. For the second morning in a row.

Nobody noticed the small, dark man. He wore jeans and running shoes and a dark brown leather jacket. Like everyone else, his head and shoulders were hunched down against the rain as he attended to his business as quickly as possible.

Algar's hair was cut short, and he was clean-shaven. From his appearance, he could have been Hispanic, Arab, Italian, or even Polynesian. His driver's license carried the name Lopez and certified that he was American-born.

He moved through the wet, floodlit darkness, reading license plates, looking at the lettering on the cabs. All of the trucks on this side of the stop were, just by being on this side, northbound. The question was, how far were they going?

Finally, the Syrian found the rig he was looking for. It had Canadian plates and it was parked right in the center of a long row of darkly gleaming trucks. Better still, it was hauling a massive tanker load. He took the time to circle the vehicle, alert for anything that might make it less than the perfect choice.

Nothing. The tanker truck was perfect for his purpose. He swung around, scanning the lot for anyone who might be watching him or who might note his presence. Nobody was in view, and he quickly ducked under the trailer, up in front where it joined the tractor.

Pulling a small cloth-wrapped bundle from under his jacket, Algar unwrapped a rectangular, mottled brown-black metal box. Then he swiped at the underside of the trailer with the cloth, making sure no water or grease would interfere with the magnets attached to one side.

As he'd been taught by his Iranian instructors at Masegarh, Algar placed his burden exactly in the center, just ahead of the attachment point with the tractor unit. The magnets took hold with a strong clack, almost jerking the box out of his hands. As a test, he tried to shift it, and found it nearly impossible.

Half hidden in a cluster of cables and wires, the box blended nicely with its surroundings. Just to be sure, he splashed muddy water from a puddle over it, completing the camouflage.

He flipped a switch, arming the device. The box beeped once, indicating it was armed and ready. The switch also enabled an antitamper circuit, so that any attempt to remove it would fail catastrophically.

Satisfied, the Syrian quickly stood up and looked around again as he wiped his muddy hands clean on the cloth. Still nobody in sight.

Algar gratefully went back to his old blue Chevy Nova and ducked in out of the hated rain. He'd parked the car so he could watch the only exit out of the parking lot. Now, he thought, the only hard part was to stay awake while he waited.

About thirty minutes later, the Syrian spotted "his" truck lumbering out of line and turning toward the exit. He started his own engine, pulled out, and fell in behind the tanker. Its size made it easy to follow, and he took up position a few car lengths back. He checked his watch. It was almost 6:00 A.M. Even better. The truck driver was probably a little behind schedule. They were heading into the first wave of the morning rush hour.

Jane Kelly cursed her luck that rainy morning. The darkness and wet streets had slowed traffic, and that, combined with a five-minute delay in getting out the door, had completely screwed up her timing. If she wasn't pulling into the garage at work by 6:45, backups and traffic jams slowed her down and then she didn't get in until 7:30. Her boss was going to raise merry hell—again.

Right now, at 7:10, the thirty-three-year-old CPA maneuvered her three-year-old Nissan through the clogged traffic, heading north on I-5. She sighed. At least it was moving this morning. She didn't notice Hamid Algar's car behind her, any more than she noted the tanker truck one car ahead. Cars behind her weren't a problem, and those in front were merely obstructions. The tractor-trailer ahead was a large one, and it blocked her view of the lane forward, but what would she see? Just more wet cars.

*   *   *

Hamid Algar watched the Canadian tanker truck with satisfaction. The driver had driven straight north in the thickening traffic until Seattle's skyline appeared out of the low clouds and mist.

He had no trouble staying behind the tanker as it followed Interstate 5's winding curves. He had driven the route many times, and even taken some of the possible alternates—each time with the sensing device in place. It had functioned as advertised. In a job like this, one hundred percent reliability was the only acceptable performance.

Algar had already moved over to the right lane when the truck passed the Madison Street exit. There was only one path it could follow now, and with a sense of farewell, he took the exit and drove off into the city center. He'd take Highway 99 south back to Burien. The interstate was much too crowded.

Jane Kelly didn't see the Syrian leave. And even if she had spotted his battered blue Nova behind her, it would only have been one of a dozen cars turning off at Madison. She was nearing her own exit, Denny Way, less than a quarter mile away.

Traffic was still moving, thank goodness, although her speedometer now hovered at the fifteen-mile-an-hour mark. Up ahead, the highway curved a little to the left as it went under Olive Way.

The Olive Way–Boren Street underpass was especially wide, almost a tunnel. Above the highway, the two arterials intersected less than a block away, and the entire area had been roofed over.

The tanker truck passed beneath the intersection and out of the rain. The street surface was dry and lit by bright lamps on the ceiling of the underpass.

Hamid Algar's box sensed the change in the surrounding light. Although small, the increase was enough to register on a sensitive photocell. A microchip brain attached to the photocell noted the change—and began tracking the time. Unlike the bright beam of a passing headlight, this light lasted—a tenth of a second, two-tenths, three, four. Five-tenths was enough. The microchip triggered a tiny electric pulse.

Inside the box, a firing squib detonated a shaped-charge warhead. The squib also ignited a magnesium flare. Designed to punch through inches of armor, the warhead penetrated the tanker truck's milled steel shell easily, pushing a superheated jet of gas and metal into the liquid propane tank through a jagged, glowing hole.

The explosion died.

In its place, liquid propane began boiling out of the three-inch hole with a sound like a steam calliope jammed on high, changing to a gas as it hit the air. But when the streaming gas hit the box's hissing magnesium flare, it ignited into a roaring jet of flame. The heat of the jet, hotter than a blowtorch, opened the hole larger and larger in a chain reaction until the entire front of the steel tank disintegrated. Propane gas mixed freely with the air. At that point, only milliseconds after the bomb went off, the rest of the tanker's cargo disappeared in a devastating explosion.

The near-dawn darkness was overpowered by a searing orange-white fireball. Trapped by the ceiling of the underpass, the leading edge of the fireball spread out horizontally ahead and behind, but a final, titanic blast split the overhead structure and peeled it back. Slabs of concrete and steel weighing hundreds of pounds landed half a mile away, smashing through roofs and flattening cars and pedestrians crowding Seattle's busy streets.

One car length behind the explosion, Jane Kelly had only a single, anguished second to understand what was happening before the roaring, mindless wall of flame engulfed her Nissan.

She and all the others trapped in the four-lane underpass were incinerated. More than a dozen other cars and trucks on either side of the explosion were also scorched and burned. The vehicles on Olive and Boren streets above were either flipped over or fell through into the inferno below.

Half a minute after the echoes of the enormous blast faded

away, stunned motorists left their cars on the highway and stood staring in shock and terror at the burning mass of twisted steel and concrete clogging the gap where the overpass had once been. Buildings on either side of the highway were burning, and the agonized screams and shrieks of those who were trapped and on fire tore through the sudden silence.

Burien, Washington

Hamid Algar and his two comrades, Anton Chemelovic and Jabra Ibrahim, watched the television in rapt fascination. Coverage of the disaster had started only moments after Hamid had returned to their apartment, and now, like the rest of Seattle and America, they viewed the live television feed. But while the rest of the country watched in horror and fascination, the three Iranian-trained commandos were performing battle damage assessment.

The picture now on television came from the roof of a nearby office building. From above, the destroyed overpass looked like nothing more than a giant, blackened hourglass filled with rubble and twisted metal. Emergency vehicles surrounded the crater.

The reporter now on camera, stunned by the carnage and rattled by the lack of hard information, kept repeating the single, inadequate word: "tragedy." It had been a tragic accident, there had been a tragic loss of life, and so on. Area hospitals were jammed and some of those with less critical injuries had been farmed out to smaller clinics. At the moment, the death toll stood at twenty-five, but that was expected to climb rapidly as searchers pulled apart the rubble. Sixty-three had been seriously hurt. Seattle's burn wards were full.

The National Transportation Safety Board had already dispatched an investigative team to the area. They would land at Boeing Field at 2:10 P.M.

Algar, Chemelovic, and Ibrahim all relaxed slightly. At least initially, the Americans were treating the tanker blast as an accident. They would find no immediate clues that this was a terrorist attack. When the NTSB's investigators discovered the truth later, their trail would be days old, and it would be a very faint, very cold trail.

They nodded to each other. Tehran would be pleased.

Chemelovic, a Bosnian, had actually made the bomb. His gift for electronics had earned him special training in demolitions at Masegarh, and now both of his teammates praised his work. Algar told him several times exactly how he had placed the device. By the time the Syrian finished retelling the story, Chemelovic had a grin covering half his face. His skills had won a great victory in the war against the godless West.

Jabra Ibrahim rose from the couch and snapped the television off. "Come on, both of you. Help me pack."

Ibrahim, a Lebanese, had provided security and cover for the three-man cell. He'd rented the apartment, done the shopping, and organized all the logistics during their short, one-week stay in the Seattle area. He was the conscientious one, the one who'd worked on their laptop computer while the others watched television.

Their personal gear went into one duffel bag, and their tools and weapons into another two. While Algar and Chemelovic cleaned up, Ibrahim meticulously went through each room, each closet, and each cupboard looking for anything that belonged to them or came from them. A scrap of paper, a button, anything that might provide a link to them.

When Chemelovic and Algar returned from loading their gear into the Nova, they helped in the search. A few small items were found, a tool under a piece of furniture and a sock, one of Algar's, under another. Shamefacedly, he took possession of the offending article and stood next to Chemelovic as Ibrahim, the team leader, berated them both for sloppy security.

Finally, he handed each of them a rag and a bottle of cleaning solution. Systematically, they wiped down every smooth surface, every wall and every object capable of holding a fingerprint.

While none of them had ever been fingerprinted by the American government, a print here might link them to some past act or location, or some future one.

Just after noon, they were finished. The three piled into the blue Nova and pulled out of the lot. Ibrahim drove, and he stopped in front of the apartment complex's rental office. Grabbing an envelope, he jumped out of the car and ran in.

The day manager, a stout, middle-aged woman, glanced up from her crossword puzzle. "Oh, Mr. Rashid. You here to check out?"

Ibrahim nodded. "Yes, Mrs. Hume. We all finished the program this morning." He'd rented the three-bedroom apartment on a weekly basis with the story that he and the others were reps from a Silicon Valley data processing company who had come to the Seattle area to attend courses at Microsoft University. It was a common and believable cover—one which no one felt compelled to check.

"And how did you do?" the manager asked, busy counting the money in the envelope he'd handed to her.

Ibrahim smiled. "We received top marks, Mrs. Hume. Straight As."

NOVEMBER 9

Special Operations Headquarters, Tehran

(D MINUS 36)

LYNX Prime via MAGI Link to MAGI Prime:
  1. Attack successful. Preliminary damage assessment attached.
  2. LYNX Bravo confirms cell in movement to Portland, Oregon. Security unbreached.
Standing by for further orders.

General Amir Taleh finished reading through the latest status reports from his widely scattered forces and nodded in satisfaction. The first two of his planned attacks had been carried out—with perfect attention to detail. A third, set for the Houston area, had been scrapped at the last moment to avoid tighter security at the intended target—a railroad crossing near a poor, predominantly black and Hispanic neighborhood. He shrugged. His field commanders had acted intelligently there. It was too soon to risk compromising the whole operation to press home an attack against higher odds.

He looked up at Captain Kazemi. "You understand I wish to see the latest videotapes as soon as they arrive?"

His aide nodded crisply. "Of course, sir. I've left explicit orders at the communications center."

Besides the trained agents in embassies and elsewhere who made up his official intelligence network, Taleh found himself relying increasingly on news reports from the United States to monitor the progress of his covert war. Curiously and foolishly left uncensored by their government, the networks were a unique and useful source of information. They mirrored, and often led, American public and political opinion.

And from what Taleh had seen so far, the right notes of hysteria were beginning to be sounded over the American airwaves. He picked up the phone on his desk and punched in the internal code for the head of the operations planning section. "Colonel Kaya? Come to my office immediately. Bring the next set of strike orders with you."

He hung up and rocked back in his chair, envisioning the havoc his next set of signals would wreak on the United States.

Every attack against America sprang from his mind—from his will. When he saw the results, it was a personal satisfaction. It was partly revenge for all the evils the Americans had inflicted on his beloved country over the years, but he knew revenge by itself was pointless. That was where his predecessors had failed. His terror operations only had merit if they were part of a larger campaign.

Taleh smiled fiercely. The initial stages of SCIMITAR had gone well. It was time to increase the tempo.

CHAPTER 13
ABOMINATIONS

NOVEMBER 12

Chicago, Illinois

(D MINUS 33)

Bundled up against the cold, Nikola Tomcic stood on the sidewalk beside an idling green Dodge minivan. He wanted a cigarette, but the short, stocky Bosnian Muslim suppressed the urge. They'd already cleaned out the cheap basement apartment that had sheltered them for the past several weeks, and his tobacco was packed away with the rest of his personal gear. He would simply have to wait. As his instructors had said so often, patience was one of the qualities of a good soldier.

Bassam Khalizad, his team leader, sprinted back from the mailbox and clapped him on the shoulder. "They'll get the keys in a few days," the Iranian remarked, his smooth face oddly boyish without its customary beard and mustache. "Not that the fools will care."

Tomcic nodded sourly. Although the lackadaisical management at the old brownstone apartment house had made it attractive to Khalizad's team, he still thought the landlords were
sloppy—even decadent. The wizened old man and woman who
owned the building were clearly used to renting out their property to all manner of deviants—drug users, alcoholics, boy-
lovers, and the rest. So long as they were paid in cash, the
landlords paid no attention to their tenants.

Khalizad motioned the young Bosnian into the back of the
minivan and slid onto the seat beside Halim Barakat, their
driver. "We're set. Let's go."

The sallow-faced Egyptian grunted and pulled out into the
light, midday traffic. He threaded the van through the streets
with ease. Tomcic had once heard him say that navigating
through Chicago was nothing to one used to driving a taxi
through Cairo's teeming alleys. Since the team had slipped
across the border with Canada, it had been his job to study the
terrain, to know this American city as well as a skilled general
knows his chosen battlefield.

Once a member of the Muslim Brotherhood—Egypt's violent
Islamic faction—Barakat had fled to Iran and into the hands of
General Taleh's recruiters following a government crackdown
on dissent. For him and for millions of Egyptians like him, the
murdered Anwar Sadat and his moderate successors were nothing more than American and Israeli puppets. The chance the
Iranians offered Barakat to lash out against Islam's enemies had
been irresistible.

Barakat kept to the larger streets, but he included one or two
random turns, paying close attention to his sideview mirrors
each time. It didn't appear that they were being followed. Good
enough. He turned his attention to the road ahead, driving with
extra precision and care. There were so many things to worry
about: the chance of an accident, a random police stop, a carjacking. While the odds of any of them happening were low,
and a carjacking would certainly not succeed, anything out of
the ordinary could compromise their mission. That worried him
most. It worried them all. Their orders from Tehran were clear:

Security was paramount. They could not risk discovery. They must not be captured.

Barakat gripped the steering wheel tighter, focusing on his job as they bounced and jolted over the potholes that dotted this city's streets. It was important that they all concentrate on their jobs. He drove, Khalizad planned, and the others, well, the others had their own special tasks.

This part of Chicago was a checkerboard of middle-class neighborhoods and run-down public housing. The racial lines were almost as clearly drawn, with white on one side, blacks and Hispanics on the other. And all of the poverty-stricken public housing projects were overrun with crime, with drugs, and with gangs.

Barakat eyed the passing cityscape grimly. A product of the Cairo slums himself, he knew only too well how easy it was to set such places ablaze with hatred.

"Pull in here." Khalizad nudged him gently and pointed to a deserted block of mostly boarded-up houses and businesses. Fair-haired Emil Hodjic, another Bosnian, was waiting for them behind the wheel of another van, this one dark blue, parked in front of a small abandoned grocery store. He had rented the vehicle that morning, using a forged Illinois driver's license and a credit card issued in the same false name.

Barakat pulled in behind Hodjic's vehicle. Led by Khalizad, he and Tomcic scrambled outside lugging duffel bags containing their weapons and other gear. The Egyptian took pains to lock the Dodge behind him. They would need it again soon enough, and the iron bars protecting the empty store's windows and doors spoke volumes about the kind of neighborhood they were in.

Hodjic met them near the rental van's rear doors. "Gloves!" he reminded them sharply.

The Iranian and his two companions nodded and paused long enough to pull on thin, flexible leather gloves—usual enough wear against the biting November winds blowing westward off Lake Michigan. More important, wearing the gloves should make sure they left no damning prints for later investigators to find.

Barakat slid behind the wheel and took a moment to familiarize himself with the controls. Behind him, the other three got to work.

Stripping off their winter jackets, they opened the duffel bags and pulled out body armor, black coveralls, and black ski masks. Each of the coveralls bore a white sword on the back, hilt upward to resemble a cross. The body armor went on first, followed by the coveralls and masks.

A weapons check came next. Each man carried a military-style assault rifle and a pistol in a shoulder holster. Hodjic passed a tiny TEC-9 machine pistol up to Barakat, who laid it on the seat beside him and covered it with his coat. He was not expected to need it, but graduates of the harsh training at Masegarh learned early on not to take chances.

Khalizad snapped a thirty-round magazine into his M16 and glanced at Tomcic and Hodjic. The two Bosnians nodded back silently, tightly gripping their own weapons. They were ready.

Barakat put the rented van in motion, and the three men in back checked their watches. They were seven minutes away from their objective. Plenty of time. Like paratroopers preparing for a combat jump, they checked each other over, looking for loose gear or forgotten items.

Finally, they crouched facing the rear door. They had to brace themselves against the twists and turns of the van, but the Egyptian was taking the shortest route he could and driving as carefully as he could. A fender bender now would be an unmitigated disaster.

The minutes ticked off slowly, almost interminably. Crouched beside Khalizad, Tomcic felt the sweat pooling under his ski mask. After the cold outside, the enclosed van felt like a steam bath.

"One block!" Barakat called out over his shoulder.

The Iranian reached up and unlocked the back doors. Soon.

Tomcic muttered a short prayer under his breath. The mullahs had said that he and the others were the very hands of God in this war—guided by the will of the infallible and incapable of error. They had said that none of the innocent blood that must be shed would fall on his head—that all who died sinless were necessary martyrs in the struggle against the Great Satan and assured of a place in heaven. He earnestly hoped the mullahs were right.

The van braked sharply and came to a complete stop.

"Now!" Khalizad shouted. He threw open the doors and leaped out onto the pavement, with the two Bosnians right behind. All three moved rapidly, spreading out to take up carefully rehearsed positions.

The Iranian team leader went to the left, toward the curb. Tomcic went with him. Hodjic spun right, covering an arc behind the van. On the far side of the narrow two-lane street was a row of small, decrepit shops: a check-cashing center, a shoe store, a little grocery, and a liquor store on the corner.

On the near side was the Anthony A. Settles Elementary School.

It was precisely 11:35 A.M., five minutes into recess on a sunny day, and the playground was filled with children, laughing and running and jumping in noisy, gleeful fun. Almost all were African-American or Hispanic. The playground was separated from the sidewalk only by a chain-link fence.

Tomcic dropped to one knee at the fence and poked the muzzle of his Russian-made AKM through one of the gaps. Khalizad moved in beside him but remained standing.

Only seconds after the van squealed to a stop, and before anyone even consciously noted their presence, the Bosnian pulled the trigger. All his doubts vanished in the sudden, hammering pulse of the assault rifle against his shoulder. He was here, deep in the heartland of a nation that had let his people and his Faith be crushed by their foes, striking back. It was an instant where fierce joy and blood-red rage met and mingled.

Tomcic's face, hidden by the mask, matched the intensity of his emotions—his eyes gleaming, his lips pulled back in almost a rictus of anger. He remembered to aim low.

His first long burst caught a cluster of children on a merry-go-round, knocking them off the ride in a welter of blood. Sparks flew wherever his bullets slammed into metal. He walked the burst to the left, toward the entrance to the school building. Halfway there, his first thirty-round clip ran dry. With a practiced motion, the Bosnian switched the empty out, slid in a new clip from a pouch at his waist, and yanked the AKM's charging handle back, chambering a round and cocking the hammer. In seconds, he was firing again.

Settles Elementary, only blocks from the crime-ridden Cabrini Green housing project, was no stranger to gunfire, and the teachers tried to do as they were trained—screaming at their students to lie flat or duck inside the building. While that might have worked against a random shooting or a gang gunfight, it was utterly useless against trained special warfare troops.

As Tomcic tore his targets to shreds with 7.62mm rounds from his AKM, Khalizad scanned the schoolyard, shooting adults—anyone who looked as though they might interfere. He had a better view of the carnage the Bosnian was inflicting, not only because he was standing but because his vision was not focused over the muzzle of his weapon.

Children screamed hysterically and wept, crouching behind anything or nothing at all as they tried, instinctively, to escape the deadly fire. Older kids tried to help younger ones to safety. Some, too young to understand what was happening, simply stood and cried, and were cut down. Many teachers tried to bring the children inside to safety, or shield them with their bodies, and died at Khalizad's hand.

The second Bosnian, Emil Hodjic, heard the firing and screams from the playground, but kept his attention and his own AKM locked on the street in front of him. His job was to protect the team. He had to keep the road open for their planned escape.

There were cars crowding the intersection half a block away. Hodjic began shooting, firing short, precisely aimed bullets into windshields and tires. He was the team marksman and sniper. As a teenager he had practiced his trade a hundred times in the deadly hide-and-kill games played amid Sarajevo's artillery-shattered high-rises.

Now he searched for pedestrians, for customers coming out of stores, and for car drivers. Witnesses. Those who fled, he generally ignored. Hodjic was after the ones who watched.

Still firing on the playground, Khalizad heard one long beep on the rental van's horn. One minute gone. Thirty seconds left. There were no immediate threats in his field of view, so he consciously widened his search beyond the corpse-strewn asphalt. There were shocked and stunned faces pressed up against the windows of the school. The Iranian shot them out, pumping a steady stream of 5.56mm rounds through glass and brick and flesh.

Hodjic also heard the horn—the first of the signals the sniper had been waiting for eagerly. The past sixty seconds had seemed like sixty years. To his victims, he was a fearsome figure—dressed and masked in black, firing into the cityscape like some nightmare come to life. Only he and his teammates understood their vulnerability and the risks they were running by taking direct action.

During the planning for this attack, the likely law enforcement response had been carefully measured and assessed. The police would not be halfhearted, but every calculation showed the attackers should have enough time to strike fast and flee. The nearest Chicago police station was more than two minutes away, and it would take several minutes more to assemble a reaction force. No, Hodjic was more worried about the possibility of a roving patrol car or an armed response from some unexpected direction. He'd already killed one shopkeeper who appeared at his door with a shotgun. Many in America's cities owned weapons. At this point in the campaign, one unexpected bullet could smash General Taleh's grand design beyond repair.

The Bosnian sniper searched the area carefully, trying to suppress the fear and excitement surging through his body, trying to keep a clear head so that he could spot any movement, any possible threat. By now, the intersection half a block away was a jumble of abandoned cars, their windshields starred or shot out altogether. Bodies dotted the pavement along with shattered glass. He pivoted, sighting over the AKM's muzzle. There. He saw someone crouched behind a car that had driven up over the sidewalk and plowed into a storefront. He fired twice. An elderly black woman slumped forward and sprawled, unmoving, on the sidewalk.

The van's horn beeped again—twice this time. It was time to go.

Hodjic stared hard along the muzzle of his assault rifle, making sure it was safe to turn his back for ten seconds. He whirled and dove through the open rear doors.

Khalizad heard the horn too and turned, but Tomcic showed no signs of leaving. He was still firing—still flailing away at the heaped corpses on the playground. The Iranian had to grab his shoulder to break his fierce concentration.

The Bosnian turned his head slightly, but his expression was unreadable under the mask.

Khalizad yanked on his shoulder again, stabbing a finger toward the van. He said nothing. Except in dire emergency, their standing orders prohibited speech during a mission. No one must hear the accents that would give them away as foreign-born.

This time, Tomcic shook his head as if coming out of a trance. He rocked back slightly. Then, without another look at the schoolyard or his victims, he rose and dashed into the van.

Khalizad was the last one in. He pulled the doors shut and shouted over his shoulder to their driver, "Go! We're clear!"

Barakat took off with a screech of tires, peeling out into the street and away at high speed. As soon as the van started moving, the three men in back stripped off their masks and began shoving their weapons into the duffel bags. Reaction to the enormous stress left them utterly exhausted, and only their training carried them through the routine now. Both Khalizad and Tomcic were actually trembling, shaking uncontrollably.

Tomcic slid his AKM out of sight and sat down heavily, emerging fully now from his murderous daze. His emotions were running wild, cycling through deep satisfaction and unappeased fury. He'd had his revenge, but he still felt unsatisfied. America's crimes against his people and his homeland were too great to be expunged with just one punishment.

They were back at the other minivan in five minutes, still apparently unnoticed and unpursued. While Khalizad and the others threw their gear into their own Dodge minivan, Barakat made a fast, thorough search of the rental vehicle. He found no traces, not a shell casing or any other evidence. All they left behind was the stink of powder.

Barakat scrambled into the Dodge and started the engine. They drove off, taking the Kennedy Expressway north to the Edens and then on into Wisconsin on the Tri-State Tollway. They stopped only once, so that Khalizad could make a short call from a pay phone to other members of his command, reporting their success and triggering the message claiming responsibility for the attack.

By the time the police found the abandoned rental van, the four men were crossing the Wisconsin border. They had new orders.

News Bulletin, WBBM radio, Chicago

". . . Police have now set up barricades around the Settles School to reduce crowds and allow access for emergency and police vehicles. A helipad is being set up for the medivac flights needed to transport the most critically wounded to area hospitals.

"Parents are asked to please refrain from going directly to the school. All uninjured students and faculty have been taken to Fellowship Baptist Church. Officials at the church are maintaining a list of casualties and the hospitals where they are being treated.

"In another key development, police spokesmen have confirmed the written statement anonymously delivered to our sister station WBBM-TV as authentic. It matches one eyewitness account of the attackers wearing emblems identified as belonging to the New Aryan Order, the same hate group believed responsible for blowing up the National Press Club seven days ago. FBI agents arriving at the scene of the massacre have said they are proceeding on the assumption that the group is responsible."

South Side Islamic Center, Chicago

The words rang out, full of anger and loathing. " 'We have begun the holy task appointed to us, the destruction of the Soldiers of Satan. The black race will be exterminated. We call on all true whites, all true Aryans, to fight for the purification of our Christian faith and race.' "

The Reverend Lawrence Mohammed lowered the paper from his thin, almost ascetic features. His face was purple with rage, but every word he spoke was carefully shaped and controlled.

Reciting the last of the New Aryan Order's message from memory, he finished, " 'This is only the beginning of the decisive campaign to cleanse America of all impure races.' "

He paused, gazing out over the sea of appalled and outraged faces. The Islamic Center's vast meeting hall was crowded—packed with people far past any legal capacity. It was impossible to move in that space, almost impossible to breathe. No fire marshal would be checking the hall that night, though. The angry, grieving crowd would brook no challenge from anyone in authority. Thousands more, unable to make their way inside, jammed the streets outside the center, listening to the speech on loudspeakers.

All listened to Mohammed's words in dead silence. He'd been speaking for half an hour, since seven in the evening of that horrible day.

The Black Muslim community had begun congregating at the

South Side and other Islamic centers in Chicago almost as soon as the first reports of the massacre began airing on local TV and radio. Other crowds gathered at the city's predominantly black Christian churches. Chicago's African-American population was shocked by the slaughter at the Settles School—almost paralyzed by its overtly racist nature, the most heinous in American history. Local, state, national, and even international leaders had issued statements all day, consoling the families of the victims. Some had promised justice, others reform. Most had urged calm.

But not all. The Reverend Lawrence Mohammed and the Black Muslim community were not calm. Some of the parents in the crowd before him wept uncontrollably with recent loss. Mohammed had spent much of the afternoon counseling and comforting them, before talking with confused, harried police who had told him what they could, which wasn't nearly enough. They had nothing—no hard leads, no clues—nothing. Just an abandoned vehicle and a playground littered with dead children.

Mohammed scowled. His brand of Islam was not strong on conciliation or patience, and it drew a sharp line between black and white. For all their talk of "energetic investigations" and "methodical searches," he did not believe the FBI and the police would find the schoolyard butchers. In his heart, he did not believe the authorities really wanted to find them. All his life he had seen the police for what they really were—merely the slave-catchers of old in a new guise.

But now, perhaps, more of his brothers and sisters would come to realize the truth of his vision.

Already traumatized by the death of Walter Steele and other mainstream leaders in the press club bombing, America's black community was on edge. Many had wondered openly whether that attack was the last gasp of a former racist era, or just the beginning of a new time of persecution and murder. For many, the Settles School massacre had answered that question.

And now they were here—hanging on his every word, waiting for a call to action, a call to arms.

Mohammed leaned closer to the microphone, speaking quietly at first. "And so now our enemies openly gather round us, my brothers, my sisters. These men, these evil men, threaten our people, all our people, with extermination—with genocide." His voice rose, gathering strength gradually. "And what is the law doing? They're sitting, that's what they are doing! Sitting while we die!"

The crowd growled.

He nodded flatly. "They're being careful, they say. They don't want to miss anything, they say. It all takes time, they say." He shook his head. "Oh, yes, they are taking their time—taking time and giving it to the killers. Handing precious hours, precious days, to those who use it to murder more of our children!"

Lawrence Mohammed's voice rose higher to an angry shout. "These evil white men, these devils in sheets, strike, and strike again, and the police are no closer to catching them. They will never be closer, because the police are part of the same problem!

"We have been betrayed by our brothers on the police force and in City Hall! The police are one arm of the white establishment, the racists are another!"

Mohammed shook his head in disgust and asked, "Now, can one hand fight the other?"

As one the crowd roared out its resounding answer, "No!"

"Can two hands work together?"

"Yes!"

"Are those two hands aimed at us?"

"Yes!"

"Are they aimed at our children?"

"Yes!"

Mohammed paused again. He seemed to look each man and woman there in the eye, and his next words were quieter, softer. "Now, as long as I have had someone to preach to, I have preached pride, solidarity, and strength for our people. Did you ever wonder why?"

All of those filling the hall and the streets outside were silent, holding their breath in a collective hush.

He said it again, louder. "Did you ever wonder?"

The silence broke in a shout from thousands of throats. "Yes!"

Mohammed nodded, satisfied. "I'll tell you why! So we could have the power to fight this white man's war on us!

"If a man strikes at your children, do you turn the other cheek?" His voice rose again as he asked the question.

"No!"

"If a man strikes at you, do you give him time to strike again?"

"No!" The shout rang out, deeper and uglier this time. Men and women were already moving toward the exits, pouring out onto the streets in a fury.

The Reverend Lawrence Mohammed stood back from his microphone and watched with pride as they left. His words had become weapons. These white devils of the New Aryan Order had struck the spark, but now he would turn the flames against them—and against their more powerful masters.

Bravo Company, 2nd Infantry Battalion, Illinois National Guard, State Street, the Loop, Chicago

Chicago was on fire by nightfall.

Gunfire echoed above the keening wail of police and fire sirens—the single, distinct cracks of pistol shots interspersed with the echoing thumps of shotguns and the rattle of automatic weapons. The National Guardsmen scrambling down out of their canvas-sided, three-quarter-ton trucks stopped in midmotion and looked south in apprehension. Their olive-green battle fatigues, Kevlar helmets, and M16 rifles looked eerily out of place against the elegantly dressed mannequins visible in the display windows of the Carson Pirie Scott department store.

Lieutenant Richard Pinney, a lawyer by day and soldier by weekend, glanced at his company commander in shock. "Jesus Christ, Captain, what the hell's going on? A full-scale war?"

A harassed-looking Chicago police sergeant standing nearby saved Captain Philip Jankowski from answering. "That's it exactly, pal." He wiped a hand across his weary, red-rimmed eyes and nodded south down the broad expanse of State Street. "Things are totally out of control down there. What was a protest march up Martin Luther King Drive turned into a pushing and shoving match with our crowd control guys. And then that turned into a riot with looting. And now, shit, now it's a goddamned civil war."

Jankowski's jaw tightened. It was clear that the hurried phone briefing he'd been given by city officials before leaving the armory was already way out-of-date. He stared down State Street, peering intently through the pall of smoke and soot cloaking the area. Flickering orange-red glows several blocks away marked fires that were steadily consuming the rows of retail stores lining Chicago's north-south commercial axis.

He turned back to Pinney. "Get the men formed up, Dick. You know the drill. Make sure everyone's in full gear. Flak jackets, helmets . . . the works." He swore softly. "Damn it. I wish we had more troops."

The sudden activation order from the governor's office had caught everyone by surprise. By the time Bravo Company moved out of its North Side armory, barely half its one hundred men had reported for duty. Jankowski had left another lieutenant and sergeant behind with orders to bring the rest down south as soon as they showed up. He only hoped they wouldn't be much longer. He also earnestly hoped Bravo wasn't the only outfit being summoned to emergency duty.

The lieutenant nodded hesitantly. "What about our weapons, sir?"

More gunfire rattled through the darkness.

"Make sure they're loaded, Dick. I don't want anybody opening fire without my orders, but I don't want anyone going down that street without a full magazine and several spares. Clear?"

Pinney nodded, eyes wide under his helmet.

"Okay. You and Crawford get 'em organized." Jankowski pointed toward the exhausted police sergeant. "The sergeant and I are gonna pay a visit to the local CP to find out where they want us."

Five minutes later, Jankowski emerged from the police radio van being used as a temporary headquarters even more worried than he went in. The earlier reports calling the situation in the Loop area "volatile" had been about as accurate as calling a tornado an "atmospheric disturbance." Police commanders weren't sure where the largest pockets of looters and rioters really were. They weren't even sure where very many of their own men were. Sporadic reports came in from small bands of regular police and riot squad officers cut off by the mob and forced to hole up for safety. There were unconfirmed reports that several of those tiny groups had been overrun. All communications circuits were jammed by a flood of frantic calls for fire and ambulance service.

Jankowski shook his head in dismay. One thing was clear: Many among the rioters were well armed and fully prepared to use their weapons against anyone who got in their way. Apparently, Chicago's notoriously violent street gangs were out in force to settle old scores with each other, with the police, and with the "white establishment"—especially with those who owned stores selling jewelry and consumer electronics goods.

He was pleased to see that Pinney and his noncoms had the men deployed and ready to move. The formation he had chosen was simple. Two squads up front, one on each side of State Street. They would scout for the main body of about thirty men following about fifty yards back.

Jankowski took his place with the largest group and raised his voice. "Bravo Company! Fix bayonets!"

A succession of metallic scrapes answered him as the fifty guardsmen snapped bayonets into place on their M16s. The captain did not seriously expect his men to use cold steel in combat, but he earnestly hoped the sight of the long blades moving closer might prove intimidating to at least some of the rioters.

He stepped forward and shouted again. "At my order, Bravo Company will advance!" He paused, looking right and left one last time to make sure his outfit was ready. Pinney and the sergeants nodded back. They were set.

Jankowski faced forward again and squared his shoulders. "Advance!"

Moving with a measured tread, the small force of National Guardsmen went forward into the smoke.

They stumbled into a scene out of hell within minutes.

Waves of heat radiating from fires burning out of control in every building of the 200 block of South State Street washed over the advancing soldiers. Sheets of flame roared out the ground-floor windows of the Berghoff restaurant, a Chicago institution since 1893. The dense smoke billowing over the area was already making it hard to breathe, and now the soaring temperatures made it even more difficult. Corpses were strewn in every direction. Some of the dead were probably rioters gunned down by the police. Others were probably unlucky bystanders caught by the mob or in the cross fire. Several bodies were clad in the tattered remnants of police uniforms.

Dead and dying horses lay among the murdered humans. A patrol of mounted policemen had been ambushed near the intersection of State and Adams. Now wounded horses screamed and writhed in anguish on the torn pavement, trying desperately to rise on bullet-shattered legs.

Jankowski gagged and turned away, unable to look any further. Why hadn't someone, anyone, put the poor beasts out of their misery? He glanced back, trying to find Pinney to order him to have a detail take care of the job.

Suddenly, the wall of the building next to him exploded in a spray of concrete chips, torn up by a tearing fusillade of automatic-weapons fire. Guardsmen scattered in all directions or fell prone. Two were hit and thrown backward off their feet.

Someone slammed into Jankowski from behind and knocked him flat. It was Pinney. More bullets whipcracked past their heads.

A sergeant wriggled closer to them, moving faster than anyone had thought possible in their weekend training sessions. "Jesus Christ, Captain! We're taking heavy fire from a barricade up ahead!" the noncom shouted, gesturing southward. "The scouts say some of the sons of bitches have blocked the street with abandoned buses."

Against his orders, the troops ahead of him began firing back into the smoke, pumping bursts from their M16s down the street toward the unseen gunmen. No matter, Jankowski thought in a daze. They were committed now. Bravo Company had been sucked into the maelstrom sweeping northward through Chicago.

Emergency Broadcast System bulletin, aired over WMAQ radio, Chicago

". . . the martial-law zone has now been expanded to include the area north of East Sixty-third Street, south of Wacker Drive and the river, and east of the Dan Ryan Expressway. Do not, repeat, do not attempt to enter or leave this area. The police and National Guard units now manning this perimeter have orders to shoot curfew violators and looters on sight. All citizens in the Chicagoland area are urged to stay at home and off the expressways.

"Reports from inside the area show widespread looting, arson, and rioting. Casualties and damage are both heavy, but there are no accurate counts yet. Field hospitals are being set up at the Navy Pier and Grant Park to accommodate the overflow of wounded from area hospitals. The Red Cross has put out an urgent appeal for all types of blood, especially O positive. If you live outside the martial-law zone and wish to donate blood, go to the nearest hospital, and they will accept your donation there.

"To quell the rioting, Governor Anderson has expanded his call-up of the National Guard to all Illinois units. Officials in the governor's office also report he has been in communication with the governor of Wisconsin to arrange a selective mobilization of that state's National Guard units as well.

"Governor Anderson is currently en route from Springfield for consultations with the mayor. Informed sources have indicated they are considering asking for federal troops to help restore law and order."

CHAPTER 14

RABBIT PUNCH

NOVEMBER 13

The White House

An emergency conference on domestic terrorism had replaced the President's standard morning briefing on foreign military and political developments. The rapidly developing internal crisis took precedence over slower-moving global concerns.

The first minutes of the White House meeting were played out before an array of television cameras and print journalists. With opinion polls showing a public that was increasingly fearful, the President's political and policy advisors all agreed on the need to convey the impression of an administration on top of events and working hard to put things right. Pictures of the nation's chief executive conferring with the Attorney General, the Chairman of the Joint Chiefs of Staff, and the heads of the FBI and CIA were an integral part of that confidence-building process.

But the real work of the gathering began only after the last members of the media were ushered out of the Cabinet Room. Jefferson T. Corbell, the President's top electoral tactician, slipped in a side door and dropped into one of the empty chairs.

The President waited for Corbell to settle himself before dropping his tight, confident smile. He stared across the elegant, polished table at his assembled advisors. "Well?" he asked sourly. "Are we any closer to putting a cap on this goddamned situation?"

Nobody spoke up immediately.

"Well?"

David Leiter, the Director of the FBI, cleared his throat. "I'm afraid not, Mr. President."

"And why the hell not?" the President demanded angrily. He jerked a thumb toward the television set parked in the corner of the Cabinet Room. The sound was off, but the picture was on. Right now it showed aerial shots of Chicago's South Side. Whole city blocks were burning. "This country's third largest city is under martial law and tearing itself to pieces. One of the country's biggest civil rights leaders has been blown to hell— along with a couple of hundred other important people, congressmen included. Jesus Christ, *Nightline*'s running broadcasts asking whether or not this is the first battle of a full-scale American race war! What am I supposed to tell the American people? That we're still twiddling our damned thumbs while this army of white-power maniacs is out there killing at will?"

Leiter and the others sat stiffly, waiting for the fiery burst of executive temperament to fade slightly. Years of service to this President had taught them how to ride each storm out.

"There's no solid evidence to suggest that we're facing an army of terrorists, Mr. President," the FBI Director said quietly. "Even assuming the press club bombing and the schoolyard massacre were conducted by different people, we're still talking about less than ten individuals, possibly no more than five. Taking the time between the two attacks into account, I suspect both were carried out by the same group."

"Well, then, these five or ten fanatics of yours are making quite a mess, David," Sarah Carpenter said sharply. There was little love lost between the Attorney General and the head of the FBI. In the past, they'd repeatedly locked horns over Justice Department policy and spending priorities. Now she saw an opportunity to score a few points at his expense. "If you hadn't dragged your heels when I ordered you to increase surveillance of the neo-Nazi extremists, we might not be facing this crisis today!"

Leiter glared back at her. "With all due respect, Madam Attorney General, I doubt all the electronic eavesdropping in the world would have picked up the slightest hint of either the bombing or the school massacre before they occurred. The people conducting this campaign are not stupid."

He turned back to the President. "Frankly, sir, my behavioral sciences people are puzzled. Neither of these attacks fits the pattern we've come to expect from the extreme right in this country. They tend to be an impulsive, often poorly educated lot. But both the National Press Club bombing and the slaughter in Chicago bear every indication of sophisticated, intricate planning and flawless execution."

"So?" the President prompted impatiently.

"I think we're facing a small number of uncommonly skillful and resourceful terrorists. Probably with military training or experience. And, given their choice of targets, their political orientation seems clear." Leiter shook his head glumly. "But I seriously doubt they're in our files as active members of existing neo-Nazi organizations. We're checking out every possible suspect anyway, but so far, we're coming up empty."

"What about a foreign connection?" Admiral Andrew Dillon, the Chairman of the Joint Chiefs, asked. "I understand your agents have been investigating a possible tie-in to Germany's neo-Nazi organizations."

"That's correct, Admiral." The FBI Director nodded toward his counterpart from the CIA. "With help from Bill's people we've been trying to rule the possibility in or out."

"Have you made any progress?"

"Nothing significant. At least not so far." Leiter shrugged. "Several hundred thousand Germans visit the U.S. every year on business or as tourists. That's rather a large haystack to hunt through for what must be a very small needle."

"Terrific, Mr. Leiter," the President ground out. "Do you have *any* good news to report—or just more about all the things you *don't* know?"

The tiniest flash of irritation crossed the FBI Director's face, but then vanished beneath a bland mask. "Some good news, Mr. President. Our investigative teams are just beginning to work the Chicago crime scene, but we do have a few leads in the National Press Club bombing."

"What kind of leads?"

Leiter started ticking them off one by one. "First, we've been able to track the explosives used to their point of origin—a manufacturer in Arizona. One of Special Agent Flynn's teams is combing through their records right now—"

"To find the buyer?" the President interrupted.

"Possibly." Leiter shrugged. Privately, he doubted the people they were up against would have made so elementary an error. He fully expected to learn that the C4 plastique had been purchased by a dummy corporation with a forged certificate. But it seemed impolitic at the moment to explain his low expectations on that score. He pushed ahead. "We've also definitely identified key components of the various explosive devices—electrical cabling, shards of electronics junction boxes, and pieces of a rigged VCR and video camera."

The President looked closely at him. "And that's significant?"

Leiter nodded. "Yes, sir. For example, Flynn informs me that his experts have concluded the bombs were *manually* armed."

"So the son of a bitch was there? Right in the room?"

The FBI Director nodded again. "Yes, sir. The various devices were concealed among all the other television and radio equipment in the room."

"Were your investigators able to pick any prints off the debris?" the CIA Director, William Berns, asked softly.

"Two," Leiter confirmed. "One thumbprint. And one partial from an index finger. Both off what was left of the video camera case." He saw the surprise on the other faces in the Cabinet

Room and explained. "Fingerprints often survive even the intense temperatures and pressures in an explosion. If the bomber has ever had a run-in with the law or served in the military, for example, we should be able to identify him—given enough time at least."

For the first time in the meeting so far, the President's features relaxed slightly. "Anything else so far, David?"

Leiter nodded. "Yes, sir. Some of the lettering on the camera case also came through the blast intact. The letters ECNS. We think that stands for 'European Cable News Service.'"

"And?"

Berns, the CIA Director, answered that. "We checked, Mr. President. No such organization exists. It's a complete fabrication."

"Shit," the President muttered.

Leiter took up the tale. "But that does confirm that the bomber gained access to the press club by posing as either a technician or a correspondent. Flynn's people are busy interviewing all the survivors again, looking for anybody who might have seen this person. If we can work up a good physical description from what they tell us, we can plaster it over every square inch of this country."

The President nodded his understanding. "Keep Flynn and his team hard at it then, David." His mouth tightened. "I want results I can take to the nation. And soon."

"Excuse me, Mistah President." Jefferson T. Corbell's soft Georgia drawl cut through the murmurs of agreement from everybody else around the table. He stabbed a slender finger at the television. It was still showing pictures of looters roaming Chicago's smoke-filled streets. "Catching these people is all well and good, but what the country wants to know—right now—is what you're going to do about *that*."

"True enough, Jeff," the President said reluctantly. It was no secret that he preferred prolonged and theoretical discussions to hard decision-making. He looked around the room. "Both the mayor of Chicago and the governor of Illinois have officially requested federal troops to help restore order in the martial-law zone. I need your views on that." He glanced at the white-haired Chairman of the Joint Chiefs. "Admiral Dillon?"

Dillon sat up straighter. "I've conferred with the Army's Chief of Staff, General Carleton. He informs me that we could have a full mechanized infantry battalion from the 1st Infantry Division at Fort Riley on the ground in the city within twenty-four hours, with the rest of a brigade in place in two days."

"What about the 82nd Airborne or the 101st?" the President asked, clearly somewhat surprised by their omission. "Aren't they part of the contingency force?"

"Yes, sir," the admiral answered patiently. "And that is why General Carleton would prefer to use the 1st Infantry. Both the 82nd and the 101st are our immediate reserve against a crisis somewhere overseas. Committing either one to a domestic peacekeeping role would measurably strain our readiness."

"I see." The President sounded unconvinced. His limited experience of military operations had taught him that the American people were reassured by the sight of the two elite divisions swinging into action. Their use was also a clear signal of serious intent and firm resolve.

Shaking her head vigorously, the Attorney General leaned forward. "Mr. President, I strongly advise against sending federal troops to Chicago. It would be provocative and an unnecessary infringement of civil liberties." She frowned at the television. "Frankly, I believe both the mayor and the governor have already overreacted badly—turning a peaceful demonstration into a full-fledged riot. Committing Regular Army units to the fray would only compound that error."

Corbell made sure the President could see him and nodded slightly, privately signaling his own agreement with the Attorney General's heated comments. The Georgian kept his own reasoning quiet. Though the alliance had been frayed by the lack of progress so far against these radical white-power terrorists, black Americans were still one of the administration's most loyal constituencies. Seeing federal soldiers shooting black Americans in the streets of Chicago would only inflame an important political bloc they would need desperately in the next election.

"What are you proposing, then, Sarah?" the President asked sharply.

"I suggest that we focus on the real enemy here—the radical right. They're the real menace—not the inner-city poor. So I propose a renewed push by you for much tighter gun laws. This is a golden opportunity to move our legislation through the Congress." Carpenter's eyes gleamed. "After all, if we can disarm the crazies, we'll solve most of this terrorism problem—once and for all."

She shrugged. "Beyond that and pressing the FBI's ongoing investigations forward at a rapid pace, I see no need to panic."

Along the Potomac, near Georgetown

(D MINUS 32)

Two miles west of the White House, the quarter-mile-wide Potomac River drifted lazily past a wooded northern shore. A national park established to preserve the remnants of the historic Chesapeake & Ohio Canal separated the capital city's elegant and exclusive Georgetown district from the river. Across the expanse of slow-moving water, the modern steel and glass skyscrapers of Rosslyn, Virginia, dominated the southern skyline.

On mild days, the clerks, waitresses, and waiters who worked in Georgetown's trendy boutiques, antique stores, and restaurants found the canal park and the Potomac waterfront a pleasant place to eat lunch or read a book. But it would be far too cold for that today. Even the light breeze coming off the river intensified the chill. The weak sun was blocked by scattered high-altitude clouds, giving the morning light a gray, thin quality.

Sefer Halovic sat with studied calm in the back seat of their chosen transport for this operation—a black Ford Econoline van. Ali Nizrahim sat next to him, nervously glancing out the side windows from time to time. Nizrahim was a light-skinned Iranian, a small man with long experience in the use of special weapons. Khalil Yassine, their Palestinian driver and scout, was behind the wheel. They were parked facing the exit of the small car lot near the tree-lined Chesapeake & Ohio Canal. Only the steady rumble of rush-hour traffic heading into downtown Washington along the elevated Whitehurst Freeway broke the early morning stillness.

Yassine had stolen the Econoline in Maryland the night before. Now it bore North Carolina license plates—stolen weeks before and held in readiness for just such a use.

All three men were dressed in jeans, running shoes, and dark-colored winter jackets. All wore black gloves. Their outfits were effectively anonymous, devoid of anything distinctive that might draw attention to them now or that potential witnesses might remember later.

Both Halovic and Nizrahim carried 9mm pistols in shoulder holsters under their jackets. Yassine had their heavier small-arms firepower hidden beneath the empty seat beside him—an Israeli-made Mini-Uzi with a twenty-round magazine. With luck, Halovic thought grimly, none of their personal weapons would prove necessary. The park had been empty at this time and in similar weather on previous days.

Besides his sidearm, the Bosnian also carried a small walkie-talkie clipped to his belt. It was tuned to National Airport's Air Traffic Control frequency, but right now it wasn't producing much beyond static and the occasional squawk. Yassine had a larger tactical radio with better reception up front, and he wore headphones that helped cut out background noise. His radio was tuned to the same frequency.

Halovic laid a hand on the two long green tubes propped up against the seat beside him. He stroked the cold metal appreciatively. These were the real reason they were here.

He shifted slightly and checked his watch. This was ordinarily a busy time for the airport as the early morning flights from all over the country began arriving with planeloads of families bent on touring their nation's capital, government workers on assignment, and lobbyists determined to shape laws for their clients. The timetable for this mission was fairly precise— molded by the minimum intervals between incoming flights and their scheduled arrival times. But Halovic also knew that the vagaries of weather and mechanical malfunction could throw the timetable off.

That was why he'd kept the plan simple.

Yassine looked up sharply, with one hand held to his head-phones. He glanced into the back seat. "We have one! He just turned on to final." The Palestinian quickly craned his head, scanning the area around them again. "All clear!"

Halovic nodded and slid the Econoline's side door open. He hopped out onto the asphalt and pulled first one and then the other of the shoulder-fired surface-to-air missiles off the seat. They weighed more than thirty pounds apiece. Nizrahim scooted out beside him as soon as the way was clear. Each man grabbed a tube and sprinted toward the water's edge.

Halovic's walkie-talkie came to life. This time he heard a fragment of the air traffic controller's conversation through the static. "Roger, Northwest Flight Three-Five-Two. We have you four miles north and west. You're cleared for Runway One-Eight . . ."

Barely two minutes out from the airport, the Bosnian realized, mentally calculating the incoming jetliner's position and likely bearing. He thumbed a safety switch on the missile launcher. It took about five seconds for the nitrogen in a small sphere to cool the missile's infrared seeker. He was rewarded with a low buzzing growl from the weapon as he ran. The system was ready to fire.

The Bosnian and his Iranian subordinate reached the shore in seconds, only slightly winded by their short dash.

Halovic searched the sky rapidly. Nothing. He turned more to his front and relaxed as he saw the bright red plane there, hang-ing in the air against the tall skyscrapers of the urban northern Virginia skyline.

Northwest Flight 352

Northwest Airlines Flight 352 was a Boeing 757, a twin-jet airliner with a crew of nine and more than one hundred passengers aboard. Captain Jim Freeman, the senior pilot, had been in the air almost six hours since starting his day in Denver. His red-eye flight had landed in Minneapolis–St. Paul for a one-hour stop before continuing on to Washington, D.C.

So far the weather had been fair and the flying without incident. Now Freeman knew he had only the always difficult landing ahead before calling it quits for the day. He was scheduled to take another flight out to Detroit early the next morning.

National Airport lay on the western side of the Potomac River, just south of the center of the District of Columbia. Because of the many sensitive and historic sites in the capital city, jetliners approaching from the west flew first over the northern Virginia suburbs near Tysons Corner before swinging southeast toward the capital city. Just over the Georgetown Reservoir they always made a sharp turn south to follow the Potomac in a slow, winding approach that taxed any pilot's skill.

Freeman kept both eyes and all his attention on the job at hand while his copilot, Susan Lewis, ran through the landing checklist. He was a former Navy attack pilot, and right now he missed the heads-up displays and sophisticated electronics of frontline military aircraft. Putting the 757 down safely on one of National's notoriously short runways required a precision juggling act involving altitude, speed, and distance.

Getting something that goes very fast to slow down safely and quickly is a delicate task. While a Boeing 757 cruised at 450 knots, its approach speed was only 130 knots—just above stall speed. Any loss of power, any maneuver that slowed the plane too much, would drop it right out of the sky.

Add to this low altitude. Any problem in the air usually means losing altitude, so height gives a pilot time to act. But Freeman's aircraft, caught in the landing pattern, was only a thousand feet up.

Three miles out from National Airport, Northwest Flight 352 was low and slow.

Along the Potomac

Sefer Halovic had spotted the passenger jet when it was almost abreast of him, passing from right to left. Now he raised the SAM launcher to his shoulder and pressed his eye against the sight.

The Boeing 757 leaped into view. The Bosnian knew he had only seconds to fire. The missile had a decent range, but when fired from behind, its effective range dropped because it was chasing the target.

He held the airliner in the center of the crosshairs and heard a buzz from a small speaker in the sight. The buzz became stronger and higher-pitched, verifying that the missile seeker had locked onto the 757's heat signature.

Halovic fought the urge to pull the trigger instantly. Instead he pressed a switch that "uncaged" the heat seeker. Now the infrared sensor would pivot freely inside the missile's nose, and he didn't have to hold the missile precisely on target.

He angled the SAM launcher upward at the nearly forty-five-degree angle needed to make sure the missile cleared the ground after firing. The buzz continued. At last, sure that the seeker still had a solid lock on the airliner, he pulled the trigger.

A dense, choking cloud of gray and white smoke enveloped him, and the echoing roar made by the rocket tearing skyward seemed incredibly loud—more appropriate for a battlefield than a peaceful park. Through the clearing smoke, he looked for Nizrahim and saw the Iranian also sighting on the airliner, still as a statue.

Nizrahim's finger twitched, and he, too, disappeared in a thick acrid cloud. The second SAM streaked aloft—a small bright dot at the end of a curving white smoke trail.

Halovic's own missile was already closing on the lumbering airliner.

NATO designated the shoulder-fired, heat-seeking SAMs they were using as SA-16s. The Russians who had designed the system called it the Igla-1, the Needle.

The missiles used in this attack were manufactured by the North Koreans, not the Russians. Iran had bought Igla-1s and training equipment from the Russians for its Army, but those purchases were aboveboard and easily traced. The North Koreans, experts at selling arms to nations who valued their privacy, had exported others to the war-torn Balkans. And once in that chaotic region, Taleh's agents had found it easy to covertly appropriate one of the shipments intended for the Bosnian Serbs.

Little more than a four-foot tube with an attached sight and grip, the Igla-1 was a popular design. It had first entered Russian service in the early 1980s and was a great improvement over earlier shoulder-fired SAMs. The missile could attack a target from any angle, and its seeker was sophisticated enough to ignore some early forms of IR jamming and decoy flares. The weapon's chief flaw was its small warhead, just a few pounds of high-explosive, but Iglas had shot down coalition warplanes during DESERT STORM and NATO attack aircraft in the Balkans.

Compared to a wildly maneuvering military jet, an undefended passenger airliner flying straight and slow made a perfect target.

Halovic stood motionless, still holding the now-useless missile launcher. By rights, he and Nizrahim should be back in the van, speeding away from the scene. This waiting was foolish—even dangerous.

But he had to stay. He had to know if the missiles worked. He had been trained well enough to know how many ways the weapon could fail. And so, like two children watching a model plane fly for the first time, Halovic and Nizrahim stood, immobile, watching their SAMs arcing in for the kill.

Northwest Flight 352

WHAMM.

Captain Jim Freeman's first sign of trouble was a loud bang from the left and behind. The 757 shuddered abruptly, bouncing around in the air as though its port wing had slammed into something. Startled, he checked the altimeter. That was impossible. They were over the river and still at a thousand feet.

The pilot's eyes raced over the array of gauges and dials, looking for the problem. Lord. There it was. The rpm gauge on the port engine was dropping fast. The 757 dipped left, and its airspeed began falling.

Freeman instinctively pushed his throttles forward, increasing power to both engines. He snapped out a quick, "Power loss on the port engine, Sue!"

"Understood." Susan, his copilot, stopped monitoring the plane's altitude and distance from the runway and started a frantic check of her instruments. That bang suggested an explosion of some sort, but it was better to go by the numbers. Her eyes flicked first to the fuel flow gauge. No problem there . . .

The 757's port wing was still dropping.

Freeman clicked his radio mike. "National, this is Three-Five-Two. Declaring emergency. Repeat, declaring . . ."

WHAMM.

Another explosion rattled the plane, but this time the resulting shudder went on and on, growing rapidly worse. Both Freeman and Lewis heard a wrenching, tearing screech from the wing.

Halovic's SAM had functioned perfectly, literally flying up the tailpipe of the airliner's port engine before exploding. Fragments from the blast damaged the afterstages of the compressor fan, resulting in a rapid power loss. But jet engines are relatively tough, and the plane could still have landed safely.

Nizrahim's missile finished the job.

The Igla-1 blew up only a few feet from the port engine pod.

Pieces of shrapnel peppered the pod's metal skin and sliced into the engine inside. They cut the fuel line and wrecked the digital controls, but most important, they weakened the afterstage of the compressor fan again. Spinning at more than ten thousand revolutions per minute, the fan tore itself and the rest of the engine apart.

Freeman saw the port engine gauges run wild and then go dead. Still fighting the wing as it dropped, he looked aft and saw the ruin of the port engine, now little more than a pylon with sharp-edged scraps of metal attached. Damn it.

"Give me full power on the right!" Freeman screamed. He strained on the control yoke, trying to get the port wing up. They were sliding off to the left, veering off course toward downtown Washington. He could see the gleaming white roof of the Lincoln Memorial ahead. Oh, Christ.

He silently cursed their slow speed. They were too close to the ragged edge of the 757's envelope. The shattered engine pylon was now a liability instead of an asset, creating drag instead of power.

"Gear up!" he shouted.

"It's already up," Lewis replied desperately. She'd raised the wheels in an effort to reduce the drag.

Behind them, they could hear shouts and screaming through the bulkhead. "Pass the word back to brace for impact."

Freeman had reached the end of a distressingly short list of things to try. He looked at their airspeed. Still falling. They weren't going to make the runway.

Along the Potomac

Halovic followed the dying 757 with satisfaction. The airliner was lower now, and canted to the left. Black smoke trailed from its damaged wing, and even at this distance he could see the shattered left engine.

"Oh, my God!"

The horrified shout from behind them brought the Bosnian out of his trance. He whirled around and saw a tall, stout, middle-aged man in a tan topcoat staring upward at the stricken plane. A small dog, a tiny white poodle, tugged unnoticed at the leash in the American's hand.

The man's eyes flashed from the falling aircraft to the SAM launchers still on their shoulders. Horror turned to sudden, appalled knowledge and then to terror. He dropped the leash and turned to flee.

Alexander Phipps had not run anywhere in his life for years. The wealth accumulated over a lifetime of shrewd business dealing had ensured that other people did the running—not him. Now all that money meant nothing.

Gasping in panic, he dodged off the canal park path and crashed into the trees. He heard shots behind him and felt a slug rip past his ear. It seemed to pull him along and he ran faster. Another bullet gouged splinters off a tree in front of him.

Phipps skidded on the wet grass and fell forward onto his hands and knees. An impact from behind threw him facedown in a flood of searing, white-hot pain. The world around him darkened and vanished.

Halovic watched the American shudder and lie still. It had been Nizrahim's shot that felled him.

The Iranian trotted over to the slumped figure and fired once more—this time into the man's head. Then he calmly holstered his weapon and walked back toward Halovic. He stopped a few feet away and asked flatly, "What about the dog?"

The little white poodle had emerged from its hiding place and now stood nuzzling its fallen master, whimpering softly. The Bosnian shrugged. "Leave it."

He turned away, striding toward the missile launchers they'd thrown aside to hunt down the dead man. It was time they were on their way.

Northwest Flight 352

The crippled airliner was down to three hundred feet above the Potomac.

Freeman yanked desperately on his controls and felt the 757 roll right a hair—not much, not more than a couple of degrees. It was just barely enough.

The white bulk of the Lincoln Memorial flashed past the cockpit's portside window and vanished astern. They were heading back for the center of the river. Then he felt the controls go mushy under his hands and grimaced. He was out of airspeed and out of options.

The jetliner dipped again, sagging toward the water.

Susan Lewis screamed suddenly, staring straight ahead.

Freeman looked up and saw the long, gray, car-choked span of the Fourteenth Street Bridge filling the entire width of the cockpit windscreen. He sighed softly. "Oh, shit."

Northwest Flight 352 slammed nose-first into the bridge at more than one hundred knots and exploded.

The Pentagon

The thundering, prolonged sound of the titanic blast barely half a mile away penetrated even the thick concrete walls of the Pentagon's outer ring.

On his way back down to the ILU's Dungeon after another unsuccessful sparring match with his counterparts in other DOD intelligence outfits, Colonel Peter Thorn paused with his hand on the staircase and stood listening. What the devil was that?

A young naval rating thundering down the stairs behind him supplied the answer. "A passenger jet just hit the Fourteenth Street Bridge, sir! Saw it out my window!"

The young man kept going.

Jesus. Thorn stood stunned for a split second and then took off after the sailor, taking the stairs down two at a time. He didn't stop to think about it. If anybody on either the plane or the bridge had survived the impact, they were going to need help, and soon.

By the time he reached the ground floor, the hallway was filling up with dozens of men and women, most in uniform, some in civilian clothes. All were racing toward the Pentagon's northeastern exit, the one closest to the crash site. He joined them.

A blinding cloud of thick black smoke hid most of the Fourteenth Street Bridge from view until Thorn crested the highway embankment and gained a clear line of sight. What he saw was worse than anything he had imagined.

Orange and red flames danced across the entire length and width of the span, fed by thousands of gallons of spilled aviation fuel and gasoline. The cars and trucks that had once crowded the bridge were unrecognizable—mere heaps and lumps of blackened, torn, and twisted metal. The impact itself had gouged an enormous crater out of the roadway at the midpoint across the Potomac. Only one scorched wing of the passenger jet remained visible—obscenely protruding above the water near a buckled bridge support like a giant shark's fin.

A small cadre of Pentagon security officers, Virginia state troopers, and U.S. park policemen were already on the scene, frantically and futilely trying to fight the nearest fires with handheld extinguishers. More and more civilians from the vehicles bottlenecked on the jammed highway were rushing forward to lend a helping hand.

Against all Thorn's expectations, there were survivors emerging from the tangled chaos on the bridge. He could see them stumbling and staggering toward safety. Most were bleeding, their clothing in tatters. A few were on fire—human torches running madly in agonized circles amid terrifying shrieks and screams. People dashed toward them carrying coats and blankets to douse the flames.

Beneath the smoke pall, the kerosene-stained waters of the Potomac bubbled as debris from the sunken fragments of the airliner's fuselage broke free and popped to the surface. Bright orange flotation seat cushions, jagged pieces of cabin ceiling insulation, and other unidentifiable odds and ends bobbed in the river.

Thorn came to the western end of the mangled bridge and stopped, staring downward into the black fog, straining to see clearly. Was that someone out in the water, drifting facedown in the midst of all the other debris? He caught a flash of long golden hair and made his decision without conscious thought. Nobody else was in a position to see what he saw or to act in time.

He stripped off his uniform jacket, kicked off his shoes, and dove straight into the Potomac—straight down into the black, icy waters.

For a terrible instant, Thorn feared the frigid cold had paralyzed him—that he would never taste the air again. But a single frantic kick brought him to the surface. He sucked in a welcome lungful of oxygen and spat out the sickeningly sweet taste of the jet fuel clogging his mouth and nostrils. Then he started swimming, covering the distance toward the bobbing head he'd glimpsed so faintly with a powerful crawl stroke. As he swam, he tried to keep his bearings with quick glances toward the shattered bridge.

Twenty yards. Forty. He was starting to tire now, weighed down by the cold, the water saturating his shirt and trousers, and the kerosene burning its way down into his lungs. Where was she? Had she already been dragged under?

Thorn pushed a charred seat cushion out of his path and began treading water, pushing himself above the surface as he spun slowly, peering in all directions. There! He spotted the tangle of golden hair drifting just a few yards away.

He lunged out and grabbed the floating woman from behind. With his right arm locked around her chest to pull her face out of the water, he used his left to turn around and kicked out for shore, sculling vigorously against the slow current pushing him down toward the burning Fourteenth Street Bridge. The distance, the icy cold, and the weight dragging at his hip all fused in one long, nightmarish journey without a clear beginning and without a visible end.

Thorn could barely move by the time he reached the shallows. He was only dimly aware of the sudden rush of volunteers who came thrashing into the Potomac to help him out onto the long grass at the water's edge. He lay shuddering for long moments, gasping for air. When an Air Force sergeant knelt down to drape a spare jacket over his shoulders, he recovered enough to lever himself to his knees.

"What about the woman? Is someone helping her?" he heard himself ask hoarsely.

The sergeant's face fell and he looked away. "I'm sorry, Colonel," he said softly. "It was no good, sir. You couldn't have done anything for her. No one could have."

Thorn stared past the noncom to where the blond-haired passenger lay faceup, staring blindly at the sky. She was quite young, he realized. And quite pretty. But there was nothing left below her thighs but a few dangling scraps of bloodless flesh.

On the Virginia shore, near the Fourteenth Street Bridge

The rescue crews were still hard at it well into the night, working under hastily rigged floodlights to gather corpses and personal effects. Park Police and Coast Guard patrol boats motored back and forth across the searchlight-lit Potomac as they fished more bodies and more debris out of the river. Teams of divers in heavy wet suits were already conducting a coordinated search for the aircraft's black boxes—the 757's flight data and voice recorders.

Helen Gray climbed wearily out of the official car she'd borrowed and made her way slowly down the steep embankment. The smell of burned metal and flesh hung everywhere—in the air, on the roadway, on the grass, and in her clothes and hair. Earlier during that long, terrible day, she'd led a cadre of FBI volunteers in desperate rescue efforts on the D.C. side of the river. Now she'd taken the longer way around via the still-intact Memorial Bridge to find the man she loved.

Exhausted soldiers still plainly shaken by what they had witnessed directed her toward a small clump of senior officers gathered near the water's edge.

One, a gray-haired Navy captain, nodded when she asked after Peter. "Colonel Thorn? Yeah. He's around here somewhere, ma'am." He looked up, squinting further down the riverbank against the floodlights. Then he pointed toward a lone figure staring out across the water. "That's him."

Helen nodded her thanks and moved on.

Peter Thorn looked up at her approach. His drawn face held a look of anger and sorrow stronger than any she had ever seen before. "This was deliberate?" he asked grimly.

She nodded. "Several hundred eyewitnesses have reported seeing two or three distinct missile trails merging with the plane. And we know where the terrorists fired from. The canal park. They killed an innocent bystander there. We found the body this afternoon."

His jaw tightened.

"I'm afraid it gets worse, Peter," she said gently. "Somebody blew up the main fuel storage tanks at Dallas/Fort Worth International two hours ago. Several hundred thousand gallons of jet fuel went up in seconds. They're still trying to fight the fires and make some estimate of the damage and casualties, but it's pretty bad."

She paused briefly before delivering the rest of her news.

"The local papers here and in Dallas have already had phone calls claiming responsibility for both attacks. They seem genuine."

"From the goddamned New Aryan Order?"

Helen shook her head. "No. These came from a group called the African Liberation Front. They claimed they were retaliating against the 'Nazi white establishment.' "

"Christ. That's all we need." Peter looked away again, out toward the floodlit river. His eyes were full of pain. "I became a soldier to fight the kind of bastards who would do something like this. The kind who shoot down airliners full of women and kids just to make some lousy political point. But now it's happening right here at home, and I can't do a single thing to stop it."

She moved closer, into the circle of his arms. "I know," she said softly.

He held her tighter, softly stroking her hair—taking what comfort he could from her presence and her warmth.

CHAPTER 15
REACTION TIME

NOVEMBER 15

JSOC headquarters, North Carolina

Officers from three separate services and several different units filled the JSOC's main conference room. Delta Force officers mingled with their counterparts from the Navy's SEAL Team Six, the Air Force's air commando units, the Army's Ranger forces, and the 160th Special Operations Aviation Regiment, the Night Stalkers. While they waited for Major General Sam Farrell to appear, they chatted quietly among themselves, exchanging theories about why they had been summoned on such short notice.

Colonel Peter Thorn finished talking to Bill Henderson, his successor at Delta's A Squadron, and moved off toward the water cooler. His throat still hurt from the kerosene he'd swallowed in the Potomac, but the Pentagon doctors had cleared him for continued duty, with the sternly worded proviso that he significantly increase his fluid intake for the next seventy-two hours.

"Attention."

The single, crisp order cut off every conversation in midsentence. Every man turned toward the entrance to the conference room and came to attention.

The commander of the JSOC appeared there suddenly, flanked by his top operations officer, Colonel Raymond Ziegler. The general had a grim, set expression on his face. Ziegler's face was studiously blank.

Farrell waved them into the chairs surrounding a long, rectangular conference table. "Please take your seats, gentlemen. We have a lot of ground to cover this afternoon."

The general strode to the head of the table while Thorn and the other officers found their assigned places. He didn't waste any time on the regular briefing platitudes. "I just got off the phone with the Joint Chiefs. As of 1500 hours today, all elements of this command are on full alert. All leaves have been canceled, and my staff is already issuing an immediate recall order to all affected personnel."

Despite the earlier speculation, Thorn was surprised. Before he'd flown down to Pope Air Force Base earlier that morning he'd seen no signs of unusual activity at the Pentagon that might explain this sudden order. Washington's policy makers, the FBI, and the American people were still in a state of shock over the twin disasters at Dallas/Fort Worth and National Airport. Had someone stumbled across the headquarters of a terrorist cell big enough to warrant all this military attention?

Farrell's next words dashed that faint hope. "Gentlemen, the President has authorized a number of emergency measures in a coordinated effort to safeguard air travel over the capital and this country's other major cities. This operation has been designated SAFE SKIES."

The general was careful to keep his tone neutral, but Thorn could sense that he disagreed with aspects of the plan he was busy laying before them. He'd known Sam Farrell for too long to be taken in by his poker face. "As approved by the White House this morning, Operation SAFE SKIES has several key provisions.

"First, effective immediately, the FAA has prohibited all private flights into and out of the Washington, D.C., area.

"Second, the government is exerting pressure on the airlines to sharply curtail the number of commercial flights in and out of both National and Dulles. Similar measures will be applied to all airports of significant size across the United States."

Thorn and several other officers around the table whistled softly in amazement. Disrupting the normal flow of civilian air traffic to that extent for any length of time would seriously affect the national economy. Certainly, it would cost the airlines, commercial freight companies, and a host of other businesses dearly in lost revenue and efficiency.

"Third, the Air Force will begin an around-the-clock program to retrofit commercial jetliners with the jammer and flare dispenser systems already used by our military transport aircraft."

That, too, was astounding. On a per-plane basis, the costs of such modifications were not exorbitant, Thorn knew, but the total cost of such a program would be enormous. The U.S. airlines alone operated around five thousand passenger jets.

Farrell paused to let the magnitude of the planned federal effort sink in before continuing. If anything, the expression on his face grew even more dour. "These measures are designed to make our job in this operation more manageable."

Thorn shifted closer to the edge of his seat. What role could the military's special forces possibly play in this expensive extravaganza? The steps the administration planned were reactive—not proactive.

"The President signed a special National Security Action Directive this morning, gentlemen," Farrell said with emphasis. "And NSAD-15 authorizes the use of the armed forces within the continental United States to carry out the objectives of Operation SAFE SKIES. Under that directive, we have been ordered to deploy units of Delta Force, SEAL Team Six, and the Night Stalkers to northern Virginia, Maryland, and the Washington metropolitan region."

Thorn glanced to the left and right. The faces of the officers in view all mirrored his own confusion. What the hell did the White House have in mind?

Farrell answered their unspoken questions in a flat, official voice. "Using ground surveillance teams, helicopter sweeps, and quick-reaction forces, we will be responsible for securing designated air corridors into both Dulles and National airports." He held up a hand to still the sudden buzz. "Units of the 101st Air Assault Division and the Army and Air National Guard will conduct similar security sweeps around all the other major airports—Dallas/Fort Worth, Chicago's O'Hare, LAX, and the rest.

"That's the short and sweet of it, gentlemen." The general nodded to his chief operations officer. "Colonel Ziegler will brief you on the details in a moment. But before he begins, does anyone have any preliminary questions or comments?"

"I do, sir." Thorn spoke up first. Unlike the other men in the room, he didn't hold a field command—not at the moment at least. He had less of immediate value to lose by speaking bluntly. "May I speak frankly?"

Farrell nodded. "Always, Pete."

"Well, sir, first of all, this is not the right mission for our troops. Delta and the SEALs are trained as hard-hitting assault forces, not as glorified military police outfits. Using them this way does not make good military sense."

The general's face was impassive. "Anything else, Colonel Thorn?"

"Yes, sir. You know what the areas near most of those airports are like. Christ, around D.C., it's a mix of heavily wooded countryside and heavily congested population centers." Thorn shook his head decisively. "Under those conditions, there's no conceivable way that a few hundred soldiers and a few dozen helicopters can adequately secure enough ground against terrorists equipped with handheld SAMs. All we'll succeed in doing is dispersing a large part of the troops and equipment we may need later somewhere else."

There were murmurs of agreement from around the table.

"What's worse, sir, is that I'm convinced this whole operation is way too late," Thorn said flatly. "From what we've seen so far, the terrorists conducting these attacks are too damned good to risk sticking their necks into a highly publicized buzz saw. They'll move on to safer targets instead. I'm afraid we're going to wind up guarding the barn door while these bastards are burning down the farmhouse!"

Farrell said nothing for several seconds, leaving Thorn to wonder briefly whether he had finally gone too far. Delta and the other special forces units operated with a high degree of informality away from outsiders and behind closed doors, but a two-star was a two-star was a two-star.

At last, the general simply shook his head. "I understand your concerns, Pete. I know for a fact that some of them have been raised at higher levels. But I also know what's politically possible and what's not in this situation. Right now, the President wants action ASAP and he wants it from us. And the Chiefs aren't going to get in his way to let us off the hook. So we're all just going to have to shut up and soldier—and pray for the chance to do things the right way when it counts. Is that clear?"

Thorn knew the only possible answer to that. "Yes, sir. Perfectly clear."

NOVEMBER 16

Andrews Air Force Base, near Washington, D.C.

A C-141 transport touched down on the main runway at Andrews Air Force Base and taxied slowly toward the four other Starlifters already parked on the tarmac. Dozens of reporters and cameramen were on hand to record the first military movements in the administration's highly choreographed and scripted Operation SAFE SKIES.

Soldiers in black coveralls, Kevlar helmets, and body armor trotted out of two of the C-141s, forming up facing away from the reporters with the easy grace of disciplined troops. Even in the full glare of publicity guaranteed by their dramatic arrival, the officers and men of Delta Force's B Squadron wanted to keep their faces off television.

Air Force and Army crewmen swarmed near the open rear cargo ramps of the other Starlifters, readying for flight the twelve small helicopters they had ferried in, the MH-6 transports and AH-6 attack craft belonging to Delta's own aviation company. More helicopters belonging to the 160th Aviation Regiment were scheduled to arrive on transports throughout the night.

NOVEMBER 17

Tehran

(D MINUS 28)

MOST SECRET
General Staff, Armed Forces of the Islamic Republic of Iran
Operations Order 4

FROM: Chief of Staff
TO: CINC, Army
    CINC, Air Force
    CINC, Navy

SITUATION UPDATE:

Recent news reports confirm earlier indications of large-scale troop movements within the boundaries of the United States. The American political authorities are reacting as we predicted. Most significantly, the Americans are dispersing essential elements of their special warfare and rapid-reaction force structure—units of their elite 101st Division and the Delta Force commando battalion. These formations are being committed piecemeal to security details stationed in major American cities. Effectively, they are chasing ghosts.

ORDERS:

1. All units slated for SCIMITAR should be brought immediately to full operational readiness.

2. First-wave formations should begin moving to their preassigned assembly areas NO LATER THAN 3 December.

CHAPTER 16
OVERLOAD

NOVEMBER 21

Anaheim, California

(D MINUS 24)

Newly refurbished as part of an ongoing corporate effort to maintain the glamour and profitability of Disney's oldest theme park, the Disneyland Hotel stood as a tribute to the power of "imagineering" and the American love of glitter and fun. The "guests"—mostly parents with small children and teenagers—heading for the monorail ride to the park itself were brought to a fever pitch of excitement by their surroundings. They moved through a maze of enticing sights, smells, and sounds emanating from an array of restaurants and souvenir shops. Live entertainers—musicians, magicians, and actors inside larger-than-life character costumes—mingled with the crowds.

With an effort, Hassan Qalib concealed both his disgust and his amazement at the sight of so much godless luxury and so much waste. Everywhere the young Somali looked he saw excess and idolatry. Idolatry in the way these Americans taught their young to love and worship these mythical beasts, these cartoon characters. Excess in the half-eaten food they so casually discarded. The trash cans were full of hamburgers, hot dogs, french fries, and other foodstuffs that could have fed a family in Mogadishu for nearly a week.

Qalib caught sight of himself reflected in a storefront and scowled inwardly. He, too, appeared contaminated by this evil land and way of life. Three months on a typical American diet had added kilos of muscle and fat to a normally bony frame. The extra weight made him less conspicuous, but it also made him look bloated and alien when compared to the older self of memory.

To complete the masquerade as a park-goer, he wore typically American casual clothes: khaki slacks, brown loafers, and a light gray windbreaker over a more colorful Mickey Mouse–emblazoned sweatshirt. In his right hand he carried a large plastic bag full of gift-wrapped packages purchased several days ago from one of the hotel souvenir shops by another member of his special action cell.

Ahead of him the jostling crowds began forming lines as they approached a row of turnstiles and uniformed employees at the entrance to the Disneyland Hotel monorail station. He joined one of the lines.

With an effort, Qalib forced himself to smile politely as he showed a young white woman his Magic Kingdom passport. The ticket guaranteed him all-day admittance to the park and all its attractions. It also cost more than most people in his starving homeland earned in a month. The Somali was careful to smile with his mouth closed. Anyone who saw his stained and broken teeth would not have mistaken him for a college-age, middle-class American black man. She glanced at the passport and nodded him through the turnstile with a chirpy, impersonal "Have a nice day!"

Still smiling faintly, he took the stairs up to the platform and blended in with the other eager tourists waiting for the futuristic transport that would take them to the "happiest place on Earth."

He did not have to wait long.

The sleek bullet shape of the train came into sight almost immediately, gliding noiselessly along a gleaming monorail that ran above the vast Disneyland parking lot and crossed the street to the hotel station. Doors slid open as soon as it braked to a complete stop. People leaving the theme park disembarked in a chattering rush. Only a smattering of them, Qalib noted. The arriving train had been almost empty. That was good.

Once those leaving were clear of the platform, he and his fellow passengers were allowed to board. Each car held up to sixteen passengers, and the Somali chose one near the middle. A man and woman holding hands with a bright-eyed toddler took the seat facing him. The door hissed shut behind them.

Qalib ignored them, and concentrated instead on double-checking the routine the train attendants followed before departure. What he saw was reassuring. A single uniformed employee hurried down the row of compartments, hastily making sure the doors were properly secured. The young man paid little attention to anything or anyone else.

The Somali nodded to himself. Corporate cost-cutting had been shrinking Disneyland's total workforce for years. And now, with the start of the flu season, the park was said to be particularly shorthanded. That would make his task easier.

With a barely perceptible jerk, the monorail slid out of the station and accelerated toward Tomorrowland Station.

Several minutes later, after a rapid run around the back half of the park, the train braked as gently as it had accelerated, gliding to a stop at a platform overlooking a large artificial lagoon. The gray and white bulk of the Matterhorn loomed in the middle distance. The ride was somewhat shorter than he'd expected, Qalib realized, but still well within the time parameters laid down by his controller.

The Somali stayed behind when everybody else got off. Nobody paid much attention to him. Anyone with a valid ticket to the park could ride the monorail as many times as they wanted.

As he had hoped, there were only a handful of people waiting to board for the return trip. It was still early enough in the day so that tourists were pouring into Disneyland, not out of it. This time, as the train pulled out, he had the compartment all to himself.

Qalib swung into action, moving rapidly through an often-rehearsed series of actions. First he dipped into his windbreaker pocket and pulled out a tube of fast-drying epoxy. Then he reached under the top layer of gift-wrapped packages in his bag, took out a metal case painted to match the compartment interior, and set it on his lap. It was six inches long, six inches wide, and three inches high. "Property of Disneyland" had been stenciled across the case's outer face. There were adhesive strips attached to its underside.

He flipped the top open and pressed a button on a small digital watch attached to the inside front. Instantly, the display shifted from the current time to a preset number—and began counting down. A quick scan of the wires leading out from the improvised timer showed no loose connections. Satisfied, he shut the case and sealed the top with a blob of epoxy. That should stop any prying hands for the short time needed, he thought.

The young Somali glanced up from his work. The monorail was just beginning its long arc over the crowded Disneyland parking lot. Careful to keep his hands away from the adhesive, he leaned over, set the metal case against the compartment wall at his feet, and tamped it into place.

He slid across the monorail compartment, closer to the door, and surveyed his handiwork for a brief moment. Placed below eye level, the case blended fairly well with its surroundings. It should escape immediate notice.

The train began slowing. They were almost back to the hotel.

Qalib recapped the epoxy, dropped it into his bag, and stripped off his windbreaker. That was the easiest form of disguise. Whites could rarely tell blacks apart by their facial features. The station attendants should see no immediate connection between the gray-jacketed black man who'd gotten on the monorail only minutes before and the young man in a bright Mickey Mouse sweatshirt who was coming back.

When the doors slid open, the Somali walked unhurriedly toward the stairs, completely ignoring the milling crowds waiting to board. They were no longer his concern.

Ten-year-old Brian Tate mumbled a favorite swear word under his breath as his freely swinging ankles jarred painfully against that dorky raised bump that stuck out from the side of the compartment. He sneaked a fearful look toward his parents to see if they'd heard him. Nope. He relaxed. Both of them were way too busy pointing out the sights to his bratty younger brother and sister. They were crossing over that stupid submarine ride he'd taken two years ago. He sneered. You didn't see anything cool, he thought. Just swimming pool water and some stuffed fish. Even the submarines were on tracks.

Curious now, Brian bent over to inspect the wall. His hands brushed against the bump and came away sticky. This was definitely very weird. Whatever it was, it wasn't part of the train. It was a metal box.

The ten-year-old looked up. "Hey, Dad! Check this out . . ."

Inside Qalib's metal case, the timer blinked from 00:00:01 to 00:00:00.

Thirty feet over Tomorrowland, the Disneyland monorail exploded, torn from end to end by a powerful blast. A ball of fire pushing razor-edged shards of steel and aluminum roared outward in a searing, deadly tide that surged over the tightly packed people waiting in lines below and left them charred or broken and bleeding on the ground.

Most of the warped, burning remnants of the monorail were blown off the track and plunged hissing into the lagoon.

New Hope Baptist Church, near Churchill Downs, Louisville, Kentucky

The deep, joy-filled voices of the New Hope Baptist Church choir were loud enough to be heard in the parking lot outside the whitewashed, wood-frame church. A special night service full of prayers for civic and racial peace was in full swing. Other gatherings were planned later in the week in churches of other denominations. Louisville's religious and political leaders wanted to calm emotions that were boiling dangerously near the surface as racial attack after racial attack rocked the country.

To help keep the peace and make sure there were no ugly incidents, two officers from the Louisville police department sat in a parked patrol car outside the church.

Officer Joe Bailey listened to the music for a few moments before rolling his window shut. He grinned over at his rookie partner. "Fine singing, Hank. Mighty fine singing. Just kind of reaches down and picks your spirit right up, don't it?"

Hank Smith nodded politely without saying anything. Music was one of the things he and the older policeman would never agree on. His own tastes ran more to U2 than to country or gospel.

The younger man turned back to the pile of routine reports on his lap. Paperwork was always the bane of any cop's working life, especially when you had a sly old fox like Joe Bailey for a partner. Fifteen years with the Louisville police department had taught the older man every trick there was to avoiding work he didn't enjoy. Work like filling out arrest reports in the triplicate and quadruplicate so loved by bureaucrats.

Smith sighed under his breath. At least pulling guard duty outside a church on a quiet night offered him a chance to cut into the backlog a little. For several minutes, his pen scratched steadily onward through page after page, accompanied by the faint, off-key sound of Bailey humming and by the occasional crackle of voices over their car radio.

Halfway through one report, Smith stopped, his pen poised over a blank line. He sat chewing his lower lip absentmindedly while mentally running through the rules, regulations, and legal information he'd crammed in at the academy. Finally, he gave up. He turned toward the older man. "Say, Joe, what's the code for felonious—"

Bailey's head exploded. Blood and bits of brain matter blew

across the rookie policeman's horrified face. The older man shuddered once and slumped sideways across the seat with his bulging eyes fixed and staring at nothing. Bright red arterial blood spilled across the papers in Smith's lap.

The young policeman pulled his terrified gaze from the dead man at his side and turned slowly toward the shattered side window. A dark figure stood there just outside the patrol car, still, calm, and poised—a faceless man dressed in black from head to toe. Smith's eyes widened as he saw the pistol aimed at his forehead.

His mouth opened in a frantic, whispered plea. "No . . ."

The last thing Hank Smith saw on earth was a blinding burst of bright light.

Salah Madani lowered his silenced 9mm automatic and stared into the car's blood-spattered front seat for a moment. Neither of the two policemen showed any signs of life.

Sure now that they were dead, the Egyptian turned away and signaled the rest of his team into action. Four men wearing the same kind of black overalls and black ski masks to hide their features darted out of an alley and loped across the parking lot toward the New Hope Church. Two of them held shotguns at the ready, guarding another pair lugging heavy, bulging backpacks.

Madani stayed by the police car—ready to abort this mission at the first sign of trouble. Not that he expected any. Not now. America's cities averaged only two full-time law enforcement officers for every thousand or so of their citizens. Spread so thinly across such a vast population, the police simply could not be everywhere and protect everyone all the time. This would be even simpler and safer than his cell's earlier work in Dallas.

A soft whistle from the alley caught the Egyptian's attention, and he saw another figure in black there giving him a thumbs-up signal. Antonovic had finished setting his charges ahead of schedule.

Men and women and children dressed in their Sunday best packed every pew and aisle of the New Hope Baptist Church, swaying in time with the music as they sang. Sweat beaded up on shining faces and foreheads. With so many people crowded so close together, the temperature inside was climbing rapidly, but nobody wanted to break the spell—the overwhelming sense of fellowship and community—by opening the church doors or windows. Perhaps later, perhaps when the minister began his oration, they would seek comfort in the cool night air. For now, though, the congregation was content to stand and shout out its joy to the Lord in hymns of praise and celebration.

None of them heard the faint, muffled thump as an explosive charge knocked out an electrical switching station two blocks away.

The power went off in a five-block radius around the New Hope Baptist Church. Streetlights and homes went dark instantly. But the loss of electricity knocked out more than lights. It also disabled fire alarms and sprinkler systems.

Inside the church itself, the hymn stumbled to a stop in the sudden darkness. Voices rose in consternation as people called out for lights or for their husbands, wives, parents, and children. Other voices urged calm and asked everyone to stand still until the electricity came back on. Two of the ushers standing in the back tried to open the main doors to let the congregation filter outside.

They were chained shut.

Seconds later, the incendiary charges Madani's men had planted around the outside of the church began going off.

Washington, D.C.

Although it was close to midnight, most of the lights in the massive FBI headquarters building were on. More bright lights shone on the streets surrounding the imposing structure. Television crews from around the world were camped out there, relaying a constant stream of reports to their viewers about the progress, or lack of progress, of the FBI's special counterterrorist force. Normally, D.C.-area investigations were run out of the Washington Metropolitan Field Office at Buzzard Point on the Anacostia River. In a bid to present the public with a confidence-inducing backdrop, the FBI's powers-that-be had insisted that Special Agent Mike Flynn run his task force from the more imposing and accessible Hoover Building on Pennsylvania Avenue. As the weeks slid by without results, many of them were beginning to think that had been a mistake.

Just through the building's main doors, Colonel Peter Thorn finished signing in at the security desk and clipped a visitor's badge to his uniform jacket. "Where do I go now?" he asked.

A grim-faced guard slid his briefcase back across the desk and pointed toward a small open area near a bank of elevators. "Just wait there, sir. Agent Gray will be right down."

Thorn spent the next few minutes watching a sporadic stream of other visitors run through the maze of security precautions. Like every other important government building and military base, the Hoover Building was locked up tight—shielded from terrorist attacks by concrete barriers outside and metal detectors and armed guards inside. So far none of the right-wing or left-wing terrorist groups they were hunting had tried to target a secure installation, but no one was taking any chances.

Helen Gray stepped out of an arriving elevator into the waiting area. She smiled as soon as she saw him, but even the smile couldn't hide the fact that she was dead tired and deeply troubled. There were faint worry lines developing around her eyes.

Thorn knew that expression. It was the same look he saw on every face inside both the Pentagon and the Hoover Building. It was the same look he saw every morning in his mirror. It had been sixteen days since the first bomb blasts rocked the National Press Club. Sixteen days. And yet, despite the application of massive investigative manpower and every piece of advanced forensic technology at the FBI's disposal, they seemed no closer to solving any of the dizzying parade of terrorist attacks that were coming with increasing frequency. They were losing ground, not gaining it.

Helen stopped a few feet from him. "Hello, Peter," she said softly.

"Hi." Thorn struggled against the temptation to take her in his arms. They were on public ground and near the inner sanctum of her professional life. Flaunting their personal relationship inside the Hoover Building would only damage her hard-won credibility with her superiors. "I've got those patrol overlays you asked for."

"Great." She nodded toward the elevators. "We can go over them in my office, if you'd like."

"I'd like that a lot."

On paper, Thorn was here to help coordinate Delta Force's operations in and around Washington with the FBI's counterpart counterterrorist unit, the HRT. In reality, he hoped to obtain more hard data than he could glean from the PR-flack news briefings the Department of Justice held at irregular times. Virtually the only good thing about the administration's ill-conceived Operation SAFE SKIES was that it gave him a better excuse to prowl around inside the Bureau's hallowed halls. He was still looking for some way to make himself useful to his country in this snowballing crisis.

Helen led him into an elevator and punched the number for the floor set aside to hold Flynn's special counterterrorist task force. They rode up in a companionable silence. The security cameras and microphones visible on the car ceiling precluded any meaningful conversation.

They emerged into a bustling hallway. Plush carpeting, soft lighting, and freshly painted pastel walls testified to the administrative clout of those who ordinarily worked in this part of the headquarters building. Now the administrators and bureaucrats were gone, crowded onto other floors by Flynn's task force.

Everywhere Thorn looked he saw agents and technicians hard at work—hunched over computer terminals or blown-up crime-scene photos, standing over humming fax and copier machines, or hurrying from room to room carrying hard-copy files or disks. But there were also more untenanted offices and empty desks than he'd expected.

Helen saw his quizzical look and nodded wearily. "We're running short of warm bodies and good brains. Between Chicago, Dallas, and Seattle, we'd already lost a lot of manpower. Two more teams left for Disneyland and Louisville tonight. I'm afraid we're getting close to the breaking point."

Thorn knew exactly what she meant. For all its influence in American law enforcement, the FBI was a comparatively small organization. Just over eight thousand agents worked out of the Bureau's fifty-five field offices, and only a small percentage had the training and experience needed for top-notch counterterrorist work. In 1995, the investigation of the Oklahoma City bombing had tied up most of the FBI's available forensics specialists and terrorism experts for weeks. Now the Bureau was being forced to cope with the terrible equivalent of a new Oklahoma City attack one or two times a week. Flynn's task force was the only place to find the people needed to staff additional investigative units. Caught in a constant reshuffling as new teams were formed and dispatched to the field, the strain was clearly beginning to tell on the agents assigned to each case. There were only so many investigators, so many hours of computer and lab time, and so many hours in the day. It was no wonder that all of them were beginning to feel like they were floundering around in the dark, waiting helplessly for the next blow to fall, the next bomb to go off.

Helen opened the door to a large office suite and led him through a crowded central area. Panel partitions broke the room up into smaller cubicles, each one just big enough for a single desk, two chairs, two phones, and a network-linked personal computer. None of the people closeted in the cubicles looked up as they passed through.

Helen had her own tiny office off to one side. It wasn't much—just four walls, a door, and a desk—but it offered her some much-valued privacy. She used it to catch up on paperwork whenever her HRT section was out of the duty rotation.

She shut the door behind them and kissed him passionately, almost fiercely. Then she stepped back and smiled again, a shade more happily this time, at the surprised expression on his face. "I've been waiting to do that since I last saw you, Peter."

For the first time in days, Thorn felt his spirits lift a bit. He moved closer. "It *has* been a while. I guess I'll just have to prove my good intentions all over again."

Helen's eyebrows went up. She backed up to her desk and held up a warning hand. "Sorry! No fooling around on federal property, mister." She shook her head in regret. "We'll have to save that for later. After we're both off duty."

Thorn nodded slowly, briefly reluctant to come back to the grim reality they faced. "Fair enough." He set his briefcase down on the floor and took the chair she indicated. "So. Fill me in. From what I hear, nothing's working."

Her smile slipped. "Worse." She sat down in the only other chair. "We keep running into dead ends at every turn. We've got fingerprints from the press club bomb, but they don't match anyone in our files. Even the C4 used was bought by an untraceable dummy corporation. It's the same story everywhere."

"I thought you had a picture of the bomber."

Helen nodded. "One of our guys spotted him on the videotapes shot by the Metro surveillance cameras. Wearing that damned fake ECNS jacket and carrying all his gear. Flynn's releasing it to all the news services tomorrow morning."

Then she shrugged. "Not that it'll do much good. Here." She rummaged around in the papers stacked on her desk, pulled one out, and slid it across to him. It was a blowup of a photo taken by one of the Metro cameras.

Thorn studied it and saw right away what she meant. The man framed in the picture was dark-haired, thin, of average height, and wore dark glasses and a mustache. Even if he still looked anything like the photo, and that was doubtful, there were millions of men all across America who might fit that description.

He handed it back to her without saying anything.

"We have even less to work with in Chicago," Helen said tiredly. "Shell casings from the scene would help us ID the weapons used . . . if we could only find the weapons. And that rental van we found was useless—wiped clean."

"What about the rental agency?" he asked. "Anything from them?"

"Zip. They think the guy who rented it had blond hair and blue eyes . . . but they're not sure. What we are sure of is that he used a fake credit card and a fake driver's license."

Thorn nodded. Again, that wasn't surprising. Credit card fraud and forged identification were a multibillion-dollar business in the United States. "And there's nothing new from any other site?"

"Not a thing. The explosions and fires in both Seattle and Dallas/Fort Worth took care of most of the evidence. We know now they were both deliberately set—not accidents. We don't know much more than that."

Thorn set his jaw, fighting memories that were still painful. "What about Flight 352?"

Helen's gaze softened. She had her own nightmare visions of that terrible day and night by the Potomac. "The lab says the solid-rocket exhaust residues we picked up on the shore near Georgetown probably came from Russian-designed missiles—either SA-7s or the newer SA-16s. Our divers and the Park Police are still dragging the river for any bits and pieces we could use to confirm that."

"Wonderful," Thorn said softly. There were so many SA-7s and SA-16s piled up in military and terrorist arsenals around the world that tracing the weapons used for this particular attack would be almost impossible.

"What about on your end, Peter? Have you and the Maestro zeroed in on any of our guys who might have gone bad?" Helen asked.

"Only a handful." Thorn spread his hands in a gesture of negation. "And none I'd lay any money on. One's in prison, so he's out. Another's overseas working as a bodyguard for a Saudi prince. I understand most of the others had airtight alibis when your people checked them out. Anyway, none of them showed any signs of having the kind of connections or money they'd have to have to jump all over the country without getting caught."

Suddenly, he shook his head. "I just don't buy this, Helen. I could swallow the Bureau not spotting one or two small, sophisticated domestic terrorist groups . . . but three or four or five? Where the hell are all these bastards coming from?"

"Believe me, Peter, we've all been asking the same question," Helen said quietly. She lowered her eyes to the pile of reports and photos on her desk. "Our intelligence people honestly thought they had a handle on every group likely to cause trouble. But it's a big country out there and the evidence is pretty clear that we screwed it up somehow. Maybe we counted too much on these people slotting neatly into our psychological profiles. Or we relied too heavily on informants who weren't tracking the right organizations."

She looked up again. "All I know is that we're getting hammered by terrorists of all stripes using different techniques and weapons to hit different types of targets in different parts of the country. And the only thing I can see that they've got in common is that they're damned good at what they do."

Thorn grimaced. "True." Every separate attack showed clear signs of careful advance planning and attention to detail. That was one of the factors that had first led him to believe someone with military training might be involved. Something else about the terrorist strikes tugged at his memory. Something about the communiqués claiming responsibility . . .

Helen's phone buzzed, breaking his train of thought. "Special Agent Gray here."

Thorn sat still while she listened to someone on the other end.

"Right. I'll be there." Helen hung up. She looked sadly at him. "I have to go, Peter. Flynn's called a meeting in five minutes to go over the preliminary reports on the monorail bombing."

"Is he still giving you grief about sharing information with me?" Thorn asked seriously.

"Not much." One side of Helen's mouth twitched upward for an instant. "Mike Flynn's got a few too many other things to worry about right now. So I think he's pretty well decided to turn a blind eye on us—at least as long as he doesn't trip over you every time he turns around."

Thorn forced some humor into his own voice. "Got it. I'll practice tiptoeing on eggshells." He stood up. "I'll talk to you tomorrow?" he asked.

She nodded and came around the desk to kiss him good-bye. "Tomorrow."

Thorn was on the Metro before he remembered what it was that had been bothering him about the terrorist communiqués. Every one of them had been written or spoken in precise, textbook-perfect English. At first he'd thought that was because the terrorists wanted to avoid giving the FBI's language analysts any regional accents or speech patterns that could be used to identify them later. But what if there was another reason? A simpler reason? Did all the statements sound like textbook English precisely *because* they were taken out of a textbook?

He thought hard about that all the way back to the Pentagon.

NOVEMBER 22

NBC News morning briefing, "Terrorism in America"

NBC had built a special set in its New York broadcast studios as a backdrop for its daily reports on the terrorist campaigns convulsing the nation. A giant electronic map of the United States framed the news desk and NBC's top anchorman. Pulsing red lights scattered across the map marked areas officially confirmed by the FBI as terror attacks. A large monitor showed the grim, determined face of Senator Stephen Reiser, the Senate majority leader. He was being interviewed by satellite linkup with the Capitol Hill television studio.

"If I understand you correctly, Senator, you believe that the administration's response to this wave of terrorism has been too weak and too hesitant. Is that right?"

Reiser nodded flatly. "That's right, Tony." He frowned. "For God's sake, we know the kinds of people responsible for these atrocities. I see no reason on earth to keep tiptoeing around the way we've been doing. A little police or FBI raid here or there isn't going to stop this thing."

"What exactly are you proposing?" the interviewer asked curiously. Reiser was a rare politician—one noted for his blunt talk and acid wit.

The senator did not disappoint him.

"A knockout blow. Something that would stop these terrorists in their tracks. I think the President should get up off his duff and declare a nationwide state of emergency. We should slap every known member of these extremist groups into preventive detention until we can sort out the guilty from the innocent. And if the police and FBI are too damned shorthanded, I think we should deploy the Army and Marines to do the job!"

"Wouldn't the ACLU and other civil rights organizations object to—" the interviewer began.

"The hell with the ACLU!" Reiser interrupted sharply. "We're at war, whether those idiots know it or not."

South-Central Los Angeles, California

Officer Carlos Esparo swore softly as the scene in his binoculars swam into sharper focus. He and his partner were stationed seven blocks from the improvised roadblock thrown up across a major street leading into one of L.A.'s poorest and most dangerous neighborhoods. The roadblock wasn't much—not yet. Just a few old clunkers parked sideways across the street. But it was manned by punks. By gang members wearing their colors. By armed gang members. Most wore pistols tucked into their pants, and he could see at least one shotgun. The LAPD officer was

willing to bet they had automatic weapons too. He'd had too
many run-ins with the local street gangs not to respect their
firepower.

They were stopping every car and truck headed into South
Central. Only those driven by blacks were allowed through the
roadblock. The others, those driven by whites, Hispanics, or
Asians, were waved back with menacing gestures and shouted
insults.

Esparo clicked the button on his radio mike. "No, sir. There's
been no violence. Not yet anyway. But I still think—"

The voice of his watch commander cut him off. "Don't think,
Carlos. The orders come right from the top. You just stay put
and observe the situation. Got it? Don't intervene unless they
start getting out of hand. And even then, you check with me
first. Is that clear?"

Esparo gritted his teeth. "Clear, sir." He understood the reasoning behind his orders even if he didn't like them very much.
With racial tensions climbing every day, the LAPD could not
risk sparking another disastrous riot. Even his request for a
SWAT sniper team on standby had been refused. They were too
busy guarding vulnerable installations and city officials.

NOVEMBER 23

Oak Brook, Illinois

The coils of razor wire strung across the quiet, suburban street
west of Chicago seemed utterly out of place. So did the hunting
rifles slung over the shoulders of the well-dressed, mostly middle-
aged men clustered around a tiny portable heater. Their breath
steamed in the freezing late autumn air and they seemed acutely
uncomfortable. But they also looked angry and utterly fixed in
purpose.

Against police advice, Oak Brook's various Neighborhood

Watch groups had decided to arm themselves against what they saw as a rising tide of terrorism and civil strife. Their members, mostly wealthy lawyers, doctors, and stockbrokers, were taking turns away from work to patrol the streets and to man checkpoints at key locations. All of them were determined to make sure that no "undesirables" bent on murder, rape, or pillage menaced their homes or families.

America's social fabric was starting to come apart at the seams.

CHAPTER 17

BLACKOUT

NOVEMBER 24

On the Potomac River, near Leesburg, Virginia

(D MINUS 21)

A severe autumn storm—the howling, roaring creation of high winds and driving sheets of ice-cold rain—tore across Maryland and Virginia just after dark. The long, black wall of clouds came pouring down out of the Blue Ridge Mountains, scudding eastward across rolling hills, woods, and open farmland toward the Chesapeake Bay. Thirty miles northwest of Washington, D.C., the storm swept over the tall steel towers of the PennMarVa Electrical Intertie.

The intertie's transmission lines linked Pennsylvania, Maryland, and Virginia electric utilities together in a common power pool. Under normal conditions, the network enhanced each company's market and power supply position. Lines running north gave them access to cheaper hydroelectric power routed from Canada. The intertie also made it possible for member utilities to swap electricity back and forth to meet unexpected demand or to make up for out-of-commission generating plants.

Now, though, the power transmission network was a liability—a weak point open to attack. Its long high-voltage lines were especially vulnerable where they crossed the Potomac.

Sefer Halovic turned his face to the bitter, cleansing wind with something very like exultation in his soul. For him the storm was a manifestation of God's power—a vast and elemental force lashing out at America's sophisticated technology and its material works. It was surely a sign of divine favor for his own secret war.

Strengthened by this revelation, he swung back to the task at hand.

A massive electrical transmission tower loomed out of the darkness above him like some primeval monster. As warning to low-flying aircraft, a ruby-red light blinked at its peak, one hundred and fifty feet above the ground. The fierce wind keening through the tower's steel girders rose and fell in eerie counterpoint to the low, crackling hum of raw electricity coursing through the 500-kilovolt lines it supported.

Halovic peered through a blinding torrent of rain, following the swaying power lines northward across the Potomac until they disappeared in the swirling darkness well short of the Maryland shore. Another tower soared there, visible only as a hazy, pulsing glow in the distance. Truly, this was the place to strike, he thought. Once again, General Taleh's planners had done their work well.

He felt a hand on his shoulder and turned.

Khalil Yassine had to yell to be heard over the wind and rain. "The charges are in place!"

"Good!" Halovic patted the backpack slung from his left shoulder. "I will place the detonators myself. Use the radio. Find out how Nizrahim and his men are coming along."

The young Palestinian nodded sharply and slithered down the rain-soaked slope toward where they'd parked the vehicle they were using tonight—a dark-colored Jeep Wrangler. It held the automatic weapons they would need later, spare explosives, and communications gear.

Halovic moved in the opposite direction, toward the nearest leg of the giant transmission tower. He knelt beside the white blocks of plastic explosive Yassine had molded to the steel, and reached inside the backpack for a reel of detonator cord. More blocks of C4 were visible on another of the tower's four supports. Ignoring the freezing rain soaking through his jacket, the Bosnian began his delicate work. First, he stuck sections of the detcord into all of the charges the younger man had placed. Then he spliced the separate lengths together. He did not hurry. Men who took foolish chances when rigging demolitions rarely lived to regret their haste.

Satisfied that his splices would hold, Halovic started back toward the Wrangler, carefully trailing the detonator cord behind him. Again, he took his time, making sure of his footing before taking any step. Slipping in the mud now could undo all his hard work.

The Bosnian would have preferred using a surer, easier means to set off his explosives, but that was impossible. This close to a high-voltage source, timed or electrical detonators were too likely to malfunction or go off prematurely.

Yassine rejoined him halfway down the slope. "Nizrahim says they are almost ready. He is standing by."

Halovic nodded without looking up.

Five minutes later, he knelt again, this time on the muddy access road next to their stolen Jeep. This far away, the transmission tower was only a half-seen blur through the pouring rain. A dirt embankment offered rudimentary cover. He pulled more equipment out of his backpack. In quick succession he taped the end of the detcord around a nonelectric blasting cap and then attached a time fuse and fuse lighter. Ready.

Halovic climbed up the embankment and gently placed the detonator assembly on the ground within easy reach. Then he slid back down the embankment. Set.

Yassine crouched beside him holding the walkie-talkie to his face as though it were a sacred talisman.

The Bosnian reached up and gripped the pull ring on the fuse lighter. He glanced at his companion and nodded sharply. "Go!"

The younger man clicked the transmit button on the walkie-talkie. "Fire!"

In that same instant Halovic yanked the pull ring out of the lighter and flattened himself against the embankment. The blasting cap exploded, sending fire racing through the detonator cord at 21,000 feet per second.

THUMMP. THUMMP. Harsh white light flared against the dark, rain-drenched sky as their plastic explosives went off, shearing through hardened steel supports as though they were butter.

Two more explosions echoed across the river as the charges Nizrahim's team had set on the Maryland tower detonated.

Halovic cautiously raised his head over the embankment to check his handiwork.

With two of its four steel supports shattered, the Virginia-side transmission tower shuddered, whipping back and forth through the rain. Then gravity and its own enormous weight took hold. Girders and bolts buckled under stresses they were never designed to withstand. Slowly first and then faster, amid the wrenching scream of tearing metal, the tower swayed sideways and toppled.

The long, twin 500-kv lines fell with it, whirring downward through the air, smashing through trees, and splashing into the white-capped Potomac. On the way down, they made contact and shorted out. Streamers of hellish blue light arced back and forth between the swishing wires like bolts of lightning trapped in a narrow space. Abruptly, everything went black.

Halovic blinked away the dazzling afterimages and turned toward his staring, openmouthed companion. "Come, Yassine. We have much more to do before we are done."

The Palestinian nodded and followed him down the embankment to their waiting vehicle.

PennMarVa Intertie Emergency Control Centers

As planned, the terrorist attack came at the worst possible time—the hour just after sunset when the demand for electricity peaked. Streets were now brightly lit against the gathering darkness. Office lights, computers, and copiers were still on. And millions of people coming home from work or school were flipping on lamps, televisions, ovens, and microwaves.

So when the PennMarVa Intertie's 500-kv line went down, it created havoc in seconds. Current was still flowing south with nowhere to go. Emergency circuit breakers tripped automatically, desperately shunting the electrical load to secondary 230-kv lines. But the cascading load was too much for them to handle. Line temperatures rose rapidly, climbing toward the danger zone. More circuit breakers blew out across the entire system.

As alarms blared through several utility control centers, their computers swung into action, fighting for precedence among themselves as they tried to bring transmission lines back up. Power outages hopscotched across a vast area—south from Gettysburg all the way to Williamsburg, Virginia. More and more substations and secondary lines went black as they were knocked off-line. The edge of each outage was easy to see. On one side of a street the houses and streetlights were bright and warm. On the other side there was nothing but cold darkness.

By the time the situation stabilized, more than 300,000 homes and businesses were left without power.

VEPCO trouble crew, off Route 7, near the Potomac

Rain pounded the red and gray VEPCO truck lumbering up the rutted access road. Water crashed down across the windshield in waves that drowned vision for seconds at a time. Branches scraped across metal as the fierce winds whipped the trees on either side of the narrow road into frenzied motion. For an instant, the truck skidded sideways as its tires lost traction in the mud.

Almost anybody with any choice was either at home or heading there as fast as the weather allowed.

Ray Atwater and his partner, Dennis Greenwood, didn't have a choice. Both men had seen the weather coming and had said good-bye to their wives, not expecting to see them again until the storm stopped, whenever that was. While everyone else hunkered down, Virginia Electric Power crews worked to keep the lines up and everyone warm.

Right now Greenwood drove while Atwater pored over maps and diagrams of the power grid. Raised in Michigan's stormy winters, Greenwood fought the rain-slick roads like a pro. Atwater was a rarity, a native of the area, and he was more than willing to let the other man have the wheel.

Their first job was to find the line break and see how bad things really were. In a sense, they were scouts for the construction crews assembling at utility yards throughout northern Virginia.

Atwater shook his head as he used a penlight to scan the intertie map. The first sensor reports showed that they'd lost the 500-kv line at one or both of the river transmission towers. He hoped the sensors were wrong. Even in good weather, trying to string new line across the Potomac would be a delicate, ticklish job. Under the current conditions, it would be all but impossible.

The troubleshooter put his charts away as the truck nosed out of the woods onto the long, mostly open slope leading to the intertie Potomac crossing point. He stared through the streaked windshield, straight into the center of total darkness. It was no good. He couldn't see anything up ahead—no steel latticework and no red warning light. Nothing but rain-flecked blackness in the headlights.

Atwater glanced at his partner in surprise. "Where the hell's the tower?"

He rolled down the window on his side, letting in the cold and wet, but also improving his view. Still nothing. "Shit."

He thumbed the transmit switch on his radio mike. "Dispatch, this is One-Five—"

Rippling flashes lit up a small grove of trees only yards away. The windshield blew inward.

Both Atwater and Greenwood were killed instantly by a stuttering fusillade of automatic-weapons fire that ripped them apart. The utility trouble truck rolled on for a short distance and finally came to rest against the access road embankment. One lone headlight still gleamed, shining across the twisted wreckage of the 500-kv transmission tower.

HRT ready-response section

A sudden gust bounced the UH-60 Blackhawk up and down through the choppy air. The clattering rotor noise rose to a new pitch as the helicopter's pilot fought to maintain his control over the machine. They were only five hundred feet above the wind-whipped surface of the Potomac. Between the wind, the rain, and the bitter cold, flying conditions were right on the margin between dangerous and suicidal.

Seated right behind the cockpit, Helen Gray gripped her MP5 submachine gun tighter, trusting that her safety harness would hold. As the Blackhawk nosed down into forward flight again, she leaned closer to the copilot's helmeted head. "How much further?"

"Not far." He turned his head toward her, eyes invisible behind a set of night vision goggles, and gestured through the windscreen. "Maybe another half mile or so."

Helen slipped her own goggles down and stared hard at the wooded slopes ahead. It was difficult to make out any details through the downpour.

"There. About five hundred yards ahead. Just out of the tree line." The pilot's voice crackled through her earphones. "Looks like a vehicle. It's not moving."

Helen saw the VEPCO trouble truck at almost the same moment. It was slewed across an access road just below a pile of debris that must be the transmission tower they'd briefed her on. The driver's-side door hung open. "Take us in."

"Roger."

The Blackhawk swooped closer to the hillside, shuddering again as it flew through more turbulence. HRT troopers in full assault gear slid the helo's side doors open, bracing themselves against the sudden onslaught of rain and wind.

Helen leaned out through the opening, focusing on the ground rushing upward toward them. They were at one hundred feet. Fifty. Twenty-five. Her fingers unsnapped the safety harness holding her inside. "Here we go, people! Get set!"

The Blackhawk flared out just above the ground and hovered there, rotor pounding.

"Move! Move!" Helen threw herself through the side door and dropped prone with her MP5 out and ready. The rest of her section spilled out after her and took up firing positions, forming a defensive ring on both sides of the helicopter. The instant they were all out, the Blackhawk transitioned to forward flight and climbed away into the darkness.

She waited for the sound of its engines to fade, scanning the ground in front of her for signs of movement. Tree limbs swayed in the wind, but she saw no evidence of anyone still lurking in ambush. "Anyone see anything?"

No one did.

Helen nodded, unsurprised. As she had feared, they were undoubtedly too late. Unsure of what had happened to its men and suspecting only a simple communications failure in the bad weather, VEPCO had delayed reporting any problem for nearly an hour. When the call came in, Flynn had immediately dispatched her HRT section to the scene. He had also asked both the Virginia and Maryland state police agencies to set up roadblocks in a wide perimeter around the power line crossing. She frowned. By now the terrorists were snugly and securely hidden among the D.C. area's several million inhabitants.

Helen's lips pursed as she sighted through her goggles at the bullet-riddled VEPCO truck. Why should they linger on at risk, when they had so easily and swiftly accomplished their mission?

Knocking down the two intertie transmission towers merely created a onetime inconvenience for several hundred thousand people. By killing the men sent out to cope with the problem, though, the terrorists had multiplied the effectiveness of their attack a hundredfold. How many utility crews anywhere in the United States would venture out to repair a line break or downed power pole until they were sure that SWAT teams or military units had secured the area? So power outages and other problems that once would have lasted only minutes or a couple of hours were bound to drag on for several hours or days.

Helen rose cautiously to her feet with the bitter taste of yet another defeat in her mouth. Whoever these sons of bitches were, they'd succeeded in throwing another monkey wrench into the intricately meshed gears of modern American life.

WJLA late night news, Washington, D.C.

Rita Davis, one of the station's star reporters, stood framed against the floodlit front steps of the Hoover Building. The petite, dark, curly-haired woman seemed dwarfed by the harried-looking man next to her.

"This is Special Agent Michael Flynn, the man heading up the FBI's special task force on terrorism. I've just filled him in on the phone call we received from the New Aryan Order, and he's agreed to speak with us for a few minutes."

The camera swung up and over to Flynn, who was clearly impatient and unhappy at being on TV. Davis couldn't say so on camera, but she would certainly crow later to her colleagues about peeling Flynn away from the layers of public affairs people screening the FBI's top investigator. Bartering hot information for interview time had worked.

"Agent Flynn, can you tell us how this most recent attack may fit into an overall neo-Nazi plan to set off a race war in this country?"

The FBI investigator frowned but answered smoothly. "As far as we know, Ms. Davis, there is no overall plan. Some of the terrorist groups may be loosely coordinating their operations, but we haven't even found any hard evidence of that."

One of Davis's finely sculptured eyebrows rose skeptically. "No plan? Then how do you explain the wave of terror that's been spreading across this whole country for the last three weeks? Is this all just a terrible coincidence?"

Flynn refused to rise to the bait. "I'm not prepared to discuss details of our investigations at this time, Ms. Davis. But I will say that an organized, nationwide conspiracy seems unlikely. Historically, none of these radical groups have trusted each other enough to work effectively together."

"And you have no other explanation?" prompted the reporter.

"The best way to get answers is to find and arrest the men responsible."

"And just how close are you to doing that?"

Flynn looked grim. "I can't comment on that. We're making some progress." The tall FBI man turned away with a final, curt "That's all I have time for, Ms. Davis."

The camera followed him striding back into the building, surrounded by security men and aides, and then cut back to Davis. She addressed the studio-based anchorwoman. "Well, Fran, there you have it. Despite an intense effort, the FBI seems no nearer to stopping this deadly terrorist campaign than they were at the very beginning. This is Rita Davis, reporting live from the Hoover Building."

NOVEMBER 25

Over Bushehr, Iran, on the Persian Gulf

(D MINUS 20)

Captain Farhad Kazemi felt the C-130 Hercules transport plane bank sharply, beginning its descent over the blue waters of the Persian Gulf. They were on final approach to Bushehr's tiny airport.

He glanced forward toward where General Amir Taleh sat reading—deep in one of the unit readiness reports that consumed so much of the general's time these days. Nearly sixty heavily armed soldiers wearing the green beret of Iran's Special Forces filled the rest of the C-130's troop compartment. Perhaps too many, Kazemi thought, but his near-raw nerves demanded that he take every measure imaginable to ensure his commander's security.

When Kazemi was a young officer candidate, Taleh had saved him from execution by a Revolutionary tribunal, and ever since he had dedicated himself to keeping the general alive. That was getting harder to do.

The commander of Iran's armed forces was playing a dangerous double game. His real plans were still a closely guarded secret. But opposition to his publicly stated policies was on the rise among Iran's religious fanatics, some in the bureaucracy, and the survivors of the discredited Pasdaran. Taleh's military and political reforms had wrecked many careers, most with good cause, but they had also left behind many angry men without much to lose. Such men were dangerous.

Kazemi felt himself pressed back into his seat as the Hercules bounced once and then braked sharply before taxiing toward one of the hangars at the airfield's far end. They were down.

The Special Forces troops trotted down the C-130's rear ramp and fanned out across the airfield, securing the small terminal building and the closest hangars before Kazemi allowed the general to emerge.

As a further precaution, Taleh would ride into town in one of three identical staff cars. The captain also dispatched a squad to scout the route ahead. Bushehr's sunlit streets might make a pleasant change from Tehran's crowded, polluted, frigid avenues, but they could prove just as hazardous.

Even though this was an unannounced inspection tour, Kazemi had no intention of taking unnecessary chances. Arranging some of Taleh's own "incidents" had taught him just how vulnerable they were outside the well-defended precincts of their Tehran headquarters.

Headquarters, forward logistics base, Bushehr

The sleepy little town of Bushehr jutted out into the Persian Gulf at the end of a narrow, waterlogged peninsula. Sand-colored mud-brick houses with balconies, latticed windows, and flat roofs lined the old city's narrow, winding alleys and waterfront. Street urchins played leisurely, seemingly endless games of soccer, sticking to the cooler shadows wherever possible, dodging in and around brightly clad women out on their own slow, daily errands.

During the 1700s the town had been the country's principal port. But when it was bypassed by the trans-Iranian railroad in the 1930s, it had fallen steadily in importance and value. Exposed to repeated air and missile attacks during the war with Iraq, Bushehr had sunk further as a viable commercial harbor.

Now the port's main business came from the Iranian Navy. During the war, Pasdaran Boghammer speedboats had used Bushehr as a base for raids on Iraqi and Kuwaiti shipping with some success. Since then, the Regular Navy had begun moving some of its activities northward from its crowded main base at Bandar-e Abbas.

Kazemi felt himself start to relax only when their well-armed convoy of staff cars and troop carriers passed through the military checkpoint marking the logistics base perimeter. This was now friendly ground.

One week before, contingents of Iranian Army troops had occupied the old warehouse district adjoining the Bushehr naval base. They'd repaired and erected fences and barbed-wire entanglements around the area, boarded up warehouse windows, and set up a ring of bristling sentry posts to keep the curious out and some of Taleh's secrets in.

Military equipment and supplies of all kinds were pouring into Bushehr. Convoys of trucks piled high with tank, artillery, and small-arms ammunition had begun arriving from the north—mostly at night and always under heavy guard. Other matériel arrived at the airfield, flown directly from overseas arms dealers.

Taleh had handpicked a trusted officer, one renowned as a master logistician, to manage the all-important buildup here. Now it was time to see if he was doing his job properly.

Surrounded by a small cluster of his own aides, General Shahrough Akhavi was waiting for Taleh in front of the headquarters building, an old commercial shipping office taken over by the Army. He was a short, solidly built man, but his wire-rimmed glasses and full beard gave him a bookish air, like a university professor or a bookstore proprietor. He wasn't one of Taleh's inner circle, but the general had marked him as a fine officer, another man with Western training who had suffered at the hands of the Revolutionary Guards.

Taleh emerged from the car, and the two generals greeted each other warmly. Kazemi ignored them and concentrated instead on rechecking his security arrangements. What he saw pleased him. The Special Forces detachments were in place, ubiquitous but unobtrusive. There were no signs of trouble in any of the surrounding buildings. Good.

The captain turned back to his superiors.

Akhavi was introducing his staff to Taleh. As each man stepped up and saluted, Kazemi studied them closely. He always found it interesting to watch the faces of junior officers when they first met the Chief of Staff of their nation's armed forces. Fear was common, as was awe, and sometimes open admiration. He was possessive enough about his commander to take something of a proprietary interest in their reactions.

One man, a tall, scarred major, seemed to keep his emotions very carefully under control when he met Taleh. But as he turned away, a flash of some strong emotion rippled across his features. He looked as though he'd smelled something bad or seen something disgusting. The expression was gone as quickly as it had come, but seeing it raised the hairs on the back of Kazemi's neck.

A bad attitude like that was not conducive to a smoothly running operation, and this was too important a post to let the matter pass. The captain resolved to discuss Akhavi's staff with Taleh at the next available opportunity.

The group, led by the two generals, started up the steps into the headquarters building. Kazemi hung back as was his habit, to make sure the security people were keeping up.

There was the tall major again, he noticed, moving quickly, maneuvering through the crowd of officers to approach Taleh from behind. The man's right hand was held tight and flat over his pistol holster, slowly lifting the flap.

For an instant, Kazemi froze. The major was not simply a disgruntled staff officer. He was an assassin.

The captain started moving, racing up the steps without calling out. The security detail was too far away and the would-be assassin too close for an outcry to do Taleh any good. He could see the man's pistol slowly coming clear of the holster. No!

Desperate now, Kazemi shoved a fat colonel out of his way and lunged up the last few steps. Still moving full tilt, he crashed into the assassin from behind, knocking him to the ground in a tangle of flailing arms and kicking legs. The pistol skittered away, unfired.

Shouts of surprise echoed above him, and Kazemi caught fleeting glimpses of men running, some away from the struggle, others toward it. He felt the other man attempting to rise and slammed an elbow into the back of his neck—hard enough to stun him. In seconds it was over.

A pair of hard-faced Special Forces troops arrived at a run and yanked the would-be murderer to his feet, pinioning him between them. Another retrieved the cocked automatic and held it out for all to see. That was all the indictment required. At Taleh's curt nod, the guards hustled the dazed assassin away for interrogation.

Kazemi picked himself up, bruised and scraped but barely winded by the brief struggle. He looked around him. General Akhavi's look of horror seemed genuine enough, and the staffs of both generals were confusion personified. There appeared to be no more immediate danger.

Flanked now by guards with their weapons drawn, Taleh walked over as the captain brushed himself off. Concern filled his voice. "You are all right, Farhad?"

"Yes, General."

"Once again it appears that I owe you my life."

"It is yours to take, General." Kazemi smiled, half in pleasure at his own success, half in knowing Taleh was safe.

The general touched his arm. "Can you take charge of the investigation? I must still hear General Akhavi's report."

"Of course, sir." Kazemi actually would have liked a quiet cup of coffee somewhere, but he knew the time to act was now, before any other conspirators escaped or fabricated convincing stories. He hurried off to find his opposite number on Akhavi's staff.

Two hours later, General Amir Taleh emerged into the bright afternoon sunshine, blinking. He'd sat quietly through Akhavi's prepared briefing, projecting an image of stability and confidence. He was fairly sure that the logistics expert had not been involved in the attempt on his life, and he wanted to show his trust in the man—both for Akhavi's sake and to reassure his staff. The Bushehr base was too important to the success of SCIMITAR to leave in unwarranted turmoil.

But while half his mind had listened to the reports, the other half had been busy running through the possible implications of this sudden, unexpected attack. His security arrangements were so tight and well managed that the possibility of a betrayal or a conspiracy within his own personal staff was very slight. Nonetheless, such a thing could not be completely discounted.

Taleh made another mental note to review their procedures with Kazemi if the young man's investigation turned up nothing more here. The alternative was even more frightening than betrayal by one of his own men. It was the possibility that some of the officers in the Army were so disaffected by his reforms and by his apparent rapprochement with America and the West that they were willing to shoot him on sight—even at the certain cost of their own lives.

He shook his head slowly. Perhaps his hold on power was even more tenuous than he had imagined. His shoulders stiffened. Well, then, all the more reason to press ahead with his plans.

His operations here and in the United States were nearing a critical stage.

It was time to use one of his most jealously guarded and sophisticated weapons—the special weapon his agent had acquired in Bulgaria so many months ago.

NOVEMBER 26

(D MINUS 19)

Special Operations Order
MAGI Prime via MAGI Link to WOLF Prime:
　　1. Effective immediately, activate OUROBOROS.
　　2. When possible, transfer your base of operations outside the affected area and reestablish positive communications with this headquarters.

CHAPTER 18
DIGITAL WAR

NOVEMBER 27

The Midwest

(D MINUS 18)

OUROBOROS went active at noon, central standard time.

At 12:01 P.M. Bill Rush, a farmer outside Red Wing, Minnesota, picked up his phone and started punching in the number for his feed supplier. He stopped, three numbers in, when he realized he wasn't getting a dial tone. He whapped the receiver against the heel of his hand, but it remained silent. Resolving to get a new phone tomorrow, he stomped off to do his chores.

At 12:02 P.M. Fred Wong, a commercial real estate broker near Chicago's Loop, tried to dial one of his clients to let her know he'd be a little late for their meeting. Instead of a steady tone, the receiver was silent. He tried line two and, when that didn't work, his cellular phone. Nothing.

"Wonderful," he fumed, "an outage." Grabbing his suit coat, the Realtor sprinted for the elevator. His client was all the way across town, so he had no time to waste.

Three minutes after OUROBOROS activated, at 1:03 P.M., eastern standard time, Jeri Daniels, a salesclerk in Detroit's trendy "The Cache," ran a Visa card through the reader, her first sale since coming back from lunch. The small box didn't seem to be working. The window displayed "dialing" as always, but then changed to "no connection."

"Annette?" Jeri called to another salesclerk. "Have you had any problem with the card reader?"

Shaking her head, the other woman came over to help.

One minute later, in Fort Wayne, Indiana, Mrs. Ruby Jeffers shuffled quickly over toward the telephone. That old electric space heater in the back room of her apartment was sparking and smoking, and she hadn't made it to eighty-three by sitting around. She would call the fire department, if only to have them unplug the thing.

Arthritis forced her to move slowly, and the smoke was a little thicker by the time she made it to the kitchen. She picked up the receiver and frowned. Nothing. No dial tone at all. Not even static. Just silence. She dialed 911 anyway, but there was no response.

"Oh, my Lord," she breathed.

Dropping the useless telephone, she left the kitchen almost running, ignoring the pain shrieking through her joints. The smoke was thicker, and the front door seemed a hundred miles away.

Precisely at 1:00 P.M., eastern standard time, all of the switching computers for the Midwest Telephone company had suddenly ceased to make connections. Occupied with some internal, mysterious task, they were no longer taking any calls.

Inside a service area that spilled across two time zones, Midwest Telephone was relied on by 40 million Americans living in Minnesota, Wisconsin, Iowa, Illinois, Michigan, and Indiana for telecommunications service.

1:05 P.M., EST

Detroit

Officer Bob Calvin tried to phone his girlfriend from the fast-food joint he'd stopped at for his lunch break.

Calvin was of medium height, with a very dark complexion, only one shade removed from jet black. He kept his hair cut high and flat on the sides, emphasizing his lean, narrow face. He was in his late twenties, a seven-year veteran of Detroit's police force. Although smaller than some, he kept a lot of energy in his frame, and he could move fast and hard when necessary.

He had the 0800-to-1600-hours shift, driving a police car through one of Detroit's tougher neighborhoods. Come the afternoon and graveyard shifts, they'd have two men in the car, but in the daytime one cop per vehicle was all the force could spare. Usually, he didn't mind riding alone in this neighborhood. He'd grown up here. He'd even volunteered for this beat. Now, though, he'd been around long enough to know just how close it was to the edge.

Hell, the whole city was . . . Calvin realized the phone he was holding wasn't working and hung up.

He left the restaurant and climbed back into his patrol car. He reached under the seat and pulled out a small cellular phone. Although they were expensive to use, many cops bought them as backups for the car radio, or to make personal calls when phones weren't available—like now.

He pressed the dial and 1 buttons and heard the phone dialing. But the message window displayed "no connection." He tried again, with the same results. What exactly was going on?

He put the portable away, a scowl on his face. The bum phone meant another long explanation to Linda, he thought irritably. He enjoyed her company and her conversation, but she was not a patient woman. The dangerous aspects of his job also worried her, and she often needed to hear that he was still okay.

"All units on this frequency, all units," the radio crackled as he settled himself and started the engine. "Repeat, all units. Landline phone service is out. No incoming or outgoing calls from Dispatch can be made. The problem may be citywide."

"Wonderful," Calvin muttered sarcastically. The city was on the verge of blowing up, and now the utilities were on the blink. At least that explained his problem.

He often missed having a partner—not for backup, but just someone to keep him company and bitch to at times like this. He could share his worries with another cop, but not with Linda.

The nationwide, tit-for-tat wave of white racist and black supremacist terrorism was threatening to tear Detroit apart. He'd seen some of the confidential memos circulating through the department. Many in high places were increasingly worried by the prospect of major trouble between the city's poor, black inner-city neighborhoods and its affluent, white suburban neighborhoods. Far too many of Detroit's people were already choosing up sides. Plenty of "black spokesmen," radicalized by the violence or radical to begin with, spoke of "taking the war back to the whites." And too many of their white counterparts were talking the same kind of garbage. The ugly reality of a race war seemed to lie just around the corner.

Calvin shook his head. He'd broken up a lot of interracial arguments lately. Vandalism and other low-level crimes were way up, and gang activity was at an all-time high. He saw the murderous punks all the time now, in packs on the streets, just hanging or cruising from somewhere to nowhere, just looking for trouble. All they needed was a spark to set them off.

Even as he worried, a small corner of his mind relaxed, imagining the tack he could take with Linda. "I tried to call you, honey, but the phones were out." Best excuse in the world.

But he knew that the solution for his small problem with his girlfriend had created a much bigger problem for the city as a whole. Well, with luck, the phone company would uncross their wires in short order and bring everything back on-line.

Resolving to cover as much ground as possible, Officer Bob Calvin pulled out of the hamburger restaurant's trash-littered parking lot and started his patrol. He still had half his shift to go.

1:10 P.M., EST

Midwest Telephone's primary operations center, near Fort Wayne, Indiana

Maggie Kosinski pulled a printout out of the printer so that she could see the data for herself. The traffic counters all read fine. The links to the other Baby Bells throughout the rest of the country were busy too. It was just that no calls were getting through anywhere in the company's service area.

She temporarily ignored the shift operators clustered around her as they all tried to suggest possible courses of action at once. She was the boss, the person in charge of operations at the center. She'd been summoned only moments after the outage began. Unfortunately, ten minutes of analysis told her nothing.

Kosinski had worked for the phone company for almost twelve years, starting after a tour in the Air Force as a communications technician. She'd paid her dues as a technician and operator before becoming a supervisor and then operations manager.

She was pretty, a little over average height, and had short blond hair. She kept her hair short and dressed down at the office so she wouldn't be accused of using her looks to get promoted. Today, for instance, she wore a plain black sweater and cream-colored pants, little makeup, and small, gold hoop earrings. Hopefully, they'd pay more attention to her brains than her outfit.

Her second-in-command looked up from his desk. "Maggie, it's Jim Johnston on the E-phone."

Jim Johnston was Kosinski's boss, the man in charge of company operations. She ran to pick up the special line. Midwest Telephone had its own backup system for maintenance and for emergencies like this.

"What have we got, Maggie?" asked Johnston matter-of-factly.

She started spelling out the symptoms, using the same straightforward tone. "The whole system's locked up tight. We're getting traffic readings, but nothing's really being passed."

There was a moment of silence on the other end as Johnston tried to digest news that was worse than anything he'd anticipated. "What have you tried so far?"

"We aren't getting any hardware faults. So first we tried isolating each of the switching computers from the others. That didn't help. So we've stripped as much of the load as we can. But that still isn't making any difference."

Because Johnston had once held her job, she only needed to give him a shorthand picture of the system's condition and their first attempts to fix it. Kosinski was more worried than she wanted to admit. She'd seen a lot of different problems in her time, but all the standard fixes, plus a few imaginative ones, hadn't done a thing. There were only a few options left. And none of them were very palatable.

"All the switching computers are down?" Johnston asked.

"All within a minute of each other, all over the region," she replied. It was hard to believe. This had never happened before, in her experience or in the experience of anyone in the operations center. Still, working with computers, you learned to expect the impossible.

"The system may be corrupted," Kosinski ventured reluctantly. "Either by a bug or by damage to the code."

"Meaning a virus," Johnston said flatly. The chance of a bug in mature software was very remote.

"It's possible," she admitted. "The code's clearly been corrupted somehow. I recommend that we shut everything down and reboot from the master backups."

That wasn't her decision to make, thank goodness. Shutting the system down and restarting it from scratch would guarantee that all telecommunications services in the Midwest would be off-line for at least another thirty minutes. The company's own losses and financial liability were probably already running somewhere in the tens of millions of dollars. Another half an hour out of commission might increase that by an order of magnitude.

There was silence on the other end of the E-phone for several seconds.

"Can you salvage the accounting data?" Johnston asked finally. The system's RAM held a significant fraction of the day's billing records in temporary storage. Shutting the machines down would wipe all of that information, adding millions more to the company's losses.

"I don't know, Jim. We've already dumped all that we can, but it looks pretty bad."

Another silence. This one lasted longer.

"Well, go ahead. The quicker we start, the quicker we'll be back in business. I'll call public relations." She could hear the frustration in his voice. "Christ, they're gonna love this."

Maggie hung up, turned back to the shift crew, and started snapping out orders. She was determined to bring the system back on-line in record time, if only to shorten Jim Johnston's discomfort.

12:15 P.M., CST

Chicago

The Chicago Mercantile Exchange sat quiet, almost as silent as a tomb.

Jill Kastner, one of the hundreds of commodities traders milling around in confusion, wished they'd kill the power as well and make the effect complete. She had never seen the brightly lit trading floor so still. It made the whole vast room seem alien and utterly unfamiliar.

Ordinarily, the exchange handled millions of dollars of business a minute. Pork bellies, gold, stock market indices, foreign currencies, and hundreds of other commodities. They all moved from seller to buyer amid the shouting, yelling, and waving chaos of the separate pits. Ultimately, though, the traders and their customers relied on near-instantaneous communications and information retrieval. The exchange's computer terminals were linked by phone lines to a sophisticated net that spanned the globe. Without those phone lines, the exchange was just another large, paper-littered room.

Jill Kastner frowned. They had been out of business for fifteen minutes so far. Fifteen minutes that had cost her and her partners tens of thousands of dollars of potential profit.

Some of the traders scattered around her were trying to catch up on their paperwork. Others read the paper or tried the telephones over and over, hoping to be the first back on the electronic web that made their business possible. A few had already left the building for a quick drink or a walk to blow off steam.

Jill was too competitive to walk away from a problem like that. She simply tapped a pencil on the counter in front of her, tried to clear her mind, and waited. Whenever the phone company fixed the problem, she'd get back to work. The problem was, with the phones out, she couldn't even prepare for the godawful mess she knew would appear when they came back on.

1:20 P.M., EST

Detroit

The Napoli was a small Italian restaurant on Detroit's West Side. It wasn't a four-star or even a three-star restaurant, but it served a good lunch and had a regular dinner clientele.

Joe Millunzi, the owner, spotted trouble as soon as it came in off the street. Three black kids in their teens, dressed in dark, dirty, loose-fitting clothes. They all wore Detroit Pistons hats or shirts—gang colors, probably. They glided in the front door in a carefully studied strut, hard looks on their faces. He knew his customers, and these people were not here to buy lunch.

One hung back by the door while the others headed for the cash register and his daughter, Carla. Millunzi shivered. Carla was busy with a customer. She hadn't noticed the boys.

He had been standing a few yards away at the entrance to the dining room, going over the reservations book. Moving as quickly as he could without running outright, he managed to get to the register before the two gangbangers. Whispering "Get Mama and everyone out the back!" he shooed her toward the kitchen.

They saw Millunzi come up and watched the girl leave, but they didn't seem to care. They just stopped in front of the register, coldly regarding him. He was a big man, over six feet and a little overweight. The two teenagers were both shorter, possibly not even fully grown.

Millunzi felt like a slab of meat being inspected.

His hands were hidden as he desperately pressed a small button on the underside of the register stand. The alarm system was linked via a dedicated phone line to an alarm service and from there to the police. In a few minutes the cops would know there was a robbery in progress. And Millunzi knew there were usually two police cars in this area at this time of day. He'd made it his business to know. With luck, the police could be outside in five minutes. Ten tops. Just keep cool, Joe, he thought nervously.

The two teens looked around to make sure no one else was paying much attention. The shortest pulled his hand out of his jacket pocket, showing Millunzi a silver-gray automatic pistol. It looked immense in the boy's hand.

"Give us the money, man," the teenager demanded in a small, even voice. Having shown his weapon, he then folded his other hand over it and stood quietly, waiting arrogantly for his chosen victim to comply.

Millunzi nodded hastily, swallowed hard, and rang up "No Sale" on the register. It beeped and spat the cash drawer out at him. He carefully scooped up the twenties, tens, and fives, and offered the wad of cash to the one with the gun.

"All of it, fool!" the taller, older teen said in a harsh voice. He savagely grabbed the bills out of Millunzi's hand and stabbed a hand down at the register again.

The restaurant owner nervously gathered up the ones and rolls of coins and started to offer it to them, but the triggerman snarled, and showed him the gun again. "Not that shit! Give us what's under the drawer!"

Millunzi sighed and lifted the cash drawer, showing three bundles of twenties in bank wrappers. He pulled them out, fighting the urge to look at the clock or check his watch. It had been at least a minute. Maybe two. Probably not three. Were Carla and Rosa out the back? His brain seemed to be spinning, overheated with fear. Where were the police?

The two robbers smiled triumphantly as the older one took the bundled cash. They both turned away toward the door, but the one holding the gun suddenly swung around, whipped the gun up to point at Millunzi, and fired.

The first round caught him in the stomach and slammed him back against the wall. He instinctively clutched at his belly and groaned aloud—gasping as a wave of sharp, piercing agony struck him.

The triggerman fired twice more, this time into Millunzi's chest. As the restaurant owner's consciousness faded, he noticed that the teenager still wore the same, small, triumphant smile.

＊　　＊　　＊

The patrons in the restaurant reacted to the noise by turning startled faces toward the cash register. They saw Joe Millunzi sliding down the blood-smeared wall behind the cash register and the young black men in dark-colored Pistons jackets walking quickly outside.

Three blocks away, Officer Bob Calvin continued his patrol. He never saw the three robbers, who escaped without a trace. There would be many clean getaways that afternoon.

1:25 P.M., EST

Detroit

Bob Calvin's radio pulled his attention away from the heavy traffic building up on the neighborhood streets.

"All units, this is the watch commander. This phone outage is a big one. We're getting radio calls from neighboring jurisdictions. Their land links are out too.

"Latest word from the phone company is that it's going to be some time before they fix the problem, so the commissioner has decided to mobilize the force. We're also coordinating with the hospitals and the fire department. Ambulances and fire engines will be dispersed throughout the city. Everyone look sharp, and we'll let you know when things get back to normal."

Calvin whistled sharply. This situation must be even more serious than he'd first thought. Mobilizing the force meant pulling all shifts in and keeping everyone on duty until the emergency was declared over. It also meant calling up the city's police reserves. The reserves had only limited arrest powers, but they were armed.

Mobilizing the force and its reserves would put a lot more needed manpower on the streets—although at the cost of overtime pay. On the other hand, Calvin realized, under the present circumstances, ordering a mobilization was a lot simpler than carrying it out. Without phone service the department would have to send someone to knock on the door of every officer or reservist being summoned to duty.

Still, that was the smart move to make, even if it meant he had to stay on for a second shift. The city was ready to blow, and it was their job to keep the lid on.

Of course, Calvin thought to himself with a tinge of regret, his date with Linda for tonight was now in jeopardy. A citywide emergency was not an excuse, not in her eyes, and she'd be worried sick. He was scheduled to get off at four, and their date was set for eight. Surely, Midwest Telephone would have its technical glitches sorted out by then.

1:30 P.M., EST

CNN Headline News

The piece was third, after an update on the continuing and fruitless FBI counterterrorist investigation and the equally fruitless Balkan negotiations.

"Midwest Telephone technicians are scrambling to deal with a major telecommunications outage affecting the company's entire service area."

A map flashed into view behind the anchorman's head showing the six affected states. Together they formed an irregularly shaped red blob in the heart of the country.

"For more than half an hour, the outage has paralyzed industries, businesses, stock markets, and commodities exchanges across a vast area. Phone company spokesmen reached by emergency satellite downlink are unable to explain the cause or offer a firm estimate for the resumption of service . . ."

1:45 P.M., EST

Midwest Telephone's primary operations center

"You're sure the masters were clean?"

It was a stupid question, even if Johnston did have to ask it, and Maggie Kosinski shot him a hard look. "They're only three months old, Jim. We made a new set after the last software revision."

Johnston had come down from his upper-floor office to watch them bring the system back on-line. First the switching computers were powered down and all the operating disks and tapes were removed. When the computers were brought back up, Kosinski's technicians reloaded master copies of the system software and rebooted.

It was an exacting, step-by-step procedure, one as carefully planned as a satellite launch. It also hadn't worked. No calls came in, no connections were made.

The two of them stood intently studying the operations center's main control console. Banks of CRT screens offered them a visual representation of the telephone system's cybernetic organism. They shook their heads simultaneously, utterly baffled. By rights, the machines should be fine.

"Taylor's gonna be pissed," was Kosinski's only comment.

John F. Taylor was the president and CEO of Midwest Telephone. He was not an easy man to bring bad news to.

"It's gotta be hardware, then," Johnston insisted.

There were only two things that could go wrong with a computer. The complex set of instructions, the software, could be bad in any one of a hundred different ways. Alternatively, the hardware, made up of thousands of complex components, could fail. It had to be one or the other. There was no third alternative.

"We isolated and tested each of the CPUs, remember?" Kosinski was adamant. "The equipment is fine. Besides, what conceivable fault could create this kind of problem?"

Johnston spread his hands. "If it's not the CPUs, then the problem has to be in the hookup somewhere in the system—how they interact."

"Could be." Kosinski frowned. "Geez, that could be either a hardware or a software screwup . . . or some weird combination of both." Part of her mind groaned at the thought. Debugging the intricate interactions of the machines and code as they communicated with each other would be a brain-burning exertion.

She shrugged. It was necessary. Then she brightened. If she was the one who brought the phone system back into operation, she would get the glory. Of course, she was also the one who would take the fall if the system stayed down.

Kosinski got to work.

2:00 P.M., EST

CNN Headline News

"Our top story this hour is the continuing phone outage in the Midwest.

"Phone service in Minnesota, Wisconsin, Iowa, Illinois, Michigan, and Indiana remains at a complete standstill. While some attempts to place calls have been successful, Midwest Telephone spokesmen estimate that only one in a thousand or even one in ten thousand calls are being connected.

"The outage remains confined to the six-state region, but the rest of the nation's telecommunications companies are reported to be closely monitoring the situation.

"In an exclusive radio interview with CNN, an assistant to John F. Taylor, Midwest Telephone's CEO, hinted that the company suspects outside interference with its operations. Apparently, Midwest Telephone has requested emergency assistance

from both the FBI and the Federal Communications Commission . . ."

2:15 P.M., EST

Detroit

Randy Newcomb stood with the rest of the crowd watching the
fire gutting old Mr. Romano's house. The fire department was
nowhere in sight.

He felt strangely detached. Neither the sight of the fire nor
the old geezer's loss meant anything to him.

Randy lived on the corner with an older brother and an alco-
holic mother. Just eighteen, he'd been drifting in and out of
high school for more than a year. He was a bright kid, and his
brains had earned him leadership of the F Street posse. But they
hadn't been enough to keep him off crack.

The fire was just one more unimportant event in his drab existence. The only color was provided by small vials of crack.
Getting the money for the next vial and the one after that occupied his entire being. Nothing else was worth much thought
or worry.

Newcomb heard the neighbors talking about the phones
being out, and complaining about not being able to call a fire
truck or an ambulance. That struck a sudden spark in his brain.
If people couldn't reach the fire or emergency services, they also
couldn't alert the police to any trouble, he slowly realized, smiling.

Drifting away from the crowd, he trotted back to his own
house and grabbed the car keys. He had to collect a few of his
friends. If they moved fast before the phones came back on,
they could really score.

He turned the key, and the old Ford turned over. Reaching
under the seat, he pulled out a 9mm automatic. He checked the

magazine and patted the weapon affectionately. This was going to be fun. After all, the police couldn't possibly be everywhere at once.

2:30 P.M., EST

Detroit

Newcomb wasn't alone.

Ninety minutes after the phones went dead, Officer Bob Calvin had the frustrating feeling of knowing there might be crimes going on all around him, but of being unable to do more than sweep up. He'd found out about the Napoli restaurant robbery only when someone flagged down his car and told him about the shooting.

By then, it was far too late for Joe Millunzi. All Calvin had been able to do was summon the detectives and the coroner. Even that took extra time, because the coroner's office was not normally on the radio circuit. Someone had finally passed them a walkie-talkie, but until then Dispatch had to send a runner over to their office. Calvin had the sinking feeling that Detroit's medical examiners would be busy today.

He scrambled back into his patrol car still trying to think of a way to increase his chances of stopping the bad guys before they struck again. It was the old story. Walking a beat instead of driving would make him more accessible to the community but it would also cut the ground he could cover by a factor of ten. Using a motorcycle or bicycle instead of an enclosed car would have been a compromise, but just looking at the freezing weather outside made him shiver at the thought. Bike patrols were practical in the Sun Belt—not here.

Detroit's police force had operated with radio dispatch for years, and before that they'd used a call box system for the beat cops. But both those communications systems depended on people phoning the police when they spotted trouble. You just couldn't protect a large city any other way.

Now the city's officials were scrambling to patch together a makeshift replacement for the telephone system. Neighborhood watch patrols and citizens with CB radios were already taking to the streets, but they were sometimes more of a hindrance than a help. He'd already heard of an incident where one officious idiot thought a radio in his car gave him arrest powers and tried to stop a liquor store holdup on his own. The man had paid for his overzealousness with his life.

The CB nets were confused too. Most of the people using them lacked the discipline and training needed to manage a communications net efficiently. Multiple callers on a limited number of channels often turned the airwaves into a static-laden Towel of Babel. There were even some jokers actually putting out false alarms—sending an already strained police force off on wild-goose chases across the city.

But then again, maybe they weren't just pranksters, Calvin suddenly thought. The street gangs and other criminals infesting Detroit's poorer neighborhoods knew what was happening around them. Maybe some of the smarter bastards just wanted to make sure they were left to run wild unmolested.

He slowed as a knot of people on the sidewalk ahead drew his attention and his concern. What he saw was unusual, and today anything unusual was bad.

Storefront shops and run-down apartments lined both sides of this two-way street. As he drove closer, he saw that the crowd he'd spotted was clustered around an appliance store. People were moving quickly in and out of the store, and even from this distance he could see a shattered window.

Wonderful.

He picked up the microphone. "Dispatch, this is Unit Five-Three-Two. I've got looting at Concord and St. Paul. I need some backup."

The dispatcher's voice came back through the radio speaker, relaying his request to the closest patrol cars. "Any units to assist Five-Three-Two at Concord and St. Paul?"

The responses were not reassuring.

"Unit Five-Two-One, I'm stuck here for at least fifteen more minutes."

"Dispatch, this is Two-Four-Four. Negative on that. I'm tied up with two in custody."

"Unit Two-Three-Two, I can clear and go. But I'm ten out."

Shit. Ten minutes was way too long. Calvin thumbed his mike again. "Roger, Dispatch. I'll do it myself. Out."

He shook his head. Trying to break up a crowd alone violated not only standing department policy but common sense. Handling a mob this size ordinarily required half a dozen men. But the times were not ordinary and he'd studied the crowd's behavior while the dispatcher made her futile calls. He had a glimmering of an approach that might pay off.

He was facing about twenty or thirty people, most of them adults. They seemed more intent on getting into the store and getting out with boxes or items in their arms than in physical violence. He didn't see any gang members nearby with bloodier ideas on their tiny minds.

Calvin parked the car half a block up from the store and hopped out, taking the riot gun with him. He stood behind the driver's side door for half a moment, surveying the situation one last time. No one in the crowd paid much attention to the lone cop car and the lone cop.

"Time to restore the peace and earn my pay," he muttered under his breath. He pumped a round into the riot gun and trotted toward the appliance store. His heart started to pound.

A few people at the edges of the crowd saw him coming and faded away, some pulling friends with them, the others just hightailing it up the street. The rest were still trying to force their way inside. The looting must be just starting, Calvin concluded. Good. Now was the time to stop it.

He pulled the trigger on the shotgun, firing it into the air. The weapon bucked in his hands, and the roar easily drowned out the mob's confused babble. "Everyone on the ground now!" he shouted.

More of the crowd, maybe half, broke and ran. The rest stood their ground, apparently trying to gauge their chances. After all, they were many, and he was only one.

Calvin sensed their mood and fired the shotgun again, closer this time but still over their heads. Most of the rest took flight. He pumped another round into the riot gun and leveled it at the few who were left. "Go on, get out of here!"

Needing no further instruction, they fled.

Even as they disappeared into alleys and doorways, Calvin suddenly realized he wasn't breathing. Letting the air held in his lungs out with a whoosh, he took a breath and felt the tightness leave his body. He took off his cap and wiped the sweat off his forehead. "Shit, maybe that was stupid, but it worked."

Trotting toward the shattered storefront, he sighed. With enough backup, he could have arrested them all, but the jails would already be full tonight. Anyway those weren't the kind of people he wanted to lock up. He'd seen their worn-out winter coats, and lean, careworn faces. They were just taking advantage of something started by someone else—some thief or gang-banger who'd broken in the store's windows.

Calvin reached the store and stepped inside, picking his way through the jumble of boxes and broken glass. Almost immediately, he spotted the bodies. One lay by the front door, while another sprawled behind the counter.

He knelt by the closest, a Korean man in his forties who had been shot at least twice. He checked the man's pulse quickly, but it was obvious from the head wound that he was stone-dead. Damn it.

Calvin turned to the other victim. This one was a Korean woman—probably the dead man's wife since they were almost the same age. She lay on her back near the smashed-open cash register, almost spread-eagle, and with a single wound in the chest. The bullet must have gone all the way through, he realized, looking at the pool of dark blood all around her.

She was still alive, but she wouldn't be for much longer—not in the cold and not after losing that much blood . . .

He sprinted back to his patrol car and pulled up next to the shop. As he drove the short distance, he reported to Dispatch, asked for an ambulance, and checked again on his backup.

"Backup is still five minutes out, Five-Three-Two. Ambulance delay is currently twenty minutes or more."

Calvin swore. Without adequate communications, the city was losing its ability to deliver emergency care with the necessary speed. Another link to civilization had broken.

After quickly applying field dressings from the first-aid kit in his car, he loaded the wounded woman into the backseat and sped off for Mercy Hospital, fifteen minutes away. He knew the looters would come back as soon as he left the scene, but there was nothing else he could do.

Mercy Hospital was a mess. The emergency room was crammed, of course, nothing new about that, but the injured were coming in so fast that a triage team had been set up in a nearby meeting room.

Detroit was falling apart. The drugged-out thugs and drunken punks who perpetrated Devil's Night every Halloween were taking full advantage of the developing crisis. The fire department had been swamped by hundreds of small fires, any of which could flare out of control if not contained in time. Besides the fires, a wave of looting, robbery, and revenge killing was spreading through the city as police response times lagged further and further behind.

After leaving the wounded Korean woman in the hands of a haggard surgical team, Calvin reported in.

"Roger, Five-Three-Two," the dispatcher acknowledged urgently. "Code Three to the commercial district. Report to the mobile CP at Michigan and Woodward."

Calvin sprinted back to his car and tore out of the hospital driveway at high speed. Code Three meant move it, lights and siren. Something big and bad was going down.

Detroit's biggest tourist attraction was the Renaissance Center, a glittering, high-rise collection of shops and offices right on the water. Part of an extensive redevelopment plan by the city, it had become a symbol of Detroit's hope for better economic times.

Now the Renaissance Center was on fire, and Calvin could see the smoke billowing skyward as he raced up Michigan Avenue. He pulled up to the command post, a cluster of police cars, vans, and ambulances parked a few blocks from the complex. As he drove up, an ambulance pulled away, screaming back down the avenue.

The command post was close to the Center, but far enough to be out of immediate danger. Calvin could hear the dull roar of a crowd out of control just a few blocks away. He could also smell smoke and tear gas. The streets had been blocked off.

The commander-on-scene was a middle-aged, harried-looking lieutenant hurriedly briefing and assigning policemen as fast as they reported in. His name tag read "Haskins." He grabbed Calvin by the arm and pointed to a street map spread in front of him. "Set up a roadblock at this intersection. Nothing goes south toward the Renaissance Center. You're part of a cordon around the area. Got it?"

Calvin nodded and drove off to take up his position.

4:30 P.M., EST

Riot control cordon, near the Renaissance Center, Detroit

Beneath an overcast sky, it was already twilight. Off to the east, the blazing towers of the Renaissance Center glowed orange against a black horizon.

Despite the cold, deepening as the sky darkened, Bob Calvin waited outside his police car. So far he hadn't had much to do beyond waving off those few idiotic motorists who somehow hadn't heard the news.

To Calvin that seemed almost impossible. He'd been listening to the radio transmissions describing the disaster overtaking Detroit's city center for more than an hour.

Someone, nobody seemed exactly sure who, had firebombed two of the Center's towers, trapping hundreds of workers inside. The arsonists hadn't fled when the fire department arrived on scene. Instead, they'd begun sniping at the firemen and rescue workers, forcing them to fall back until a police SWAT team showed up.

But then, in turn, the SWAT team was driven back by a new wave of angry, young black men pouring out of the run-down row houses only a few blocks from the Renaissance Center. Word of the arson and looting attracted many who seemed determined to burn the soaring towers to the ground, along with anyone, black or white, still inside. More police units were fed in to regain control.

For the first few minutes, despite the increasing furor, Detroit's law enforcement units had seemed to have the upper hand over the rioters. To Calvin's trained ear, the reports of arrests, disturbances, and requests for ambulances had been rushed and excited but indicated that the officers were still in control.

Then, almost as soon as true darkness began falling, the radio transmissions changed. Now there was real trouble.

Calvin heard someone, a sergeant he knew only by voice, suddenly transmit, "Jesus, Tactical! We've got more bad guys swarming us! Too many! We need immediate assistance!"

There were sporadic gunshots audible over the radio now.

"Say again! Shit! Tactical, we're getting fucking overrun—"

And that was it. Nothing more.

Calvin listened to the static hiss for a moment more before scrambling back inside his patrol cruiser. He reversed away from the barrier he'd been manning and headed east toward the Renaissance Center. He considered calling the CP to ask for permission to leave his post and then scratched the idea. There wasn't enough time. His buddies on the police line needed him now.

He skidded to a stop at a line of black and yellow traffic barriers blocking off the wide, divided boulevard that ran past the Renaissance Center.

The Center's landscaped grounds were filled with a tangled mass of people, overturned cars, and burning emergency vehicles. Flickering light from the flames and from spotlights showed him a huge crowd, more than a thousand strong, on the rampage. Shots rang out from time to time, but it was impossible to tell who was firing at whom.

The mob had a small group of police and firemen at bay more than a block away from the Center itself. Officers were loading and firing tear-gas canisters into the crowds, most of whom now seemed intent on rolling and torching a couple of fire trucks.

There were bodies littering the ground behind the police line, some motionless, others writhing in pain. They were being rushed into ambulances as the riot police fell back, giving ground slowly to win time for the medics to load up and escape. It was clear that the police had not only lost control of the Renaissance Center Plaza, they were actually fighting for bare survival.

Calvin abandoned his vehicle and sprinted toward the retreating police line. He was careful to hug the sides of buildings and duck behind cars or any other available cover whenever possible. Right now the mob was an aimless, angry animal, searching for prey. He did not want to draw its attention.

He spotted a figure behind the line issuing orders and hurried over. There was enough light to see that it was Lieutenant Haskins. Blood ran down the lieutenant's face from a cut on his forehead, and he had one arm hanging limply at his side—splinted with a riot baton.

Haskins didn't bother asking why he'd abandoned his position. Instead, he yelled, "Get on the radio and pull in the rest of the cordon! They're about all the help we're going to get!"

That would only give them about ten more officers to reinforce the line. Stunned, Calvin exclaimed, "Isn't the department going to send anyone else?"

Haskins shook his head, then winced at the motion. "The department's got other problems besides us. The whole goddamned city's going up tonight!"

Still shocked, Calvin found the nearest intact police car and relayed the lieutenant's orders. As he headed back, another shot cracked out from the mob. He saw a cop fall, clutching his leg. Another officer fired back.

Calvin hoped the man had a clear target.

He ran toward the injured policeman, but two paramedics beat him there. They dropped to the ground beside the groaning man, feverishly stripping off his riot gear as they tried to treat his wound.

Calvin knelt close by, putting the riot cop's helmet, gas mask, and bulletproof vest on as fast as they came off. He snatched up the fallen officer's baton and clear Plexiglas shield, and took his place in the shrinking police line.

He could see the crowd more clearly now. They were only a hundred yards away—close enough to make out individuals. Somehow, though, the rioters all looked the same. Young men in dark clothing ran, shouted, and taunted the police. All were black or Hispanic. Bottles and other missiles flew out of the darkness toward the police line. Most fell short. A few clattered off their upraised shields.

Calvin slid into position and immediately felt a little more secure, although he knew that was illusory. He was part of a disciplined line of trained men, but the chaos they were facing made him feel like an island of sand facing the raging ocean.

He stiffened, readying himself, as a band of screaming young toughs suddenly shoved their way forward out of the crowd. Some were waving baseball bats or tire irons.

THUMMP. A tear-gas canister sailed over his head and landed in the middle of the advancing teens. They scattered.

A ball of flame blossomed skyward in the middle of the plaza. Calvin guessed that was a car's fuel tank cooking off.

The command came for them to step back, and he backed up in line with the others.

Now Calvin could hear a bullhorn blaring somewhere out in front. Somewhere out in the middle of the mob. He couldn't hear the words, but he could hear their rhythm and pitch. Did this beast have a brain? The thought frightened him, and only his training steadied him. They stepped back again.

The crowd actually drew away from him and the other riot

police, and for a moment he hoped they had grown bored or
were more interested in easier prey. Then he saw that they were
clustering around the bonfire from the burning car. The voice
shouting through the bullhorn was still indistinct, but he could
hear cheers and answering shouts from the throng.

Suddenly, almost as one, they turned to face the police, and
Calvin knew what the man with the bullhorn had been saying.
The cops are the enemy. Kill them. Take their weapons. Simple,
brutal instructions—commands the crowd was ready to obey.

The mass started to move forward, and he fought down a feeling that the whole thing was headed straight at him. He tried to
pick out individuals at the edge and saw that while they were
eager to shout, they were reluctant to challenge the police line
physically. Pushed from behind, though, they did advance, first
walking and then running.

Calvin heard more feet slamming onto the pavement behind
him, and knew that the line was being extended as every able-
bodied officer joined them. Would it be enough? If they were
outflanked . . .

Haskin's voice bellowed, "Guard!"

He brought his baton up, ready to take the shock and defend
himself. The mob seemed as big as the ocean, and the tide was
coming in.

"Advance!"

Calvin blinked. The tactical manuals said the best defense
was a good offense, but who ever heard of a shoreline advancing
to meet the waves? Nevertheless, he took one step in unison
with the officers on either side, paused a moment, and then
went forward again, falling into the well-drilled rhythm designed to cow an unruly crowd.

More tear-gas canisters landed right in front of them. The
yelling people nearest to the gray haze recoiled for a second and
then were pushed forward by the vast throng behind them.
Some fell, retching, and were swallowed up.

With a heart-stopping, guttural roar, the mob slammed into
the advancing police line.

A short, skinny teenager rushed Calvin first, trying to grab his baton. The policeman easily dodged his outstretched hands and brought the baton around in a slashing blow. The boy screamed and ducked back, clutching a broken wrist.

Another man, older and much larger, tried to tear the shield out of Calvin's grip. Pain shot up his forearm as he slammed the baton down across the attacker's arm and then again across the man's head. The rioter went down in a boneless heap.

After that, the struggle disintegrated into a flurry of half-seen, half-felt, and half-remembered blows and counterblows, strike and counterstrike. His earlier fears submerged by the primal urge to survive, Calvin fought calmly and effectively. But no matter how many rioters he knocked down or drove off, there was a seemingly endless supply of others still surging forward in an effort to tear him apart.

Twice he heard Haskins pulling the police line back to tighten its sagging formation. He saw another policeman dragged down and grimaced. They were running out of men and maneuvering room.

And still the mob came on.

Calvin felt a bullet whiz past his head and heard the deafening sound of a shot close by in the same moment. His eyes focused on a man in his twenties, heavy-set and bald, coldly aiming a pistol at him at point-blank range.

Oh, hell.

The man fired again and Calvin felt his shield take the bullet this time, deflecting it, but the shock of its impact ran up his arm. It felt like his elbow had been hit by a ball peen hammer. He staggered backward.

The gunman fired a third time. This time the round tore through the Plexiglas shield and slammed into his bulletproof vest. At such short range, the 9mm slug had enough velocity to shock and bruise him, but the shield and vest stopped it from doing more damage.

His assailant snarled in frustration, acting as though the policeman had broken the rules by not falling down dead. The man raised his aim, pointing the pistol straight at Calvin's unprotected face.

No! He didn't have time to draw his own weapon.

Calvin lunged forward and slammed the point of his baton into the gunman's sternum. As the man doubled over in agony, he slashed downward, striking him across the back of the neck, just below the skull. That was potentially a killing blow, but the policeman didn't give a damn. There was only one law operating right now—the law of survival.

He looked up, gasping for breath, and realized that he was surrounded by screaming, shouting rioters. His lunge had carried him well out into the midst of the mob.

People swarmed past him, pouring through the sudden gap in the police line. Others dove on top of him, knocking him over as they tried to pull off his helmet or grab his weapons. His shield protected him from many of their blows, but it also trapped one of his arms. Punches and kicks rained down in an unrelenting hail. Something sharp stabbed into his leg. He felt himself being driven down into unconsciousness.

Calvin struggled desperately to get up off the ground. Staying down meant dying.

A baseball bat swung overhand caught his shield and knocked him back down. Someone else stomped on his wrist and grabbed his baton away. The world blurred in a red fog.

Shots rang out suddenly. Calvin felt the pressure on him slacken as his attackers turned away in surprise. Seconds later, another ragged volley cut across the crowd noise. Somebody was firing tear-gas guns—a lot of them. A dozen brilliant beams of white light lanced into the plaza, blinding rioters caught staring at them and turning night into artificial day.

Clouds of gray mist billowed up from each gas canister. The mob began coughing, gagging as the tear gas rolled over them. Their shouts changed swiftly in tone from anger and hate to fear.

Calvin heard the growing roar of diesel engines moving closer.

The crowd began backing away, slowly at first, and then faster. More and more of them turned to flee.

Still barely clinging to consciousness, Calvin lifted his head just high enough to see what was going on. Hundreds of soldiers in full battle gear and gas masks were advancing across the wreckage-strewn Renaissance Center Plaza. Armored personnel carriers mounting searchlights trundled behind the troops.

Suddenly, Bob Calvin lay alone. He tried to get up, but his right leg crumpled under him and he landed heavily on the pavement. The ground seemed very cold. He heard someone calling for a stretcher as he surrendered at last to the pain filling every corner of his being.

11:30 P.M., EST

ABC News Special Report: "Shutdown"

The ABC News Special Report showed signs of being hurriedly assembled. Half the video aired was live or only minutes old. And none of the news was good.

The Midwest's phone system was still down, and it would remain down for the foreseeable future. Caught without the ability to communicate, tens of thousands of businesses had been forced to close, idling millions of workers. So far the only beneficiaries of the disaster had been messenger services. Most normal commerce had ground to a halt. The economic losses alone were already estimated in the tens of billions of dollars.

But there were other, far more serious losses. Detroit was not alone. With police and emergency services degraded, every major city in the region had experienced a vicious crime wave. The governors of Minnesota, Wisconsin, Illinois, Indiana, and Iowa had all mobilized their National Guard units by midafternoon and instituted an immediate nighttime curfew. Hundreds were already dead, and hundreds more were seriously injured in the continuing civil disorder.

Pressed hard for an explanation, company representatives now blamed "an external cause, most likely the deliberate sabotage of the switching network by a highly sophisticated computer virus."

This claim was immediately backed up by several electronics and computer experts. In the blink of an eye, the phone company went from villain to victim. The news also transformed the ongoing catastrophe from an unavoidable act of God to an act of deliberate, calculated terror.

The final piece of the ABC News Special was an interview with Senator George Roland, one of the few survivors of the National Press Club bombing. Since the attack, Roland had acquired immense standing, and he used every ounce of it in making his points.

"There is no doubt that these terrorists are bent on destroying American society. The government can no longer deny that these attacks are part of a larger plan. Unless the administration acts swiftly, strongly, and positively, our nation may not survive."

No one disagreed.

NOVEMBER 30

Midwest Telephone's primary operations center

With Jim Johnston standing next to her, Maggie Kosinski dialed the boss's number. Light-headed, almost shaking with fatigue and excitement, she hit the last digit and then looked again at the diskette on her desk. The label read simply "Alpha Virus."

An urgent, pleading voice answered on the first ring. "Yes?"

"This is Kosinski in Operations," she announced. "We've got it!"

"Hang on."

After a short pause, she heard, "This is Taylor." Midwest Telephone's CEO sounded almost as tired as she did, almost as tired as they all were. Nobody had gotten much sleep in the past three days.

Kosinski forced herself to speak calmly and distinctly. "We've confirmed our initial diagnosis, sir. We were able to track down the virus and its source, and we've started a reboot. The whole system will be back on-line in forty-five minutes."

"Thank God!" Taylor breathed. His voice sharpened. "Where was the damned thing hidden?"

Kosinski prodded the diskette on her desk with a pen. She didn't even want to touch it with her bare hands. "In one of our printers, sir."

"What?!"

She explained further. "Some clever bastard hid the virus inside our laser printer ROM chip—piggybacked onto its normal code in several pieces. Every time we rebooted, it would reassemble the pieces and reinfect the system from scratch." She shook her head at the vicious intelligence behind the attack, half in unwilling admiration and half in anger. "We got lucky or we'd probably still be looking for it. One of my techs turned the printer off to clear a paper jam and forgot to turn it back on. While it was off, we rebooted the system again and everything started to come back on-line. But as soon as we powered up the printer, the virus reappeared."

"Good God!" Taylor exclaimed. He hesitated. "Have you discovered any more nasty surprises lurking out there?"

"Yes, sir." Kosinski's lips thinned. "We found the same type of altered ROM chip in every switching center's printer. They'd all been serviced in the past two months."

"Son of a bitch."

"Yeah." Kosinski prodded the diskette on her desk again. "This is no virus I've ever seen or heard of, sir. I've already passed the ROM chip we found here to the FBI and the Computer Emergency Response Team. It's their baby now."

Personally, she wished them luck. Virusland was a mysterious and spooky place, full of secrecy and strange personalities. It took a special kind of weirdo, she thought, to write a program that deliberately fouled up a computer.

And someone out there, some terrorist, had gone straight to the top of a very twisted bunch to find this little gem.

CHAPTER 19

BACKLASH

DECEMBER 2

Falls Church, northern Virginia

Helen Gray fought off the last clinging tendrils of a nightmare and woke up, suddenly aware that she was all alone in the rumpled bed. She opened her eyes. The glowing digits on his bedside clock read 1:41 A.M. Where had Peter gone?

She pushed herself upright and looked around the room. The lights were off, but her eyes were adjusted to the darkness. Her lips curved upward in a smile as she noticed the pieces of clothing strewn across the floor from the half-open door all the way over to the bed. Someday she and Peter Thorn were going to have to learn to set a somewhat slower, less frantic pace in their lovemaking.

But not now. After weeks of strain and enforced separation, neither of them could have been expected to restrain themselves for very long. And they hadn't.

With her section on a twelve-hour stand-down, Helen had

driven straight to Peter's town house. She remembered falling into his arms as soon as he opened the front door. Her memories after that were a tangled mix of roving hands, parted lips, motion, warmth, and finally, a swelling, crashing wave of sheer ecstasy.

Sleep had come after—a welcome slide into restful oblivion that had been broken only by an old nightmare from her childhood. A nightmare of being hunted through an endless maze of narrow, dead-end corridors and impossible turnings. It was an evil dream that had come back to haunt her in these past several weeks as she and her fellow FBI agents grappled with their faceless, nameless foes.

Helen glanced at the empty place beside her and guessed that the nightmare had begun only after Peter left her side. She shook off the last wisps of sleep.

Her nose twitched as she caught the welcome smell of coffee wafting in through the open doorway. She slid out of bed, threw on one of his shirts, and glided quietly out into the hallway.

The lights were on in the guest bedroom Peter used as a work space. She pushed open the unlatched door and went inside.

Wearing only a pair of ash-gray Army sweatpants, Peter Thorn sat at a desk, paging steadily through a stack of reports she had forwarded from the FBI task force. Under enormous pressure from above for results, Special Agent Flynn's initial reluctance to share their information with the government's other counterterrorist units had faded somewhat.

Peter had pinned a large map of the United States to the wall above his desk. Color-coded pins marked the location of different terrorist attacks. His light brown hair was tousled and his green eyes looked weary. A forgotten cup of coffee sat cooling beside a calculator and a pocket calendar.

Helen leaned over and put her arms around him. "Couldn't sleep?" she asked softly.

He looked around with the same wry, boyish grin that had first attracted her to him. "Nope. Sorry." He tapped the disordered pile of papers in front of him. "I just can't seem to stop going over and over these reports in my mind."

"What are you looking for?"

Thorn shrugged tiredly. "I'm not sure exactly. Maybe some pattern we haven't spotted yet. Some common method of operations or choice of targets."

She nodded slowly. "Not a bad idea, Peter. Nobody on our task force has the time or energy to look very hard at the big picture. Everybody's locked into the little piece of the puzzle they're directly responsible for investigating."

"What about Flynn?"

Helen shook her head. "He tries. But every time he starts pulling all our data together, it seems like somebody from the White House calls for another briefing. Or he has to fend off the press or the Congress. There are too many distractions. Too many conflicting demands on his time." She nodded toward his desk. "So, are you finding anything interesting in all of that?"

Peter grimaced. "Nothing solid. Just an ugly sneaking suspicion that we're looking in the wrong goddamned place for these bastards. I'm beginning to think we're not dealing with domestic terrorism at all. That maybe most of what's been happening is something that was planned and organized overseas. That we could be facing a single, coordinated terrorist effort."

Helen straightened up to her full height, suddenly very alert. "Explain."

His mouth turned down even more. "I wish I could. It's more a feeling than anything else." He pushed some of the FBI incident reports to one side. "Look, discount the background noise—the murders and penny-ante bombings conducted by the second-raters and punks we've already caught. Right?"

She nodded. Each large-scale terrorist massacre or bombing seemed to spawn half a dozen or more copycat acts—most by known psychos or members of hate groups already under FBI surveillance. The legwork involved in running those incidents down consumed precious time and resources, but it never seemed to bring them any closer to the people who were doing the real damage.

"Well, then, take another look at what's left. Bombings and massacres that jump from D.C. to Seattle, to Chicago, then back to D.C., and on to Dallas. More bombs that hit L.A. and Louisville on the same day. Then another series of bombs and ambushes back in this area. And now this communications virus in the Midwest." Thorn jabbed a finger at the map as he spoke, pinpointing each separate incident. "Every attack is professionally planned and executed. Every attack strikes a new area and a new type of target. And every attack spreads our personnel and resources across a wider and wider area."

"Sure." Helen frowned slightly. "But, Peter, several groups with very different agendas have claimed responsibility for the worst attacks."

"Sure. Groups that no one had heard of before this all started. Terrorist organizations that never showed up on any law enforcement agency's radar screen. Terrorists with access to plastic explosive, SA-16s, and now computer viruses, for God's sake!" He shook his head forcefully. "It's just too damned much, Helen. Every instinct I've got tells me that there's someone lurking out there pulling the strings and watching us jump."

"Who?" she asked quietly.

"God knows. I don't." Some of the fire went out of his eyes. "Maybe those German neo-Nazis we heard about after the synagogue hostage-taking you smashed. Maybe the people who recruited those Bosnian Muslims Rossini and I tried so hard to find earlier this year."

"So you think the terrorists, or some of them anyway, are foreigners?"

Peter nodded. "Yeah, I do. I think that's why none of your people have ever been able to find a print they could match at any of the crime scenes. Plus, there's at least one piece of supporting evidence that backs up my hunch."

He sorted through the stacked documents and pulled out a stapled collection of transcripts and photocopied letters. "Take a gander at those."

She glanced through them and looked up. "The oral and written communiqués issued by the different terrorist groups?"

"Uh-huh. Supposedly issued by everybody from the New Aryan Order to the Black Liberation Front. But they've got one thing in common. Rossini and I both checked them over to make sure." Peter paused to take a sip of his cold coffee, set the cup aside again, and continued. "Every single message is perfect. Not a single spelling error. Not a single misplaced comma. Not a single piece of slang. They're all absolutely grammatically perfect."

Helen vaguely remembered hearing or reading something similar. Had it been in a memo from the FBI's own language experts? She frowned. So many documents had crossed her temporary desk in such a short space of time that she'd often suspected the task force would drown in paper before finding its first terrorist. Still, how had she missed something like this? How had they *all* missed something like this?

She already knew the answer to her question. The FBI task force had been swamped right from the day it was formed—hit from all sides at every turn by new demands on its time and its limited resources. If Peter's guess was right, that had been an important part of the terrorist plan from the very beginning. Her face darkened in anger.

He reached out and took the material out of her unresisting hand. "I think all of these little propaganda pieces were written by the same people. By people with a thorough, but very academic, knowledge of American English."

Helen nodded slowly, still rocked by the stomach-turning possibility that the Bureau task force had been walking right past an important clue. "God, Peter, I think you're probably right." She hesitated. "But . . ."

"But I don't have a single shred of solid proof beyond those communiqués," he finished the sentence for her.

She shook her head. "I'll talk to Flynn tomorrow morning anyway. We've been focusing all our energies on the domestic angle. Maybe it's high time we widened our search."

Peter smiled crookedly. "You think Special Agent Flynn's really going to listen to a wild-eyed theory from an Army grunt?"

"Coming from a *smart* Army grunt? He might. Mike Flynn's got a good head on his shoulders," Helen countered. "He doesn't put up with bullshit, but I've never seen him turn away a good idea—no matter where it came from."

"That's nice," Peter said, still clearly unconvinced. He bit down on a yawn and glanced at his watch. Then he pushed back his chair and stood up. "Look, maybe we should try to get some sleep. You've got to report back, and I've got a date with Rossini a little later this morning."

"Oh? A date with the Maestro?" Helen asked, slipping her arm around his waist. "Is there something I should know about you, Colonel Thorn?"

He laughed softly, almost against his will. "Not that kind of a date, Agent Gray." His smile slipped. "Rossini wangled a copy of that damned computer virus out of the Computer Emergency Response Team. We're going to run it by somebody he knows— a guy the Maestro says is a Grade A computer whiz."

He shrugged. "Of course, it's probably just a waste of time. God knows, every cybernetics expert in the federal government is already doing the same thing."

Helen hugged him tighter. "You just keep at it, Peter." Then she stepped back and held out her hand. "Now come take me to bed."

Thorn's grin returned. "Yes, ma'am. Anything you say."

Herndon, northern Virginia

Joseph Rossini took the Dulles Access Road out toward Herndon, relying on their official Pentagon identity cards to get them through the tollbooths without having to scratch around for exact change. He also drove fast, exceeding the speed limit by at least fifteen miles an hour.

The older man caught Thorn watching him out of the corner of his eye and lifted his shoulders. "I hate poking along, Pete. Going fifty-five's just not efficient."

Thorn hid a smile by pretending to take an interest in the passing scenery. Saddled with a loving wife and a multitude of kids, the Maestro had obviously decided to settle for the first half of the male equation seeking "fast cars and loose women."

They sped past what looked like a military encampment. It was a staging area for one of the security patrols established under the President's vaunted Operation SAFE SKIES. Two Blackhawk helicopters and a couple of Humvees sat under camouflage netting in a clearing off to the side of the road. Soldiers wearing the Screaming Eagles patch of the 101st Air Assault Division tramped through the mud left by another hard rain. They looked thoroughly bored and uncomfortable.

Thorn looked away, still angry at the clear waste of good manpower. He turned back to Rossini. "You're sure this guy Kettler can handle the job?"

"Uh-huh. Without breaking a sweat."

Thorn hoped the Maestro's confidence wasn't misplaced. The man they were on their way to see, Derek Kettler, made his living as a freelance software designer and consultant. Apparently, JSOC had hired him once before to craft special security and antiviral programs for its intelligence section.

"Kettler lives and breathes computers, Pete," Rossini continued. "The guy's a little unusual, but he practically *dreams* in machine code. He's good. One of the best."

"Just how unusual is he?" Thorn asked skeptically.

Rossini shrugged. "He telecommutes so he can work alone. He likes being alone. He hates having to take orders. In fact, he hates just about anything to do with authority or control."

Thorn arched an eyebrow. "Then why work with computers? Hell, they're nothing but rules and instructions . . ."

Rossini shook his head. "Those are physical limitations, like gravity or the speed of light. It's people telling him what to do that Kettler has trouble with."

Great, Thorn thought. They were off on a visit to the Computer Hermit of Herndon.

The older man pulled off the Access Road, fast-talked their way past the local tollbooth, and followed a series of treelined streets to a newer part of the town.

The housing development still showed signs of newness. A

Dumpster loaded with construction scraps marked the corner where they turned off the main road, and two of the end units still had raw, muddy earth instead of lawns. The homes were attractive, brick-fronted, two-story town houses. Different gables and copper trim gave each a small bit of identity otherwise lacking in their construction.

Derek Kettler's house was third from the left in a row of ten. They parked, and Rossini muttered, "Stay here in the car for a minute, until I signal. He agreed to meet with us over the phone last night because he's dying to see this new virus, but he really wasn't very happy with the idea of a face-to-face chat. Like I said, he prefers dealing by modem."

Swell. Thorn sat stiffly in the front seat, watching Rossini climb the front steps to Kettler's town house.

The Maestro knocked, and then, after waiting a few moments without any apparent response, pressed the bell. Even in the car, Thorn could hear the sound, not of a bell, but a fierce animal roar. Rossini seemed to expect it and looked apologetically toward the car, shrugging.

The door opened, and Thorn saw Kettler for the first time.

His immediate impression was a 1960s-style hippie without any of the tie-dyed color. Rossini's computer genius wore a gray sweatshirt, jeans, and sneakers, all of which looked rumpled—even the shoes. Kettler himself was in his thirties, slightly overweight, and badly in need of a haircut. His black hair and beard were long and lank.

Thorn watched the two men speak for a few minutes. Kettler kept nervously glancing toward the car while Rossini made soothing gestures. Finally, the computer expert disappeared, still shaking his head, and the Maestro motioned for Thorn to come on up.

He trotted up the steps and followed Rossini inside.

He first noticed the smell, a mixture of stale food and mustiness and other things he didn't want to identify. The front door opened into the living room, which was dominated by a six-foot-high, ten-foot-wide entertainment center. Thorn considered himself something of an audiophile, but this system was incredible. It included a CD player and a tape deck, but it also contained a reel-to-reel tape player and a turntable. There was even what looked like a CRT and a computer keyboard built into the system.

A mass of scattered clothes, magazines, and paperback books surrounded the wall unit, covering about half the carpet. Empty potato chip bags punctuated the mess.

If Thorn expected the living room to be the worst of it, he was mistaken. When they walked back past the kitchen, he spotted countertops littered with dirty dishes and empty soda cans. The room's main fixture seemed to be a large green plastic trash can with so many pizza boxes stuffed into it that they overflowed onto the floor.

Kettler led them upstairs.

A converted bedroom was obviously the heart of the house. A large U-shaped desk filled the center of the room, with computer boxes and electronic components on the desk, on shelves over the desk, and on the floor beside it. Bookshelves crammed with thick hardcovers and trade paperbacks lined one wall. They were all computer-related, with titles like *Numeric Process Control Codes*.

Thorn didn't even feel tempted to open that one.

Like the rest of the house, the blinds were closed, and he doubted if they were ever opened. In stark contrast to the rest of the house, though, the desk and the room were comparatively neat, although he could see small piles of debris in the corners.

Kettler's system was already on. Several large-screen monitors displayed brightly colored geometric designs against a darkened background. The center monitor, a huge two-page display, showed a blue and white emblem surrounded with the words "United Federation of Planets."

Cute. Very cute.

"Gimme the disk," demanded Kettler.

Rossini handed it over without apparent qualm, violating several federal laws in the process. Thorn winced a little, but kept his thoughts to himself. The diskette passed to them by

CERT bore only a handwritten label identifying its contents as "MidTel Virus, Unknown."

Kettler handled it like it was red-hot.

He sat down in a swivel chair and started typing. "Okay, Maestro, I'm going to reconfigure my system. I'll isolate one CPU, and then we'll see what this beast looks like."

Rossini explained to Thorn what they were seeing while Kettler typed in commands and threw switches on a homemade junction box. The software designer had four computers wired together. One was a server, or file manager. Another did nothing but log on to bulletin boards, download files, and screen them for material he was interested in. The final two were paired processors, hooked up in a special rig that allowed Kettler to designate which processor would handle a task. Isolating one of the units would protect the rest of his system from damage if the virus started running wild.

Despite his misgivings, Thorn had to admit he was impressed by the sheer amount of linked hardware in the room and by the evident ease with which the other man handled his equipment.

New lines of text popped into existence on the central monitor.

"All right, here we go," Kettler muttered to himself. He slid the disk into a drive and typed in another set of commands.

"All right, it's just one big file. Okay, baby, let's see if we can find out just what you're made of." Kettler conducted a running monologue with himself while he started running a series of keyboard controlled tests, probing around the file's periphery. Rossini stood over his shoulder, answering questions about the known behavior of the virus.

"Oh, yeah." Kettler nodded knowingly. "Same kind of trick we're supposed to have pulled on the Iraqis during the Gulf War."

Thorn looked at Rossini. "Is that true?"

"Uh-huh," the older man agreed. "The story showed up in a number of the journals. According to them, we planted a virus in the printers inside their air defense computers in Baghdad. It would have worked pretty much the same way."

Thorn whistled sharply. Maybe Amir Taleh's belief that Iraq was behind the effort to rebuild radical Islam's terrorist forces was right after all. Was this a case of an eye for an eye, a tooth for a tooth?

The big monitor suddenly filled with jumbled numbers. "Yes!" Kettler exclaimed.

Thorn looked over Rossini's shoulder. "That's it?"

"Yeah, in octal code," Rossini answered.

"This will make more sense," Kettler announced, and hit a key. The numbers vanished. They were replaced by text grouped in three-letter combinations.

Assembly code, Thorn realized. That was one step up from octal, but it was still Greek to him.

Kettler, however, studied it as if he were reading a road map. Tracing his finger across the columns of code, he scrolled the screen up and down. There were pages of the stuff. Oblivious to the two men, he murmured to himself and scratched notes on a pad.

Thorn fought the urge to check his watch.

After what seemed like an eternity, Kettler shouted, "All right!" for the umpteenth time. Spinning around in his chair to face them, he smiled, almost beaming. "It's the Bulgarian!"

"You're sure?" Rossini demanded.

"Absolutely," Kettler asserted. "This is his stuff. I know viruses. I have to in my line of work. See?"

The computer expert took a key from his pocket and unlocked one of the desk drawers. He pulled it open and lifted out a long disk box that had been marked with yellow-and-black striped tape.

He held the box carefully, as if afraid to jostle its contents. "This is my collection. Every virus I've ever heard of, including some that were stopped before they hit the street." He patted it almost lovingly.

Rossini looked at the box in horror, as though the codes it contained were about to leap out and infect him personally. Like any good analyst, he was instinctively repelled by the idea of a program deliberately created to destroy information.

Kettler flipped open the lid and pulled out three neatly labeled disks. "All three of these babies hold viruses created by the Bulgarian, and the similarities are unmistakable. Some of the subroutines are identical."

Rossini saw Thorn's impatient look and explained. "He's right, Pete. Programmers are like other artists. They've each got their own styles and their own bags of little tricks—favorite techniques they use to achieve specific ends. To somebody who knows how to read this stuff like Derek here, those are as good as fingerprints or signatures."

Kettler was still engrossed in the machine code showing on his monitor. "God, Maestro, this is beautiful work! Whoever paid to have this little monster made sure went to the right place."

Unable to contain himself any longer, Thorn cut in. "Much as I hate to break up this little mutual admiration session, can either of you tell me just who the hell this Bulgarian guy is?"

Rossini filled him in, with Kettler interjecting occasional comments.

Only a few viruses had ever been traced back to people with names. Several, the nastiest of a nasty breed, had been linked to a mysterious individual— "the Bulgarian."

Nobody knew his name, but detective work, much of it unofficial, had traced some viruses back to Bulgaria and to a master programmer working covertly there. Bulgaria's secret service had always had an evil reputation. It had been involved in several assassinations, and even linked to an attempt on the life of the Pope. As a result, many in the computer world assumed the Bulgarian had originally been trained and paid by that country's now-defunct communist government, probably as part of a plan to wreak havoc on the technologically advanced West. Whatever he had once been, it was now clear that the virus-maker was working as a cybermercenary—selling his destructive wares to the highest bidders.

Kettler finished by saying, "Whoever made the deal for this program paid pretty dearly for it. There's all kinds of gossip on the Net, the computer bulletin boards, about what the Bulgarian charges to do his thing—including some pretty wild guesses. But I'd bet you're talking at least a couple of million bucks to craft this baby, and probably a lot more."

"Several million dollars?" Thorn raised an eyebrow and looked at Rossini. "You believe that a white racist group or a band of black radicals could raise that kind of cash without anybody hearing about it?"

"Not a chance. That has to be a government's money," Rossini said flatly. "Whichever it is, I'd say your theory is looking better and better. This campaign is being orchestrated from overseas."

Kettler stared at both of them. "Let me get this straight. You guys think these terrorists are working for some foreign government?"

They nodded slowly.

"Wow." Kettler shook his head. "Far freaking out. This'll sure rock some boats on the Net." He pawed through the diskettes on his desk and came up with a stack of four. "See these? That's almost four megs of traffic on the terror wave alone. Practically everybody with a modem and two brain cells to knock together has his or her own theory about what's going on."

The computer expert slipped his diskettes back into place and shrugged. "Between this terrorism shit and the code controversy, I've been on the Net almost constantly."

"Code controversy?" Thorn asked.

Rossini nodded. "Some government agencies wanted to restrict commercially available E-mail encryption programs to ones the government could break . . ."

"Hell, no, Maestro. Not that old gripe. That's yesterday's news," Kettler interrupted. "This is a privacy issue deal. It broke out a couple of months ago when some guy started bitching about unbreakable, coded E-mail he'd spotted on CompuNet, one of the worldwide computer bulletin boards. Said he'd been intercepting a ton of scrambled posts from somewhere in England to a bunch of users scattered across the country—all using an encryption program he'd never seen before. Boy, did that set off fireworks!"

The computer expert smiled at the memory. "Geez, you should have read all the screaming about the sanctity of private electronic mail, and the First Amendment, and all the usual shit . . . ."

"Hold it," Thorn broke in, his mind racing in high gear. Two or three months ago? The timing could be coincidence, but he'd been wondering how the terrorists coordinated their attacks. Were they using computer hookups to communicate? He looked down at the younger man. "Are you saying someone has spotted coded messages coming *from* a foreign source *to* people here in the U.S.?"

"Yeah," Kettler answered with a nonchalant shrug, "and as far as I'm concerned, they can put them in left-handed Swahili. I don't give a rat's ass. I'm just getting a kick seeing how loud all the Net prudes squawk about it."

Thorn took a step closer and spoke slowly, intensely. "You're missing the point. We've got terrorist attacks going on right and left, and now you're telling me someone's been intercepting coded messages?"

Kettler nodded, a little taken aback, but starting to understand. "Yeah. But that's not necessarily unusual. A lot of E-mail these days is PEM, privacy-enhanced E-mail. It's just that these messages are using a real high level encryption program nobody's ever heard of." He shook his head. "Like I said, a bunch of us have been arguing the issue on some of the Net forums. It's not general knowledge. Cripes, if CompuNet or any of the other public bulletin boards knew that someone was routinely breaking into their private message files, they'd have a conniption fit."

Thorn cut him off sharply. "I don't give a goddamn about the legalities, Mr. Kettler." He leaned forward, towering over the openmouthed computer expert. "Do you know the person who's been making those interceptions?"

"Only by his handle. He calls himself 'Freebooter,' " Kettler replied hesitantly. "He's a real top-gun hacker. He's a little strange."

Thorn didn't say anything, though his mind reeled slightly at the thought that the computer expert could find *anyone* else odd.

Rossini joined in. "Can we contact this guy, Derek?"

"I can dial him up, I guess. I know where he usually hangs out in cyberspace." Kettler absentmindedly scratched his beard. "Freebooter won't talk to you directly, though, Maestro. You work for the Man." He didn't even mention Thorn.

"Whatever. Just do it." Rossini almost pushed Kettler into his chair. "Do you think he'll be there?"

Kettler nodded, typing fast again. "Freebooter's always there. He practically lives on the Net."

The strange lines of machine code vanished as he shunted back to the CPU he had dedicated solely to monitoring the computer bulletin boards.

A speaker suddenly spat out a dial tone, followed by the sound of a number being punched in at high speed. The screen flickered and then blinked into another image. This one showed a rippling black flag emblazoned with a white skull and crossbones. Bold text letters spelled out: WELCOME TO THE PIRATES' COVE.

Kettler looked apologetic. "It's a hacker's BBS. I like to keep my ear to the ground here . . . you know, just kind of see what's new." He bent over the keyboard again, fingers flashing through long-practiced combinations as he logged on and called up a list of those currently on-line. He leaned closer, scrolling through the names and then nodded sharply. "There he is!"

Thorn focused on the list and saw it. A line read: FREE-BOOTER, IN THE TAVERN.

The computer expert punched a few more keys and leaned back. "Okay, he's chatting with someone else right now, but I just paged him."

"Good," Thorn said simply. "Now, you know what we want?"

Kettler nodded rapidly. "Yeah. A data dump of every en-crypted message he's collected, right?"

"Right."

"Okay," Kettler said. "Listen, lemme work on him for a while. This could be kinda tricky. Freebooter's a touchy bastard. If we screw this up or he gets spooked, he'll drop off the Net, change his handle, and then we'll never find him."

Thorn frowned. Despite Kettler's demonstrated computer expertise, he was reluctant to trust something so important to someone so flaky. Still, he had to admit the bearded whiz kid knew a hell of a lot more about the strange subculture they were fishing in than he did. He nodded. "All right, Mr. Kettler. We'll do it your way. You reel him in."

Kettler hesitated. "There's just one more thing."

"Yes?"

"This guy won't do shit for free, Colonel Thorn. He lives on secret knowledge. It turns him on. Makes him feel good. Know what I mean?"

Thorn nodded. He'd seen others in the intelligence game with the same compulsion.

"So we've got to offer him something," Kettler continued. "Trade stuff he'd be interested in for those message files."

Thorn nodded again. He thought fast. "Does Freebooter usually blab his secrets? Or try to sell them?"

"No." Kettler shook his head. "At least, I don't think so. I think he only started posting stuff about the codes because he got so frustrated that he couldn't crack them. He even dropped out of the Net debate once he realized no one there had the kind of decryption software he needed."

"Fine. Then you offer him what we just learned about the Midwest Telephone virus. The Bulgarian connection. The fact that we now suspect the terrorist campaign is under foreign control. The whole bit. You emphasize that it's knowledge that only a very few people in the U.S. government possess. And you promise a first look at whatever our code-breakers come up with if they can crack those messages. Think that'll make him bite?"

Thorn carefully avoided looking at Rossini as he spoke. What he was proposing was a massive breach of security. But damn it, they needed those message files. Trying to track them down on their own would take too much time.

Kettler nodded slowly, thinking it through. "Yeah. That

might do it. Freebooter knows I've got some Pentagon connections."

He sat upright as text began appearing on his display. "Here we go. He's answering my page." His hands came down again over the keyboard.

Thorn felt Rossini's touch on his arm and stepped back. Nothing more would be served by crowding Kettler now. Strange as it might seem, he would have to rely on the oddball computer expert who was busy wheeling and dealing over the ether to acquire illegally obtained information from an electronic Peeping Tom. It was an uncomfortable, if unavoidable, position.

The time dragged by, punctuated only by a steady clicking as Kettler typed in offers and responded to counteroffers.

Thorn paced impatiently, matched almost step for step by Rossini. His mind whirled with the information that might be contained in those encrypted messages. Proof that a foreign government was behind this wave of terror. The hiding places and plans of the separate terrorist cells. A target.

That was what he wanted. What the whole country needed. Something or someone to focus their anger on, to strike back at—to destroy. Knowing their enemy would change everything. Maybe.

"Got it!"

Thorn's head snapped up at Kettler's triumphant cry. He crossed to the computer expert's side in two long strides. "Where?"

"There." Kettler pointed to the blinking red light on one of his machines indicating a hard drive in operation. "I'm downloading Freebooter's files now. Shouldn't take more than another minute."

This time Thorn stood impatiently by, waiting for Kettler to pull up a directory of the files he'd just received. There were more than a hundred of them, some dating back to early October when the mysterious Freebooter had first stumbled across them. Others were more recent.

"Pull that one up," he ordered, pointing almost at random.

"Right." Kettler complied swiftly, his own curiosity now clearly engaged.

All three men stared at the message that popped onto the display.

From: magi@univ.london.com SAT NOV 22 00:15:35 GMT
Received: from sub-ingul.xby by relay7(comnet.com) with SMPT
(2.34.281.278/M8) id AA 314935146; NOV 22 00:15:35 GMT
Text follows:

The main body of the message was an indecipherable hash of numbers, letters, and characters.

"Go to another," Thorn commanded. He barely noticed Rossini pulling in chairs so that they could all sit grouped around the monitor as Kettler began dancing through the encrypted messages—first at random and then in chronological order.

Even a cursory check of the time/date stamp each message contained began to reveal a distinct pattern. Communications from a single, unidentified, foreign source, "Magi," were being sent to at least ten separate users in the United States. And those users communicated only with Magi—never with each other. More damning still, there appeared to be a rough correlation between the messages from Magi, the deadliest terrorist attacks, and the messages back to Magi.

Thorn felt his pulse starting to accelerate. To his trained eye, the sequence was a familiar one: operations orders and postaction damage assessment reports. He felt the strange elation of seeing a long-sought enemy moving into his sights. He was willing to stake his career on the belief that he and Rossini had found the communications network the terrorists were using to conduct their campaign.

CHAPTER 20

TRACKING

DECEMBER 2

Andrews Air Force Base, near Washington D.C.

With its navigation lights blinking steadily, an Air Force C-20 Gulfstream slid down out of the night sky onto a floodlit runway. Slowing, the aircraft rolled past the control tower and darkened hangar buildings and stopped near a group of vehicles at the far end of the field.

Without ceremony, Major General Sam Farrell emerged from the transport plane, followed by several members of his staff.

Colonel Peter Thorn stepped forward to meet him at the foot of the stairs and saluted.

The head of the JSOC snapped a return salute and shook hands with him. "How's it going, Pete?"

"Better, sir."

Farrell nodded. "You have those encrypted messages ready to go?"

"Yes, sir." Thorn handed him a computer diskette. "They're all on that."

The general handed the disk off to a young captain. "On your way, John. Download 'em to Fort Meade on a secure line. You know the number."

"Sir." The captain headed toward one of the waiting cars.

Farrell turned back to Thorn. "After I got your fax, I got on the horn with the NSA's deputy director of operations. His people are eager to see if they can crack these mystery messages of yours."

Thorn nodded his understanding. The National Security Agency was responsible for cryptanalysis and code-breaking. Access to its trained experts and supercomputers was essential. From what Kettler had said, only the NSA had a chance at turning the gobbledygook on that diskette into readable text. If it contained anything worth reading, that is.

"This could still be just a blind alley, sir," he warned quietly.

Farrell shook his head. "I doubt it." The taller man put a hand on Thorn's shoulder. "You're one of my best officers, Pete. I trust your instincts and judgment. That's why I'm here instead of still down at Pope. If you're right, this damned situation could start breaking open fast. And I want to be in a position where I can talk some sense into the Chiefs if the balloon goes up."

Paced by Thorn and his staff, the general strode toward the vehicles waiting to take him to the Pentagon. "You ready to take this discovery of yours to the FBI task force?"

"Yes, sir. I have an appointment with Mike Flynn early tomorrow."

"Good." Farrell lowered his voice. "Be persuasive, Pete. The Bureau's bound to be pissed-off if they think we're muscling in on their turf. Make it clear that we know this investigation is still in their bailiwick."

"Understood, sir," Thorn said, hoping he could pull that off. Diplomacy had never been his strong suit. "I'll do my level best."

Tehran

(D MINUS 13)

General Amir Taleh listened with satisfaction to the brief assembled by his staff. Despite a natural caution that had served him so well for so long, he had to admit to himself that his intricately designed plan was working perfectly—holding precisely to its preset schedule. The short video montage his officers had assembled from American news broadcasts summed up the situation in a few dramatic pictures.

Shots of burning buildings, troops moving in armored vehicles down city streets, and rows of bodies in makeshift morgues were telling evidence of his special operatives' efficiency. In effect, the pictures of soldiers moving through civilian neighborhoods told the whole story. America's police were no longer able to keep order without help from their National Guard. Soon, he thought coldly, even they would not be enough.

His gaze turned from the television screen to the small staff grouped in front of his desk. These men were his closest intimates—the only men in Iran he trusted with full knowledge of his plans.

"Are you satisfied that we are ready to begin Phase IV of SCIMITAR?" Taleh asked quietly.

His question was largely a formality. The tight movement schedules needed to bring his forces into place at the proper moment required an intricate juggling of Iran's transportation resources—its trucks, trains, and ships. Unnecessary delay at this point might throw the whole operation out of kilter. Nonetheless, nothing could begin without Taleh's express authorization. He had taken great pains to ensure that all the strands of military power ran through his hands and his hands alone.

His senior operations officer, an elderly, precise man, nodded. "We are ready. Our meteorological reports also indicate a patch of bad weather coming in, which we may be able to use to our advantage."

"Excellent," Taleh replied. Their troop movements had all been timed to avoid American reconnaissance satellites as much as possible, but cloud cover would simplify matters. Truly, God was showing his favor to the Faithful.

His eyes sought out Farhad Kazemi in the back row and moved on. He knew that the young captain was increasingly worried about his personal security, but he was sure the internal opposition to his policies would fade once the full magnitude of his plan became clear to all. Victory always had a thousand fathers.

He made his decision.

"We are very close, brothers," Taleh said firmly. "In a very short time the West will understand just how badly they have misjudged us."

DECEMBER 3

Washington, D.C.

Gray, gloomy light seeped in through the windows in Special Agent Mike Flynn's office. It was just after dawn.

The FBI agent stood silently, watching Thorn spread printouts of the still-encrypted messages across a long conference table filling one corner of the room. Without offering any comments of his own, he listened intently as the soldier described the suspicious pattern he discerned in the E-mail transmitted between London and users in the United States. Short messages from this mysterious "Magi" to a given user were usually followed within a day or two by a new terrorist outrage. And in every case, the same user sent a much longer post to Magi within twenty-four to thirty-six hours after each attack. To

Thorn, the messages all slotted neatly into an identifiable chain of orders and after-action reports.

"I believe what we're looking at are communications between a higher headquarters and a group of operational terrorist cells. I think that's how they've been coordinating this campaign right under our noses. Basically, these bastards have been using our own high-technology and computer networks to run rings around us," Thorn finished quietly.

Flynn stayed silent for several moments more. Finally, he looked up. "Let me get this straight, Colonel. The NSA still can't make heads or tails out of this stuff?"

"No, sir," Thorn admitted. "But they've only had the material for about eight hours. I understand their experts believe the program used to encrypt these messages is extraordinarily sophisticated—far beyond anything available commercially. Like the Midwest Telephone virus, it appears to be purpose-built. That's another reason I believe these intercepted communications are significant."

"Maybe." Flynn sounded dubious. "But for the moment, Colonel, your theory of a grand terrorist conspiracy hatched overseas basically rests on an operational pattern you claim to see in messages none of us can read."

"Not entirely," Thorn said stiffly. "What about the Bulgarian virus? Where would a bunch of racist fanatics get the kind of money and connections they'd need to buy something like that? And what about the practically identical language all these supposedly separate terrorist groups are using to claim responsibility for their attacks? Is that just a coincidence?"

Flynn heard him out impassively, just standing there with his arms crossed. "I've already talked to Agent Gray about that, Colonel. You've raised some intriguing points. But I've spent too many years in this business to dive headfirst at the first plausible theory I hear."

Thorn gritted his teeth, biting down an angry retort.

In the abstract, he could understand the FBI agent's skepticism. He *was* making a lot of assumptions about the contents of that intercepted electronic mail. More important, both of

Flynn's superiors, the FBI Director and the Attorney General, had already invested a lot of their political prestige backing the notion that American neo-Nazis and radical black extremists were the driving forces behind the wave of terror. Convincing them that they had been wrong would certainly take a lot more evidence than a few indecipherable computer messages.

Appearing more curious than anything else, Flynn watched him struggle to hold his temper in check.

"So you're not interested in pursuing this angle further unless the NSA can crack those messages?" Thorn asked finally, instantly aware of the bitterness apparent in his voice.

The FBI agent snorted and shook his head. "That is not what I said." He smiled wryly at the surprise on Thorn's face. "I may be a skeptic, Colonel. But I'm not an idiot. And I've never turned my back on a promising lead in my life."

He nodded toward the E-mail intercepts spread out across his conference table. "We'll check with CompuNet's managers to see what they can tell us about this stuff." He looked up at Thorn. "In the meantime, Colonel, I suggest you try to light a fire under those folks at the NSA. See if you can get 'em to crank those supercomputers along a little faster."

Flynn smiled humorlessly. "I'd feel a lot safer telling the Attorney General she's been a Grade A idiot if I had a few more aces up my sleeve."

Thorn felt his spirits lift. Helen had been right. He had been misjudging the head of the FBI task force. Mike Flynn was one of the good guys after all.

The Pentagon

The telephone call Thorn had been expecting came shortly after noon.

"Any more luck on those codes, Colonel?" Flynn asked.

"Not yet, sir," Thorn admitted. "The NSA is still stumped. They say the system used to encrypt these messages is definitely better than anything they've ever seen in private use. It's more sophisticated than many of the data encryption systems used by other governments."

"I see," the FBI agent said quietly. "Then we may have to do this the hard way."

"You mean, you'll have to work in from the other end," Thorn reasoned out loud. "Find out who these users are first—before we get a read on the kind of data they're sending and receiving."

"Right on the money, Colonel. I talked to CompuNet's operations director after you left this morning," Flynn explained. "Once I put the fear of God, or more precisely, a Presidential National Security Directive, into him, he agreed to release the billing information for your mystery E-mail users. More important, he also agreed to let us trace any future calls they make to CompuNet."

Thorn nodded to himself. By itself the billing information would have been nearly useless. Once you were signed up with one of the computer networks, you could dial in from anywhere in the world. Permission to trace their incoming calls was the key to pinpointing the people sending and receiving these messages.

Zahedan, Iran

(D MINUS 12)

The order reached the headquarters of the 12th Infantry Division shortly before midnight.

General Karim Taleghani roused slowly at his orderly's shaking. He had been driving his division hard, retraining both it and himself according to Amir Taleh's new directives. The old, easy patterns of garrison life had been completely disrupted. Now he and his troops were up well before dawn and asleep only when their work was done.

"Sir, please, you must wake up. We have movement orders for the division."

The orderly's frantic words finally penetrated the fog and Taleghani came fully awake. "Give the message to me," he mumbled.

"Sir." The orderly passed him the message form and reported, "Colonel Beheshti has already ordered the staff to assemble."

Taleghani frowned slightly but then nodded. Beheshti was an efficient officer, if sometimes a little too willing to assume authority not fully his. "Inform the colonel I will be there in five minutes."

The orderly vanished.

Left alone, Taleghani scanned the decoded dispatch. It told him to ready his division for movement to the port of Bushehr. The schedule attached told him when to expect fuel and additional trucks, what supplies to take, and when to arrive. Significantly, the message ordered him to take his entire force. A much smaller Pasdaran brigade would take over the division's mission of guarding Iran's border with Afghanistan and Pakistan.

He stood up and started moving. Even as he automatically went through the motions of dressing and washing, his mind raced through the possibilities. Was this only another drill?

Taleghani had received a similar emergency alert from Tehran six months ago, and the result was an utter disaster. Only one of his battalions had been able to load on schedule, availability of vehicles was much lower than had actually been reported, and many critical jobs were found to be occupied by untrained officers and men.

In the aftermath of that fiasco he had been paid a visit by Taleh and his shadow, that young Captain Kazemi. Taleghani still shivered at the promises Iran's new military leader had made. Stories he had heard whispered down the Army grapevine made him sure they were not idle threats.

Driven by fear and by a prideful determination not to be caught napping again, his division had done much better during a second surprise alert two months ago. Two of the 12th's three brigades had been ready to move on schedule that time.

Did the Army's new master want to see if they could get it completely right given a third chance? Taleghani shrugged. Well, then, he would show Amir Taleh what the 12th Infantry Division could do when it was ordered into action.

By the time the extra trucks dispatched by Tehran arrived at dawn, his troops were mustered in long lines, loaded with packs and weapons. The division's own transport was already filling up rapidly.

Taleghani stood with his staff, watching closely as a mile-long column of military vehicles—the first of many convoys—roared out through the Zahedan Garrison's main gate and turned onto the Kerman Highway. Brand-new, Russian-made armored personnel carriers loaded with troops, prime movers with towed artillery pieces, others with antiaircraft guns, freshly refitted tanks, Chinese multiple-rocket launchers, supply and maintenance vans all flowed by in a camouflaged, olive-drab river.

The river would flow for days. It took time to shift ten thousand men and all their gear from one place to another.

Taleghani wondered where his men and equipment would all end up. He had waited in vain for a message canceling the movement—for a signal telling him that it was all an exercise. But no such order had arrived.

Perhaps this was not a drill.

As God wills, he decided.

Hamir Pahesh watched the convoy as well, from a very close viewpoint. Loaded with artillery shells, his truck's suspension groaned as it lumbered over the poorly maintained Kerman road.

A few days ago, the Afghan had reported to his company's dispatcher's office for a new assignment. He'd found the place in chaos. Everyone who could drive was driving anything that would move. Along with a score of other truckers, he had been ordered to the eastern end of Iran. There was no explanation given, of course, but something big was happening. That was obvious.

From the cramped cab of his truck, Pahesh had watched with interest as the 12th Infantry Division stripped its storerooms and magazines. Now the entire division was pulling out of its garrison, headed west. He had overheard enough to know that this was not a temporary move. They were going to be replaced by another unit. What was going on? A redeployment? Not the way everyone was hurrying. This had to be it—whatever "it" was.

CompuNet network management center, outside Baltimore, Maryland

The beauty of CompuNet's worldwide network was that it largely ran itself. Automatic switching systems handled incoming calls. Intricately crafted software managed everything from billing to file and electronic-mail transfers. Even better from a corporate view, volunteer systems operators, or sysops, monitored the various user forums and roundtables on their own time. The sysops policed them when flame wars—slanging matches—erupted, and coped with newbies who couldn't get the hang of navigating through the system on their own. Usually, the network required professional human intervention only when its software and hardware crashed.

The result was that CompuNet's small permanent staff spent most of its shift time playing computer games.

BEEP. BEEP. BEEP.

Byron Wu, CompuNet's senior technician on duty, swore and hit the pause key on his auxiliary system. His space fighter had been within seconds of dumping a plasma torpedo into an

enemy base. It had already taken him a dozen tries to get even
this far in the mission. This interruption was going to screw up
his reflexes.

He spun his chair around to look at his main monitor. Beneath the glowing schematic that showed the network in operation, a small red flag pulsed: USER 1589077 CONNECTED.

"So who the hell cares?" Wu muttered irritably. He tapped a
function key, calling up management's reasons for layering this
alert into the system. His eyes widened as he read the first line
aloud. "Emergency network tap authorized by Federal Bureau of
Investigation . . ."

Below the scrolling, boldfaced memo, the red warning flag
changed: TRACE COMPLETED. CONNECT NUMBER IS
703-555-3842.

The Pentagon

"You've got an address here in northern Virginia?" Thorn asked
into the phone again, scarcely able to believe that some of the
information they were seeking had come in so quickly. He
checked his watch. It was just after 10:00 P.M. It was too easy to
lose track of time under the Pentagon basement's fluorescent
lights.

"Yeah," Flynn said. "One of the Magi group users logged onto
CompuNet less than an hour ago. We traced the number they
gave us to an address in Arlington."

"Oustanding."

"Yeah." The FBI agent sounded pleased. "I'm putting a team
in straightaway to scope the place out . . . to see what we can
find out about the people living there."

"Why not launch a raid right away?" Thorn asked. "If that *is* a
terrorist safe house, why risk giving them time to scoot or
launch another attack?"

"It's that 'if' I'm having trouble with, Colonel," Flynn said flatly. "Point A: We still don't know who this so-called Magi and his electronic pen pals really are. It could just be a god-damned lonely hearts club, for Christ's sake! Point B: I need more than illegally obtained E-mail to get a warrant. If these are some of the bad guys, and we take 'em down without a warrant, the whole prosecution will be tainted from day one. So unless we want these sons of bitches to walk, we're going to have to do this by the book."

Thorn frowned. He hated the prospect of more wasted time. Delay only benefited the enemy. "Damn it."

"Too true," Flynn agreed. "Look, Colonel, don't sweat it. Thanks to you and this Maestro of yours, we've finally got a shot at what may be a real target. So if my people pick up even a whiff of something bad at this place, I'll get a search warrant and send an HRT section in on the double. Any terrorists inside that house will be dead or behind bars before they wake up."

DECEMBER 4

Near Kerman, Iran

(D MINUS 11)

Hamir Pahesh looked back, toward the campfires and the road beyond. He cursed the half moon, but in the next second was grateful for the hints it gave him about the ground under his feet. After fourteen hours of driving in convoy, all he wanted to do was join his countrymen at the fire, eat, drink a little sweet, hot tea, and go to bed.

Instead, here he was picking his way across a pitch-black, rocky ground looking for something, anything, that would give him cover. The treeless landscape held nothing higher than a weed or two, and he needed more.

The bundle he had smuggled out of his truck cab was small enough so that it could be tucked under his coat. But the rest of the drivers thought Pahesh had left the convoy to attend to nature's needs, so he could not afford to be gone too long.

There. A low rise, little more than a fold in the ground, seemed to offer an acceptable solution.

Kneeling on the cold, stony ground, the Afghan ignored the lumps under him, hoping none of them would start moving. He unzipped a small case and fumbled in the darkness with the unfamiliar device it contained.

The antenna was easy enough, but there was a small lead that had to be plugged into the case, and for a moment he could not remember which side it went into.

In the quiet darkness every click and scrape seemed deafening. He paused for a moment, listening for the crunch of a footfall in the sand, or some more ominous sign, but all he heard was singing and faint chatter from the roadside several hundred meters away.

Ah. Pahesh found the socket for the antenna cable, then the rocker switch for the power, and turned the machine on. He typed in a series of digits he had computed earlier, based on the date, and hit the start button. While the transmitter sent out its signal, he slipped on a set of earphones and picked up the microphone.

A small indicator on the front told him the transmitter had found a satellite, that it had acknowledged his signal, and that he had entered the proper code. Only a moment later, a voice answered, "Watch officer."

Pahesh hoped this man knew what to do. "This is Stone," he started. Trying to speak clearly and whisper at the same time was difficult but he dared not speak louder. "I have a flash message for Granite."

His own code name was Stone. He'd never met his controller, Granite. Indeed, the Afghan didn't know if Granite was one man or more, or where this signal was being received.

All he knew was that the Americans couldn't wait until the end of the week to hear what he'd learned. He'd gathered more information at the noontime break, and still more just now, with the convoy stopped for the day.

"Roger, Stone, ready to copy."

Pahesh recited his message—composed, changed, and polished a hundred times as he drove. "Iranian 12th Infantry Division left barracks in Zahedan zero six hundred hours today, 4 December, with all elements and extra fuel and ammunition. Another unit, identity unknown, may be arriving in Zahedan to take over its duties. Convoy passed through Kerman in the afternoon and is now headed for Shiraz. Ultimate destination is unknown. Message ends."

The American voice at the other end read back the message, then said, "Received and understood. Please stand by."

"Stand by?" wondered Pahesh. He looked around nervously, but could see nothing in the darkness.

"Stone, this is Granite." The voice was different, more purposeful. "Could this simply be a routine redeployment?"

The Afghan shook his head in reflex before he remembered they could not see him. "No. The Iranians have an urgent deadline. Two officers have already been punished for not meeting their schedules."

There was what seemed a long pause before the American replied. "All right. Can you give us an update in twelve hours?"

"Yes." Then Pahesh corrected himself. "I will try. I must go now."

"Understood."

Pahesh turned off the machine and hurriedly repacked it. He was late. He hadn't counted on an extended conversation. The others would be looking for him.

Tucking the satellite radio pack under his coat again, he strolled as quickly as possible back to his truck. As soon as there was enough light, he checked his watch. Only twelve minutes had passed since he'd left the roadside. He felt the tension ease.

Fatigue replaced the tension, and he quickly unrolled his pallet near one of the fires. Pahesh crawled in, reasonably sure the Komite, Iran's hated secret police, were not going to arrest him before dawn. Before he dropped off to sleep, he found himself going over and over his brief communication with the Americans. It was good to know they were taking him seriously. Instincts honed by years of war told him this long road march was the first stirring of an evil wind.

CHAPTER 21

HORNET'S NEST

DECEMBER 4

Washington, D.C.

Outside the Hoover Building, the capital city's streets were filling up with rush-hour traffic. Even in the present crisis, the
hundreds of thousands of workers employed by the various government agencies, businesses, and law firms seemed to be determined to carry on as much of their daily routine as possible. For
all the outward show of normalcy, however, the unpredictable,
ever more frequent, and apparently unstoppable terrorist attacks
were striking nerves already worn raw.

False alarms were triggered more and more often, with less
and less provocation. Whole buildings emptied into the streets
at the sight of a package without a return address. Phoned-in
threats prompted widespread closures of the Metro or the region's major highways. Entire neighborhoods, from wealthy,
trendy Georgetown to the hopelessly poor northeast sections of
the city, barricaded themselves in by day and by night, desper-

ately hoping they could seal themselves off from the terrorist contagion. The drab, olive-green Army Humvees and Bradley armored fighting vehicles posted to cover the capital's major intersections and traffic circles only increased the sense of crisis.

London had been bombed flat during the Blitz and periodically targeted by the IRA, but Washington, D.C., had existed in relative peace for many years. Not since the riots following Dr. Martin Luther King, Jr.'s assassination had racial tensions been so high. And not since Jubal Early's tattered Rebels fell back toward the Shenandoah Valley in 1864 had so many in the American capital felt the oppressive dread of knowing that a deadly enemy lurked close at hand.

Around-the-clock television coverage fed the public's barely controlled panic. The first pictures of each new terrorist outrage were played over and over again on every news channel, magnifying their scope and impact. In the fiercely competitive war for exclusives, every wild rumor found a reporter to repeat it, deny it, and then repeat it afresh—often the same reporter and often within the same hour.

Even the headquarters of the Federal Bureau of Investigation was not immune to the general paranoia gathering force across the country. The security detachments manning its entrances had been reinforced by U.S. Army Rangers. Razor-wire entanglements surrounded the building, keeping pedestrians, the press, and potential terrorists at a distance.

Deeply worried by the signs of widespread, almost crippling fear he saw all around him, Peter Thorn followed Helen Gray into the conference room adjoining Special Agent Mike Flynn's office.

His Metro ride over from the Pentagon had been instructive. Uniformed D.C. policemen were posted on every train coming into Washington. They were backed by heavily armed SWAT contingents conspicuously stationed at every subway stop. Passengers embarking and disembarking were subject to identity checks and random searches. While the heavy security presence provided some deterrence against terrorist attack, it also reinforced the overwhelming feeling of entering a city under siege.

Thorn frowned. The nation's capital seemed to be nearing a breaking point. They were running out of time.

There were only two men waiting for them inside—Mike Flynn and his deputy, Tommy Koenig. Both looked exhausted. That was understandable. They had worked straight through the night trying to follow the lead he and Rossini had given them.

"Thanks for coming, Pete. I'm glad you could make it," the head of the FBI task force said quietly. "You have any trouble getting through our watchdogs?"

Thorn shook his head, inwardly noting with some amusement the other man's decision to use his first name. Evidently, he'd been promoted from nosy, Pentagon pain in the ass to helpful, fellow investigator overnight. Interesting. Well, better late than never. He took the chair next to Helen and set his uniform cap aside.

"What's the skinny, Mike?" she asked.

"We've got a preliminary read on the CompuNet address," Flynn answered. "Andy Quinlan's team checked in an hour ago."

Helen leaned forward, her eagerness apparent. "And?"

"I think we have a target."

Thorn felt himself relax slightly. More than anything, more than he had wanted to admit to himself, he had feared that he and Rossini were only stumbling down the wrong path—and dragging everyone else along with them. But they had been right. Their instincts were on target.

Helen, though, appeared unsatisfied. "You think? Or you know?" she pressed.

Flynn shrugged. "Let's say the evidence Quinlan and his people have assembled is mighty suggestive, but it's not conclusive." He glanced at his deputy. "Tommy can take you through it piece by piece. He rode herd on the investigative team every step of the way."

Koenig nodded. "Mike made it clear that we didn't want to

spook these people prematurely—whoever they are. So Quinlan's been working around the edges for the last twenty-four
hours."

He flipped open a file. "Basically, what we've got is this: The
phone number CompuNet gave us belongs to a house in Arlington just off the Columbia Pike. The place was rented nine
weeks ago by a blond-haired man with a slight, but discernible,
European accent. He told the Realtor his name was Bernard
Nielsen and that he worked for a Danish import-export firm—a
company called Jutland Trading, Limited. Apparently, this guy
Nielsen told her his bosses wanted him to explore business op-
portunities in the U.S. and that he needed a home base to come
back to between trips. He signed a six-month lease and paid his
security deposit in traveler's checks. Since then, he's paid one
time—by mail—using personal checks drawn on a local bank."

"Not from his business or from a Danish bank?" Thorn asked.

"Nope. Curious, isn't it?" Koenig looked up from the file.
"One of our guys took a little walk through Nielsen's account
records. There's been a steady movement of cash money in and
out—but the balance has always been over five thousand dollars
and always under ten thousand."

Thorn heard the shorter FBI agent's emphasis on those figures and nodded slowly. Again, that made sense. Five thousand dollars in a checking account made bank managers smile
at you and generally kept them from asking too many inconvenient questions. On the other hand, ten thousand in cash triggered an automatic report to the IRS. It certainly looked like
this Bernard Nielsen liked cruising in a comfortable financial
zone that guaranteed him both flexibility and relative
anonymity.

Helen frowned. "Does this Jutland Trading company even
exist?"

Koenig shrugged. "We're still working with the Danish authorities on that. The phone number our blond friend gave the
Realtor only connects to an answering service. The Danes are
trying to follow the trail further, but it'll take some time to generate results." He smiled grimly. "I can tell you this. I spent the

morning breathing down some necks in the Commerce Department. And Commerce sure as heck doesn't have any record of a Jutland Trading company registered to do business here in the States."

"What a surprise," Thorn said flatly.

Flynn nodded. "After I heard that, I gave Quinlan the go-ahead to dig deeper near the house itself."

Thorn looked at Koenig. "And what did they find?"

The shorter man's grim smile faded. "That's the inconclusive part," he admitted. "It's a transient neighborhood. Lots of rentals. Lots of people moving in and out on temporary assignments with the Pentagon or other government agencies. Lots of people who go to work early, come home late, and go right to sleep. Nobody really knows much about any of their neighbors."

"Nobody's noticed anything?" Helen asked, surprised. "Nothing odd at all?"

Koenig spread his hands. "We did find one retired couple who said they'd seen several suspicious men coming and going from the house at odd hours . . ." His voice trailed off.

"But?" she prompted.

"But this Mr. and Mrs. Abbot are both a little blind and hard of hearing. Plus, we checked with the Arlington police. They say the Abbots average reporting one prowler, rapist, or drug dealer a week. The cops don't usually bother investigating their calls anymore."

Thorn grimaced. Perfect. If this rented house in Arlington was a terrorist safe house, whoever had picked it had done a brilliant job. He turned to Flynn. "So what's the next step? Surveillance?"

That would be the standard procedure, he knew. Find a house nearby, move the occupants out, and put in a stakeout team to monitor the suspect's comings and goings, phone conversations, and associates. Once enough evidence of possible wrongdoing had been collected, the FBI would obtain a search warrant from a sympathetic judge and move in. For a by-the-book guy like Flynn, that would be the best and safest way to proceed. But it would also gobble up hours and days he wasn't sure they could afford.

Flynn surprised him. "No, Pete. We go in as soon as possible." He pointed upstairs and growled, "When I briefed the Director and the Attorney General this morning, both were adamant that we take any action necessary to break this thing open."

From his tone, Thorn suspected the senior FBI agent was leaving a lot unsaid. If anything, the country's political and media elites were even more spooked by the terror campaign than the general public, and the political pressures to act were enormous.

Flynn turned to Helen. "The Attorney General herself is seeking a search warrant authorizing an HRT raid. Once we have the warrant in hand, I'm assigning the mission to you and your section. You know the general area pretty well and you're damned good—the best I've got, in fact. John Lang concurs."

"Okay." Helen nodded flatly, taking the compliment in stride without any false modesty. She glanced at Koenig, getting down to business without wasting any more time. "What do we know about the house right now, Tommy?"

"Not as much as I'd like." He slid a faxed copy of a real estate brochure across to her. "The place is fairly large—about twenty-five hundred square feet. Four bedrooms. Two and a half baths. One story aboveground and a good-sized basement below. A one-car garage attached to the house."

"Brick exterior construction?" she asked.

Koenig nodded. "Hardwood floors upstairs. Concrete covered by carpet in the basement."

Helen looked up from the brochure. "I need more than this. Can we get a set of blueprints from the builder or the county records?"

"We're working on it," Koenig confirmed.

"Good. Now, what about numbers inside the house? Any data on that?" she asked.

"Nothing solid. We risked one drive-by earlier this afternoon and spotted two vehicles in the driveway—one minivan, one

Toyota Camry. There was another car, a Taurus, parked along the street out front. The Camry is registered to this Nielsen. The other vehicles trace back to different names and addresses. Based on that, we're guessing a minimum of two suspects and a maximum of six."

"I see." Helen sat back in her chair, her eyes distant as she considered her options for several seconds. Finally, she turned back to Flynn. "Okay, Mike, what are my rules of engagement for this operation?"

Thorn knew that was the key question. The rules of engagement, or ROE, would determine the Hostage Rescue Team's tactics. The looser the rules were, the more options Helen would have in laying out her assault plan. If she could assume the people inside were hostile, she and her agents could bring significantly more firepower to bear in the early stages, and they could use their weapons a lot more freely.

Flynn looked troubled. "There's a snag. Without clear-cut evidence of wrongdoing, I can't get the AG or the Director to sign off on unlimited ROE. They're too afraid we might nail some innocent civilians by mistake. So we have to tread lightly at first. I'm afraid you can't go in with guns blazing on this one."

Helen nodded slowly, hiding her concerns behind an impassive mask.

Thorn knew his own face was less controlled. He didn't like the sound of this—not at all. Taking out terrorists was a lot different from conducting a sweep against a suspected crack house. Success always depended on the maximum application of controlled violence in the minimum amount of time. Without that, the risks to the assault force—to the woman he loved—went up dramatically.

Despite his relief that the FBI was moving at last, he couldn't help worrying about Helen's safety. Concrete evidence or not, he firmly believed that house in Arlington held some of the terrorists they were hunting. If he was right, Helen and her comrades could be walking right into a buzz saw.

"I'd like to move in after midnight," she said calmly. "We'll have a better chance of catching these people asleep, or at least at a low ebb, then."

Flynn nodded his understanding and approval. "I can buy that much time from the Director."

"Good." Helen paused briefly, thinking again, and then went on. "That should also allow us to covertly evacuate the nearest neighbors. I don't like increasing the chances that we'll be spotted, but I think it's imperative. If there are terrorists inside, we have to accept that they have heavy weapons and that they'll use them if they get the chance. I don't want civilians caught in the cross fire if we can help it."

"Agreed. Anything else for now?"

When Helen shook her head, Flynn checked his watch and stood up. "Okay, then let's start moving things into place. The clock is running fast on this one."

Determined not to be left wholly on the sidelines, Thorn leaned forward. "I have one request, Mike. With your permission, I want to ride along as an observer."

The senior FBI agent stared hard at him for a moment before replying. Then Flynn glanced at Helen, obviously making sure she had no objections. Finally, he nodded abruptly. "Okay, Pete. I guess you've earned the right to be in on the kill. We'll find you a place in the command van."

Thorn sat back, partially satisfied. He couldn't do anything to reduce the risks she'd be running, but he knew he'd feel better if he were at least close by.

Much as he longed to lead the planned raid himself, he couldn't think of anyone better qualified for the assignment than Helen. She had more tactical ability, fighting skill, and sheer guts than anyone else in the FBI—or even in the Delta Force for that matter.

Amazing. Six months ago, he would never have imagined himself thinking that of a woman—any woman. And now he couldn't imagine being left without her.

DECEMBER 5

Arlington, Virginia

Somewhere off in the distance, a church bell chimed once and fell silent.

Despite her Nomex coveralls and body armor, Helen Gray shivered. It was well below freezing outside and the need to stay motionless only intensified the cold. She lay burrowed in a hedge bordering the street and sidewalk across from the suspected terrorist hideout. Her post offered her a good view of the front of the house.

She studied it carefully, looking for the slightest evidence of anything wrong—anything that might indicate they had been spotted. Even with her night vision goggles down, she couldn't see anything out of place. From the outside at least, the house appeared a perfectly ordinary suburban dwelling, identical to thousands of others throughout northern Virginia—all the way from its sloping shingle roof to its red-brick walls and the white trim around its curtained windows. There were no lights showing behind those curtains.

Well, Helen thought coolly, it was time to find out exactly what was hidden inside that quiet house.

She keyed her mike and whispered, "All Sierra units, this is Sierra One. Everybody set?"

Voices ghosted through her earphones as her teams checked in, one right after the other. Sierra Three and Four, Paul Frazer and Tim Brett, were around the back, poised to enter through the rear door on her signal. Five and Six, Frank Jackson and Gary Ricks, were crouched behind the rear of the Ford minivan parked in the driveway. They would take the front door. Sierra Two, Felipe DeGarza, lay prone beside her as a reserve. Her own two-man sniper teams, Byrne and Voss, and Horowitz and Emery, occupied positions in the surrounding homes.

She would have preferred to lead the assault teams herself, but with the situation still so murky, Flynn wanted her in a position to exercise tighter tactical control over her sections if things didn't go according to plan. Leading from the rear wasn't her style, but orders were orders.

The head of the FBI task force wasn't taking many chances. As a safeguard against an attempted breakout by the suspects, he had deployed a cordon of local police and other special agents in a wide net around the neighborhood. He even had a Blackhawk helicopter standing by on the local elementary school's playground—prepped for immediate flight if a pursuit became necessary. From the absence of any media nearby, she guessed that Flynn had also stomped hard on the Attorney General's notorious tendency to curry favorable publicity.

Helen took a deep breath. Her next signal would open the ball. "Hotel One, this is Sierra One. We're ready. Initiate shutdown sequence," she said softly.

"Roger, Sierra," she heard Flynn say.

Helen clicked her mike again. "All Sierra units, stand by. Wait for my mark."

She waited without moving for the next reports to be repeated over the command circuit. It was crucial to take the suspected terrorists out while they were deaf, dumb, and blind. CompuNet already had instructions to block incoming and outgoing E-mail from the target address. Now it was time to take more direct measures.

"Landlines down."

The telephone company had cut its service to the immediate calling area.

"Cell down."

All cellular phone communications were down.

"Lights down."

The streetlamps on this block blinked out as technicians switched off all electric power to the vicinity. Now!

"Go! Go! Go!" Helen ordered, sighting down the barrel of her submachine gun at the front of the house.

Jackson and Ricks were already on their feet and heading for the front door. They carried a door-breaker, a heavy battering ram with twin handles, slung between them. The restrictive rules of engagement prohibited the use of the HRT's two favored methods for opening locked doors—breaching charges or shotgun blasts direct to the hinges.

One. Two. Three. Helen found herself mentally counting the seconds it took her lead team to reach the front steps and get into position. They were there!

Jackson and Ricks rocked back on their heels and then slammed the battering ram into the front door. The smashing, tearing thud seemed loud enough to wake the dead—let alone the suspects they were trying to surprise. The door sagged under the impact but stayed stubbornly shut.

Again! Another heave and more nerve-shattering noise. This time the front door gave way and fell open.

"We're in!" Helen heard Ricks' triumphant report as he dropped his side of the door-breaker and darted in with his weapon ready.

WHAMMM. The doorway disappeared in a dazzling orange and red explosion that lit the whole area. Caught full on by the blast, Ricks was blown in half. Jackson, two steps behind, flew backward off the front porch and landed on the lawn screaming in agony. He flopped around on the dead grass like a gutted fish.

"Jesus Christ!" Helen snarled. A booby trap. Those bastards inside had rigged their front door with a booby trap as a precaution against unwelcome nighttime visitors. Part of her mind was silently screaming in shock and in time with Jackson. Another part, colder and more analytical, realized that knocking down the door had triggered the explosive—probably a sheet charge mounted in the side jamb. Simple. Classic. And totally unexpected.

She tore her eyes away from the boiling cloud of smoke and still-falling debris at the front door. Ricks and Jackson were out of action, but she had other forces in motion. She keyed her mike. "Three, are you in yet?"

Frazer answered immediately. "Negative! Negative! They've reinforced the back door! It's backed by steel!"

"Can you rig a breaching charge?" Helen demanded. The tactical situation was going from bad to worse at a rapid, breathtaking pace.

It got worse.

Gunfire crackled suddenly from somewhere in the back of the house.

"Shit! Shit!" Frazer shouted over the radio. "We're taking fire! Christ!" The noise doubled in volume as he and Brett started shooting back. "We're pinned down, One! Can't go forward! Sure as hell can't go back!"

Helen gritted her teeth. She called the leader of the sniper team posted to cover the rear of the house. "Byrne! Take that bastard out!"

"Trying, Sierra One," the sniper replied calmly. She heard him pause and caught the muffled crack of his high-powered Remington rifle. "Gonna be tough. Hostile has a flash-suppressed weapon. I'm having a hard time drawing a bead on him."

Lying beside her in the hedge, DeGarza suddenly stiffened. "I've got movement in the right front window, boss."

"Great." Helen peered through her goggles, zeroing in on the window he had indicated. Was that a curtain stirring?

More gunfire erupted—this time from the front of the house. The Ford Taurus parked on the street rocked crazily back and forth, hammered by the stream of rounds that tore through its doors and shattered every window. Sparks flew off metal in wild, corkscrewing patterns. Whoever was inside the house was making sure there were no attackers hiding behind the vehicle.

Helen saw brick dust and splintered wood puff up around the house's front windows as her snipers opened up in an attempt to silence the still-unseen gunman. The curtains jerked wildly— shredded by each bullet—but the hostile fire continued without pause. She shook her head decisively. This was too slow. "Emery!" she ordered. "Smoke 'em out!"

In response, a grenade launcher thumped once from behind her, hurling a tear-gas grenade toward one of the house's windows. But instead of sailing on through into the rooms beyond, the grenade bounced back outside onto the lawn and lay hissing, spewing its gray cloud of tear gas harmlessly into the open air.

Helen swore sharply to herself. The defenders must have strung netting behind the curtains. She grimaced. Booby traps, reinforced steel doors, and now grenade netting. She and her section were attacking a fortress.

Alerted by the attempted grenade attack, the gunman inside shifted his fire away from the mangled Taurus to the homes across the street.

Helen and DeGarza burrowed deeper into the hedge as rounds whipcracked past their heads. The chattering roar of automatic-weapons fire rose higher. Someone else inside the house had opened up, systematically shooting into every piece of cover that could shelter an attacker.

"Jesus," the stocky HRT trooper whispered into her ear. "Who *are* these guys?"

She shook her head impatiently. Their enemies were damned good. That was all that was important now.

Her gaze darted across the flame-lit, bullet-torn landscape in front of her as she evaluated and then rejected courses of action in the blink of an eye. That bomb-blasted front door gaped open invitingly, but getting to it would be impossible. There was too much cleared ground to cover. Anyone trying to cross that street would be gunned down before they took three strides.

The back door was out too. Frazer and Brett were still pinned down there, unable to get close enough to slap the necessary breaching charge in place. What did that leave?

Helen's eyes narrowed as she made her decision. It was time to gamble. They were running out of time and options. Every passing minute gave the terrorists inside more time to destroy the information they needed or to prepare for a mass suicide.

She tapped DeGarza's helmet to get his attention and wriggled back out of the hedge. The other agent followed her. Crouching low to avoid the bullets still flying past overhead, she made another radio call to the sniper team covering the front. "Horowitz! Keep shooting! Keep these bastards busy! Emery! Fall back and meet us at the school!"

FBI command van

With half its interior taken up by the radio and other equipment needed to manage a surveillance operation or raid, the
five men inside the back of the command van were crowded together almost cheek-to-jowl. They were parked out of sight, two
streets away from the pitched battle now raging around the terrorist safe house.

"Damn it!" Peter Thorn slammed his fist into his thigh in
frustration as he listened to the rising crescendo of gunfire outside and the desperate radioed reports from the stunned HRT
assault force. He couldn't just sit here idle while Helen and her
section were cut to ribbons. He yanked off the headphones he
was wearing and whirled around to face Flynn. "Your people
need help now! Give me a weapon and three men and I'll lay
down a base of fire on that frigging house long enough for them
to break inside!"

For an instant, the older FBI man seemed tempted. Then he
shook his head. "Not possible, Pete! You don't have any jurisdiction here."

"Screw the fucking jurisdiction!" Thorn snarled angrily. He
started to stand without really being sure of where he planned
on going or what he planned on doing.

"Sit down!" Flynn barked. His voice softened. "Look, Pete,
think it through. Things are already bad out there. You really
think throwing in another set of strangers with guns—in the
dark—is gonna make them better?"

Thorn shook his head numbly, unwillingly admitting to himself that the other man was right. His instincts urged him into
action. His brain told him an unplanned, unrequested intervention now could be disastrous. Plenty of soldiers and police officers were killed by friendly fire in the dark or in the swirling
confusion of battle.

"Let Helen do her job," Flynn said quietly. "She's in command. If she wants help, she'll ask for it."

Arlington

Lugging her submachine gun and a pack carrying extra gear, Helen Gray dashed across the playground toward the waiting Blackhawk helicopter. DeGarza and Emery, similarly burdened, ran right at her heels. They ducked low under the helo's turning rotors and scrambled up into the troop compartment.

"We're in! Take us up!" Helen shouted to the pilot over her command circuit.

"Roger."

Turbines howling, the Blackhawk climbed skyward, already spinning left to head toward the battle. It leveled off just fifty feet above the ground.

Helen crouched in the helicopter's open doorway, staring down as they slid low over the street. Orange flames and black, oily smoke billowed out of the burning Ford Taurus. She could see Jackson's body sprawled on the front lawn. They were over the roof of the house in seconds.

The Blackhawk pilot's voice crackled through her helmet headset. "You ready?"

Helen craned her head to check with her teammates. They both nodded and gave her a thumbs-up signal. She whipped back around and confirmed that for the pilot. "We're ready. Let's do it!"

Rotors whipping through the rising smoke, the Blackhawk went into hover only a few feet above the roof.

Without pausing, Helen dropped out through the helo's open side door. Robbed of her natural grace by her weapons and extra equipment, she landed awkwardly on the sloping asphalt shingles. She teetered there for a second, fighting briefly for her balance. Breathing hard, she regained it and knelt down—already tearing open the equipment pack she'd been carrying. DeGarza and Emery made the same leap and moved to her side.

Helped by DeGarza, she extracted the thin, rolled-up sheet of explosives she'd been digging for, unrolled it, and started tamping the charge into place on the roof. Emery crouched nearby, aiming his M16 downward.

Helen finished securing her end of the breaching charge and carefully attached the detonator. They were almost set. She looked across at DeGarza . . .

And rolled away from a hail of splinters as bullets blasted through the roof directly in front of her, fired upward from inside the house. She felt a sharp, stinging pain in one cheek and wiped away a smear of bright red blood with one gloved hand. Some of the splinters must have caught her in the face. "Jesus!"

Emery fired back, using three-round bursts to punch new holes in the roof. Suddenly, the FBI sniper jerked upright, caught by a bullet under the chin. The top of his head blew off, and he toppled backward, sliding rapidly out of sight.

Hell. Helen blinked away tears and felt the welcome inrush of a cold, focused, killing rage. At least three of her men were down—dead or dying. She intended to make the bastards inside this house pay for that.

Her fingers raced through the last adjustments, setting the detonator for a five-second delay. "Done!"

Four. Three. She and DeGarza scrambled up the sloping roof and over the peak. Then they threw themselves flat, hugging the shingles. Two. One.

The house rocked under them. Flame spurted skyward, but most of the blast was directed downward—through the roof.

With her ears still ringing from the enormous explosion so close by, Helen pulled herself back upright and peered at their handiwork. The breaching charge had torn a jagged, five-foot-wide hole in the roof. Smoke and dust boiled upward through the new opening.

She clapped DeGarza on the shoulder and shouted, "Come on!"

Then she unslung her MP5, skidded down the roof, and dropped straight through the ragged opening. Speed was life. They had to strike before the stunned terrorists inside the house recovered.

Helen landed heavily on a tangled heap of debris—torn shin-

gles, pieces of charred support beams, and the mangled corpse of
a man. One of the terrorists had been right below the charge
when it went off. Good, she thought coldly. One less to kill.

Ignoring the sharp, stabbing pains shooting through her legs
and rib cage, she rolled off the still-smoking pile of wreckage
and came up into a crouch with her submachine gun ready to
fire. DeGarza followed immediately after her and came up facing in the other direction. He swung around after making sure
they were alone in the room.

Helen summoned up memories of the blueprints she'd studied. They were inside what had been a living room before the
HRT's bullets and their breaching charge ripped it apart. She
rose and moved toward a hallway that ran the width of the
house. A hand signal sent DeGarza right—toward the two bedrooms and bathrooms on the ground floor. She turned left—toward the dining room, kitchen, back door, and the stairs leading
down into the basement.

Gliding quietly across the dining room's scarred hardwood
floor, she skirted past a dinner table and chairs and drew closer
to the open arch connecting to the kitchen. Every sense, every
perception, she possessed was at its highest possible pitch.

"One, this is Two. All clear." DeGarza's hoarse whisper rang
loudly through her earphones. "Coming back your way."

Helen froze. She could see part of the kitchen now. Not
much of it really, just the glint of a glass-fronted microwave on
one of the tiled counters. Was there something reflected in that
dark glass? An arm? Perhaps a weapon?

Conviction crystallized without conscious thought. She
shifted her aim and fired a burst through the edge of the doorway, tearing away chunks of wood and plaster. Before the stuttering echoes faded she was moving again, charging sideways to
bring more of the kitchen into her line of sight.

There! She spotted a moving shape near the opening.

Helen squeezed the trigger again, holding her submachine
gun tight on target as it spat out another three rounds.

The terrorist, already hit at least once, jerked again convulsively and fell back against a refrigerator, sliding slowly to the

floor. His eyes were already open and fixed before his arms and legs stopped twitching. Helen's eyes took in the dead man's dark hair and light skin before moving on to inspect the rest of the room. It was empty.

"Two, this is One. Kitchen is clear. Come ahead," she breathed into her mike.

DeGarza followed her in, his weapon still sweeping through controlled arcs as he checked potential hiding places.

Helen stopped facing a door left ajar. It led down into the basement. Her gaze fell on a dark smear on the door handle. Blood. Another of the terrorists must have been wounded in the earlier exchange of fire with Frazer and Brett.

She moved closer to get a better look at the staircase and frowned. It turned sharply at a right angle halfway down. This was going to be a bitch. And there wasn't time to summon reinforcements.

She signaled DeGarza into position on one side of the half-open door and crouched on the other. Then she tugged a flash/bang grenade out of her leg pouch and looked across at the stocky agent. He nodded.

Counting silently to herself, Helen tugged on the grenade's pull ring, slammed the door open, and lobbed the cylinder down the stairs, trying to bounce it around the bend. DeGarza followed the grenade down, taking the stairs two at a time. She hurtled after him.

They rounded the corner at high speed and took the last few steps into a long, low-ceilinged room lit only by the blinding strobes thrown by the exploding grenade. Helen sensed rather than saw motion in the far corner and yelled a warning. "Down!"

She and DeGarza dropped prone just as a third terrorist reared up from behind a sofa and fired a long, tearing burst from an assault rifle. He missed. They shot back from the carpet. Shredded by multiple hits, the man collapsed across the sofa, bleeding into the ripped stuffing and exposed steel springs.

Helen breathed out. These bastards *were* good—good enough

to shake off the effects of a stun grenade and fight back. Well, she thought wearily, maybe this one had been the last.

More gunfire rang out suddenly inside the basement, muffled only slightly by distance and closed doors. Crap.

Helen surged to her feet and sped down a hallway that led to the last two bedrooms and bath. DeGarza dogged her heels.

Without pausing, she kicked open the door to one room and rolled back away as the other HRT agent dove inside. She risked a glance and got a hasty impression of a small, starkly furnished room containing nothing but an unmade bed and a few closed suitcases. A bullet-riddled portable computer lay in pieces near the bed. That explained the gunfire they'd heard.

Damn it! They'd needed the information that shattered machine had once contained.

She swore again in sudden realization. If the man who'd destroyed that computer wasn't in there, then . . .

Helen whirled as the door to the bedroom behind her flew open. A fourth terrorist, this one a fair-haired man with pale blue eyes, stepped out into the hallway, already raising an AKM assault rifle in her direction. He was too close, and there wasn't any cover she could reach in time.

The world around her slowed to a crawl. In the long, seemingly endless blink of an eye, she recognized the face she had stared at for so many weeks. The face captured in black and white by a Metro security camera. The cruel, arrogant face of the man who had planted the National Press Club bomb.

Reacting instinctively, Helen threw herself forward and slammed her submachine gun down across the AKM's longer barrel, pushing it toward the floor. Her finger tightened on the MP5's trigger.

Both weapons fired at the same time.

Helen felt something punch across her thigh and ignored it at first. Then she was falling backward as her leg buckled. She felt a second impact, as another steel-jacketed round ricocheted off the concrete floor and slammed into her lower back below her body armor.

She tumbled to the floor still clutching her submachine gun.

Clenching her teeth, she raised her head high enough to see the terrorist she'd shot. He lay propped up against the doorjamb. Her bullets had torn his chest open.

The fair-headed man stared back at her, breathing in shallow, gasping pants as the blood pumped out of his wounds. "A woman," he whispered in amazement. One corner of his mouth twisted upward in a terrible smile and then froze. He was dead.

Helen shivered, suddenly horribly, terribly cold—colder than she had ever been in her life. She could sense something wet spreading across her back, but she couldn't feel anything below her stomach.

"Oh, my God." DeGarza dropped to his knees beside her and smacked his hands over her thigh, desperately trying to hold back the blood spouting out of her severed femoral artery. "Hotel One, this is Sierra Two! I need a medic! Sierra One is down and hit bad!"

Helen slid slowly into an icy, black void.

HRT medevac flight

With an ashen Mike Flynn at his side, Peter Thorn pushed through the crowd of grim-faced policemen and FBI agents surrounding the Blackhawk. Medical teams were busy loading stretchers into the helicopter as it spooled up for an emergency hop to the trauma unit at the Walter Reed Army Medical Center. Blankets covered most of the faces. All four terrorists caught inside the shattered safe house were dead. Two members of the HRT assault force, Ricks and Emery, were also dead. Helen and Frank Jackson were still alive—but only barely.

Thorn saw Helen lying motionless on one of the stretchers already aboard and stopped, rooted in place by his own despair. Paramedics surrounded the stretcher, working feverishly to stabilize her condition long enough to get her into surgery. One had his hands clamped around her thigh, holding the artery closed, while another slid a blood pressure cuff as high up as he could over the wound and started pumping it up, using the device as an improvised tourniquet.

An FBI agent he didn't recognize stepped in front of him, motioning him away. "Sorry, sir. Medical personnel only. You'll have to move back."

A red mist floated in front of Thorn's eyes. He moved forward, ready to fight his way through.

Flynn grabbed the agent and pulled him aside. He turned back to the blank-faced Army officer. "Go on, Pete," he said gently. "Ride with her. I'll take care of things here."

Still not trusting himself to speak, Thorn nodded abruptly and climbed into the waiting helicopter. He crouched next to Helen's stretcher, trying to ignore the muttered exclamations from the paramedics working on her.

"God, what a mess! I've got a major impact wound right near the sacrum . . . Jesus, it shattered her pelvis . . . bone splinters everywhere . . ."

"She's deep in shock and bleeding out . . . keep that pressure up!"

"Trauma, this is Medevac One-One. Request immediate clearance. Suggest you alert surgical team . . ."

Helen's eyes opened suddenly, bright blue against skin so pale it was almost transparent. She looked up into his worried face and said in wonder, "Peter?"

He leaned closer, whispering, "I'm here. Remember that I love you."

She smiled drowsily and closed her eyes. "First time you ever told me that . . ." She slid away into unconsciousness.

The Blackhawk lifted off, climbing steeply as it flew north toward the hospital. Peter Thorn sat silently, holding Helen's hand. Tears ran unnoticed down his face. He had some of the answers he had been so desperately searching for.

But the price had been terribly high. Too high.

CHAPTER 22

TARGET ACQUISITION

DECEMBER 5

Trauma Unit, Walter Reed Army Medical Center

"Colonel Thorn?"

Peter Thorn stopped his pacing and turned abruptly at the sound of his name. He found himself facing a haggard, unhappy-looking man still wearing a surgical smock.

"My name is Doyle. I'm one of the trauma unit surgeons here. I understand you're waiting for news about Agent Gray?"

Thorn nodded, holding his breath. He'd been besieging the medical center's volunteers for information since the paramedics first wheeled Helen off the helicopter and straight into emergency surgery. After making an awkward call to her parents back in Indiana, he'd been left with nothing to do but stare at the pastel walls in the visitors' lounge. Either that or to sit watching the clock as the hours ticked past.

He fought to control his voice and asked, "How is she?"

"Not good, Colonel," Doyle said bluntly. He shook his head.

"She suffered two very serious wounds. The first injury, the one to her femoral artery, was bad enough. We've repaired the artery after some pretty delicate vascular surgery. But she'd already lost a lot of blood and she was pretty shocky when she came in. Despite the units we've put into her, her blood pressure is still abnormally low."

The surgeon frowned. "I think that's from shock, but I want to monitor her very closely over the next several hours. If her pressure doesn't start coming back up soon, that could be a sign of continued internal bleeding. I'd have to reopen her to make sure we didn't miss anything the first time through."

Thorn nodded grimly. He'd seen enough soldiers wounded in combat to know how dangerous shock could be. It was often the first killer. Helen had survived the first crisis point, but going back into surgery in her weakened state might be more than she could stand.

"Frankly, though, Colonel," Doyle said slowly, almost reluctantly, "it's Agent Gray's second wound that worries me."

The surgeon lowered his voice. "She took a 7.62 mm ricochet that shattered her pelvis. The impact pushed bone splinters and bullet fragments into her peritoneal cavity." He spread his hands helplessly. "So we're looking at a severe risk of infection—even a likelihood, I'd say. I'm starting her on a massive multi-antibiotic regime to fight that off, but it'll be touch and go for the next forty-eight to seventy-two hours."

"Christ." Thorn closed his eyes in pain for a moment and then opened them. "Is that the worst of it?"

Doyle paused. "No, sir. I wish it was. You see, that second bullet struck very near the plexus of nerves at the base of her spine. If those nerves were irreparably damaged . . . well, she might never walk again."

Thorn stood silent, afraid to trust his own voice. The thought of Helen, so alive and so graceful in every movement, permanently confined to a wheelchair was too terrible to contemplate. Finally, he croaked, "Can I see her?"

The surgeon shook his head firmly. "Not now, Colonel. She's in intensive care and we have her sedated. Leave me a number where I can reach you and I'll contact you as soon as a visit would be advisable."

He reached out and put a hand on Thorn's shoulder. "We'll do our best for her, Colonel. I promise you that. She's young and she's strong. She has a fighting chance to pull through. That's more than a lot of people who come in here start out with."

Thorn nodded blindly, barely noticing when the other man left him. After his father's long, losing battle with cancer, he'd shut part of himself off from others, preferring loneliness to vulnerability. But then, despite all his defenses, Helen had found her way into his heart. What would he do if he lost her now? And if she lived, what would she do if she found herself reduced to a life so dependent on others?

"Colonel Thorn?" The young student volunteer's hesitant contralto cut through his misery. "You're wanted on the phone. It's a priority call, sir."

He took the portable telephone she offered him without comment. "Thorn."

"Pete, this is Joe Rossini." He could hear the deep concern in the older man's voice. "How's Helen?"

Fear and sorrow gave his answer a harsh, monosyllabic character. "Not good. She may die. If she lives, she may not be able to walk."

"Jesus, Pete. I'm sorry." Rossini stopped for a second and then continued. "Maria and I will pray for her."

"I'd appreciate it, Joe." Thorn had known that the Maestro and his wife were fairly devout Catholics. He'd always been something of a skeptic himself, but agnosticism was cold comfort now. Prayer might not help Helen, but it certainly could not hurt her. If he had ever needed to believe in the existence of a just and loving God, it was now.

"Have you been able to visit her?" Rossini asked gently.

"Not yet," Thorn answered. "She's in intensive care. From what one of the doctors just told me, it might be days before she'll be out of danger."

"You can't stay there that long, Pete. Not now."

"I know." Thorn knew he had to set his personal anguish

aside—at least for the moment. The nation still faced a crisis, and Helen and her HRT teammates had put their lives on the line to obtain the information he and his analysts needed. His job now was to make sure their sacrifices hadn't been in vain. "Has the Bureau turned up anything useful in that damned house yet?"

"Some," Rossini said guardedly. "Look, Pete . . . this isn't really a secure line."

"Hell. Sorry." Thorn ran a hand across his weary eyes. He must be losing it to overlook something so elementary. He'd come dangerously close to blabbing classified information over the open airwaves.

From the first breathless television news bulletins he'd seen, Flynn had handled the situation perfectly. The FBI had sealed off the entire area around the terrorist safe house. No residents or media people were being allowed anywhere close by. The Bureau's preliminary statements said only that its agents had surprised a suspected neo-Nazi group inside the house, and that there had been a prolonged firefight—one in which all the terrorists were killed. Reporters were being told that the house itself had been utterly destroyed by fire—either in a blaze set accidentally or tear-gas grenades or as part of a suicide pact by those trapped inside. They were also being told that all the bodies found inside the ruins were charred beyond easy identification.

There were still other terrorist cells operating in the United States, and Flynn was determined to conceal just how much information the FBI had been able to recover from the safe house.

"Sam Farrell wants you back pronto, though," Rossini advised. "I'm told there's a helo en route to Walter Reed now."

Though his sorrow remained, Thorn felt part of his fatigue drop away. If the commander of the JSOC wanted him back at the Pentagon that badly, the information recovered in the raid on the terrorist hiding place must be pretty hot. "Understood, Maestro. I'm heading for the pad."

The Pentagon

Thorn scrambled down out of the helicopter and hurried toward the nearest entrance. Rossini was there waiting for him. Already briefed, the security guards and soldiers stationed at the doors passed the pair of them through with a minimum of fuss.

Thorn returned their salutes impatiently and glanced at the older man. "How much have Flynn's people been finding?"

To his relief, Rossini clearly understood that he needed to work right now more than he needed a sympathetic ear. The analyst started filling him in, limping slightly as he tried to keep up with the rapid pace Thorn set through the Pentagon's corridors. "A lot. That place the HRT knocked over was a miniature armory. The FBI's still cataloging all the weapons and explosives they found, but they've learned enough to tie the people inside to the press club bombing and those blown-down transmission towers for sure. The C4 and detonators match the traces left at both scenes."

"What about the bodies?"

"No firm identification yet," Rossini answered. "Two were clearly Caucasian. The other two could be either Hispanic or Middle Eastern in origin . . ."

"Some rabid, neo-Nazi group," Thorn interrupted bitterly. "Those bastards were pros."

"Uh-huh. Looks like our hunch was right," the older man agreed. "Mike Flynn said pretty much the same thing. He's having the bodies shipped to their D.C. lab for more detailed examination."

Thorn nodded. The FBI's forensics experts should be able to develop a fair amount of information about their dead terrorist John Does. Even if their fingerprints were not on file here or anywhere abroad, dental work and the evidence of old injuries or illnesses could provide useful clues as to their places of birth or prolonged residence. That level of forensics work would take time, however—certainly days and probably weeks. He had been hoping the HRT raid would produce more immediate re-sults. "Any documents or papers turn up?"

Rossini shrugged. "Several sets of false ID—passports, driver's licenses, even credit cards. All top-notch work."

"Naturally." Thorn started down the stairs leading to the Pentagon's basement. "Nothing else, though?"

"Nothing on paper, Pete." Rossini limped after him. "But the NSA's still going over the laptop computer Helen found."

"What?" Thorn stopped dead, narrowly avoiding a collision with the older man. "I thought that was destroyed. Flynn said one of the suspects blew it to hell with an AKM burst."

"Maybe. Maybe not," Rossini said. He explained. "Apparently a round clipped the hard drive, but the NSA techs think they may still be able to recover some of the data it contained. They're working on it now."

National Security Agency headquarters, Fort Meade, Maryland

Greg Paige, a gangly, twenty-something computer specialist in the NSA's T Group, finished readying the damaged hard drive sent over by the FBI for his data retrieval attempt. Not a particularly difficult job, he thought with a mild trace of contempt for the cyber-challenged. A portable computer's hard disk was less than three inches wide and barely an inch thick. It was also buried inside a concealing case. Wrecking the information a portable contained by hitting a target that small was staking more on luck than most people realized. And in this case, the shooter had not been lucky.

One round had utterly mangled the machine's floppy drive and internal modem. Another had torn a gaping hole in the computer's battery. But a third bullet had only scored the outer casing of the hard disk itself. The drive's bearings and heads were completely undamaged. Finding out what it contained required little more than transferring the assembly to another machine and running a simple diagnostics program.

Humming a made-up tune off-key, Paige finished making the last cable connections and hit the power switch. He swung back to his keyboard as the new machine's monitor blinked on.

"Piece of chocolate cream cake," the NSA specialist mumbled to himself. He quickly scrolled through the hard disk's directory, ignoring standard listings for off-the-shelf commercial word processing, communications, and accounting programs. If he didn't find anything else more intriguing, he could always go back through those—hunting for signs someone had buried other, less innocent pieces of code inside them.

As he had expected, a few of the disk's sectors were damaged—rendered unreadable when the bullet clipped its casing—but most were fine.

Paige stopped scrolling when he reached a program whose name he did not recognize: BABEL.EXE. He shook his head in disbelief. "Well, well, well . . . how very cute."

Someone the FBI was interested in had a very dry sense of humor.

He probed deeper into the program, summoning up its inner workings. Line after line appeared on the screen—an intricate interweaving of complex algorithms clearly intended to turn plain text into meaningless gibberish and back again. Paige smiled. Pay dirt.

To make absolutely sure he was right, he fed one of the pieces of E-mail intercepted from CompuNet into the suspected encryption program. Seconds later, a complete, plain-text message flashed onto his screen.

Paige read through the translated E-mail once in surprise and then a second time in growing horror. Still staring at his monitor, he reached out for the phone on his desk and punched in an internal number. "This is Greg Paige with Group T. I need to speak to the deputy director. Right away!"

The Pentagon

Rossini poked his head into Peter Thorn's office. "Pete? I think you'd better come see this." The Maestro sounded strained.

Thorn looked up from the investigative reports Flynn had faxed over from the terrorist safe house, slowly realizing that he had been staring at them for minutes without really seeing them. His brain still seemed to be functioning at half-speed. Despite his determination to throw himself into his work, he was finding it difficult to focus on anything beyond Helen Gray. So far his hourly phone calls to Walter Reed had yielded little more than the news that she was still in critical condition and still in intensive care.

He made an effort to gather his scattered thoughts. "See what?"

"The NSA found the encryption program they were looking for on that computer Helen captured. They're downloading the complete set of decoded E-mail from our terrorist friends into our database now." Rossini looked almost ill. "It contains a damned ugly surprise."

Thorn was on his feet instantly, following the older man next door into his cramped office. "Show me."

Rossini handed him a printout without comment. A time/date stamp at the top showed that it had been transmitted from London on October 12.

Special Operations Order
MAGI Prime via MAGI Link to LION Prime:
    1. Activate Phase II of SCIMITAR.
    2. Your field operations will commence on 5 November. Target selection BRAVO
TWO is approved.
    3. Go with God.

Message Authentication: TALEH, MAGI Prime, VXE115

Thorn stared down at the printout in his hands in shock. Taleh? Amir Taleh had organized this terror campaign? The terrorists posing as American extremists were *Taleh's* creatures? His *friend* was the man responsible for these atrocities against innocent civilians? The man ultimately responsible for Helen's terrible injuries? The man whose actions might cost him the one person who meant more to him than anyone else in the world?

It was insane—utterly unbelievable. How could the man who had been like a brother to him all those years ago be capable of such evil? How could Taleh have changed so much?

Thorn's face darkened. Maybe Taleh had not changed after all. Perhaps the evil had always been inside him—a core of malice hidden behind a mask of honor and friendship.

He crushed the sheet in his hands without thinking, caught up in cascading images of the past months. The Iranian had conducted a brilliant and cunning masquerade to conceal his true intentions. Taleh's attacks on the HizbAllah, his push for renewed U.S.-Iranian diplomatic relations, and even his offer to help track down the missing Bosnian terrorists—all had been nothing more than a gigantic deception, a blindfold pulled over American eyes while he readied his organized butchery.

Thorn tossed the crumpled printout aside in sudden, blind fury. Clearly, he had been one of the Iranian's favorite dupes—a trusting conduit of disinformation to the highest reaches of America's counterterrorist forces. His hands curled into fists. The bastard had *used* him. Taleh had asked him to come to Iran to renew their friendship and to seek new ties with America— all the while plotting to use his old friend's trust as a shield for this murderous campaign.

Brought face-to-face with the magnitude of the Iranian's treachery, Thorn's whole view of the world wavered. He was accustomed to making fast, accurate judgments about people and then trusting those judgments with his life. Taleh's betrayal struck at the heart of his confidence, weakening his own faith in himself.

His breathing slowed as reason returned. The anger remained, but it was now an icy, calculating enmity.

Amir Taleh was obviously a man of hidden malice, but he was not a fool. The Iranian must have realized that the United

States would eventually discover his nation's responsibility for this terrorist offensive. No sane man could hope to keep so large an operation secret forever. He had to know the kind of awful vengeance that would descend on Iran's head once his duplicity became clear.

Peter Thorn stood motionless in Rossini's office, staring at nothing while his mind grappled with questions that seemed to have no rational answer. Why would Taleh involve himself and his country in this slaughter? What could he possibly gain that would make the inevitable price worth paying?

DECEMBER 6

It was well past midnight.

Thorn and Rossini sat on opposite sides of a desk piled high with maps, satellite photos, transcripts of intercepted Iranian military communications, and reports published by a dozen different U.S. and foreign intelligence agencies. Some of the data came from the files pulled together earlier that year by the Maestro's tiny team trying to track down those first rumors of Bosnian Muslim terrorists. More had been scraped up by JSOC-ILU researchers held long after normal hours and sent out to scour the Pentagon's voluminous databases. After reading through Taleh's E-mail to his terrorist teams, Thorn had put the entire unit on a de facto war footing.

Both men were exhausted, but neither of them was willing to break for sleep. Their growing certainty that Taleh had something else up his sleeve—something even worse than the terrorist campaign—drove them onward.

Thorn put down the fragmentary telecommunications intercept he'd been studying, pulled a map of Iran closer to him, and scrawled a hasty note on the map next to one of the Iranian Army's garrison cities.

Rossini looked up from his own pile of papers. "Another one?"

"Yeah." Thorn slid the intercept across to the older man. "One of our VORTEX satellites picked up part of a conversation between the commander of the 25th Parachute Brigade and one of his battalion COs. They're going to full readiness—all leaves canceled, extra practice jumps, full equipment draw. The works."

"Jesus." Rossini scanned the sheet quickly and then eyeballed the map Thorn had been working on. "There's a hell of a lot of movement going on over there, Pete."

Thorn nodded. Although the picture of recent Iranian military activity they'd been putting together was by no means complete, it was increasingly ominous. Significant portions of more than six elite Iranian divisions were either in motion or preparing to move—somewhere. Air and naval units scattered across the Islamic Republic were also being brought to higher states of alert.

So far, no one else in the U.S. defense and intelligence communities had spotted the full scope of the Iranian maneuvers. That was understandable. Viewed in isolation, the various clues and bits of evidence meant very little. Few analysts were in a position to see *all* of the information gathered by America's satellites, signals intercept stations, and spies. Lulled by Taleh's phony U.S.-Iran détente and immobilized by the terrorist attacks at home, nobody in authority had paid much attention to the tiny warning bells going off.

"Colonel? Maestro? You got a minute?" Mike McFadden came bustling in, clearly excited.

"What've you got, Mike?" Thorn asked.

"This just came down the wire from Langley. It's a summary of the latest Satcom transmission from that Afghan truck driver, 'Stone.'" The young, red-haired analyst held out a two-page color fax with blue stripes running down one side of the cover sheet. The stripes indicated the fax contained information from a CIA agent. "He just reported the final destination for the Iranian 12th Infantry Division and most of the other convoys."

"And?"

McFadden stabbed a finger down on the map in front of Thorn. "They're moving to Bushehr!"

Bushehr? Thorn stared at the map. Why Bushehr?

Suddenly, the data they'd been accumulating bit by bit began falling into place with dizzying speed.

"My God," he said softly. He turned to Rossini. "I'm going to see Sam Farrell."

The older man looked confused. "Why?"

"To make sure he demands an immediate emergency meeting of the National Security Council."

"To do what, exactly?"

Thorn showed his teeth in a grim, bitter smile. "To persuade the President and the NSC that we have to kill General Amir Taleh before he kills us."

The White House

The White House Situation Room was packed to the rafters. The President and his Secretaries of State and Defense sat around a long rectangular table flanked by the Directors of the CIA and the FBI, the Attorney General, the National Security Advisor, and the uniformed Joint Chiefs of Staff. Notepads, pens, and glasses of ice water were precisely squared away in front of each man and woman at the table, along with briefing books hastily prepared for this meeting. Chairs lining the walls were filled by civilian and military aides.

"Major General Farrell, is your officer ready to brief us?" The President's familiar voice sliced through the buzz of uneasy speculation and concern. Word of Tehran's complicity in the wave of terrorism had already swept through the administration's upper circles like wildfire. So far, the threat of prosecution for leaking classified information had kept it away from the media. That and the realization that revealing the information prematurely would shatter an administration that had rested so much of its reputation on the mistaken assumption the terrorists they were fighting were homegrown radicals.

"Yes, sir," Farrell nodded. He glanced at Thorn. "You're on, Pete."

Thorn appreciated the symmetry of Farrell's decision to let him conduct the brief. He had played an unwitting role in Amir Taleh's diabolically clever deception plan. Now he was being given an opportunity to make amends by punching a hole through the tissue of lies surrounding Iran's true objective.

He rose from his chair and moved to the plain wood lectern at the front of the room. Its raised front concealed an array of buttons, knobs, and switches that gave the briefer control over the room's computer-driven displays.

By rights the concentrated gaze of the most powerful political and military leaders in the United States should have made him nervous. Instead, he felt nothing beyond the same cold anger that had filled him since he first learned of Taleh's treachery.

"Mr. President, ladies and gentlemen, my name is Colonel Peter Thorn, and I command the JSOC's Intelligence Liaison Unit. This briefing is based on satellite photography, signals intercepts, and on human intelligence from CIA assets inside Iran—much of it received over the past seventy-two hours," he began in a quiet, confident voice. "By now you all know that General Amir Taleh, the Chief of Staff of Iran's armed forces, is the prime mover of this terrorist campaign directed against us."

Heads nodded around the table, some of them impatiently. This was old news by Washington standards. Most of them had read the intercepted dispatches proving that the terror groups operating in the United States were receiving their orders from the military high command in Tehran.

"What you do not know," Thorn continued firmly, "is the reason we believe General Taleh has committed his country to such a risky course of action."

He tapped a button on the lectern. The large video monitor behind him came on, showing a map of the Persian Gulf region.

Blinking symbols on the display showed Iran's armed forces in motion.

"As you can see," Thorn said flatly, "a sizable fraction of Iran's conventional military forces are on the move. These forces include Tehran's most elite divisions and its most sophisticated ships and aircraft. Although the Iranians are making significant efforts to conceal the full scope of this sudden mobilization, we now know that the majority of these units are heading here—to Bandar-e Bushehr." He touched another button, highlighting the port city.

Thorn paused briefly to let the President and his advisors take in the vast size of the Iranian buildup and then went on. "Put bluntly, Mr. President, Taleh's open diplomatic overtures toward us and his covert terrorist campaign here have all been nothing but a smoke screen—a calculated and successful effort to conceal Iran's true objective for as long as possible. He has been buying the time he needs to complete these massive military preparations."

"And what exactly is this man's real aim, Colonel Thorn?" the President asked. His eyes were still fixed on the outlined port of Bushehr.

Thorn answered him quietly but with absolute conviction. "General Taleh is preparing to conduct a major amphibious operation across the Persian Gulf within the next seven to ten days. He intends to invade Saudi Arabia."

There were gasps around the crowded table and throughout the room.

"Surely that's not possible!" the President exclaimed, clearly stunned. His eyes roamed around the Situation Room, seeking someone, anyone, who would contradict such a dire prediction.

"On the contrary, Mr. President. Such an operation is not only feasible—it is likely to succeed," Thorn cut in decisively. He was determined not to offer any excuse for inaction or delay. "Taleh has systematically strengthened Iran's armed forces. Their weapons are better. Their maintenance and supply units are better. Most important of all, the Iranian officer corps is more professional and more capable than at any time since the fall of the Shah. Iran is once again a major military power in the Gulf region."

"Hold on, Colonel," the Secretary of Defense, a quiet, scholarly man, protested. "Aren't you jumping to conclusions prematurely? Isn't it possible that these Iranian troop movements indicate a possible offensive against Iraq—and not against Saudi Arabia?"

"No, sir," Thorn said. "First, Iran's elite divisions and Air Force units are moving away from its land border with Iraq— and there are no signs of any higher alert there. Second, why would General Taleh conduct a murderous campaign of terrorism on our own soil simply to distract us from a planned attack against Baghdad?"

Silence greeted that. Although no one welcomed the thought of another war, few could doubt that Washington or its allies would strenuously object to seeing the Gulf region's two most powerful and troublesome states again entangled in conflict. The same could not be said of Saudi Arabia. The vast oil reserves controlled by the House of Saudi were vital to the world's developed economies and to U.S. national security.

"What about the Saudi armed forces?" an aide asked aloud. "They're well equipped. Can they defeat this Iranian invasion on their own if we warn them in time?"

Thorn shook his head grimly. "Not a chance! Most of the Saudi troops are deployed in the north against Iraq, around Riyadh guarding the Royal Family, or as security forces for the holy cities of Mecca and Medina. Even if they could be redeployed in time, their military value would be nil."

The military men inside the Situation Room nodded. Saudi Arabia's armed forces had performed reasonably well during DESERT STORM—*after* intensive retraining by American advisors. Since then, however, the Saudis had slipped back to their older, more slipshod methods of operation. Much of their high-tech weaponry was out of commission, awaiting repair. Once ashore, Iran's revitalized divisions could slice through the weak Saudi Army practically without breaking stride.

"If this is all true, then clearly we must deploy our own forces to the Gulf . . . as a deterrent," Austin Brookes, the Secretary of State, said. He looked horribly depressed. Thorn knew that the successful rapprochement with Iran had been one of his cherished projects. The public revelation that it had been nothing more than a ruse in an undeclared war would finish the elderly man's career as the nation's chief diplomat. It would also rob him of any hope of future reputation. "We simply have no other choice."

A medley of raised voices around the room contradicted Brookes. There wasn't time to deploy a sufficient force to Saudi Arabia. Even using the prepositioned equipment stockpiled in Kuwait, it would take at least four days to put a lone mechanized brigade in the region. Additional forces would take far longer to arrive. U.S. aircraft could be on the ground at Saudi airfields in forty-eight hours—but it would take far more time to move the munitions, ground crews, and spare parts required to conduct a prolonged campaign against the revamped Iranian Air Force. Once the Iranian invasion actually began, all U.S. troop movement bets were off. The ports and airfields needed by arriving American reinforcements were bound to be among Taleh's first targets.

"Even if we had enough time, Mr. Secretary, it would be impossible for us to conceal the signs of a major military move into Saudi Arabia," Thorn added flatly. "And that could easily trigger the very thing we are attempting to prevent—an Iranian invasion. Taleh's preparations are so advanced that he can launch his attack on virtually a moment's notice."

At Farrell's quiet signal, he stood back from the lectern, listening as the discussion grew more and more heated, and more and more desperate. The level of rancor did not surprise him. Clearly, the President and his national security team were all too aware that they faced a political and military disaster. Command of the Saudi oil reserves would give Tehran a potential stranglehold over the global economy. Catapulted to status as the most powerful Islamic nation in the world, Iran would be free to smash its foes and reward its friends at will. Decades of diplomacy and the careful application of American military force would be erased in the blink of an eye. The West would face its ultimate nightmare: a powerful Islamic alliance domi-nated by one able and ambitious man, Amir Taleh.

He kept his eye on Sam Farrell. The head of the JSOC had a fine sense of timing and the ability to navigate smoothly through troubled political waters. Both men had agreed on the only possible course of action before the meeting began. And both men knew the first hurdle would come in persuading their superiors to take the high-stakes gamble needed to stop Taleh's invasion before it got off the ground.

After the futile wrangling had lasted for several minutes, he caught a tiny nod of Farrell's head. Thorn mentally crossed his fingers. It was time to pitch his plan.

"We have only *one* viable option, Mr. President," he broke in suddenly. "We must launch a special forces operation aimed at destroying the Iranian high command *before* Taleh and his gen-erals can strike. Taleh is the focus of political and military power inside Iran. He is also the mind controlling the terror offensive in our own nation. Kill him and the Iranians will be disorga-nized—even vulnerable."

Heads swung his way. Most of the men and women around the table were clearly astonished by his abrupt suggestion. A few, those with a better understanding of Iranian politics, looked thoughtful.

"If we're lucky," Thorn continued forcefully, "eliminating Iran's top military leaders will force them to abandon their inva-sion plans. Even at worst, it should sow enough confusion to buy us the time we need to strengthen Saudi Arabia's defenses."

Austin Brookes stared at him, clearly appalled by his pro-posal. "You cannot be serious, Colonel!" The Secretary of State turned to the President. "Surely, sir, no responsible government can support a plan to assassinate its foreign rivals? Our own laws clearly prohibit killing rival heads of state. Such conduct would be infamous!"

Infamous conduct! Thorn thought angrily. What the hell did Brookes consider the murder of American women and children? Still on the rising crest of his anger, he rode roughshod over the older man's objections. "Taleh is *not* Iran's official head of state. He's a military leader—and a legitimate target in time of war. And that, Mr. Secretary, is exactly what we're facing here—a war."

Brookes sat back, pale and clearly flustered at being contradicted so abruptly by someone so much his junior.

No one around the table jumped to the Secretary of State's defense. Thorn realized suddenly that most of the senior people in this administration were old hands at reading the prevailing winds. They could sense the growing sentiment in favor of eliminating Amir Taleh. It was the only course of action that offered any hope of avoiding the catastrophe he had so vividly conjured.

The Chief of Naval Operations spoke up strongly. "The colonel is dead right, Mr. President. We have to wipe out this General Taleh and his top aides."

Then he shook his head. "But he's wrong about the means, Mr. President. Putting Delta Force troops on the ground inside Tehran is far too dangerous. Too many things could go wrong. Too many American lives would be at risk." The admiral leaned forward so that the room lights gleamed off his balding pate. "We hold a decisive technological superiority over Iran. I suggest we play to our strengths, not to our weaknesses. I say we leave the job of crippling their high command to a massive, time-on-target, Tomahawk attack, followed by air strikes using precision-guided munitions."

The Air Force's Chief of Staff nodded his agreement with the admiral's proposal. "We can put together a strike package that should blow the hell out of this Taleh's headquarters within seventy-two hours, Mr. President."

To Thorn's relief, Sam Farrell intervened. In a clash of brass on brass, the JSOC chief's general's stars carried more weight than the eagles on his own shoulders.

"Blowing apart a building is not the same thing as killing a man, sir," Farrell said. He turned to the others grouped around the table. "During DESERT STORM, we used hundreds of

Tomahawks and laser-guided bombs in an effort to kill Saddam Hussein. We failed."

They nodded their understanding. America's air war and lightning land campaign against Iraq's dictator had driven his forces out of Kuwait. But it had not killed him or driven him from power.

"No, sir." The head of the JSOC shook his head grimly. "The only way we can be sure we've eliminated Taleh and his top aides is to root them out on the ground—up close and personal. Anything short of certainty means risking the loss of the Saudi oil fields to invasion."

Farrell turned his gaze on the President. "My troops have trained hard for just this kind of mission, sir. They know the risks. They can do the job. Just say the word, and we'll start moving!"

The President nodded slowly, looking far older than his years. While his top aides sat fidgeting, he studied the blinking symbols on the electronic map in silence, apparently hunting for other, less risky options. That was understandable. If the Delta Force failed, the repercussions and resulting casualties would tear his administration apart. But the risks of inaction were even more appalling.

Finally, he shook his head. Something about the set of his shoulders told Thorn that he had made up his mind.

The President turned to Thorn and Farrell. "All right, gentlemen," he said hoarsely. "Draw up your plan for a Delta Force raid on Tehran! But I want to see it before I make a final decision."

Before Thorn could protest any further delay, Farrell caught his eye and shook his head slightly. He sat back. The general seemed satisfied by what they had accomplished. Presumably, the older man knew enough about the way this White House worked to be confident the President would approve their final plan.

Thorn just hoped the JSOC commander's confidence was justified. They were already pushing the outer edge of the time envelope for planning, organizing, and carrying out a large-scale commando attack.

He paid little attention to the meeting's closing formalities. His mind was already far, far away—wrestling with the challenge of inserting a strike force deep into the heart of an enemy country.

A tiny, ill-dressed man stopped him on the way out the door. Thorn recognized Jefferson T. Corbell, the administration's political guru, from news photos.

The small Georgian snorted. "Well, I guess you and General Farrell won your point, Colonel. You mind telling me just who you think will lead this suicide mission?"

Thorn did not hesitate. "I will, Mr. Corbell."

CHAPTER 23

PREPARATIONS

DECEMBER 7

Bushehr airfield

(D MINUS 8)

General Shahrough Akhavi looked up from his cargo manifests as another C-130 Hercules touched down on Bushehr's short main runway. The short, stout logistician turned toward the taller Air Force colonel at his side. "There are the last of your missiles, Imad."

"Thank you, General." The colonel smiled and nodded toward the airport perimeter. "Now, with God's blessing and some hard work, my men and I will have all of our batteries in position by nightfall."

Akhavi followed the younger man's nod, squinting into the sunlight sparkling off the blue Gulf waters. There, silhouetted against the ships crowding Bushehr's waterfront, he could just make out the low, tracked shape of an SA-6 SAM launcher.

Soldiers and technicians were busy piling sandbags around the vehicle and stringing camouflage netting over it. More men were occupied elsewhere around the field, digging in towed anti-aircraft guns and building missile and ammunition storage bunkers.

The logistician breathed a little easier. Each load of military supplies ferried in by coast freighter, train, truck, or aircraft had made the little port city a more inviting target for a preemptive strike. Now, as General Taleh's plans took final shape, Bushehr's own defenses were at last being strengthened.

Operation NEMESIS planning cell, Fort Bragg, North Carolina

Colonel Peter Thorn was practically hip-deep in maps, satellite photographs of Tehran, and intelligence reports when one of the senior sergeants assigned to his planning cell looked in the door of his temporary office. "Sir, Major General Farrell is on secure line one."

"Thanks, Hal." Thorn dumped the pile of papers in his hand to one side and grabbed the phone. The JSOC commander was still in Washington, shepherding events there while he ran things at this end. "Thorn here."

Farrell didn't waste any time. "NEMESIS is a go, Pete. The President signed off this morning after seeing your preliminary ops plan. He also confirmed you as mission commander."

Thorn relaxed slightly. NEMESIS was his plan to kill Taleh. "Thank you, sir."

Farrell snorted. "You *ought* to thank me. I've had Bill Henderson and the other guys in my face ever since they heard the news."

"Sorry about that," Thorn said without much real remorse. He wasn't surprised by his peers' reaction. In the normal course of events, Henderson or one of the other Delta Force squadron commanders would have been selected to lead the raiding force.

Certainly, no one would have expected command to fall to a staff officer—even one who was a Delta veteran with a sterling combat record. But he had been prepared to pull every string and use every chit accumulated over his career to wangle this assignment. In the end, Farrell had agreed to give him the job for two very good reasons. First, he knew the territory and Taleh's mind and personality better than any other officer in the U.S. Army. Second, the NEMESIS force would, of necessity, be a mixed outfit—one hastily drawn from the existing Delta Force squadrons. Given the limited time available, that was the only way to create a team with the needed language and combat skills. Besides, if NEMESIS failed to stop Taleh's planned invasion, Farrell's other officers would have more than enough bloody work for their own skilled hands.

There was a third reason, of course—one he and the general left unspoken. Helen Gray. Both men knew this mission would be the most difficult and dangerous operation ever mounted by the Delta Force. Much could go wrong in the blink of an eye. And both men instinctively knew the on-scene commander might need the driving force of a very personal and very compelling passion to push NEMESIS through to victory. Peter Thorn had that fiery drive for vengeance. He wanted Amir Taleh dead more than any other man alive.

"Are you getting the data you need on the Iranian HQ?" Farrell asked.

Thorn's mind came rapidly back to the present. "Yes, sir. The CIA and NSA assessments agree with our own. Taleh and his staff are definitely working out of the old Pasdaran building near Khorasan Square."

Fragments of intercepted telephone conversations, satellite photographs showing upgraded defenses, and gossip the CIA's agents inside Tehran had picked up from local residents all confirmed Amir Taleh's presence there. With their primary target locked in, Thorn's planners had kicked their work into high gear.

"You have enough to build your HQ mock-up?"

The Delta Force always tried to run its assault teams through detailed mock-ups of their targets before any major operation. In the Delta Bible, elaborate, full-scale dress rehearsals were essential to reducing both confusion and casualties.

"Yes, sir," Thorn answered. "I have the construction crews out working now. We're using satellite photos for details on the outer defenses. We were even able to dig up a set of floor plans for the interior."

Farrell whistled appreciatively. "How the hell did you manage that?"

"Before the Revolution, the Shah's secret police used the building as a prison. Apparently, our mission there tried to keep an eye on SAVAK excesses," Thorn explained. "Captain Pappas found the blueprints in an old Army Intelligence file."

"Outstanding." Farrell cleared his throat. "Look, Pete, I don't want to rush you, but you know the time pressure we're under. I need to know when you and your assault force can be ready to go."

Thorn glanced at the massive piles of paper still heaped throughout his office while he considered his reply. To lay out the detailed plans for NEMESIS, he'd commandeered talented officers and NCOs from Delta's intelligence, operations, logistics, and administration staff directorates. They had already been working nearly around the clock for more than twenty-four hours. The planning cell was making enormous strides—adding real substance to the skeletal outline Farrell had laid before the NSC yesterday. But there was still a lot of hard work and hard training left to be done.

"We need at least a week to prep," he said finally.

"That's cutting it mighty close, Pete," Farrell warned quietly. "A week is well inside the early window for the Iranian invasion."

"Can't be helped, sir. I won't send my troops into Iran unprepared," Thorn said stubbornly. They were already moving faster than was really wise. Previous Delta Force operations, even those of less inherent danger and complexity, had often required more than a month of planning and preparation. "Besides, having this CIA contact inside Tehran is critical to the mission, and Langley tells me he can't possibly be in position for at least another three days."

Neither he nor the head of the JSOC were happy about having to rely on the Afghan truck driver code-named Stone. Unfortunately, there wasn't time to infiltrate anybody else into the Iranian capital. Stone's CIA controllers regarded him as a man of the utmost integrity and reliability. Thorn just hoped like hell they were right for once.

"On the other hand," he continued, "we should have thirty-six to forty-eight hours' notice of any imminent Iranian move now that we know what to look for. If Taleh puts his plan in gear sooner than expected, we'll saddle up and go right away."

"Fair enough," Farrell said. "I'll try to keep the President and the JCS off your backs for as long as possible."

"Thanks."

"One last thing, Pete." The general's tone changed, becoming less official and more personal. "What's the latest word on Helen?"

The room seemed to darken around Thorn. "I talked to one of the surgeons at Walter Reed this morning. She's still in intensive care and still fighting off the infection. But, as best they can tell, she can't move anything below her waist. They just don't know yet whether the nerve damage is temporary . . . or permanent. He couldn't give me much more than that."

"I am sorry, Pete," Farrell said sadly. "Louisa's flying up here tonight. She plans to stay near the hospital and keep an eye on Helen for you."

Grateful beyond words, Thorn was conscious of mumbling his thanks, but he couldn't shake the feeling that he should be there himself—waiting by Helen's bedside to comfort her, to stroke her hair, to tell her again that he loved her.

The general seemed to read his mind. "Helen will understand, Pete. She has a soldier's heart. She'll know that this mission must come first. There's too much at stake."

"Yes, sir," Thorn said slowly.

Farrell's next words were in deadly earnest. "This is gonna be a rough one, Pete. Don't screw up and get yourself killed."

"No, sir."

DECEMBER 8

Special operations headquarters, Tehran

(D MINUS 7)

General Amir Taleh stood with his arms folded near the front of the chair-filled subterranean room, watching the men he had summoned assemble.

His audience was a distinguished one. It included not only the full Defense Council and staff but senior officers from each of the armed forces. Significantly, it also included the remnants of the Pasdaran command structure and many of his most powerful political enemies. All had been summoned with only a few hours' notice after morning prayers and whisked here by limousine, helicopter, and military aircraft.

Taleh had invited his enemies to his headquarters for two reasons: First, Kazemi's reports made it clear that their opposition to his declared policy of détente with America was growing stronger with every passing day. Assassination was no longer his sole concern. Some in the Pasdaran were moving closer to open revolt—particularly as many of the Army's best troops were moved further from Tehran. By asking them here, to his visible center of power, he was invoking the oldest traditions of Persian hospitality. For the duration of this meeting at least, he was their host and they were his honored guests. None of the various factions would move against him or each other under those conditions. More important, though, these men needed to be here. This was the time for truth-telling. A time to drop the mask that had so enraged them.

One worry still nagged at him. He turned to Kazemi. "Has there been any further word from Halovic's team?"

The young captain shook his head. "No, sir. Nothing since we received their December 4 situation report."

Taleh nodded. It was as he had feared when he first heard the American news reports crowing about the destruction of a neo-Nazi terrorist cell near Washington, D.C. The Bosnian and his men were undoubtedly out of action. He sighed. That was un-fortunate. He had grown fond of Halovic over the past months. Like Kazemi, the Bosnian had been a perfect weapon. "And we are sure that the Americans took no prisoners, Farhad?"

"Yes, sir," Kazemi replied with satisfaction. "Their broadcasts make it clear that Halovic and his men fought to the last—even as their house burned down around them. The Americans are still stumbling around like lost sheep."

"Good." Taleh shrugged off the Bosnian's death. Casualties were to be expected in any war and he had seen many brave men die to less purpose. Besides, his other special operations teams were still at large, undetected, and conducting terrorist attacks to keep the United States in a state of confused panic.

Colonel Najmabadi, his chief intelligence officer, stepped closer and whispered, "Sir, I believe we are ready to begin. All of those invited have arrived."

Taleh nodded briskly. "Very well." He stepped forward.

The gentle hum of whispered conversation hushed abruptly as heads turned in his direction. He was pleased to see more fear and uncertainty on their faces than open hostility. His grip on power was still firm enough.

"I am glad to see you, my friends," Taleh began smoothly. He showed his teeth in a thin smile. "Much as I regret it, I cannot waste much time on the ordinary pleasantries. Time presses in on us."

The mullahs and Pasdaran leaders stirred uneasily, clearly wondering what justified such urgency.

Taleh went on without pause, ignoring their unease. "This should be considered an operational briefing by all military offi-cers present."

That drew muttered exclamations. The terms he was using were usually reserved for times of war or crisis.

"By now, you are all familiar with the exercise currently under way," Taleh said.

Heads nodded irritably throughout the room. Code-named PERSIAN HAMMER, the exercise had been authorized as a test of Iran's ability to coordinate the movements of its ground, air, and sea forces at short notice. As part of the exercise, all military leaves had been canceled, and security had been greatly tightened around all ports, airfields, and military installations. Many of those present had condemned the endeavor as a foolish waste of desperately needed resources.

Taleh smiled again, a fighting grin this time. "What I can tell you now, my friends, is that the real name of this operation is not PERSIAN HAMMER, but SCIMITAR." He saw their puzzled expressions and delivered his bombshell. "In precisely seven days, at 0600 hours local time, the armed forces of the Islamic Republic of Iran will begin landing in Saudi Arabia by sea and air. They will conduct an offensive that will change the course of world history . . ."

As he outlined his long-held plans, Taleh saw members of the Defense Council, politicians and mullahs alike, rising to their feet in shock, ready to protest this wild, insane move. He continued speaking forcefully, glaring at them to sit and listen. Such was their fear of him that they sat.

Taleh smiled again, relishing the moment. He had saved his biggest surprise for the last. "Best of all, the Americans are in no position to intervene against us. The seeds of violence we have sown through our carefully orchestrated terror campaign are now bringing forth their own fruit. Our great adversary is tearing itself apart. By the time Washington awakes to its peril, it will be far, far too late."

More astonished exclamations greeted his latest revelation. Most of the men inside the room had followed the news of death and destruction in America with mounting delight. Only a handful had any idea that the terrorists had been trained and armed in Iran.

Taleh ignored their amazement, intent on his own great vision. "When SCIMITAR is complete, Iran will hold the balance of world power. We will command the respect of all who yearn for Islam throughout the world! We will begin the long march back to greatness—the long march back to a united Faith strong enough to subdue the infidel!"

He stopped speaking as the new Pasdaran commander rose abruptly. He was young, in his forties, and he brought zeal but no real skill to his job. A jet-black beard and mustache hid a soft face, but he was known to be one of Taleh's bitterest surviving enemies. Much would depend on his reaction.

The Pasdaran general suddenly raised his arms over his head and cried out aloud, "I praise you, Amir Taleh! You have made the Great Satan suffer as I have only dreamed! You are a worthy commander—a true leader of the Faithful! You are a man of God! A man of vision!"

Others took up the cry. In moments the entire audience was on its feet, chanting his praises. Taleh tried to remain calm, but his exhilaration would not let him.

Nothing could stop Iran now.

DECEMBER 9

Fort Bragg, North Carolina

The sound of automatic-weapons fire rattled through the Delta House of Horrors, rising in volume as more and more troopers opened up on suspected targets. Sharp thuds punctuated the noise as smoke grenades went off to cover movement down staircases and into enemy-held rooms. White smoke drifted lazily out through the building's open windows.

Peter Thorn and Sergeant Major Roberto "TOW" Diaz stood near the front steps, observing the rehearsal closely. The short, dark-haired noncom held a stopwatch in his hand.

They were watching the lead elements of each handpicked assault team show off their paces. Where possible, sections of the House of Horrors had been altered to mimic portions of Taleh's operations headquarters. Using the existing building for training was a stopgap expedient at best, but it would have to do for now. The construction crews feverishly erecting mock-ups of the buildings around Tehran's Khorasan Square were still at least two days away from finishing their work.

Thorn nodded in satisfaction as the first Delta Force troopers fell back out through open doors and windows. They had a strange, wild look about them. Like him, anyone with lighter colored hair had dyed it black. And all of the men assigned to the NEMESIS force were letting their beards and mustaches grow. Roughly half of them wore Iranian uniforms. The rest were still waiting for the seamstresses to finish sewing.

"Jesus, what a motley crew," Diaz muttered with a grin. "I keep expecting someone to raise the Jolly Roger."

"Sorry you signed on for this little jaunt, Tow?" Thorn asked.

"Hell, no, Pete!" Diaz shook his head. "Believe me, it sure beats waiting by the phone for Jimmy to call. All the kid does is piss and moan about how rough it is being a plebe! I'm looking forward to a little peace and quiet when we hit Tehran."

"Sure," Thorn said, not believing a word of it. West Point Cadet James Diaz was his father's pride and joy. Still, he was very glad to have the sergeant major aboard. TOW Diaz was the best rough-and-tumble soldier in the Delta Force, and he had a hunch they were going to need every edge they could get when they shot their way into Amir Taleh's den.

FBI Surveillance Team Six—near Milwaukee, Wisconsin

FBI Special Agent James Orr stared through a set of almost-closed blinds at the house just across the way. He could see the terrorists moving around inside again.

After a full day of close surveillance, he was beginning to put the faces and habits of these men together. There were four of them, all told. One, a short, brown-haired Caucasian, was a dedicated smoker. He was puffing away now while watching television with the sallow-faced Middle Easterner who seemed to be used mostly as a driver by the terrorist cell. The other two were out of sight somewhere in the back of the house they were renting.

Orr grimaced. This was crazy. He had these guys. He had them and now he was being told to back off. He spoke sharply into the handheld secure phone. "Jesus Christ, Mike, I'm telling you we can take these guys without breaking a sweat. Hell, my snipers could drop two of them this second!"

Mike Flynn's voice came over the line loud and clear. "Negative, Jim. I'm telling you just what I've told every other team around the country. You wait for the word. You watch those people closely, but you do not make a move on them without my direct authorization. Is that understood?" he demanded.

Orr bit back another oath. "Understood, Mike. Out."

Still shaking his head in disbelief, he clicked the phone off and went back to watching the enemies he was not allowed to touch.

CHAPTER 24

MOVEMENT TO THE OBJECTIVE

DECEMBER 11

Kilo-class submarine *Taregh,* off Bandar-e Abbas, near the Strait of Hormuz

(D MINUS 4)

Iran's submarine force sortied out of Bandar-e Abbas well after dusk on a moonless, cloudy night. Three black, seventy-meter-long shapes slid quietly past the blinking buoys that marked the main channel. One after the other, as soon as they cleared the harbor area, the diesel boats submerged and went to periscope depth.

Followed by her consorts, the lead submarine, *Taregh,* crept almost due south through the shallow Gulf waters. She was an ultra-quiet, *Kilo*-class boat, originally designed and built by the Soviets, and purchased for hard currency from the shrinking, cash-poor Russian fleet. Her forty-five-man crew was the best in the Iranian Navy.

Once he was satisfied that they were safely en route and free of any shadowers, *Taregh*'s captain picked up the annunciator microphone. "Attention to orders."

He ignored the significant looks and whispers among his control room crew. "We have been assigned an extended exercise—one which may last several weeks.

"Our mission is a simple one. We will take station in the Gulf of Oman and begin patrolling, maintaining silent status. Once on station, we will track all ships encountered, especially warships and foreign submarines. I know each man aboard will do his best. That is all."

In truth, the captain doubted any man aboard believed they were out on only a simple practice run. For two days before they sortied, working parties had sweated around the clock loading provisions and advanced torpedoes. Backed up by hired Russian technicians, the submarine's officers and senior ratings had run countless tests—double-checking every critical propulsion, sonar, and weapons control system aboard the boat. Those extra efforts and the extraordinarily tight security around the Bandar-e Abbas Naval Base were clear evidence of something serious in the wind and water.

The reality was so daunting that the captain wished he could share it openly with his men. Right now, only he, his executive officer, and the submarine's departmental heads knew their full orders.

Part of what he had said was true. They were heading for a box-shaped patrol area just outside the Strait of Hormuz. And they would indeed be tracking enemy warships. However, his instructions also required him to come up to listening depth at regular intervals. Once he received a specific coded radio signal, the boat's mission would change dramatically: *Taregh* would sink all Western warships in its patrol zone. Its sister submarines had similar orders. Together they were expected to lay a deadly barrier across the entrance to the Persian Gulf.

The captain felt a small shiver run up his spine at the thought of actual combat. Any new submarine with untested officers and crew was like an unfired clay pot. The fire might harden it, but some pots cracked in the flames.

Then he shrugged. It would be as God willed it. In any case, all the advantages were his. *Taregh* was ideally suited to hide undetected in these shallow waters and she would have complete surprise. The first enemy vessel to die would know of his intentions only when a torpedo tore into its hull.

Suddenly, he was eager for the go code.

DECEMBER 12

Near Lavan Island, in the Persian Gulf

(D MINUS 3)

Just after midnight, the passenger ferry *Chamran* slipped through the channel between Lavan Island and the rugged Iranian coastline, steaming north through the darkness with its running lights off. Five miles off her port bow, two armed Boghammer speedboats belonging to the Iranian Navy cruised back and forth in a patrol pattern—ready to shoo away unauthorized vessels intruding in what was now an unannounced restricted sea zone. There were more passenger ships requisitioned by the Iranian Navy at sea, some ahead of the *Chamran* and some behind—all moving north toward Bushehr, all at fairly regular intervals.

One hundred and fifty miles above the Gulf, an American KH-12 spy satellite passed almost directly overhead and continued silently eastward. Ground controllers had used the 40,000-pound satellite's on-board thrusters to shift it into a new orbit several days before. Using a MILSTAR satellite as a relay, the infrared photos the KH-12 took were transmitted back to the United States in real time.

Fort Bragg, North Carolina

It was still dark and bitterly cold outside when the lights began flicking on inside the Delta Force headquarters building.

Summoned by phone from their temporary quarters, sixteen Army and Air Force officers and senior NCOs were waiting inside the briefing room for Colonel Peter Thorn and Sergeant Major Diaz. Together they commanded the four twenty-man Delta troops, five Army helicopters, and three specially equipped C-17 transport aircraft assigned to Operation NEMESIS.

"Good morning, gentlemen," Thorn said briskly as soon as he came through the door.

He waved them down when they started to snap to attention. Inside its closed compound, Delta Force prided itself on its relative informality. Talent mattered more than rank among the outfit's experienced professionals. They reserved the spit-and-polish show for outside visitors.

Thorn moved to the front of the room while Diaz started setting up an overhead projector. "Sorry about interrupting your beauty sleep, gentlemen. God knows from the look of some of you, you could certainly use it."

That earned him a strained chuckle.

He didn't waste any more time. "I just got a call from Sam Farrell. The President has activated NEMESIS."

His commanders sat up straighter.

Thorn nodded. "We've run out of time. New intelligence shows that the Iranian offensive is probably now less than seventy-two hours away." He raised his voice slightly to reach the back of the room. "Ready, Tow?"

Diaz nodded and dimmed the lights.

"These satellite photos came down the wire from the National Reconnaissance Office fifteen minutes ago," Thorn explained.

The short, stocky NCO slipped each picture into the projector, keeping pace as Thorn ticked off the information they revealed. "Both the CIA and the DIA now estimate there are more than four frontline infantry divisions closed up and in their final assembly areas near Bandar-e Bushehr. Additional formations, all of them tank and mechanized units, have been spotted moving by rail to Bandar-e Khomeini."

He watched their reactions closely, pleased to see that every man appeared fully alert—and utterly focused. "Even more important than that, KH-12 and LACROSSE radar satellite passes yesterday and early today picked up signs of significant naval movements. First, the Iranians have shut down their regularly scheduled ferry services to the offshore islands. Those ships are now sailing north toward Bushehr. Second, their entire submarine force has left Bandar-e Abbas, apparently heading for the Gulf of Oman. If we needed anything else, the NSA reports that all Iranian army, air, and naval units switched to a new set of codes and ciphers six hours ago."

The lights came back to full brightness. Thorn stepped forward. "This is not a simple exercise or drill. They're getting set to go—and to go soon."

Heads nodded in agreement with his assessment. The final pieces of the Iranian operation were falling into place. Switching codes and frequencies was a classic precursor to any significant military move, and no one with any economic sense moved that much shipping around on a whim.

Thorn swept his eyes over the little group of officers and senior sergeants, picking out individuals. Keenly aware that they were looking to him for direction, he kept a tight rein on his expression. Beneath the impassive mask, however, he could feel the old eagerness, the driving urge toward action, welling up inside. He could tell they felt much the same way.

Still, he had no illusions about the dangers involved in the mission ahead. Despite their intensive work over the past several days, NEMESIS was still very much an improvised, pick-up-and-go operation. If the plan started falling apart under the stress of unexpected events, it would be up to the men in this room to pick up the pieces and carry on—against all odds and no matter what the cost.

Thorn focused on the commander of the NEMESIS helicopter detachment. "Your guys ready, Scott?"

Captain Scott Finney, a compact Texan so calm other people
often thought he was asleep or dead, nodded. "Yep. No sweat."

"How about yours, Mack?"

The tall, lanky Air Force lieutenant colonel commanding
their C-17 transports shrugged. "I wouldn't mind making a few
more practice runs, Pete, but we can do it without them."

One by one, the majors and captains commanding the four
Delta troops gave him the same answer. No one was very happy
about cutting their planned prep time short, but no one was
ready to ask for further delay now that the Iranians were poised
and ready to attack.

Ordinarily, Thorn did not believe in giving pep talks—especially not to men like those in this room. Most were already veterans of half a dozen special operations—some of them so secret
that only the barest hints had filtered out to the world beyond
the Delta Force compound. Still, he wanted to impress on them
his absolute conviction that NEMESIS, no matter how difficult
and no matter how dangerous, was a mission with purpose—a
mission with a critical and achievable objective.

"One thing we know from the computer messages we've intercepted is that Amir Taleh is a control freak," Thorn said
firmly. "Taleh is the focus of political and military power inside
Iran. He runs the Iranian armed forces pretty much as a one-
man show. All crucial orders pass through his headquarters. His
field commanders are highly unlikely to begin an invasion
without a clear directive from him personally.

"So our job is essential. If we stop Taleh, we stop this war
before it starts. Everything else is secondary. Everything. Understood?"

They nodded solemnly.

"Very well, gentlemen," Thorn said calmly. "Have your troops
saddle up. We move out for Incirlik at 2030 hours, tonight."

In the Persian Gulf

Twenty miles outside Saudi territorial waters, an old wooden dhow chugged through calm waters at a steady ten knots, relying on its auxiliary motor for power instead of its furled, lateen-rigged sails. Crates, boxes, and bales of varying sizes crowded the boat's deck. To all outward appearances, the dhow was nothing more than a simple trading vessel—one of the hundreds that plied the Gulf on a daily basis. Her crew, too, appeared utterly ordinary: a mix of wiry young lads and weathered old men clad only in T-shirts and shorts against the noonday sun.

Feeling self-conscious in his unaccustomed civilian garb, Lieutenant Kazem Buramand leaned down through the dhow's forward hatch. After the dazzling brightness outdoors, the hold below seemed pitch-black. It took several seconds before the Iranian naval officer's eyes adjusted enough to make out the ten men squatting comfortably around a mound of their own equipment.

All of them wore the camouflage fatigues and green berets of Iran's Special Forces. Besides their personal weapons, they were equipped with radios, two light machine guns, handheld SA-16 SAMs, demolition charges, directional mines modeled on the American claymore, and antitank mines.

"Is there a problem, Lieutenant?" their leader, a captain, asked softly. Scarred by Iraqi grenade fragments, his narrow face had a permanently sardonic cast that always unnerved Buramand.

"No, sir," he stammered. "But we are two hours outside Saudi waters. I thought you would like to know."

"Yes." The Special Forces officer nodded politely. "Thank you. I assume we have not received any recall order."

Buramand shook his head. "No, sir. None."

He had been monitoring the sophisticated communications gear he had brought aboard the dhow almost continuously, half expecting to hear the repeated code words that would bring this boat and the others like it scurrying back to port. Instead, he had heard nothing beyond the steady hiss and crackle of static. It was just beginning to dawn on the young naval officer that all their weeks and months of training had been in earnest.

"Very good." The captain tipped his beret over his eyes, leaned back against his bulky pack, and said quite calmly, "Then please wake me when it gets dark. My men and I will help you prepare the Zodiac rafts for our little trip to the shore."

DECEMBER 13

Loading docks, Bandar-e Khomeini

(D MINUS 2)

The Iranian city of Bandar-e Khomeini lay at the northern end of the Persian Gulf, one hundred and fifty miles north and west of Bushehr. In peacetime it served as an oil terminus. Now its docks were crowded with valuable cargo of quite another kind.

Shrill whistles blew as another heavily loaded freight train rumbled slowly down a spur line and out onto Bandar-e Khomeini's largest pier. Although heavy tarpaulins muffled the massive shapes on each flatcar, Brigadier General Sayyed Malaek's experienced eyes easily made out more of the T-80 tanks and BMP infantry fighting vehicles belonging to his 32nd Armored Brigade.

Everywhere the bearded, hawk-nosed brigadier looked, he saw signs of hurried activity. Out at the end of the long pier, working parties of his own men were busy fueling and arming the vehicles brought down from the Ahvaz Garrison by earlier trains. Dockworkers and sailors scurried among the neat rows of tanks and APCs, guiding those that were ready aboard the waiting ships.

Five vessels were moored at Bandar-e Khomeini. Three were the Navy's *Ropucha*-class tank landing ships. Together, they could carry more than seventy of his tanks and six companies of infantry. Two more vessels were car ferries hastily modified to safely lift another company's worth of the brigade's vehicles.

Malaek checked his watch and smiled. His troops were well ahead of schedule.

Bushehr Air Base

Arc lights strung around the airfield perimeter cast artificial daylight across a scene of frenzied activity.

The first echelons of the SCIMITAR strike force—more than fifty advanced combat aircraft—were parked in hastily constructed shelters spaced around the Bushehr base. Additional squadrons were moving to full readiness at fields ranging northward in a wide arc from Bandar-e Abbas to Aghajari and Khorramshahr.

Major Ashraf Bakhtiar stood near the revetments assigned to his Su-24 Fencer squadron, carefully overseeing the ordnance handlers fitting antiradar missiles and laser-guided bombs to his planes. Other teams were hard at work across the runway, outfitting the MiG-29s that would escort his fighter-bombers to their targets. Trolleys towing carts piled high with missiles, bombs, and decoy pods trundled to and fro around parked aircraft.

He raised his eyes to the eastern horizon, noting the hint of pale pink that signaled the coming dawn. The high, concealing clouds of yesterday and the day before were gone. A new front was moving in—one that would bring clear skies and light winds for the next several days.

Bakhtiar smiled and rubbed his hands together. He and his crews would have perfect flying weather. Perfect war weather.

Special operations headquarters, Tehran

General Amir Taleh looked at the bustle around him with undisguised pleasure. The Khorasan Square headquarters building was a hive of purposeful activity. In every room, staff officers hunched over keyboards or spoke into telephones, urging greater speed on the field commanders. Enlisted men updated status boards or carried messages and printouts. The long, hard months of training, reorganization, and reform were coming together perfectly. His staff was functioning like a well-oiled machine.

That was just as well. In less than twenty-four hours, he would issue the final orders setting the invasion in motion. Six hours after that, the first attack transports would depart Bushehr and Bandar-e Khomeini, bound for the Saudi coast. At this stage, even a half-hour hiccup in the schedule would have been cause for concern.

Taleh turned as General Hashemi, his senior operations officer, approached. The older man looked worried.

"Yes, Hashemi?"

"Captain Kazemi has informed me that you intend to activate his special security plan before our final staff conference."

Taleh nodded. "That is correct."

Hashemi hesitated and then said cautiously, "You realize, sir, that such a move may complicate our work at a critical moment? Since there is no sign of any unusual enemy activity, wouldn't it be more prudent to wait a while longer?"

Taleh shook his head. "No, General. I have not survived this many years by depending on foolish behavior from my adversaries. We will go on a full war footing as scheduled. In battle our soldiers must expect the unexpected. I see no reason that my staff should expect more certainty and convenience in their own lives."

Despite his native caution, Taleh was sure the first stroke would be his. SCIMITAR would fall where and when he wished, on an ignorant and ill-prepared enemy.

NEMESIS strike force, Incirlik Air Base, Turkey

Colonel Peter Thorn slipped through the side door of the massive hangar hiding his lead C-17 transport from prying eyes and stood watching the American warplanes taxiing across the field.

Officially, the NEMESIS force did not exist. Its black, brown, and gray camouflaged aircraft had been moved out of sight almost as soon as they were wheels down. Heavily armed Air Force security detachments were on guard around the three hangars allocated to his planes. Major General Farrell wanted to make sure the Iranians didn't get wind of the impending raid. The JCS and the President were equally determined to make sure the Turks didn't find out. NATO host countries tended to be picky about covert operations launched from their territory.

Inside the hangars, some of the more than one hundred soldiers and airmen under his command were busy making final checks of their weapons and gear. Others were resting—following the old Army tradition of catching up on your sleep whenever somebody wasn't actively yelling or shooting at you.

Thorn smothered a yawn. He'd tried to grab some shut-eye during the seven-and-a-half-hour flight from Pope, but he hadn't managed very much. He'd told himself that was because of the eight-hour time difference between late night in North Carolina and pale noon sunshine in Turkey. He'd also blamed his restlessness on the pressures of command and on the need to go over every last piece of his plan for the hundredth time.

The truth was both simpler and more complicated. Every time Thorn closed his eyes, he saw Helen lying helpless and in pain in her hospital bed. The last report from Louisa Farrell was not very encouraging. Although the doctors now believed she would live, they weren't sure she would ever regain the use of her legs.

He felt a sudden stab of sorrow. Helen was so intensely physical, so intensely alive on her feet and in motion. Robbing her of the ability to walk unaided would almost be worse than robbing her of life itself. What kind of life would she be willing to build

with him if her injuries were permanent? He stared out across
the runway, trying to suppress, for even a short time, his fears for
her and for himself.

The noise outside was ear-shattering. Caught unaware by
what most people on the base thought was a practice alert, Incirlik was in a sustained uproar. Pair by pair, F-15E Strike Eagles
were arriving from bases further west in Europe. As fast as they
arrived, ground crews swarmed over them, arming and refueling
each fighter-bomber at the double-quick.

Thorn shook his head. If NEMESIS and a follow-up Tomahawk strike failed to stop Taleh's attack, the planes hurriedly assembling here would be thrown into a series of desperate,
extended-range attacks against the Iranian invasion force.
Given the relative numbers of aircraft involved and the fact
that Iran's MiGs would be operating close to their own bases,
American losses were certain to be high—maybe even crippling.

Tehran

With as much patience as he could muster, Hamir Pahesh
lounged in one of Tehran's many bazaars and waited for his contact to appear. He found the waiting difficult. The normal frenzy
of the marketplace was nothing compared to the sense of urgency he had felt for the last several days.

His last radio conversation with the CIA controller he knew
as Granite had sent him straight back to Tehran at the best
speed he could manage. The journey had taken him longer than
he had planned. At every major road junction, he'd fought con-
gestion as military convoys rolling the other way strained Iran's
primitive road net. The soldiers and their vehicles all seemed to
be heading south for the coast, most for Bandar-e Bushehr.

The Afghan shook his head. Meeting the CIA's needs for this
mission had proved extraordinarily difficult. Right now, the

only thing more important to Iran's armed forces than an empty truck was a full one.

Luckily, there had been many empty trucks returning north, some of them driven by his own countrymen. Among his fellow Afghans, he had found two men he knew and two friends they trusted. All four had some experience in moving illegal goods, and they were all less than pleased with the Shiite Iranian government. They had agreed to collaborate with him on an unspecified, though very profitable, undertaking. They would join him soon.

In the meantime, though, he had other details to attend to. Two of his recruits were off buying enough black-market gasoline for their five trucks.

That left the not-so-small problem of papers. Five trucks traveling together, empty, without travel papers, were sure to be stopped at the first roadblock. He got enough grief from the Pasdaran swine even when his papers were in order. Luckily, the comings and goings of the regular military should provide the perfect cover. If, that was, the man he was waiting for came through . . .

"Hamir! My friend! Hello!"

Pahesh turned abruptly. Ibn al-Juzjani, an old acquaintance, if not truly a friend, had silently appeared beside him.

Stealth was a valuable skill in the smaller man's line of work. Pahesh knew him from his days as a mujahideen, but al-Juzjani wasn't a fighter. The little man had helped smuggle weapons across the borders between Iran, Pakistan, and Afghanistan. He was still in the same line of work.

"Peace be with you, Ibn," Pahesh greeted him languidly. It took considerable effort to appear disinterested. "You were successful, I hope?"

Al-Juzjani's sly brown eyes twinkled. "Yes, with the blessings of God. Come, follow me."

The smuggler preferred to transact his business out of a nondescript shop near the edge of the bazaar—one of many in this district selling televisions, transistor radios, and VCRs. The proprietor, a third or fourth cousin in al-Juzjani's extended clan, reserved a private room for his use.

Once they were out of sight of prying eyes, Pahesh scanned the documents the smuggler offered him. There were two sets of forged travel orders—one for a trip out of Tehran and another set for the return journey. They weren't perfect, but he'd seen enough real travel documents to know these would pass.

He nodded in satisfaction. "Good enough, Ibn. These will suit me very well." Ordinarily, he would have expected to sit, drink tea, and talk over old times with al-Juzjani, as was the custom when doing business, but he had no time left for pleasantries. He held out a wad of rials.

The other man held up a hand. "Alas, my friend, you know better than that. Rials are worth less than the paper they are printed on in my line of work. Besides," he said slyly, "my suppliers were so busy with their other endeavors that I had to pay extra to persuade them to complete your little task."

Pahesh swallowed his impatience and his resentment. He had expected nothing more from al-Juzjani. He sometimes thought the man only breathed because the air around him was free. He arched an eyebrow. "How much more do your suppliers require?"

"Another one hundred American dollars."

Pahesh considered that. Even with the clock running, it would be a mistake to simply accept the smuggler's first price. Folding too easily would only tell the little man just how important those papers were to him.

He snorted and spread his hands wide. "Alas, Ibn, that is impossible. My funds are wholly tied up in this small enterprise of mine," he lied.

"I see. What a pity." The smuggler stroked his chin and then shrugged. "Perhaps I can persuade them to accept ninety-five dollars."

They haggled pleasantly for another few minutes before settling on a mutually acceptable, if extortionate, price. He was not worried about using American currency to settle his debt with the smuggler. Tehran's black market used dollars exclusively and Iranian banks exchanged it freely—though at a terrible rate. In truth, he had never expected al-Juzjani to accept Iranian rials.

Besides, the money was of no consequence. Pahesh would cheerfully have handed over his entire, hard-earned fortune to secure those papers. They were his passport to a better life.

His little convoy of five trucks headed out from Tehran shortly after noon, plowing southward through the ever-thinning traffic on a paved, two-lane road to Robat Karim, a small town roughly one hundred kilometers from the capital. Except for a few large, expensive cars—Mercedes sedans—whose owners could either countermand or safely flout the regulations, most of the other vehicles on the highway belonged to the military.

Their forged documents got Pahesh and his companions past police checkpoints without much trouble. The papers were ostensibly issued by the Pasdaran. Even with General Amir Taleh in power, nobody with half a brain wanted to look too closely at the activities of the Revolutionary Guards.

At the town of Kasham, they turned off the highway onto a winding gravel road, heading west into a flat, dry landscape littered with stones. A few miles out of town, even the gravel surface ended, leaving only a dirt track barely wide enough for a single truck.

Despite the poor road, Pahesh kept his speed as high as he dared, and then a little higher. The sun was now only a few fingers above the western horizon. He faced it as he drove, slitting his eyes against the glare as though he were staring down an adversary.

The odometer was his master. The clock was his enemy. It was vital that he reach the right spot before dark.

Keeping one hand on the wheel, Pahesh fumbled through his duffel bag and pulled out a small device the size of a handheld calculator. He switched it on and waited. First one, then two, three, and finally five small green lights glowed on the front of the little machine. Each light represented a GPS—global positioning system—satellite whose signal it was able to receive.

With five satellites, the receiver could fix his position to within three meters.

At the moment, the receiver's readout showed latitude and longitude values almost matching those given him by Granite.

He studied the landscape ahead. There. He saw the landmark he'd been looking for—a long, low, east-west ridge that paralleled the road a few hundred meters to the north. The sun was just touching the horizon.

Once he was abreast of the hill, Pahesh pulled off the road and stopped. He clambered down out of the truck cab and stretched—well aware that he still had much work to do. A gust of icy wind warned him of the cold night ahead.

The others dropped out of their trucks and came to join him. They seemed puzzled to find themselves so far from anywhere. They stared back and forth from the long, low ridge to the straight dirt road laid across the empty landscape like a pencil line on a piece of paper.

Mohammed, a big man with an unkempt beard, was the most suspicious. "You are sure this is the right spot?"

Pahesh nodded calmly. "I've done this before," he lied smoothly. He turned to the other three men. "Move your trucks off the road and wait for us. Mohammed and I have a little scouting to do."

Without waiting to see if they obeyed him, he got back in his truck and headed west through the growing darkness. As he drove, he scanned the terrain closely. Granite's orders ran through his memory: "Make sure the road is not blocked, and that the ground is flat for at least fifty meters to either side. Watch out for potholes or large boulders."

A little over a kilometer to the west, the road curved slightly, disappearing around the ridge and into the distance.

Pahesh nodded to himself. It would suffice. The only thing in that direction was a small village another twenty kilometers further on. At night, in the winter, this should be an empty and abandoned area. Or so he hoped.

He parked at the curve and waited for Mohammed to join him. "Park your truck off the road as though it has broken down. Then build two fires, one here and one over there," he said, pointing across the road. "Keep the fires small and keep watch, but do nothing unless I say otherwise. You understand?"

The big man nodded slowly, staring down the long stretch of road to the east. "So this shipment of yours comes by air, then?"

Pahesh frowned. Since he first met the man, Mohammed had been questioning him—digging whenever possible to find out more about what they were up to. Without his friend Agdas' recommendation, he would never have taken on a man who was so nosy. Agdas, though, had promised him that the big man could keep his mouth shut when it mattered.

"Yes," he answered shortly. "The goods I am expecting are large—very bulky." That much, at least, was true—though it was cloaked in a lie. "Are you armed?"

Mohammed nodded, and lifted up his coat enough for Pahesh to see a dull black shape tucked in his waistband.

The Afghan nodded. He had expected no less. His country-men usually felt naked without at least one weapon concealed somewhere. "I will send someone to relieve you in half an hour."

Pahesh climbed back into his truck and drove off without looking back. To find the others, he followed the truck tracks with his headlights as they led him over the ridge.

The rest of his little band were gathered around a small fire of their own, and they were cooking a light supper. The circle of bearded faces, lit only by the leaping flames, reminded the Afghan strongly of the days long ago—the days in his own country when the mujahideen ruled the hills and mountains and kept their Soviet foes in fear.

He lugged his duffel a short way from the fire and set up his SATCOM radio. He did not hide his actions from others, but he did not invite them closer either.

Somewhere off in far distant America, Granite was waiting by the radio for his signal. "Granite here."

"This is Stone," Pahesh reported. "We are in Kabul." Trans-lated, that meant they were at the proper coordinates and there were no obstructions blocking the road.

Even across the ten thousand miles, he could hear the relief in the American's voice. "Understood, Stone. Expect your shipment tonight."

Pahesh paused and then said, "Wish them safe journey."

After stashing the radio out of sight again, he rejoined his compatriots at the fire.

"These friends of yours will arrive soon?" Agdas asked quietly.

"Soon," Pahesh agreed.

"Can you tell us yet what this cargo of yours is?" the other man pressed. "This is mysterious . . . even for you, Hamir."

"Yes, it is." The Afghan shrugged. "You will see soon enough."

"So what now?" one of the other men asked. "What are we supposed to do in the meantime?"

Pahesh smiled at him across the campfire. "We wait, my friend. We wait."

CHAPTER 25
NEMESIS

DECEMBER 13

NEMESIS strike force, south of Lake Van, near the Turkish-Iranian border

(D MINUS 2)

Lit red by the setting sun, November One-Zero, the lead C-17 Globemaster assigned to NEMESIS, flew eastward toward Iran at twenty thousand feet, drawing jet fuel down a boom from the giant KC-10 aerial tanker just above and ahead. The formation's two other C-17s, November Two-Zero and Three-Zero, were in position to the rear right and left, each tanking from their own dedicated KC-10.

"We're nearly full up, Mack," November One-Zero's copilot reported.

"Roger," Air Force Lieutenant Colonel Thomas McPherson replied. He spoke to the tanker's boom operator. "Ready to disconnect, Foxtrot Alpha."

"Understood, One-Zero. Pumping stopped." The operator aboard the KC-10 paused briefly and then announced, "Released."

White vapor puffed into the darkening sky as the jet fuel boom popped out. McPherson slid his throttles back a tiny bit and watched the KC-10 pull further ahead.

Within seconds the two other C-17s finished gassing up and broke away from their own tankers. November Two-Zero slid into position behind McPherson's plane, while the third Globemaster, brought this far as a spare in case one of the first broke down, slotted itself into the KC-10 formation.

"Coming up on Point Echo," One-Zero's copilot warned. They were nearing the coordinates preselected for their covert entry into Iranian airspace.

McPherson nodded. "Got it. Here we go." He drew a breath, steeling himself for the difficult flying ahead. "Navigation lights off."

"Nav lights off," his copilot confirmed, flicking switches that shut down the blinking lights on the C-17's fuselage, tail, and wingtips.

"FLIR on. TFR on standby," McPherson said. His wide-angled, heads-up display—HUD—came on, showing the dark, rugged landscape ahead and below them in clear, black-and-white detail. To allow them to fly below Iranian radar and through the middle of the jagged mountains around Tehran, Air Force technicians had specially modified each of the C-17s assigned to NEMESIS. The LANTIRN-type pod installed in each aircraft's starboard fuselage cheek contained both a FLIR, a forward-looking infrared sensor, and a terrain-following radar.

He spoke into the intercom system. "We're starting the E-ticket ride, Pete. Have your guys strap in."

Colonel Peter Thorn's unruffled voice came back through his headset. "We're all set, Mack. Let her rip."

McPherson pulled November One-Zero into a tight, diving turn to the right, angling east-southeast toward the Iranian border. He kept his eyes fixed on the altitude indicator winding down on the right side of his HUD. Trailing one thousand feet behind, the second C-17 followed him down with its own navigation lights off.

Now ten thousand feet above and several miles behind them, the three KC-10s and the spare transport curved right in a gentle, sweeping turn that would take them back toward Incirlik.

McPherson leveled off just three hundred feet above the sharp-edged, snow-covered ridges that separated Turkey from the Islamic Republic of Iran. The two American aircraft crossed the border in total darkness, flying low at nearly four hundred knots over the great salt lake of Orumiyeh and on over an arid, sparsely populated plateau.

Fourteen minutes after entering Iran, he began throttling back, slowing the C-17 to two hundred and fifty knots. The ground ahead was rising steeply, thrusting skyward to become the boulder-crowned foothills of the Zagros Mountains.

With his eyes locked to the HUD and his hands to the controls, McPherson jinked suddenly hard right, lining up with a narrow, winding valley that cut east and south through the mountains. Sheer rock walls rose above the C-17 on either side, sometimes crowding in so close that a fiery, rolling impact seemed inevitable.

The tall, lanky lieutenant colonel grinned tightly as he nimbly maneuvered the large, four-engine aircraft through box canyons and over rugged escarpments. He'd like to see some hot-shit fighter jock try following in his wake tonight. Hell, this was real flying.

Back in the C-17's troop compartment, Thorn nearly let go of his map case when another abrupt bank threw him forward against his seat straps. "Crap," he muttered.

Diaz heard him. A broad smile spread across the sergeant major's face. "You want a puke bag, Pete?" he asked helpfully. "I guess the ride's a little rough after all those cushy Pentagon executive flights, huh?"

Oh, very nice, Thorn thought wryly.

"No thanks, Tow." He shook his head and then nodded solemnly toward the two forty-foot-long shapes tied down in the middle of the troop compartment. "I was just hoping the guys who loaded those birds knew what they were doing."

The "birds" were UH-1N Hueys painted in Iranian camouflage and markings. Even with their rotors off, each weighed nearly two tons. If the chains and guy ropes holding them in place gave way under the stress and strain of the aircraft's repeated sharp turns, the helicopters would first crush the soldiers seated against the side and then smash straight through the C-17's fuselage.

"Oh, man," Diaz chuckled. "You're just full of cheerful thoughts tonight, aren't you?" He raised his voice loud enough to carry over the steady roar of the engines. "How about you, Mike? You checked your lottery ticket, yet?"

"Sure thing, Tow! You're looking at the first Delta Force millionaire."

Thorn listened to the banter passing back and forth, keeping his own growing worries to himself. The Duke of Wellington's advice to his officers at Waterloo seemed apt: "Anything that wastes time, indulge it." He and his troops were still at least two hundred and fifty miles from the landing zone. During this hair-raising, low-level flight, none of their hard-earned skills would make one damn bit of difference to whether they lived or died.

Kabul landing site, Iran

Hamir Pahesh kept a close eye on his companions around the campfire. Even his friend Agdas was growing more nervous as the minutes and hours ticked past. The others, those who had less reason to trust him, were now openly suspicious. Mohammed was the worst of all.

"These friends of yours are very late, Pahesh," the big, bearded man rumbled slowly. He scratched his stomach idly, a movement that kept his hand very near the pistol stuffed into his waistband.

"Our business does not always run on a timetable," Pahesh re-minded him sharply. "You should know that."

"Perhaps they have trouble," another man said. His gaze kept darting off into the darkness beyond the fire at the slightest change in the sound of the wind.

"Or perhaps they are leading the Komite here to catch us all sitting on our asses," Mohammed snarled, still irked at being cut short so rudely.

"Hush!" Pahesh held up a hand for silence. He cocked his head, listening. He could hear the sound of jet engines whining somewhere off to the south, drawing nearer at a rapid clip. "There! You hear them? The planes?"

They all nodded.

The sound faded abruptly.

"Pah! So where did these friends of yours go now . . ." Mo-hammed began belligerently.

He was drowned out by the rippling, piercing howl of jet en-gines at full thrust. All four men looked up in stunned surprise as a huge aircraft popped up over the low ridge and banked sharply to circle back around for a landing. Another plane fol-lowed the first only seconds later.

"Come!" Pahesh led the other four men toward the top of the ridge at a stumbling run.

They arrived in time to see the first C-17 dive, flare out sud-denly, and touch down near the end of the fire-marked dirt road. Thrust reversers kicked in with an ungodly roar as the enormous camouflaged jet rolled past them, trailing a billowing cloud of dust, sand, and gravel. It braked to a complete stop only a thousand meters from where its wheels first kissed the ground.

Bearded soldiers wearing Iranian Army uniforms were charg-ing down the aircraft's rear cargo ramp even before the second C-17 came to rest.

NEMESIS command team

Flanked by Diaz and a five-man team, Colonel Peter Thorn jogged up the ridge to meet their CIA contact. He slowed down near the crest, studying the scruffy, dirty-faced men waiting for them. They looked more like brigands than truck drivers, he thought grimly.

He mentally crossed his fingers. Dealing with local talent on a covert op was always chancy. You never knew how far you could trust them.

The oldest of those waiting for him, a scarred, thin-bearded man with a hooked nose, stepped forward and smiled. He bobbed his head and spoke in understandable, though heavily accented, English. "Peace be upon you, my friends. My name is Hamir Pahesh. The code name given to me by your CIA is Stone."

Thorn introduced himself and looked at the other man's fidgeting companions. Most still seemed stunned at the sight of so many troops pouring out of his grounded aircraft. One, taller than the rest by half a head, looked blackly furious.

Diaz caught his nod in that direction and slipped off to the side.

Thorn turned back to Pahesh. "These men are the drivers we asked for?"

The Afghan nodded. "Yes." He rattled off their names in quick succession and then asked shyly, "You have the money I have promised them?"

Thorn touched the backpack he had slung over one shoulder. "I have it, Mr. Pahesh. Twenty thousand American dollars apiece. Five thousand now. Fifteen thousand more after we reach Tehran safely."

The big man, the one called Mohammed, reared back. "You are a crazy man, Pahesh!" he sputtered in rough, broken English. "I do not put my head on the chopping block to carry spies into the city. Not for thousand of dollars. Not for million of dollars!"

Mohammed fumbled for the weapon stuck in his trousers and then froze suddenly, his eyes wide, as Diaz ground the muzzle of an M16 rifle into his ear.

"Slowly, pal. Very slowly," the sergeant major said softly. "I'd sure hate to mess up my nice new uniform with your tiny little brains."

Diaz held his weapon on target until another Delta trooper stepped in and relieved the big trucker of his pistol. Without pausing, a third member of the command team bound Mohammed's wrists behind his back and marched him away toward the parked C-17s.

Thorn turned back to the dumbfounded Afghans. His eyes sought out those of Pahesh. "It seems that Mr. Mohammed will not be joining us this evening after all. Do any of your other associates feel a burning desire to go on strike?"

The older man shrugged, amusement plain in his own expression. "I will ask them, Colonel Thorn. But I suspect they will see reason and profit in doing as you ask."

A hasty, whispered conference in Pushtu confirmed Pahesh's assessment. None of the other Afghans looked very happy at this unexpected turn of events, but none of them seemed unhappy enough to prove treacherous.

Nonetheless, Thorn planned to take out a little insurance of his own. He glanced at Diaz. "Tow, please tell Major Witt I want one of our Farsi speakers riding shotgun in each truck cab. And have these gentlemen taken back to their vehicles."

"Sure thing, Pete." Still holding his M16 at the ready, the sergeant major trotted off into the darkness. Escorted by other Delta Force soldiers, the three remaining truck drivers followed him at a discreet distance.

Thorn turned back to the older Afghan. "Now, Mr. Pahesh, if you'll come with me, I'll tell you where we need to go and what we plan to do." He led the way back down the ridge, pleased by all the activity he could see around the parked aircraft.

Nobody was wasting any time. The sixty men he was taking into Tehran were carting their weapons and equipment toward the waiting trucks. A fourth twenty-man troop would remain

behind to provide security here. They were busy deploying machine guns, antitank guided missiles, Stinger SAM teams, and
sniper teams to cover all avenues of approach to the improvised
landing strip. Aided by some of the C-17 crewmen, Scott
Finney's helicopter crews were already beginning to assemble
their birds—four UH-1N Hueys and a tiny AH-6 gunship.

Now that they all were safely on the ground inside Iran,
NEMESIS was starting to take its final shape.

DECEMBER 14

Near the Khorasan Square headquarters

(D MINUS 1)

Three hours after leaving the isolated desert landing strip, the
five canvas-sided trucks pulled off to the side of a quiet Tehran
street and parked. Their long trip northward had been unevent-
ful. The forged travel orders supplied by Pahesh got them
through the checkpoints without much trouble. After all the
military hubbub of the past several days, trucks full of Iranian
soldiers no longer drew much attention. Even the most curious
citizens and police had been sated by the sight of so many
weapons and olive-drab vehicles moving through their streets.
In any case, it was past midnight and few lights were on anywhere in the sprawling, sleeping city.

Thorn dropped out of the back of the lead truck and went
forward to speak to Hamir Pahesh. The Afghan slid out from
behind the wheel and joined him on the pavement.

The older man pointed down the road. "The headquarters is
three blocks further up this avenue, Colonel. You know the
building?"

Thorn nodded once. He'd spent so many hours studying the

blueprints and satellite photographs he felt sure he could practically find his way blindfolded through Taleh's lair.

He glanced up at the apartment houses on either side of this street. None of the plain concrete five- and six-story, flat-roofed buildings would have won any architectural prizes for elegance or style, but he was not interested in esthetics. They were important because they were the tallest buildings in this poor, run-down neighborhood and because they offered a clear line of sight to the roof of the Khorasan Square military headquarters.

Thorn turned back to the Afghan. "Will your friends obey my orders, Mr. Pahesh? You know this will be very dangerous."

"They will obey you," Pahesh said firmly. "All of us have seen war before, Colonel."

"Fine." Thorn spun on his heel and strode to the last truck in line.

Captain Doug Lindsay peered down at him through a half-open flap. With his flaming-red hair and mustache dyed black, the commander of the NEMESIS force sniper teams looked alien, almost unrecognizable.

"You ready for us, Pete?" the younger man asked.

Thorn nodded. "You know the drill, Doug. You've got five minutes to move your people into position. Then, when I give you the word, you do your stuff. Clear?"

"Clear." Lindsay swung away from the opened flap. "Everybody out. Shaw takes the building on the left. I'll take the building on the right. Let's move!"

Thorn watched the heavily laden soldiers scramble out over the truck's tailgate before heading back to his own vehicle. Without further orders from Lindsay, the snipers formed up on the street and then split apart. Four two-man teams crossed over to the other side and entered the tallest apartment building on the block. Four more teams disappeared inside the nearest tenement.

Breathing normally even under the weight of his weapon and other gear, Captain Doug Lindsay took the narrow, dimly lit stairs to the roof two at a time. Boots rang on concrete as his troops followed him up.

Farsi-speaking soldiers stopped long enough on every landing to yell stern warnings at any sleepy Iranian civilians who poked their heads out of apartments to see what was going on. "Everyone inside! This is Army business!"

Doors slammed shut again as the building's inhabitants obeyed their shouted orders. No one who lived this close to General Amir Taleh's headquarters wanted trouble with the Army.

Five flights up, Lindsay pushed open an unlocked metal door and came out onto the tenement's flat roof. It was deserted. He nodded to himself, noticing his breath steaming in the cold night air. In the summer they would have found people camped out here—driven out of their tiny, crowded apartments by the heat. Now, this close to the winter, temperatures were already dropping fast toward freezing once the sun went down.

Followed by the sergeant who would serve as his spotter and backup, the Delta Force captain moved closer to the edge of the roof. He dropped prone and started setting up his weapon, conscious of the faint rustle of clothing and scrape of metal on either side. The rest of his teams were moving into place.

Lindsay slid an eleven-round magazine into his Barrett Light Fifty sniper rifle. Nearly five feet long and weighing in at thirty-five pounds, the M82A1 Light Fifty was badly misnamed, but it had several features that made it perfect for special operations use. First, it was a simple, rugged, semiautomatic weapon accurate out to twelve hundred meters. Second, it fired the same enormous .50-inch Browning round used in the U.S. Army's heavy machine gun. More than three times the size of the 5.56mm bullets used by most modern assault rifles, the .50-inch round had enormous penetration and lethality. To handle the recoil, the Barrett Light Fifty was equipped with a muzzle brake and a thick butt pad. A bipod mounted near the muzzle helped steady the rifle.

With practiced ease, the Delta Force officer attached an ITT-made optical sight to his weapon and peered through the scope.

Two AA batteries powered an image intensifier that turned the night into day. He flicked to 8x magnification and shifted his aim to one of the emplacements on top of the squat, drab building roughly four hundred meters away. His crosshairs settled on an Iranian soldier seated behind a twin-barreled ZU-23 light anti-aircraft gun. The man looked tired and bored.

Lindsay held his aim steady. The ZU-23 was virtually useless against modern attack aircraft, but its rapid fire could murder infantry caught out in the open. He frowned. Something seemed odd. Fewer than half the defensive positions atop the enemy headquarters were manned. Maybe this guy Taleh wasn't so thorough after all.

One by one, his teams reported that they were in position.

Lindsay contacted Thorn and confirmed their readiness. "November One Alpha, this is Sierra Four Charlie. We're dialed in. Standing by."

"Understood, Four Charlie. We're moving now."

The sniper focused all his attention on the bored Iranian anti-aircraft gunner, waiting for the single command that would open the attack. He could hear motors revving up on the street below. NEMESIS was under way.

Three trucks crammed with Delta Force soldiers rolled down the Avenue of the 17th of Shahrivar, heading for Khorasan Square. A fourth truck veered right, peeling off to come in behind the main entrance to the headquarters building. The men it carried would seal off a rear exit, killing anyone who tried to escape outside when the rest of the attack force went in.

Peter Thorn rode up front now. A staff sergeant who spoke Farsi fluently sat wedged in between Pahesh and him. The sergeant, an olive-skinned man named Alberi, wore Iranian Army insignia identifying him as a captain.

Alberi also held a 9mm pistol outfitted with a Knight noise suppressor in his lap. Although the device made it impossible to fire more than a single shot without working the slide to manually feed another round into the pistol's breech, it reduced the sound of firing to that of a child's air rifle.

Thorn carried a Heckler & Koch MP2000 submachine gun. The weapon, an advance over the similar MP5, had a silencing system built in. Holes in the barrel allowed some of the propellant gases to bleed away, slowing the rounds being fired to below supersonic speed—and cutting the noise they made dramatically. For open combat, the gas bleed holes could be closed. Right now, he had the weapon set for silent fighting.

They turned into the square and rumbled straight toward the headquarter's main gate. The truck's headlights flashed across a guard post that barred direct access to an open courtyard visible beyond the gate. When they were within fifty meters, an Iranian soldier came forward, signaling them to stop. Four more sentries manned a sandbag redoubt built adjacent to the entrance. Two were talking to each other, arguing cheerfully about something. The others leaned against the piled-up sandbags near a light machine gun sited to sweep the square. One of them had a cigarette dangling from his mouth.

Pahesh stopped right in front of the gate and cranked his window open.

The soldier who had flagged them down walked right up to the truck cab, yawning slightly. The guards here must be very used to comings and goings at irregular hours, Thorn decided, vaguely surprised by their nonchalance. He had expected somewhat tighter security.

The Iranian looked in through the open driver's-side window. "Show me your orders—"

Phut. Sergeant Alberi leaned across the Afghan truck driver and shot the astonished guard in the head. The man toppled backward without a sound.

Thorn popped open the door on his side and dropped onto the street before the other stunned guards could even begin to react. His submachine gun stuttered, kicking against his grip as he walked three-round bursts across the top of the redoubt.

Sand sprayed out of torn sandbags. Blood sprayed out of torn men.

Thorn stopped firing. Nothing moved near the gate. Now for

the enemy soldiers posted on the roof. He spoke softly into his throat mike. "Take 'em out, Four Charlie."

Eight sniper rifles cracked suddenly, firing so close together in time that it almost sounded like one long, tearing shot. A few more scattered shots followed as Lindsay's snipers engaged new targets. Then the Barrett Light Fifties fell silent.

"One Alpha, this is Four Charlie," the sniper reported. "The roof is clear. Go on in."

Thorn scrambled back into the truck and waved Pahesh forward. Grinning like a madman, the Afghan threw the vehicle in gear and drove through the open gate. The other trucks followed them into the interior courtyard.

Delta Force assault teams piled out of the trucks while they were still moving, fanning out across the courtyard to cover every door and window leading into the headquarters building.

Thorn snapped a fresh magazine into his submachine gun and followed them inside.

NEMESIS command team

Twenty minutes later, the smoke from flash/bang grenades and burning papers and furniture still eddied through the bullet-riddled headquarters. Large numbers of dead Iranian soldiers and staff officers were scattered through the corridors and in several of the offices. But there were too few corpses wearing the right kind of rank insignia.

The top commanders of the NEMESIS force were meeting inside an empty office on the building's second floor. None of them were pleased. When he heard his second-in-command's first report, Thorn had to fight an impulse to smash his fist into the nearest wall in frustration. Instead he asked again, "You're sure, John?"

Major John Witt nodded flatly. "Dead sure, Pete. I went over the bodies myself. There's not a high-ranking officer among 'em." He rubbed a hand wearily across his shaved head and then continued his report. "We got plenty of majors, captains, lieutenants, and enlisted guys. But nobody else. And there's no sign of Taleh."

Christ, what a fuckup, Thorn thought in despair. At first, he'd thought their attack had gone off without a hitch—at the cost of only two Delta Force soldiers lightly wounded. They'd even secured the headquarters complex without alerting anyone outside the area. Now, though, it was clear that their intelligence had been wildly off the mark. Neither Taleh nor his top-level invasion command staff had been inside the Khorasan Square building. He and his troops had hit the wrong damned target!

His eye fell on the two troopers setting up a SATCOM radio near an open window. Once they had a clear signal, he was going to have to report the failure of their mission to Washington.

Diaz stuck his head into the office. "I have something I think you should see, Pete."

"Where?" Thorn asked tightly.

"The HQ comm center. I think we may be able to draw a bead on our Iranian friend."

"Show me." Thorn grabbed his weapon and followed the sergeant major down three flights of stairs into the basement. On the way they passed Delta Force troopers checking bodies for identity cards. Major Witt believed in being thorough.

The communications center was a large room just off the staircase. Banks of high-frequency radios, telephone switchboards, and teletype machines lined three of the walls. The fourth held a large street map of Tehran with various locations marked. Most of the equipment was old—1970s and 1980s vintage—but there were a few newer computers and fax machines on a group of desks cluttered in the center of the room. There were more corpses huddled on the floor or sprawled across the desks. The comm center at least had been fully manned.

Diaz led him straight across the room to where a Delta Force trooper, Master Sergeant Vaughn, stood tracing circuits and switches on one of the telephone switchboards. "Show the colonel what you found, Tony."

Thinner than most of the men who made it through the Delta selection course, Tony Vaughn was one of the outfit's top technical specialists and linguists. He pointed to a set of panels. "See these?"

Thorn nodded.

"They're patch panels to several remote sites. Phone calls come in here to the main center and this gear reroutes them elsewhere automatically," Vaughn explained. "Now, what's interesting in all of this spaghetti wire is that I've found a series of switches that show that several primary circuits are being routed to one site—but not to any of the others."

"They're tied into an auxiliary command post," Thorn realized suddenly.

Vaughn nodded. "Exactly." He led the way back to the desks in the middle of the room and hefted a pile of loose-leaf binders. "So that's when I started looking through their latest comm logs."

The noncom flipped the top log open to a page near the end. "And this is where I hit pay dirt." He tapped an entry. "Here's what the chief watch officer noted for 1210 hours, 13 December: 'MAGI Prime transferred to Aux Site Three. Command circuit, staff phones, emergency circuit routed to Aux Site Three.' "

Thorn swung toward the wall map of Tehran. A walled compound near the intersection of two major avenues was clearly marked as Auxiliary Site Three. A soccer stadium lay to the east just across the street. The location was painfully familiar to any Delta Force officer with a knowledge of his own unit's history. His jaw tightened. "I'll be damned! The son of a bitch has set up his new command post smack-dab in the middle of our old embassy!"

He shook his head, angry at himself for underestimating Amir Taleh's cunning yet again. With the clock counting down toward a major military move, transferring his headquarters was a reasonable precaution for the Iranian general to take. He suspected it would also give the man a twisted sense of pleasure to issue the orders that would emasculate America's economy from inside the embassy buildings Iranian militants had used in 1979 and 1980 as a prison for their hostages.

Thorn and Diaz took the stairs back up at a dead run.

Witt and the others were still waiting for them inside the second-floor office. "We're in contact with the CAC," the major said.

Thorn went straight to the SATCOM, slipped on the headset offered to him by one of his soldiers, and picked up the microphone. "Nemesis Lead."

"This is Centurion," Farrell's voice answered. To oversee the mission, the general had flown down to the Special Operations Command headquarters at MacDill Air Force Base. SOCOM's Crisis Action Center had secure computer, phone, fax, and satellite links to the Pentagon, the CIA, the White House, and every major U.S. military headquarters around the world.

"What is your status, Nemesis?" Farrell asked.

"Not good. We've missed the primary target, Centurion," Thorn reported quietly. He quickly filled the other man in on what they had learned and then said, "I recommend we delay our evac, move the force, and immediately attack Taleh's alternate HQ."

"No way, Pete," Farrell replied. "Look on the bright side. You've shot the hell out of Taleh's lower-echelon staff. That alone should throw his operations for a loop. Going for anything more now is too dangerous.

"The embassy compound is nearly eight klicks from your current location. You don't have time to drive there, set up for a new assault, and go in. Finney's birds are only twenty minutes out right now. Hell, the Navy's first Tomahawks are already on the way. You're going to have cruise missiles raining down around your ears in less than thirty minutes."

"I know that, sir," Thorn said stubbornly. "But I do not believe we have an alternative. Taleh is not going to let himself be sidetracked by one lousy commando raid and a missile strike. This is our only chance to nail the bastard. None of our missiles are going to hit anywhere close to him. We either kill the son of a bitch *now,* or he will launch his invasion and then we're screwed."

"Wait one," Farrell said finally. The satellite link went silent.

Thorn turned toward Diaz and Witt. "Start rounding the teams up. I want everybody packed and ready to move in ten minutes."

Both men exchanged startled glances. Delta Force doctrine frowned on attacking without surprise. Of course, Delta Force doctrine also frowned on suicide. They hesitated.

Thorn stared hard at them. He didn't have the time or inclination to conduct a council of war. Not right in the heart of an enemy capital. "You heard me, gentlemen. Move!"

"Yes, sir." Diaz and Witt sped off to fulfill his orders.

After several agonizingly long minutes, Farrell's voice came back over the SATCOM. "It's a no-go, Pete. I took your request all the way up to Satrap." Satrap was the code name assigned to the President for the duration of NEMESIS. "He believes the risks of continuing are too high, so he's ordered us to abort the mission. Between the damage you've already done and the inbound Tomahawk strike, he believes we'll knock the Iranian timetable off kilter enough to win any war."

"Then he's wrong," Thorn said heatedly.

Farrell's voice bristled. "What you or I think doesn't matter a damn, Colonel. Point is: That's the President's decision. So you're going to pull your people together and get out of there as per the plan! Is that clear?"

Thorn did not answer right away. Conflicting thoughts were tumbling through his mind one after another at great speed.

He understood the President's desire to take a small victory and bring the Delta Force home unbloodied rather than chance more lives in a high-stakes gamble. It was a desire he shared—a duty he owed his own men. He knew every soldier on this mission better than most men knew their own brothers. The NEMESIS assault force had been lucky so far. Its luck could not last. Pushing deeper into Tehran after Taleh meant accepting casualties—maybe a lot of them.

There was more. He had devoted his whole adult life to the military. He had sworn an oath to obey all legal orders from his superiors. But did his career mean more to him than doing what was right? Should his oath stop him from taking action that would right a great wrong and prevent an even greater evil?

The chaos sparked by General Amir Taleh's terrorists had already cost thousands of American lives. The war the Iranian planned in Saudi Arabia might easily kill thousands more. Could he fly away and let that happen? Could he leave the man responsible for Helen's wounds alive and free to plot again?

He could not. Taleh's campaign had demonstrated America's vulnerability to organized terrorism. Other fanatics and despots around the world would eagerly follow his lead—unless the United States showed plainly that it would exact a terrible price from them. That there would be no negotiations, no comfortable pensions, no forgiveness—nothing but a bullet in the head or a bayonet in the guts.

Thorn made his decision. "Centurion, this is Nemesis Lead. Regret unable to comply with your last. Mission proceeds, out." He knew those words would force any court-martial panel to convict him out of hand, but right now nothing else seemed important.

Farrell was aghast. "Jesus, Pete! Don't do this! You can't—"

Thorn switched the SATCOM off and changed frequencies on his tactical radio, shifting to the channel reserved for the NEMESIS helicopter force. "Hotel Five Echo, this is November One Alpha. This is a wave-off. I repeat, a wave-off. Primary target has shifted to a new location. Standby for the data."

"Roger, One Alpha." Captain Scott Finney's laconic voice came up over the circuit. The rotor noise in the background made it clear that Finney's Huey transport ships and the AH-6 gunship were airborne and closing rapidly on Tehran from the south.

Thorn flipped open his map case, hurriedly scanning for the grid coordinates of the old U.S. Embassy. "On my signal, new exfiltration point will be . . ." He rattled off the coordinates and listened carefully while the helicopter pilot read them back to him.

"Got one point, One Alpha," Finney said calmly. "My birds don't have the gas to loiter over the city. We're gonna have to turn back and refuel. That will put us at least another ninety minutes out. Think you and your boys can hang on that long?"

"Affirmative, Five Echo," Thorn said, praying that he was right. "We'll be there waiting for you."

Auxiliary Command Post Three, inside the old U.S. Embassy, Tehran

General Amir Taleh sat up on his cot when Kazemi came through the door to his quarters. The young captain looked distinctly worried. "What is it, Farhad?"

"We've lost contact with the main headquarters and with all elements of the SCIMITAR assault force, sir."

What? Frowning, Taleh swung himself around, stamped his feet into his combat boots, and began lacing them up. Except for his boots, he was already fully dressed. "Are there any power outages in the city? Any other unexplained communications failures?"

Kazemi shook his head. "No, sir. Everything else seems normal. There have been no reports of disturbances. But all our secure phone and telex links routed through the main building are down."

Taleh reached for the sidearm on a footlocker beside his cot and buckled it on. He looked up at his aide. "Order the Komite to send a patrol to Khorasan Square. I want a full report. Prepare a repair detail at the same time. If our communications have been knocked out somehow, I want them back up in short order!"

"Yes, sir."

"In the meantime, place the headquarters security force on

full alert. Post the troops yourself, Farhad. I want nothing left to chance, is that understood?"

The captain nodded again. "Yes, sir." He hesitated. "Should we break radio silence to contact the assault division HQs directly?"

Taleh pondered that briefly. The final preparations for SCIMITAR were entering a critical stage. Without secure links to his far-flung units, the odds of catastrophic confusion or delay multiplied greatly. On the other hand, a sudden surge in military radio traffic now was bound to draw unwelcome attention from the American and Saudi intelligence services.

No, he decided, he would not act prematurely. He would not be goaded into a mistake by ignorance. He shook his head. "Not yet, Farhad. I need more information first. Send out those patrols!"

NEMESIS force, near central Tehran

Thorn hung on tight as Pahesh threw the big truck around another corner at high speed, narrowly missing a black 4x4 tearing past in the opposite direction. He caught a momentary glimpse of bearded men wearing green fatigues when their headlights swept across the other vehicle. "Who were those guys?"

"Komite," the Afghan answered grimly.

Thorn nodded. The Iranian authorities were starting to wake up. He checked his watch. "How much further?" he asked.

"Not far. Perhaps two kilometers."

An enormous flash lit the night sky ahead of them—to the west, out near the Mehrabad International Airport. "What . . ." Pahesh started to ask. A rolling thunderclap silenced him.

"Our missiles," Thorn shouted into his ear. The leading edge of the Navy's Tomahawk strike had arrived.

There were more flashes now, spreading across the horizon and marching closer and closer to the center of the city.

Tehran's antiaircraft batteries suddenly cut loose, spewing shimmering curtains of fire into the air. Pieces of steel shrapnel from the shells they were firing began clattering down across roofs and streets. Amid the din, Thorn could barely make out a high-pitched rising and falling wail. The city's air-raid sirens were going off.

Followed closely by the other four trucks, Pahesh turned left onto a wider street. Five hundred meters ahead, the road opened up into a large public square. On the south edge of the square, the satellite towers soaring above a building surrounded by barbed wire identified the main Tehran telegraph office.

Oh, shit, Thorn thought, that's on the target list. He leaned toward the Afghan . . .

Hit squarely by a Tomahawk carrying a thousand-pound warhead, the telegraph office vanished in a searing white flash. Shattered chunks of concrete and mangled pieces of metal flew outward from the center of the blast, crashing down across the square and smashing into the other buildings nearby. The ground rocked wildly under the impact.

Pahesh slammed on the brakes.

Mounds of rubble from damaged apartment houses and hotels blocked most of the street. Many of the buildings around the square were already ablaze and the fires were growing—fed by ruptured natural gas lines.

The Afghan leaned out through his open window, already reversing as he waved the other trucks back toward a narrow side street leading north.

Outside the U.S. Embassy compound

Five minutes after the last Tomahawk cruise missile detonated over Tehran, Delta Force teams were advancing cautiously up both sides of the wide north-south thoroughfare locals still called Roosevelt Avenue. They were leapfrogging forward in pairs, using doorways and parked cars for cover. Two hundred meters behind the first assault teams, Hamir Pahesh's trucks ground forward slowly with their headlights off. More U.S. soldiers advanced beside the vehicles—ready to act as a reserve or to block any Iranians coming up from the rear.

Thorn turned his head when Diaz ducked into the doorway behind him.

"Still no reaction?" the noncom asked quietly.

"Not a peep." Thorn scanned the area ahead again through his night vision goggles. He could make out a large part of the embassy now. Barbed wire laced the top of the brick wall that surrounded the compound. There were no lights showing behind any of the windows in the upper floors of the chancery building. The Amjedeih soccer stadium bulked to the east, right across from the embassy complex.

He frowned. It was too damned quiet.

His lead teams were drawing close to Taleghani Avenue—an east-west road that intersected Roosevelt and formed the embassy compound's southern border. He planned to blow straight through the wall there, attacking north to clear the complex from bottom to top. Time constraints robbed the NEMESIS force of any hope for further tactical subtlety. The more time they spent driving around through Tehran's awakening streets, the more time the men inside Taleh's headquarters had to prepare their defenses.

"One Alpha, this is Tango Seven Bravo. Movement on the wall, near the southeast corner," one of the forward teams reported over the radio.

Rifle shots rang out suddenly, joined a second later by the staccato chatter of a light machine gun. A parachute flare soared high overhead and burst into incandescent splendor with a soft pop, spilling light across the area.

Thorn and Diaz dove for cover. Machine-gun rounds ripped down Roosevelt Avenue, blowing shop and car windows inward in a hail of flying glass. Someone behind them starting screaming.

The sound of gunfire rose in volume. Delta Force troops

armed with M16s and HK21 light machine guns were shooting back now, aiming at the muzzle flashes winking from atop the embassy's brick wall. An M203 launcher mounted under an M16 went off with a hollow thump, propelling a fragmentation grenade toward the Iranian defensive position.

It exploded right on target, throwing deadly fragments through a wide circle. The Iranian guns fell silent.

Thorn jumped to his feet, waving his troops forward. They had to do this fast. Delay only aided the enemy. "Move out!"

He and Diaz led twelve men in a rush across Taleghani Avenue toward the wall. When they were halfway across, another Iranian machine gun opened up, firing from a position near the embassy's main gate.

"Christ!" Thorn felt a slug rip past his face. He threw himself forward onto the pavement. Men all around him were falling— hit and badly wounded or dead. Diaz dropped prone beside him, calmly hunting for targets through the scope attached to his M16. Another heavy machine gun burst hammered the street and sidewalk, gouging fist-sized holes out of the concrete and asphalt.

"Can't stay here, Pete!" the sergeant major yelled to him. "We get pinned down . . . we get killed!"

Thorn nodded. He craned his neck to look behind them. Doug Lindsay's sniper teams were smashing their way into the shops and homes fronting Taleghani, but it would take them time to set up and provide covering fire. The same went for Major Witt and the reserve teams he'd stationed back by Pahesh's trucks. Wonderful.

He belly-crawled over to one of the bodies sprawled on the street. The dead soldier had been carrying an AT-4, a one-shot disposable recoilless rifle, slung across his back. Basically just a fifteen-pound tube with a cone-shaped flare on the back end and a ridged muzzle, the AT-4 was a Swedish-made weapon designed to knock out light armored vehicles and bunkers. It fired an 84mm round that could penetrate up to 420mm of armor. Two men in every assault team carried one.

Working furiously, Thorn tugged the weapon off over the

dead man's shoulder and peered through the night vision scope attached to it, sighting toward the main gate. Come on, you bastards, he thought grimly, let me see you.

The Iranian heavy machine gun fired again, sending a stream of bullets slashing right over his head. A trooper behind him moaned and then fell silent—hit several times.

Thorn shifted his aim to the center of the dazzling flashes and squeezed the AT-4's trigger.

WHUMMP. The enemy fighting position vanished in a cloud of flame and smoke.

He threw the spent tube to one side and got to his feet. He and Diaz and the five other Delta Force soldiers who'd escaped the fusillade unhurt hurried toward the shelter offered by the brick wall, dragging their wounded with them. They left four men dead in the middle of the street.

More assault teams tried to cross the avenue and were driven back by Iranian rifle and machine-gun fire—this time coming from around the soccer stadium and from the upper floors of the chancery building. Several Americans fell writhing to the ground.

"Hell!" Thorn swore out loud. His men were being cut to pieces by a dug-in enemy ready and waiting for them. Taleh's security troops had cross-fires laid on every approach to the embassy and they were showing perfect fire discipline—never shooting wildly, always waiting for the Americans to show themselves.

He glanced quickly right and left. Two of the men who'd made it safely across with him were busy administering first aid to the wounded. Diaz and the other three were already busy slapping breaching charges against the wall, but the seven of them were not going to be enough to clear that vast compound. He needed more firepower.

Thorn keyed his radio mike. "Four Charlie, this is One Alpha. I need you to suppress those people in the chancery. Now!"

"Roger, One Alpha." Doug Lindsay's voice crackled through his earphones. "We'll do our best."

Thorn contacted Witt next. "John, use half our guys to lay down a base of fire on those bastards in the stadium. I need the rest here—on the double! Got it?"

"Got it, Pete!" the major acknowledged briskly.

Thorn heard the first distinctive, high-pitched cracks made by the Barrett Light Fifties. His snipers were going into action, picking off Iranian marksmen and weapons teams sited inside the embassy compound.

The Delta Force troops deployed near the intersection cut loose, methodically shooting toward half-hidden enemy positions. Grenade launchers thumped, lobbing fragmentation and smoke grenades toward the soccer stadium to suppress and blind the Iranian defenders there.

A gray haze drifted across the street, building steadily in size and thickness as more and more grenades went off. Moving in pairs, another twelve American soldiers dashed across Taleghani Avenue. One man went down—shot through the temple and killed instantly—but the rest made it safely. The Iranians were still firing, but they were firing randomly now, unable to see their intended targets.

Thorn grabbed his team commanders as they each reached the wall and snapped out his orders for the attack in a few, terse sentences. "Here's the drill. Three breaches. Three teams. After we blow the charges, nobody goes in until we use the AT-4s to blow the shit out of the chancery building's ground floors. Clear?"

Strained faces nodded.

"Good." Thorn checked to make sure the wounded had been moved far enough down the wall to be safe and then nodded toward Diaz. "When you're ready, Tow!"

The sergeant major gave him a thumbs-up signal and bellowed out a warning, "Fire in the hole!"

WHAMMM. WHAMMM. WHAMMM. The three breaching charges went off in rapid succession, blowing huge gaps in the brick wall. And the Iranian troops defending the embassy compound itself immediately opened up, firing from concealed positions inside the chancery. Hundreds of steel-jacketed rounds came whizzing and tumbling through the empty breaches.

Thorn grinned to himself. You just made your first big mistake, you bastards, he thought grimly. He keyed his mike. "You see them, Four Charlie?"

"Yeah," the sniper commander answered coolly. "Ground floor. From right to left. One MG in the third window. Riflemen in the next two. Another MG . . ." He methodically detailed the exact location of each of the newly revealed enemy positions.

The guns gradually fell silent as the Iranians realized they were shooting into thin air.

At Thorn's signal, the six men carrying AT-4s popped up and fired their 84mm rockets into the chancery. Explosions tore across the front of the building, smashing through walls, doors, and windows and spraying deadly shards across the rooms behind them.

"Move! Move! Move!" Thorn shouted. He and Diaz were the first ones through the right-hand breach, scrambling and slipping across a mound of smoking, shattered bricks. He had his submachine up and at his shoulder as he ran, firing bursts at anything moving ahead of him.

His assault teams flooded through the breaches behind him. One six-man team peeled off through the rising smoke and dust to clear the old embassy residence used by the ambassador. The rest followed him inside the chancery.

Thorn burst in through a blown-open door. He swiveled left and right, scanning for enemies. There. Three Iranian soldiers were sprawled near a twisted machine gun. They were dead. He moved deeper into the building. Diaz and four of his men were right behind him.

They came out into a long corridor running the width of the chancery. Gunfire echoed in all directions as his troops began the ugly business of clearing the building room by room. Now where?

The sergeant major pointed to a painted sign in Farsi on the corridor wall. "The CP's downstairs! Go left!"

Thorn nodded. It made perfect sense for Taleh and his top staff to set up shop in the building's reinforced basement. Their primary concern would have been an American air raid—not a commando attack.

Weapons ready, they moved down the corridor, looking for stairs leading down.

Auxiliary Command Post Three

"Sir!"

Amir Taleh looked up from the maps he'd been studying and saw Kazemi's agonized face. "Yes, Captain?"

"The Americans have broken through my defenses. They are inside the building." The young aide swallowed hard. "You and the others must leave this place before it is too late!"

"Agreed." Taleh nodded, still staggered by the speed of the American attack. Who could have dreamed that they would demonstrate such audacity? Still, all was not yet lost. He could regain control over his invasion forces at another of the alternate command posts. He turned to his deputy. "Assemble the senior staff, Hashemi."

Most were already prepared, clutching briefcases stuffed full of hastily gathered maps and documents. Surrounded by Taleh's personal bodyguards, the group hurried toward the nearest staircase.

The Chancery

Thorn crouched at the top of the stairs, watching Diaz get set. They'd heard the clatter of boots and the metallic clink of weapons drawing closer for the last several seconds. Whoever was coming up had almost reached the bend in the stairs.

He nodded sharply and his lips formed the unspoken command, "Now!"

The sergeant major yanked the pin out of the fragmentation grenade he was holding and tossed it down the stairwell.

Taleh heard something clattering down the stairs from above and froze. A small cylindrical shape bounced into view, rolling toward them. His eyes widened in shocked recognition.

Without hesitation, Captain Farhad Kazemi threw himself forward onto the grenade just before it went off.

WHUMMP. Thorn felt concussion punch into his lungs, and buried his face against his arms to shield his eyes from the smoke and debris billowing up out of the stairwell. Then he was on his feet, charging downward with Diaz at his side.

They rounded the bend.

Iranian officers and enlisted men jammed the staircase in a tangled knot. Some were bleeding. All of them were dazed. Only one, though, was dead—the victim of his own sacrifice.

Thorn opened fire with his submachine gun, sweeping from left to right. Diaz took the other side. Each burst sent one or more Iranians tumbling down the stairs. It was a methodical, mechanical slaughter. Those who were armed were too closely crowded together to use their own weapons effectively.

He felt a single bullet tear a burning gash across his upper left arm and shot the man who'd winged him. His finger eased on the trigger. He couldn't see any more targets—any more men to kill.

Then Thorn spotted movement near Diaz out of the corner of his eye. He started to spin in that direction. He was too late. He was too slow.

A man in a blood-spattered uniform reared up from the stairs and fired a pistol into Roberto Diaz at point-blank range, aiming upward. The bullet caught the short, stocky sergeant major in the throat. He toppled backward with a surprised look frozen forever on his face.

"You son of a bitch!" Thorn squeezed off a burst that slammed the Iranian back against the wall.

"Oh, Jesus." He knelt beside his friend, fumbling desperately for a field dressing. But TOW Diaz was beyond his help.

"Peter . . ."

Thorn spun back toward the man he'd shot—toward the man who had once been another friend.

General Amir Taleh stared up at him, breathing heavily, bleeding from several wounds in the chest and stomach.

Thorn stared down in contempt. "You bastard! I trusted you. I looked up to you. I thought you were a man of honor—not a goddamned terrorist who would kill women and children!"

Taleh's face twisted in sudden pain. "What I did to your country, Peter . . . You must understand. It was war."

"No, sir," Thorn said coldly, "it was murder." He raised his submachine gun, aimed carefully at Taleh's head, and fired three more shots—one after the other.

Over Tehran

Four UH-1N Hueys flew low across the Iranian capital, dodging over rooftops and around taller buildings to throw off any ground fire. They were heading south. A tiny, rocket-armed AH-6 gunship paced them, ready to pounce at the first sign of trouble.

Aboard the lead helicopter, Colonel Peter Thorn sat silently beside a covered stretcher. Unwilling to leave the Iranians anything to desecrate, the soldiers of the NEMESIS force had brought their dead out with them. He shivered and stared down at his shaking hands.

His casualties had been high—far higher than anything he had imagined. Nearly half of his sixty-man assault force had been killed or wounded. Medics were working frantically in the rear of each overcrowded helicopter, trying to keep the worst hurt alive long enough to reach a hospital.

Thorn felt a hand on his shoulder and looked over into Hamir Pahesh's sympathetic face.

"I am sorry, my friend. I know that many brave men died in this battle," the Afghan said simply. Then he shrugged. "But you have made your enemies shake in terror. You have thwarted their wickedness. That is worth much."

Pahesh smiled shyly. "And now we go home, eh?" The Afghan's bravery had earned him the right to a new country.

"Yes, now we go home." Thorn slumped back in his seat, his eyes already closing. Home to America, he thought wearily. Home to Helen Gray.

Behind him, the fires set by Tomahawks lit the night sky.

DECEMBER 15

Walter Reed Army Medical Center

Helen Gray woke suddenly from a restless, pain-filled sleep, hearing a change in the tone of the television in her room. She'd left it on for company during the long nights. She opened her eyes.

Live satellite pictures showed a burning city. "Reports from the Pentagon now confirm that American Delta Force commandos attacked and destroyed the Tehran headquarters of General Amir Taleh early yesterday morning. Although officials claim the mission achieved its primary objectives, they also admit that casualties were extremely heavy . . ."

Helen sat rigid. Like her, Peter Thorn led his men from the front. She held her breath for a moment, fighting down her fears for his safety. She might recover. But what about Peter?

She blinked away sudden tears. What if he had been killed? How could she live without him?

A wire-service photo of a trim, bearded Iranian flashed onto the screen. "According to U.S. intelligence sources, General Amir Taleh was the man directly responsible for orchestrating the bloody terrorist campaign that has ravaged this country since early November."

The images shifted to a series of maps and black-and-white satellite photos shot from high overhead. "In a related development, White House sources have released intelligence information showing that the Iranian-sponsored terrorist campaign was part of a much larger plan to invade Saudi Arabia and, ultimately, to dominate the entire Persian Gulf. If so, the Delta Force raid has smashed Tehran's grand imperial design. There are growing reports of bitter factional fighting in Iran's major cities as various groups struggle for control over the now-leaderless Islamic Republic."

The television picture cut back to a somber announcer. "The President is expected to address the nation at six P.M., eastern standard time."

Helen lay in bed, watching the pictures flooding in from halfway around the world—desperately eager for more details. She shifted impatiently. If only her foot would stop itching . . .

She took her eyes off the television and looked down. Her foot *itched.*

Her damaged nerves might be healing. The doctors had warned her that a full recovery would take months, maybe even years, of rigorous physical therapy, but this was at least a start—a promise that she could regain the mobility and freedom she feared had been lost forever.

Helen turned her head as the door to her room opened quietly.

And Peter was there.